ONE KNIGHT'S STAND

TANVIER PEART

frenchy
PRESS

The Frenchy Press

5325 Sheridan Drive, Suite 1196, Buffalo, New York 14221-9998

thefrenchypress.com

ISBNs: 979-8-9875061-5-8 (trade pbk.)

Library of Congress Control Number: 2025927043

First Edition: December 2025

Printed in the United States of America

1st Printing

Also by Tanvier Peart

Chance at Love Series

The Seven Month Itch (available as an audiobook)
Miles Apart
Tender Offer

Standalone

Ella Gets the D
Untitled Mafia Rom-Com (coming 2026)

Buffalo Steel Rugby Series

One Knight's Stand
Buffalo Rugby Romance Book 2 (coming 2026)

Author Note

Welcome to the Buffalo Steel rugby era! I've been waiting for this for some time. Take your shoes off and get comfortable.

One Knight's Stand is a rom-com with some cussing, hunching, shenanigans, and a happily ever after. Antonio likes to lick his plate clean, so I don't want to hear a thing from my family. There are sexually explicit situations. The first three chapters follow the same timeline as *Ella Gets the D*, before Antonio becomes a professional rugby player. You *don't* need to read that standalone to follow, but do expect a few cameos as Julian is his other BFF.

There are attempted theft (not physical) and intimidation in a couple of scenes (none between the FMC and MMC). This book also includes some physical accidents, such as a wig caught on a watch, a broken nose that leads to a trip to the ER (off the page), as well as being tackled and "pistol-whipped" by a protective older sister, and falling down the stairs in hoochie shorts and heels, among other events. Everybody survives!

On a serious note, there is mention of a hospital scene (off the page) involving a parent and an appendectomy. Everyone is okay, but I wanted to flag just in case.

There is some light Spanish sprinkled throughout certain parts of the book, as Miriam (FMC) is Panamanian. I chose not to translate the words or phrases to pivot away from the expectation to cater to an English-first lens. Y'all will be good!

Oh, and if you haven't seen *The Best Man Holiday* and plan on watching, there's a spoiler in Chapter 30.

As always, please take care of yourself.

Rugby Terms

If it's helpful, here are some terms you may encounter:

Lifting block – Padded block worn around the thigh, typically for a lineout

Lineout – Restart of play after the ball goes out of bounds; "jumpers" lifted into the air by their shorts or lifting blocks

Pitch – Playing field

Scrum – Restarting play after a stoppage for a minor infringement

Try – When a player carries the ball over the opponent's goal line and touches it to the ground; worth five points

To the ones rediscovering themselves: turn up.
Just secure your wig.

THE PLAYLIST—PART I

#1 – "So Anxious"—Ginuwine

#2 – "No Air"—Jordin Sparks ft. Chris Brown

#3 – "Da Butt"—Experience Unlimited (E.U.)

#4 – "Up"—Cardi B.

#5 – "When Doves Cry"—Prince and the Revolution

#6 – "Dedication"—Nipsey Hussle ft. Kendrick Lamar

#7 – "Best Friend"—Brandy

#8 – "Vegas"—Doja Cat

#9 – "Get Money"—The Notorious B.I.G. ft. Junior M.A.F.I.A.

#10 – "Sexy Lady"—Uncalled 4 Band (UCB)

THE PLAYLIST—PART II

#11 – "Tonight"—ORGAVSM

#12 – "Friends"—Mario ft. Ty Dolla $ign

#13 – "Let's Get Down"—Tony! Toni! Toné

#14 – "U Got It Bad"—Usher

#15 – "Toro Mata"—Celia Cruz and Johnny Pacheco

#16 – "You"—Elle Eliades ft. R.L. King

#17 – "Worst Behaviour"—kwn ft. Kehlani

#18 – "DNA"—Kendrick Lamar

#19 – "Love of My Life"—Erykah Badu ft. Common

#20 – "Untitled (How Does It Feel)"—D'Angelo

Chapter 1

Miriam

Three years ago

"I'm sitting on someone's penis tonight."

I wasn't serious when I said it to Marcela, but I didn't expect her to laugh in my face like Charlie Murphy, rest his soul. She was two cackles away from needing mouth-to-mouth.

My sister didn't think I'd go out alone on one of the biggest party nights of the year. I don't go out at all, because I hate large crowds, but there was a point to prove. It surprised us both when I grabbed my keys and left. The trip was short-lived—I went to a park down the block until Marcela drove to her friend's house—but I had to commit on principle. An hour later, I was in one of her dresses, driving down I-95 with only mild anxiety to keep me company. The 495 vortex sucked me in, and, well, here I am. Sitting behind a wood column in a dimly lit bar in Adams Morgan.

Marcela

> There's still time to come over. I know your stubborn self is at the park.

> Wrong. I'm in DC. I'll pass on the hour-long drive to Baltimore to sip stale, overpriced wine and chew on Vatican crackers.

I answer my phone on the fourth ring.

"Be careful. Limit your driving, keep your location on, and text me when you get home," Marcela says with the spirit of our mother. The West Indian accent is missing, but the acting like I'm still a seven-year-old in pigtails is loud and clear.

"I'm quite capable of making it back to our father's house just fine, and I only plan to have one drink."

She sighs. "I'm serious, Miri. New Year's Eve is Halloween for perverts. Does the bar have security?"

"Please stop acting like I'm not old enough to cross the street. I'm fine. Go be with your friends. I'll see you tomorrow."

"Tomorrow? You just proved your point. Go home and watch *Buffy*."

Her comment shouldn't frustrate me, but it does.

I always do what's expected. I'm the rule follower, the one who keeps her nose in a book and never had a rebellious streak—unless you count taking a bus to the Maryland Science Center in middle school. I spent more time with my robotics kits and circuit boards growing up than I did going to the mall.

Nobody expects anything different, especially at the ripe old age of thirty-one.

Somewhere along the way, I became a fragile object everyone needed to protect. I'm not a baby anymore. I'm grown and capable of making my own decisions.

"I'm doing something different this year," I say.

"Sitting on someone's penis, if I remember correctly." Marcela's carefree laugh grates on my last nerve.

"I will if I feel like it! Lots of people have one-night stands without ending up on the evening news." I do enough research for my doctorate, and I was thorough with my internet search before I borrowed her dress. "If I want to slide into the new year with my legs in the air, I'll do it."

"You can't say 'pussy' without blushing, Miriam."

"Well, me and my—I have condoms in my purse! A pleasure three-pack."

I end the call and rip off my glasses. I don't want to hear or see her.

We spend the holidays in the home we grew up in after moving to the States. Every year is the same routine. On New Year's Eve, our father slips away somewhere, and Marcela meets up with her high school friends. I'm home alone watching *Buffy the Vampire Slayer* episodes and falling asleep before the ball drops.

My sister is the social butterfly, while I naturally shy away from big groups. I wear wide-framed glasses and have a collection of encyclopedias. While my awkwardness makes it easy to stay in the house, it's never weighed on my confidence.

Seeking validation is pointless when you're comfortable in your skin. My family doesn't see it that way. They assume my aversion to extrovert tendencies means I require saving. I'm quiet, but I've never relied on anyone to define who I am.

I might be cluelessly single, but I'm not naive about non-platonic interactions or sex. If I can follow scientific principles to design and test systems, I can enjoy force and movement for one evening.

Assuming I go through with it.

Marcela

You know I worry about you.

And I love you. Please trust that I know how to live my life.

"Want something stronger?" The bartender nods at my half-empty water glass.

"Yes. Thank you, Ben," I say to his name tag, which is across from a patch of chest hair peeking out from under an unbuttoned black dress shirt. Trimmed or not, it has to be a health code violation. "Bourbon. Neat, please."

His brows soften when I push my glasses to the bridge of my nose and wait. The chemistry of bourbon is a savory science, one often overlooked in favor of instant gratification. I've never made whiskey, but I appreciate its flavor complexities.

"House brand or something else?"

"Surprise me." My tone excites a smile.

Ben strolls to the other end of the onyx bar to retrieve a bottle from an illuminated wooden shelf. It's not at the top, which means I can afford it on my monthly research assistantship salary. "Try this." Calloused fingers extend a glass tumbler.

The burn from the first sip creeps down my throat. It's stronger than I expected. *Jinkies.* "It's good." I cough.

His chuckle rattles the chest hair that I pray isn't floating in my drink. "What brings you here?"

Entertaining the possibility of allowing a man to play in my guts.

"Wanted some fresh air," I lie.

"Fresh air," he repeats, wiping down the counter with a smirk. "There's a park not too far from here you might want to check out. Since you're old enough to cross the street."

I wince. "How much did you hear?"

He cants his head from side to side, the overhead recessed lights catching in his auburn strands. "Only that you're trying something new, which may involve your legs in the air at some point." He smiles at my groan. "Your secret is safe with me. You hear a lot in this job. No judgment. I take it it's your first time? A one-night stand?"

I push up my glasses. "What makes you say that?"

"Truth?"

"I like facts."

"You're about four hours too early to meet anyone. We won't get packed until nine," he says.

That explains why it's so empty.

Do people not come out for dinner and conversation before a night of sexual indulgence? My food takes at least thirty minutes to settle before I do any activities that exert energy.

I glance at an older couple at a nearby table.

"Early nightcap," he says. "Don't think they'll entertain a three-some."

A guy at the opposite end of the bar is wearing an ironed sweater.

"Lives next door. He got caught with two sex dolls in his car. Said it was so he could ride the HOV lanes."

Ew.

I straighten. "Maybe I wanted to eat a burger in peace before any proclivities."

"We don't sell burgers. The best I can do are marinated olives or a cheese plate."

What kind of place is this? Starvation will hit me before the courage to ask a stranger to touch me on the inside does.

"Fine." I raise my hands. "It is my first one-night stand. But I've had sex before. Twice, which might be pitiful to you and anyone else who thinks a thirty-one-year-old should be doing splits on a countertop or have more experience than Josh Alby and his bull-size nuts smacking me into a twin mattress. I have three degrees—a bachelor's of engineering, an MBA, and a master's of mechanical engineering—and I'm working on a PhD."

Ben whistles.

"Socially, I'm boring, and I might be a future bingo champion with a sequined fanny pack, but I'm sick of people telling me what to do."

Choose a different course of study, honey. You don't want to be the only female mechanical engineer.

You should live with your father while you're in college. Columbia is safer for a single woman than Baltimore.

How many degrees do you need? Don't turn into your tía who blew off men until she couldn't find one.

I point to the front door. "I'll dance in traffic before I get stuck in it again tonight. I can have a one-night stand with the next man who walks through that door."

Maybe not the *next* man. Somebody who isn't married, doesn't have a forest of body hair, and believes in cleaning thoroughly with a washcloth. Marcela's trysts were part of her "self-discovery" in her twenties. Heaven forbid I have my own in my thirties without an internal family investigation.

The notes I took in my phone about how to have a successful one-night stand said to pack condoms and lubricant. Those are in my purse, along with wipes, a toothbrush, floss, and mouthwash. None of the articles I read mentioned the last four, but oral hygiene should be a priority with safe sex.

At this point, if I could get away with propositioning a man at the grocery store, I'd do it. At least then I'd have a piece of bread and peace of mind that a nosy sibling and bartender would stay out of my business. I should quit while I'm ahead, but I don't want to give up the parking spot I found down the block. With my luck, I'll stumble into another bar that serves only grape halves and garnishes.

"Word of advice?" Ben snaps me out of my exit strategy. "Meeting someone usually works best when you stay awhile." He nods to the coat I've yet to remove. Between trying not to look desperate and the silent pep talks about having sex for the first time since I began my PhD two years ago, my mind is all over the place.

"I planned to take it off," I say, matter-of-fact.

He rolls his lips. "Tonight?"

My fingers fumble around the belt I knotted twice like I was protecting my virtue. The silk interior lining glides over my shoulders. The heat is on, but you wouldn't know it with the way goosebumps prickle my skin. I avoid attention, but tonight, it's stamped on the cleavage Ben is eyeing.

"Damn." His green eyes slide from my double-D breasts, which tonight are kissing a red square-neck dress, to my lips.

Wrestling the zipper up my spine was only part of the battle. I'm half a foot shorter than my sister. With our height difference, one would think there would be more fabric to cover my knees. The culprit is my hips, which are wider than Marcela's and eating up the hem without a care for modesty.

At least the wig I pulled into a low ponytail is still in place. I wear it for labs, and tonight I put in loose curls that took prayer and three YouTube tutorials to tackle.

"If no one comes in soon, I get off at eight," Ben says.

My brain scrambles to find a logical excuse as I dismiss him with the wave of a hand. "Ha ha." I brush off his advance.

I respond to Marcela's message and run through my notes to avoid eye contact. Maybe I'm not ready. My belly is gurgling, which could be a sign of hunger or stupidity.

"Here we go." Ben tips his chin toward the first person to walk in since my one-night stand monologue.

A heavy weight settles in my stomach. I'm not built to socialize, much less ask someone if I can play with their sexual organs for the night. What do I say? *Hi, nice to meet you. Want to stroke my walls?*

Don't look.

Don't look.

Smooth footsteps roll over concrete, prompting my attention to investigate. My pulse quickens, but it's my thighs that shift when I see leg muscles cast in a gray suit.

I should've stayed home, where it's safe. Maybe then I wouldn't be staring at DC's biggest flirt, whose former baby face is now in its rugged era and wearing a blinding smile directed at me.

Stale wine and Vatican crackers I can do. Antonio Knight is a different story.

Chapter 2

Miriam

Light glimmers over the beanie covering Antonio's fade and the tiny man bun he's determined to grow. I don't know who I personally insulted for him to walk through the door, but I'll give up sex for another two years before his penis comes near me.

Tales of "a night with Knight" are folklore across the nation's capital and its surrounding states. The care he dedicates to his partners. His stamina. His tongue.

Who needs Acroyoga with someone who bends you like Gumby?

The extent of my bedroom gymnastics is holding these thighs to my ears without scraping my knees on a popcorn dorm ceiling. And even after that I walked crooked for two days, which gave Josh a bigger ego than he deserved. Imagine what would happen after messing around with Antonio.

The first time I have sex after a long hiatus should be something I ease into, something that doesn't require floaties, a lifeguard, and a CPR team on standby. Antonio will send me straight to urgent care, and I have things to do tomorrow.

The knee-length coat draped over his wide shoulders gives way to the heavy thighs widening his stance. No one can tell me I won't need a pain reliever to handle all of that girth.

Men in expensive suits aren't a turn-on for me. Manicured fingernails and crooked smiles are never up to any good. Yet the veins in Antonio's caramel hands render me speechless. The only excuse I have for gawking is that I'm trying to guess what lotion makes the hands I've seen toss large men appear so soft.

He plays rugby with a DC team for fun. He's a flanker like Kierra, my best friend, which is the extent I know about the sport with no pads or helmets. I saw Antonio in action the few times the women's rugby team played on a field in the same park. He and I never had a reason to speak during the rare occasions I allowed her to drag me away from campus. He's him, and I'm, well, me.

I'll tell you one thing: Witnessing his muscles shift and contract as he sprinted to the goal or pummeled an opponent who easily weighed over two hundred pounds was an experience.

I discovered three things about myself while I was pretending not to watch. The first was that playful people have an off switch that makes them ruthless when necessary. Antonio wins every class clown award, but he's a menace as a rugby player. The second was a newfound appreciation for well-developed quad muscles and a gym booty. The third I'm not proud of and would never admit out loud.

A man's grunt can be as euphoric as his moan, and, my, does Antonio grunt.

His voice carried to my blanket to tease my nipples that day. I never had such a physical reaction to a man's voice, and I gathered up my things to wait in the car. I refused to be another member of his fan club trying to catch his eye—not that I would with the number of women vying for his attention. I had zero interest in one of the biggest flirts in the nation's capital whose list of sexual partners needs its own Wikipedia page.

I crane my head back to catch Antonio's tongue glisten his lower lip in a wet trail. His short, boxed beard frames a handsome square face, which crinkles at the corners in a buttery smile.

"Hello, Miriam." Antonio's voice is playful, but the brown gaze sliding down my profile to take in every curve is deadly.

"Antonio." I curl my lip in a subtle attempt to defrost my glasses and not sniff the air, which is scented with his tobacco and cedar cologne.

Ben's brows dip. "You know her?"

"We go way back, don't we?" Antonio gestures to the barstool next to me. "Mind if I join you?" He smiles at my bobblehead impression and unbuttons his coat.

I never took him for someone who wears suspenders. The tan elastic strains over the muscles packed inside his crisp white button-down. I focus on a neon bar sign above Blow-up Doll Guy's head and recite failure theories in my head.

Failure is imminent when a material's maximum principal stress exceeds its ultimate tensile strength.

Numbers and science soothe my mind whenever thoughts boomerang. My focus is on analyzing factors that impact machine components. Failure criteria applied to gears and springs.

Shafts.

The gulp of water I inhale goes down the wrong pipe.

Antonio pats me on the back at my coughing fit. "You okay?"

"Yup." I cough again and reach for my bourbon, reacquainting my heaving throat with a burn that ignites a croak. "Just fine."

This is why I stay in the house, away from all distractions. Suspender-wearing muscle men included.

Antonio could stand in for Alfie from *Emily in Paris* without anyone noticing. Kierra forces me to watch the series during monthly get-togethers that involve ordering food and never leaving the house. The same thick brows, generous mouth, and even, white teeth are currently invading my personal space.

"Two Doe sightings before the end of the year, and in this dress?" I shiver under his appraisal. It's slow, passing over the top of my shoulder, down my breasts, and eventually anchoring on the indent of my waist. "You look—"

"Like not myself?" I offer.

"Incredible." He swallows and clears his throat, motioning to the bartender. "I'll have a bourbon, Ben. Refill?"

"Sure," I say.

"So, what brings you out from your library tower and into my neck of the woods?"

"Sex," I say, taking silent pleasure at Antonio spitting his drink all over the bar. Serves him right.

"Thanks," Antonio says to Ben, who shuffles over with extra napkins. He wipes the counter. "Repeat that one more time, Doe."

I roll my eyes at the nickname. Gentle and innocent Miriam is getting laid and sprayed tonight—without the pee. I have limits.

"All anyone sees when they look at me is a brain with no human needs. I prefer the quiet of solitude, so I get written off as undesirable. People think I operate on batteries. I may spend days in a 'library tower' and not know the best words to say in social settings, but that doesn't make me someone to discard. I like the idea of sex, and I want lots of it. I just haven't prioritized it while pursuing my research. That doesn't mean I don't think about sex positions and accessories. I have lots of toys and have identified the optimum conditions for achieving orgasms."

I'm rambling. Badly.

Here I am, in my thirties, at a bar on New Year's Eve, unleashing a rapid stream of thoughts in hopes of attracting a man for the night. The words won't stop, and, oh, how I wish they would. I always do this when I overthink or anticipate judgment.

My conversation with Antonio is now a monologue about my tragic love life and abandoned vagina. It's pointless to assess his unreadable expression while I'm talking a mile a minute, but something shifted from when he sat down until now.

I clear my throat, ready to cut my losses at his hardened stare, when he does the unexpected.

He kisses me.

It's soft, but it anchors me to the barstool as he drags it between his thighs. My gasp is muffled on his lips, which are now stretched to accommodate his tongue against mine. When we come up for air, my hands are in fists next to my armpits. My chest heaves in the rise and crescendo of ragged breaths.

Jinkies.

Heat from Antonio's body pulls me like a magnet. To experience his steady gaze boring through my skin in silent expectation is...indescribable.

My first taste was months ago, at a rugby party in DC that Julian, his best friend, held. Even in a crowded room full of rugby teammates and their partners on the dance floor, Antonio's nearness overwhelmed me.

At first I assumed he was interested in Kierra. Antonio is a charmer who would take one of Blow-up Doll Guy's harem buddies if he knew he wouldn't get caught. Whatever "moment" we shared that night was a miscalculation on my part.

Tonight? His desire is pressed against my knee.

"Come home with me." His tone is low. Hungry. Needy.

"I—excuse me?"

"My condo is down the block," he says. "If you're up for the company. I'm not a stranger who meets your criteria, but I promise to cherish your mind, exhaust your body, and kick you out before eight tomorrow morning."

I grin at his arrogance. "I'd be gone by six."

"Even better."

Am I really agreeing to this?

You did put on the dress.

He isn't a stranger, which saves me money for therapy in theory and body wash for trying to scrub away a bad decision. I might still wake up with regret and fatigued muscles, but he is the safer option.

"Sex is all I want," I blurt. "Tomorrow—"

"You go back to your library tower, and we only bump into each other twice a year," he says. "I'm not looking for a relationship, and I promise not to fall in love."

"Good."

"You will be." He settles our tabs, drapes my coat over my shoulders, secures his, and extends a hand. "Ready?"

My mind sprints until he kisses my wrist, his wet lips settling over my racing pulse. Heat spreads from my belly to between my thighs.

"Don't overthink it," he whispers.

And off we go.

Finding a man I once helped with science homework attractive feels criminal. But what a man he is.

Chapter 3

Antonio

The plan tonight was simple: grab a drink, pick up dinner, and drown in my sheets. Sex wasn't on my radar until the woman whose shadow still traces the edges of my mind appeared at my neighborhood bar with demands.

At first, I thought Miriam was joking about a one-night stand. But through her *SNL* monologue of anxiety and desire, I heard her. The want to prioritize the parts of herself she pushes away for academia. The need to feel alive. Adored.

Sitting here next to her is fucking with me, not because she wants to fuck *me*, but because she's here. In front of my kitchen counter—gnawing on a chicken wing, but she's here. In the flesh tucked under red fabric that grips curves I've never witnessed this close.

Any sightings these days are like a solar eclipse. Rare and blinding. You can't look away.

"Do you usually supply your company with chicken?" Red, full lips glide over another bone. "Sorry." She sucks on whatever remnants she thinks are left. *Jesus.* "I forgot to eat before I went out."

"Do you want a rotisserie chicken?" I eye the wings she piled into a mini pyramid. It shouldn't be sexy, but it is.

"No." Her giggle is melodic. It's half Regine from *Living Single* and half Betty Rubble. "I don't pretend to eat air, but that's still too much for me in one sitting. My hips are wide as is."

"That they are." I zero in on the hips in question, soft skin spilling over my barstool. The tops of her thighs appear thicker than mine in a dress that creeps up legs I want wrapped around my neck. It takes what little concentration I have left to keep my blood from rerouting to my dick.

The invitation to come back to my penthouse slipped out before I could fully process the implications of a one-night stand with a woman who's been off-limits.

Miriam has been my crush since I was eleven. She was a real-life Ashley Banks in the form of a shy sixteen-year-old who babysat me when I was a hardheaded kid whose parents didn't trust him to stay at home alone. Did I get into more trouble on purpose to see her? Every chance I had.

By the time I was old enough to take her out, she was in a long-term relationship with her first love. School has always been her main priority, which limits any opportunity to run into her. At some point, I stopped hoping any glimpses of thick glasses and legs to match were her. Until tonight, when her smile and those brilliant dimples called to me from across the bar I drop into a few nights a week after work.

Miriam is a work of art. A masterpiece of divine lines and full hips and breasts.

"Speaking of food, where does all of yours go?" She swats at my arm and muffles a gasp at the muscles underneath my dress shirt.

I chew through a bite and wink. "I'm a big boy, Doe. Rugby and my workouts require fuel."

"Whole chickens?" she deadpans.

"You act like it was a holiday turkey," I chuckle. "I don't cook, but I eat my weight. To answer your question, I don't usually have dinner with company. Sends the wrong message."

Stuffing panties in my drawer.

"Forgetting" some random item in hopes I'll welcome her back with open arms, and not for a limited time.

"So you're saying this is special chicken."

You're special.

"Something like that," I say.

"Oh." She nods to herself, focusing on her hands in her lap.

Miriam's mind is a language I want to speak fluently. How she breaks apart words and turns them over. The way her brows narrow and her eyes shift to make sense of something that has no scientific explanation.

Every part of her intrigues me.

"So what do you do for fun besides pick up men at bars for sex?" I nudge her knee with mine and jump at her snort.

"Sorry." She chokes back a laugh with her hand and snorts again. "My version of fun is falling asleep before ten."

"*Ten?* Most of my parties don't start until then."

"Oh, I've heard," she huffs and adjusts her black-framed glasses. "I'm surprised there aren't a hundred people here for the last night of the year." Her eyes bounce from the hardwood floors underneath mid-century furniture to the steel windows and exposed ducts.

"The last New Year's Eve party I hosted was three years ago," I say. "Someone covered in vomit slept in the tub. Nine people were passed out over there." I point to the space between the sofa and the wall. I'll spare her the details of how they all fit. "Unless there's a party worth attending, I'm in the house."

That or slipping out from between a woman's legs after I stroked her past midnight. I prefer to sleep in my own bed.

The edges of Miriam's mouth tease a smile before lifting into a grin. Blush tints her mocha hue, her long lashes fanning across her cheeks. "Well, I promise not to puke on myself or mess up your tub."

Our stare unravels the space between us.

Is she...Oh, we're doing this.

Inch by inch, we lean closer, until her breath skates over mine. I caress her cheek and brush my mouth over the lips I've been dying to kiss again.

Since we left the bar, we've spent the evening talking over takeout. I'm in no rush for the night to end. Hence the chicken.

The pace of our kiss is slow, so she can dictate it based on her comfort. She parts her lips and rises off the barstool. The gentle massage of her mouth teases a years' old desire that forces its way back into my heart.

Miriam plants her hands on my thighs. The jolt from her touch reawakens the dick I told to calm down. Short nails dig into my pants. A moan slips out, and like a switch has flipped, she pounces.

I'm a hard man to tackle. I don't make it easy. The problem is, I'm not on the rugby pitch. Another is that these barstools don't have backs.

I wrap my arms around Miriam and brace for impact. My back collides with the floor in a thud. She collapses on top of me with a screech, her breasts crushing the last drops of air in my lungs.

"Sorry!"

"Are you okay?" I ask.

"Yeah," she says to my nipple as her forehead grazes it. "I'm stuck on your watch."

Light from the sconces hanging over the counter reflect off my silver timepiece, which is tangled in her curls.

"I'll fix it," I say. "Turn left."

"My left is your right."

"Turn to your left."

Miriam leans but winces. "I think that made it worse. Stay still, and I'll move back."

Huh?

Whatever response I had stalls as her hips rock over my groin. Never in my life have I prayed not to nut with a woman on top of me, but there's a first time for everything. Miriam's dress rises above her waist to expose a black thong that peeks out from under her love handles. My jaw slacks as she all but uses my dick as a personal genie lamp to rub out a wish.

"Doe—"

"It's loosening," she grunts, wiggling her hips in an attempt to scoot away. She's so focused on solving the Rubik's Cube of my watch in her hair that she's not paying attention to me hardening beneath her.

"Almost there!"

So am I.

I grip her hips to lift her up. "Let's figure out another way."

"Almost—"

"Dooooe!"

Too late.

In all of my years as a grown-ass man, I've never come from dry humping—unintentional dry humping at that. My toes curl in my socks, and my overstimulated tip pulsates at the release.

I can't look her in the face. I can't even *see* her face since she's still threaded to the watch I'm cursing myself for wearing. With her eyes pointing down, she has an unobstructed view of the mess that's settling into expensive cotton.

"I— Oh, I didn't mean—"

"Don't apologize!" I grimace. "I've been trying to get you off." Well, not like this.

"Here, let me—"

"No, it's okay—"

Too late. Again.

I lift from my elbows to sit and roll her off me but collide with her head as it swings up. The good news is, she frees herself. The bad news is, I think she broke my nose.

Blood pools out of my nostrils, and I squeeze them to stop the bleeding. *Shit*.

Miriam rushes to her feet. "Sorry! Let me get you paper towels. Actually, I might have some tampons."

"Where's your hair?!"

She pats her cornrows with wide eyes. I lift my hand to reveal her curled wig dangling from my watch.

"I'm so embarrassed!" She reaches out to pull me up with no luck. Miriam is a foot shorter without shoes.

"I got it," I groan.

"Here." She thrusts takeout napkins in my face and grabs her purse. "I'm taking you to the hospital."

I feel around the granite island for my wallet and keys, but she puts both in my hand. "What about your hair?" I wiggle the new accessory on my wrist.

"It's coming with us." She motions to the door. "Let's go."

"You should wear your natural hair out. It's beautiful," I say.

"Come on." Miriam grabs her shoes but slides into a pair of my sneakers near the door. "If I put those death contraptions back on, we'll both need the ER. Keep applying pressure."

"I've had bloody noses before." I remind her about my physical pastime...which, admittedly, doesn't involve being tackled and beat up in my own house.

"Are you smiling?" Her eyes shift to my grin.

"At least we'll spend New Year's together with a night we'll never forget."

"I should've stayed home."

"Will you be my emergency contact in case there's head trauma?"

"You already have it." She pushes me out the door. "Now shut up, and let's go."

"I feel this is the start of a wonderful relationship, Doe."

Chapter 4

Miriam

Three years later

Moving to the tundra in the dead of winter was a choice.

I have no one to blame but myself for the three extra hours it took to navigate winding roads coated in ice with the fumes of my frustration sputtering out of the exhaust. Marcela warned me not to make the six-hour expedition—that's without the scenic slowdowns and my curses wrapped in prayer—by myself. We drove my car up after New Year's, and in the spirit of *I got it*, I flew back solo, rented a moving truck, and was on my way.

Tall pines bordering a long stretch of two-lane roads finally gave way to the Rust Belt city that's home for the foreseeable future. It's much colder than the six months I spent in Panama after graduation.

The decision to trade Baltimore for Buffalo wasn't rooted in logic or theory. I did some preliminary research, but the truth is, I wanted a change after earning my PhD.

I'm starting a new chapter, and it comes with wings and a mafia of football fanatics who hurl themselves into tables in subzero temps.

Marcela and her constituents can take turns rolling the dice on whether or not their next stunt will land them in the ER with internal bleeding and unnecessary co-pays.

The tailgate leader in question sifts through my collection of dish towels. She's in a deep squat, like her knees won't crackle from the wear and tear of tossing all that booty we inherited in the club. Her slim-thick frame, E-cup breasts, and five-eleven height are compliments of our mother, who's living her best life in Panama City.

"Is there something you want to tell me?" She lifts a "When in doubt, pull it out" towel. It was a gag gift from a white elephant party years ago. There's an oven in the center, not a penis.

I shrug. "It adds personality to the room."

"For all the entertaining you do, right? Nobody but you and Jesus will see this."

"If I recall, I'm not the one who keeps the lights in front of her house off so people won't know she's home." You'd think she was dodging a process server the way she video called me in the dark. "At least I can sit in my living room with the blinds open."

"It was one time!" I dodge a swat to my overalls.

Marcela broke Buffalo's longstanding legacy of men in power as the first female city councilmember. She still goes toe-to-toe with fragile egos, but she's smashing the patriarchy one pair of stilettos at a time.

If she's anything like how she was growing up, her colleagues will learn not to question her authority. She got it from our parents before they split when I was eight. Now she bosses her colleagues around in a city with potholes deep enough to touch the earth's crust.

Cussing out the last Jefferson District councilmember—in English and Spanish—is how she won her seat. Her complaints about city budget allocations and a lack of community investments on the East Side fueled a growing resistance to the status quo. Her seventeen years of living here after graduating from Buffalo College had her fed up, and she left the corporate world for public service.

It's a third of her old pay and longer hours, but she loves it.

Fresh Marley twists sway across her backless sweater as she disappears into the kitchen. The space is a small swatch of natural oak cabinets and banana-colored walls, but it's mine.

"Have you considered my offer?"

"For you to boss me around more than you already do between nine and five? No thanks," I say.

A cork pops. "Don't forget the occasional evening and weekend for community events," she adds. "It's something to hold you over until you decide what to do."

Jobless with a PhD. That's me.

Walking across the stage for the last time changed something in me. I was done, yet all I thought about was turning thirty-four and not fully knowing the real me.

School was my safe space for so long, it became my shield. But you can't live life out of a textbook. It will still pass you by, with or without a curriculum and an advisor.

My graduation dinner was a feast of shock and tension. I waited until after my mother flew up from Panama for my commencement ceremony to tell my family that the youngest Beckford daughter turned down three job offers because she was tired. You could have cut the fruitcake with my father's glare.

Every offer was in Northern Virginia and dangled a meaty six-figure salary. On paper, they were perfect. In my gut, they didn't feel right.

I wanted a fresh start, to find the part of myself I put on hold.

"You picked a cute spot." Marcela's eyes glide over worn hardwood floors and blank white walls.

The two-bedroom, two-bathroom house I'm renting is a canvas of charming quirks. There's wainscoting, reclaimed doors, and a backyard space buried beneath accumulated snow. I lived in an apartment on campus that was more of a rest stop, a place to wash and eat. This will be home.

"It is." I smile and sip red wine from one of the glasses she brought from her house. Mine are carefully wrapped in one of the many boxes lining the living room I plan to unpack.

Marcela spins in a circle to manifest a couch that isn't here and lands on a blanket of newspapers. She stretches out her legs in distressed jeans. "No regrets?"

"None," I say.

She shakes her head. "You actually moved. When you told us you wanted a change, I expected a haircut"—she gestures to my shoulder-length bob of natural curls—"not uprooting your life to come up here. And with no job? Our father must still be staring at the wall."

It's not funny, but it is. I could've reenacted Angela's STD confession from *Why Did I Get Married?* without him batting an eye. So long as his baby girl has financial stability and a roof over her head, Benjamin Beckford won't worry.

I have one of the two, and the savings account I fed from a lack of a social life should last me nine months.

"Change was overdue," I confess into my wineglass. Everyone else evolved. Why can't I?

The occasional texts from the few friendships I managed to sustain are now family holiday cards with matching outfits, Kierra included. She met a viscount during an international rugby trip and traded DC life for French luxury. Two kids and a dog later, her new net worth could solve famine in smaller countries.

I have no *Bridgerton* fantasies to live out, but I want more than my degrees.

"Are you sure a certain 'friend' didn't inspire your relocation?" I roll my eyes at Marcela's Cheshire Cat grin and push down the memory of chicken wings and kissing that's creeping out of its lockbox.

No one knows about my failed attempt at a one-night stand, the one that ended with Antonio's head propped in my lap inside an ER. He did have a broken nose from my attempted rescue mission to free my wig from his watch.

We were both a mess. I looked like I got into a bar fight with my "*Set It Off* braids," as he called them. My skintight dress and his high-tops, three sizes too big, did me no favors in avoiding stares.

Neither did the burly man I was cradling, who had a tampon up his nose and the fragrance of dried semen coating his dress pants.

I vowed to never see or speak to him again out of pure embarrassment. That didn't stop him from asking around for my number after we parted ways and texting me until I responded.

The *Been to any good bars lately?* messages turned into weekly check-ins. Over time, we just clicked. We became friends, communicating through frequent messages and video calls I accepted when he was too excited to text. I still kept my distance from DC when I lived in Maryland, but it was nice to have someone to talk to who wasn't a PhD candidate.

I was Antonio's second call when he got the news that a developing rugby team in Buffalo was interested in him playing professionally. The subsequent offer came out of the blue, but I had my noisemaker ready once the deal with the Buffalo Steel became official.

He was my first call when I had a moment to myself after obtaining my PhD. Antonio never asked to come to the ceremony, and I never offered. That didn't stop bouquets of flowers from finding their way to my doorstep.

Aside from my sister, he's the only person I speak to on the phone weekly. Our friendship was the surprise I never saw coming.

"We're just friends," I tell my nosy sister. Since our New Year's Eve in the emergency room, Antonio and I never kissed or made attempts to hump body parts again.

Our platonic relationship aside, I'm no fool. Antonio is *repent and put a little extra into the offering plate* fine, but he's also a player.

I'm neither arrogant nor ignorant enough to think a one-night stand would've meant more to him. Erasing his scent, those eyes, his lips, and that body took more time than I'd care to admit, but I did it.

I'm not the kind of woman to trip his radar anyway. Not that I want to be.

"Where is Muscles? I'm not carrying another box upstairs," Marcela huffs. She's never met a form of physical labor she didn't cuss out.

"Probably at practice. Their season starts in a few weeks. I didn't want to bother him."

"Bother him?" She laughs. "That man would've driven down to get you and that moving truck, blizzard or not."

It's true, which is why I'm taking my time to acclimate myself to these disrespectful temps and to us being in the same city.

Antonio left DC to start his professional rugby career two years ago. We've both been in moments of transition at different times. Now that our foundations are settling, I don't want to make it weird.

He's a friend and will only be my friend.

Then why are you so nervous to see him?

Hush.

"What's on your agenda next week?" My subject change flies under Marcela's BS radar and incites a scowl.

"Too much," she says. "We're having an MLK celebration for the kids at the community center on Monday. You should come and help with the engineering station."

I grab my glass and resume pulling books out of a box. *Add "build a bookshelf" to your to-do list.* "My calendar is open. A perk of being unemployed," I say.

We manage to sort through the boxes designated for the living room and kitchen. Marcela leaves, and I end the night with a shower and some light reading on my mattress on my bedroom floor.

No thoughts of Antonio whatsoever.

Chapter 5

Antonio

"Leaving so soon?" Traci kisses up my back.

It's cold as hell in here, and she expects some parting dick?

She drapes her arms around my neck and presses her perky breasts into my skin. "I can change my flight to this evening." A hand snakes around my torso to grab my morning wood, which is doing its daily stretch. "Stay. We'll order breakfast. Keep each other warm."

I huff at the last part. We had no choice but to fuck for half the night or risk hypothermia. It's not below freezing in here like it is outside, but it's cold enough for my nuts to look like they belong in somebody's Raisin Bran. The tissue they called a comforter did us no favors, which meant relying on body heat or triggering the fire department by setting the furniture on fire. In truth, I was ready to try it. I hate cuddling, but I bit the bullet to avoid frostbite on my extremities. Penis included.

Waking up to head usually guarantees a smile on my face. Except this morning, I was praying that Traci's saliva wouldn't crystallize on my shaft for the rest of the day. ERs and I don't get along.

An image of Miriam with her hands over her face to hide the embarrassment of her wig being stuck to my watch draws a laugh.

It was a painful night, but it was one of the best of my life. I make a mental note to text her later. She's been quieter than usual.

"What's so funny?" Traci asks, her brows creased.

"This cold-ass room," I say. "What sports organization rakes in billions and picks a hotel with tiny beds that's stingy with the heat and extra blankets?" Professional rugby in the US pulls nowhere near the revenue football does, but at least we manage better rooms than this.

"So stay and let me keep you warm," she purrs.

"Next time. I have an event this morning." I kiss her frown and slip into my jeans, which are colder than the thin sheets that forced me to cocoon around the Baltimore cheerleader who mistook my hands around her waist and leg draped over her body as a declaration of love.

Traci is cool people, the spitting image of Janet during her *Control* era, and she puts her flexibility to good use. The rugby season doesn't start until next month, but we link up—once, maybe twice a year—during football playoffs, whenever Baltimore plays against Buffalo. She's five-four and a buck thirty wet but has a mean grip—hands, mouth, and pussy. I appreciate the time we spend together, but she knows what it is.

I lean over for a hug. "Safe travels back. We should've won last night. Tell your people to come up earlier. Buffalo winters are nothing to play with." They were slipping and sliding left and right, giving up plays.

Traci hooked me up with a box seat. I would've shown my ass and gone home otherwise, cold as it was. I should've talked her into coming home with me, but wrestling her out of my crib was not how I planned to start my day. Checkout time is at eight for all guests. No exceptions.

"More time for us," she says, digging her nails into the marks she carved into my skin last night. "Call me next time you're in DC." She pulls me into a kiss and wraps around me like a boa constrictor. "There's still time for a quick shower."

"Yo, chill," I chuckle while unraveling her limbs, thankful I met her at this freezing-ass hotel. I grab my phone off the nightstand and peck her mouth. "I'll take one at home before I scoop up the boys. There are no washcloths here, and the one small piece of soap looks like a shank. Save yourself and leave early. A duck bath in the airport is probably safer."

Traci's laugh gives me enough time to slip off the bed and put on my hoodie and coat. "Go, Antonio."

"Come lock up."

She pulls a sweatshirt over her petite frame and meets me at the door. "One of these days, someone will lock you down. You can't run forever."

I smirk. "Watch me."

"How much longer are we here? I'm not trying to be around no loud kids on my day off."

"Chill, *Bailey*," I say, telling Bread and his bottom lip to shut up. "We just got here." I'm not rushing back outside to dismount the car off the pyramid of snow we parked it on.

The Buffalo Steel is only in its second year, and the team needs all the publicity it can get to convert more fans from football to rugby. Our seasons don't conflict, and we leave it all on the field without pads or helmets. Last night's football division victory will hog up every news station from here to Long Island for at least a week. Coach is hopeful that smiling and playing with kids will earn us some airtime outside of the shadow of professional football. I doubt it, but I'll do my part.

"I want to get back into some pussy, not play with orphans." Bread sucks his teeth at the kids sprinting past us down the hall.

"Aren't you from this neighborhood? These kids aren't orphans, and they deserve a good time regardless." Kenneth, or Kendrick, as we call him, for his cadence and likeness to the rapper, is a man of few words when he's not leading the back line on the pitch. "Too bad you can't drill sense into hard heads."

Bread shoulder-checks Kendrick, who cuts a smile that dares him to try it.

Their tenacity during games is where their similarities end. Bread is stocky and built like M'Baku from *Black Panther*, with a drop fade and no common sense. As a tighthead prop, Bread is physically imposing and dominates the scrum. Kendrick keeps his tiny braids pulled into a small bun. He isn't bulky, but he is quick on his feet and good under pressure as our fly half, who controls the back line.

It's hard to rattle him, but play around, and he'll go full Gemini with his disrespect.

"Why are we the only ones here?" Bread complains like the big kid he is.

"Shins is somewhere with his girl since we're off. D is with his daughter. Cho, Connor, and Logan are out of town until later tonight. Half the backs are in a PT session, and everybody else is hungover or didn't make it home from Buffalo's playoff celebration," I say.

Bread sucks his teeth. "Man, how is this fair?"

"No one told you to stay out late," I point out. "And if you do, get your ass up. I didn't get home until this morning. You work hard to play hard, and this is work. Take a few pictures and play a few games. Act like Ms. Henrietta raised you before I call her."

It wouldn't be the first time I tap in Bread's mama.

"Fine," the twenty-four-year-old mumbles. "I smell eggs." He storms off, his nostrils wide, beard tipped to the ceiling. His black tracksuit disappears into what I assume is the kitchen.

"This MLK celebration in Marcela's council district wouldn't have anything to do with us being here, right?" Kendrick gives me a pointed look. "You never jump to do events that require us to get out of bed before ten."

"Don't start. It's good publicity."

"*Right*." He exaggerates the word with a chuckle. "I'll get someone to tell us where to go, Cap." He pats my shoulder and bops away in a thermal hoodie and jeans.

The team gives me shit for my calls with Miriam. Kendrick found me knocked out with the phone on my forehead more times than I can remember. Is it my fault that he and the rest of my snack-stealing teammates don't have a friend worth staying up for? Sounds like jealousy to me.

Outside of Julian, Miriam is my closest friend. I hate texting or talking on the phone, but I make an effort for her. Not that she requests it.

Getting her number was a joke at first. I didn't expect her to speak to me again after our New Year's Eve in the hospital. Since we were in a packed ER, I used the hours we waited to get to know her.

That was the first night we talked alone, outside of a group setting. Well, as grown people who pay taxes. The time before that, Miriam was telling me to read my social studies book, as if I were five and not in middle school.

I didn't want our time to end once we left the ER, but she tossed me back into the friend zone faster than she pounced on me after sharing chicken and soliciting a one-night stand. The reality of getting with my first crush would stay a fantasy. I went home with a confirmed broken nose, a splitting headache, and cum-stained drawers.

Nursing my ego back to life would take a sick day or two. That, I could get over. What I didn't want to lose was whatever version of Miriam she felt comfortable sharing with me. So I asked around and got her number to remind her that she's my emergency contact.

It took a medical report to prove I didn't have brain damage for her to answer my calls, but she did. Three years later, she's my longest nonsexual relationship with a woman—my mother excluded, for obvious reasons.

The crush is still here. I've been feeling Miriam since I was a kid, and I don't expect the attraction to disappear overnight. The more I learned about her and the quirks I studied from afar, the more I was hooked. Every conversation drew me back to her giggles and her failed attempts at humor.

I care for her, more than I have any other woman.

My phone buzzes.

Mike

> Cap, tell Jordan it's okay to warm up food in the microwave with tinfoil if you keep the heat on low.

The hell?

> Please tell me you didn't. We talked about this.

Mike

> My bad. Would you mind grabbing some milk on your way back? And a new microwave for the community kitchen?

Coach Washington had to be high the day he called me into his office to tell me I was captain of our rugby team.

Me.

The same guy who risked arrest years ago for running naked on the National Mall to helicopter my dick in the sun after a win. Now I'm lucky if I can hold it in peace or leave the house without someone trying to blow it up.

Steel House is a ten-unit building I purchased after my first year on the team. It was a real estate investment at the time, to generate revenue. Now it's a childcare facility for toddlers with muscles.

Unlike international teams, rugby players in the US aren't busting it wide open dripped in diamonds with seven-figure deals. The salary cap for our league compared to other sports is low, and that seven figures is more like five—as in, $50,000 on the high end. My investment portfolio earns more in my sleep, and that lets me focus on the game I've played since I was a kid. I can afford not to squeeze in a job between daylong practices and training. Thus, Steel House was born to pay it forward, and I've been risking premature gray hairs ever since.

At twenty-nine, I'm the oldest in a house of five starters and four reserves, which says a lot about the maturity level.

It wasn't long ago that I was tasting my way through Chocolate City. Every serving size in every position. I was young with an MBA, making money hand over fist with no responsibilities. Days were for business, Saturdays for rugby, and nights for my pleasure.

The old Antonio would run circles around my teammates' non-stop parties and revolving door of jump-offs who scream their orgasms like they're trying to hit high notes at a Mariah Carey tribute. The *older* Antonio gets handed his ass recovering from preseason training five days a week. My version of foreplay these days is face-planting into my pillow every night. It turns out I like more than four hours of sleep and my personal space. Sex is still a stress reliever, but not when I have to lock up my apartment to keep out people on a mission to sample the team. The last woman I found was hiding behind my trash can, like I couldn't see her. That led to stricter rules for hygiene and public safety.

How Professor X dealt with mutants running around his school while keeping his mind intact in that headpiece is beyond my comprehension. There are fully-formed adults sharing my address who need a superpower to take out the trash and not stink up the house with dirty clothes, used condoms, and unwashed ass.

Julian told me life changes once you have kids. Mo swears he's Mr. Miyagi now that he has a wife and kids, but he isn't wrong. I'm ready to claim one of these Frosted-Flakes-eating thorns in my ass on my taxes.

"Aye! Get your own!" Bread jogs away from a horde of kids on his tail. A stack of pancakes is in one hand, and a plate of enough eggs to feed four is in the other.

Exhibit A.

I keep Steel House stocked for him so that he doesn't act like he hasn't eaten in eighty-two days.

"You promised me a piggyback ride. Get him!" A little girl in a pink hoodie with Afro puffs leads the charge.

Bread's brows shoot up to the chipped ceiling. "Dr. King didn't die for this!" A stampede of tiny shoes sprint after him down a hallway of taped-up art. He's running for his life.

"Oh good, you're jumping right in," a shoulder-height woman in jeans, sneakers, and a bright orange sweater says next to Kendrick.

"Hi. I'm Antonio." I extend a hand. "I see you've met Kenneth. That's Bailey down there."

"Amber. Very nice to meet you both." She gestures for Kendrick and me to follow her down another hall with fluorescent lighting and dull linoleum floors. "I admit, I never watched rugby until the Steel. Thank you for the tickets to the home opener. They're part of our raffle to expand our programming."

"It's our pleasure," I say, flicking Kendrick over Ms. Amber's head for mouthing, *Captain, my Captain*.

"We hope today's MLK Day celebration gets good press. Our after-school and senior programs are in high demand," she says. "We also have career development classes, workshops, and a limited summer camp."

"Sounds like you do a lot." Kendrick stuffs his hands in his jeans and catalogs the unaddressed building renovations.

Worn classrooms with outdated technology don't take away from the Jefferson Moselle Community Center. The wild grins on these kids' faces, painted with comic book characters and unicorns, are evidence of its impact.

Growing up on 16th Street in DC's historic Gold Coast didn't stop my dad from taking me to pickup games at the center in his old Northeast neighborhood. I've seen places like this stretch their last meal and use a few loaves to feed thousands.

Kendrick and I stop in front of the gym. One look inside, and we're cracking up at Bread's big, scary ass. He's in front of a bouncy house and some activity tables, carrying the girl with Afro puffs on his shoulders. The matching daisies on their cheeks prove they settled their beef.

"You two are this way." Ms. Amber directs us away from the door that frames the hula-hooping two-hundred-sixty-five-pound rugby player.

My phone vibrates in my pocket.

Jalisa

> **Did I leave my glasses at your place? If you're home, I can swing by.**

A chuckle rattles my throat at her excuse to get back into my bed. That's the fourth attempt this month. She came over Friday, so she's had a whole two days of roaming the earth with no sight.

This is why I don't do sleepovers. Morning sex isn't worth the expectation of commitment with a side of bacon. I can't cook, and I sure as hell don't have plans to settle down with one person. The best I can do is steady dick, speak in tongues if I'm feeling you, and a car service with a forehead kiss.

The last woman who kept leaving body wash and panties behind required a locksmith and Julian as my legal witness to get her out of my house. Who handcuffs themselves to the bed in a headstand naked?

> No need. I put them in the top pocket of your backpack.

I love fucking and sucking as much as the next freak, but I've slowed down since becoming Papa Smurf at Steel House. I still get it in, but I'm too tired during the week for the Cirque du Soleil performance that women expect from a rugby player because of our thighs and forearm veins. I've had a lifetime of parties, flings, and situationships. The names quickly fade before it's on to the next.

The thrill is losing its luster. I want something else. What that is, I don't know.

A subtle hint of rose oil startles my steps.

"You good?" Kendrick whispers at my frown.

"Yeah," I lie.

Only one person I know wears that scent, and she doesn't move here until next week.

"We want to increase our STEM programs," Ms. Amber mentions.

"Engineering," I blurt out for no reason, lacking a smooth enough recovery to dodge two sets of matching stares. "It's a good field. A friend of mine is a mechanical engineer," I clarify and cut my eyes at Kendrick's smirk.

Does Miriam pop into my thoughts at random? I'll own it.

I tuck away my physical reactions to her to keep from ruining our friendship. It took weekly ice baths at first, but now it's under control. She's worth more than any one-night stand. Always will be.

We arrive at a blue and white room scented with broken crayons and sweat from the crowd of kids gathered around a table in the center of the carpet. Some are standing on metal chairs. Others are rushing to get a better look at whatever is triggering their screams.

Either Ms. Amber is running drugs, or they're high on life.

The maybe-dealer smiles at the chants. "This is a very popular room today. Kids, guess who we have with us? The Buffalo Steel!"

"Shake it harder!" a boy shouts from behind the curtain of 'fros, curls, and fades.

Sweaters and hoodies part to reveal the source of the contained chaos.

It's not the tower of toothpicks and gumdrops wedged into a foundation of brownies that's hurling my pulse over a cliff. It's the woman in a pink sweater, librarian glasses, and jeans, wearing a grin I've only seen on a screen since she patted my chest and went back to Baltimore three years ago.

She's here.

Chapter 6

Miriam

My high-tops are off the ground. Blood rushes to my temples as my body forcefully spins in a circle. I'm dizzy, my glasses smashed to my face by the forearms pinning me in place. They're larger than I remember. So are the biceps squeezing my organs together.

"Can't. Breathe," I croak.

"Shoot, my bad." Antonio sets my soles on the carpet and searches for internal damage using X-ray vision he doesn't have.

My mind quiets at another whiff of the tobacco and cedar cologne transferring to my sweater from the long-sleeved navy shirt that's molded to his torso. The scent, mixed with fabric softener, would be comforting if a chest lined with every muscle seen on a medical drama weren't cutting off my air supply.

Did he always smell like laundry?

That would require him to know how to turn on a washer.

"Still can't breathe," I wheeze from below Antonio's clavicles.

"Sorry." He steps back to give me a chance to reacquaint myself with breathing. "It's good to see you, Doe."

"You too."

I remind my body that he's always been fine.

Antonio's caramel hue and square jaw decorated in a trimmed beard are nothing new. I've seen them countless times, along with the disarming smile he brandishes freely on video calls. The live version should not have this effect on me.

Subconscious physiological responses are normal behavior. They're not a sign of lust lurking in dark corners for a friend I almost rode into the new year. The involuntary changes to my breathing are simply jitters at seeing him and all his flesh for the first time since he left Maryland.

I gulp and point to the loose waves that have replaced the man bun that never grew. "I like it."

He runs a hand over his fresh cut. "It was time for a change. Your natural hair is just like I imagined."

His praise glides over the twist-out I freed from the rotation of nonflammable wigs I wore during my college years. Grabbing one to go with my lab coat was more efficient than experimenting with a curl pattern I had no time to learn. Today's side part is nothing innovative, but Antonio stares at my coiled bob like it's the best thing he's ever seen.

"I like it." The rasp in his voice draws my frown.

Reading social cues is an admitted shortcoming. Like right now, Antonio's pinched brows and gaze that swings from my hair to my face don't match his fervor from minutes ago.

Talking on the phone provided a safety net I no longer have. There was no thinking about hand placement or whether my smile matched that of a rabid animal. Every public interaction turns awkward, except I'm not the one breaking the no-staring rule this time.

He is.

I cough, and Antonio clears his throat.

Subconscious physiological responses.

He stuffs his hands into his pockets. "So, bestie who moved a week early. What are you doing here?"

"Conducting an experiment. You mind?"

Heat fans my cheeks when Sean puts his hands on his bony hips. He's eight, with neither the height nor bass in his voice to reprimand anybody. All eyes in the room shift between me and Antonio.

"We're still waiting," Sean scolds Antonio, who backs away with his hands raised at the threat dressed in a Minecraft shirt. He retreats to a man shorter than him, who's rolling his lips.

Did Ms. Amber get Kendrick Lamar to perform?

The tug on my sweater is my final reminder to go back to judging how the built structural foundations would survive in an earthquake.

Sorry, I mouth to Antonio, whose eyes are on me and not the engineering project that's reactivating screams.

You got it, Doe, he mouths back with a wink.

"If you weren't in your mid-thirties, I'd tell your father you drove a moving truck by yourself." Antonio shakes his head. "You always complain about driving at night."

"I arrived before sunset. What does my age have to do with it?"

His shoulder lifts. "I was raised to respect my elders—ow!" His hand covers the pec I just stuck. It's the size of my head.

I smirk through my sip of apple juice.

I've been under interrogation since we left my activity room in search of food. We're on the gym bleachers with two water bottles, juice boxes, Twizzlers from the stash I keep in my purse, and a jumbo pretzel split between us. Any butterflies I had during our initial reunion have left the building. We're back to our regular quips. His pokes to prod my annoyance.

The kids who are still here after hours of play are with the other Steel players, playing Double Dutch. The Kendrick Lamar look-alike slips through the slashing ropes with a casual swagger. Winston Duke—Carbohydrate, or was it Bagel that Antonio called him?—grabs a pair of handles to speed up the rhythm and cusses when his teammate hits a crip walk.

Today's MLK Day event was a success. News cameras arrived, prompting our state lawmakers and a congressperson to take some pictures and leave faster than they had come. I had fun—minus the glares from the guy next to me, who's still pissed that I moved without him.

"You didn't think to call me? I'm hurt." Antonio pouts with a tight lip and a wobbly chin.

"I got help packing the truck." I snicker, trying to hold in a laugh. "I don't expect you to drop everything, fly down to Baltimore, and ride up with me. You're busy," I deadpan, and his phone buzzes.

Antonio can sulk all he wants. The Steel's preseason practice schedule is in full swing. He's not wasting time on unnecessary travel. Not when he can recover from a hard training session with whatever Lala is sending him three texts in less than a minute.

His phone illuminates with another message he ignores. "I would've come if you'd asked."

There's no attempt to look away. He studies me with a focus that would make me dizzy and loosen my knees if I didn't know any better. The arch of his brow, the purse of that thick lower lip, and the inventory of hard muscle is how you wind up in somebody's bushes ready to serve time.

I never had a friendship this close with a man before, let alone a man I encouraged to play in my body. Sending messages like Lala is safer than sitting on the receiving end of his stare.

$L = T\text{-}V$

The Lagrangian function is a silent recital to calm nerves that are determined to flare and act a fool.

We're friends.

Platonic and nothing else.

My "Appreciate it" is too euphoric for a conversation about moving trucks and helping hands.

"Did you and Marcela unpack everything? I know you called her for help." My sister walks by in a community center tee, jeans, and Chucks. Her camera-ready smile dissolves at Antonio's shout. "Thanks for the heads-up that she's here! I thought we were family?"

"Boy, bye!" She rolls her neck, which is anchored by a loose bun, and sets off toward a family. Constituents, no doubt.

I giggle and nudge Antonio's knee with mine. "Marcela only does manual labor when required. I'm giving myself the week to finish unpacking. My new sofa arrives on Friday, and I want the living room set up before that."

He nods through a bite of pretzel. "I'll swing by after Friday's practice. I'm free after this if you need help today."

"Sure about that?" I motion to the messages lighting up his phone. Some things never change.

"I mean, I *can* be free," he clarifies. "If you need me."

"I'll be fine, thanks. You sure someone's not dying?" I laugh at his groan. It's not funny if someone really is passing away, but I get the sense that no one is. He might want to check the bushes before he leaves.

"It's the team chat," he says, ignoring Lala and her texts that double as smoke signals. "Conditioning got bumped to ten tomorrow. My teammates are throwing another party at Steel House tonight. When did you say your sofa comes?"

"Friday, and you're not spending the night."

"Come on, Doe!" Antonio whines. "I need my beauty rest. I'll bring my own pillow."

His plea is a mix of pouted lips, a creased forehead, and brown eyes that beg me to save him from the hell he created. His baby face on a body rivaling Alan Ritchson's is a sight.

"I'll *think* about it, but I make no guarantees." After living in dorms and shared campus apartments, I crave my own space.

"Thank you, bestie!" Thick arms wrap around me, melding my body and now-crooked glasses to his. "Did I mention that I'm happy you're here?"

"I'm starting to regret coming. Can't. Breathe. Again," I mumble through smushed lips.

"Sorry." Antonio scoots back. How anyone survives his tackles is a medical miracle. His hugs are heavy.

"I *am* happy you're here," he says, his voice soft, his eyes pinned to mine.

The air hangs in silence, weighing our glances with a sensation that needles my chest. Approaching Steel players cut through our trance, and the Darcy-Weisbach equation reroutes my thoughts.

"Can we go? I played, got shit painted on my face, and didn't cuss out any kids. I need a nap," Bagel or whoever declares, his body slumped and chest heaving from keeping up with children half his size.

"Yeah," Antonio chuckles. "We can go, Bread."

"Say less. I'll be in the car. Maid Miriam—"

"Who?" I snort.

"The fox in that *Robin Hood* movie they played today," Bread says with confidence.

"Maid *Marian*, dickhead," the Kendrick look-alike corrects.

"Fuck you too," Bread tosses at his smirk. "Like I was saying, Maid Miriam, you're cool people if you can keep Papa Smurf over here from digging in our asses. Feel free to talk to him in any closet, or whatever you two do."

"You must want to walk home." Antonio stands and pulls me with him. "You good here, Doe?"

"*Doe.* Cute," Bread mocks with heart eyes. He nudges his teammate, who grins.

Antonio's sigh is that of a tired dad. "It's not even like that. She's just a friend. Go to the car."

The way he hurls the word "friend" shouldn't sting, but it does. I am "just a friend," but hearing it like that, like an afterthought, stirs the part of me that takes offense at how easily Antonio brushes me off. The person he claims to be his bestie.

"You sure you don't need us for anything?" Antonio asks again.

"Go," I say, grabbing our trash, which he takes. "Thanks for coming today. Marcela and Ms. Amber appreciated it. I'll see you around."

His stare lingers. "Friday?"

"Sure." I nod. "You have the address, so come whenever."

"Okay." He eyes me again, frustrating my inability to register what he's not saying.

"What?" I ask.

"Nothing," he says.

"Today, Papa Smurf!" Bread yells from the door on the opposite side of the gym.

I huff a laugh. "You better go. Enjoy the party."

"I won't."

Antonio leaves with his teammates. I pull out my phone and swipe to my notes app. "Make more friends" is now at the top of my to-do list.

Whatever that was, I don't want to feel it again.

Chapter 7

Antonio

"Fast feet. Sink those hips!"

Coach Titan's whistle is an alarm to my muscles, which are gasping for energy. My arms strain to push off the turf that's clawing at my knees.

I suck in a breath and speed through the agility ladder. The quick shuffle of my cleats digs through the field's synthetic fibers. Kendrick passes me the ball, and I cradle it before propelling into Shins and Nacho's pads. Sweat from my forehead spatters the reinforced vinyl shields the lock and loosehead prop use to prevent a line break. I drop my height, anchor the ball against my forearm, and drive with small, explosive steps to wedge between my teammates.

As a flanker, my position is a link between the forwards and the backs. It involves me in the offense and the defense. Making key tackles and dismantling our opponents' play requires me to stay sharp with an awareness for opportunities.

"Way to power through, Knight!" our strength and conditioning coach shouts from the sideline. He blows his whistle again, signaling the end of the drill. Each gulp of air burns my lungs.

Fuck, I hate Wednesdays.

Preseason training requires an endurance we build through intense conditioning, weightlifting, field running, and game play. All four converge on any given day, forcing us to leave it all on the field. Today started with an early gym session, followed by speed exposure and ground contact strength work.

It's a high-intensity day, one that ends in hand-to-hand combat for first dibs on the ice bath at Steel House.

"Good work out there." Shins tosses me my water bottle and joins me on the turf next to our gear.

The only time I welcome fake grass under dome lights is during a Buffalo winter. I always played rugby outside in DC, rain, shine, or otherwise.

I suck down half of the room temperature water in one go and swipe at the sweat dripping down my face with my jersey. It's another teen-degree day, but you'd never know it inside the indoor practice field.

"You and Nacho almost had me." I smirk at him sprawled out. He gives me the finger with the arm that shields his eyes from the lights beaming above us.

Shayne, called "Shins" for his leg power to drive scrums, is tall as hell. As a lock, he's a specialist at disrupting rucks and securing possessions for a lineout. He'd give me more problems if I didn't know the side he favors with his tackles for an opening to break the line.

Our positions are adjacent to each other on the field, which makes one-upping each other during practice difficult.

"How was home?" I ask about his weekend back in Glendale, Colorado.

Shins pulls off his scrum cap, doused in sweat, and tosses it. "Good," he says. "Daisy is staying in state for college."

"She playing?" It's a dumb question, and he confirms it with a sidelong glance. Everyone in the Brown family plays rugby except for the dog.

He hesitates but says, "Flanker," and mushes me at my laughter.

"Tell Daisy I got her if she wants tips." At five ten, his little sister is short for their family, but with more time in the gym, she'll be a wrecking ball in my position.

I block the roll of tape Shins chucks at my head with my water bottle. "Stay away from her," he snaps, tugging at the tape that secures the lifting block he uses to practice lineouts from one of his thighs. "That's my baby sister."

"The fact that you think I'd go after an eighteen-year-old is insulting. Give me some credit for my virtue."

One, I prefer my women older. I'm attracted to the ones my age, but there's something about a woman in her thirties or forties.

Two, Shins and Daisy share their father's face. Pass.

All three resemble the Black duke from *Bridgerton*. Dude isn't unattractive, but he annoyed me during the first season, which my mother forced me to watch last Christmas. He and Shins have the same thick brows, brown eyes, and scowl. Shins isn't into tailcoats and cravats, but he dons a stick up his ass.

"There are certain lines I won't cross," I emphasize.

Married.

Under twenty-five.

Orders sparkling water at restaurants.

He deadpans, "Are you not the only motherfucker on this field?"

I rub my beard. "Not sure. Bread helped Coach Titan get on one of those dating apps."

"Who's a motherfucker?" Quincy, our scrum-half, walks up with Kendrick.

The "backs," or backline, had a primer training session while we forwards focused on system offense. We get thirty minutes before we switch. I was hoping for a quick nap, but I see now that's not happening.

"This one." Shins points at me.

I smack away his finger. "You need to get out more."

Quincy squeezes between us with a grin. "Did you forget about Miami?"

"How was I supposed to know an opposing player's mom was scouting for dick at the bar?" Did she get what she was looking for? Hell yeah. "And that was one time," I say in my defense and kick Quincy's cleat. "Respect your elders."

The little prick is the size of a Fiat and can't grow more than two strands of chin hair. At twenty-two, he's the youngest person in Steel House, and he gets stuffed in the trash bin at least once a week for not knowing when to knock it off.

"What about the woman in Chicago, our first season?" Shins asks.

"We got stuck in a snowstorm. I was trapped in her house." My frown deepens at their laughter.

Quincy's mini 'fro scratches against the turf as he clutches the sides of his Tonka Truck muscles. Even Kendrick is hunched over, hollering like our flights didn't get canceled that game.

Phyllis had the body of Taraji with a bob to match. We met the night before my game at an upscale bar across from my hotel. I popped in for a nightcap after practice and came out with her number. We celebrated the Steel's win at her house, and I couldn't find a ride back to my room because of the road conditions.

So I used the extra time at her place eating the snacks she kept for her granddaughter and homecooked meals. I even had a bath with those fancy salts my mom bought out of Avon catalogs when I was younger. Phyllis was forty-six and expected nothing but my stamina, a willing tongue, and me not to use her decorative towels.

I left the Windy City with hickeys, mild carpet burn, and a to-go plate.

"Is it wrong to enjoy women and not discriminate based on age?" They make it sound like I bruised granny's esophagus with no aftercare.

I'm not reckless with my dick or selfish by only seeking pleasure for myself. I take pride in my stroke game and aim to leave every woman I'm with happier than she was before she came.

Except for one.

Miriam is the only woman I have never satisfied. It wasn't from a lack of trying, but it's hard to reset the mood after a broken nose and hours in the ER. Not that I would try now that we're friends.

My question falls on deaf ears from all of the cackling. "I'm switching teams." I grab my bag and stand in a huff.

"Bro, chill." Kendrick blows out a long breath through chipmunk cheeks. He swipes a braid out of his face. "We all know you ain't moving now that Miriam's here."

Shins's brows drop. "Who is Miriam?"

"Is that why you ditched the party, being all antisocial?" Quincy presses a fist to his mouth at Kendrick's nod and squeals. "I knew it!" His cocoa complexion reddens as he punches the air like he won the lottery. He's the clown on the team, who looks like Marlon Wayans's love child.

"Someone want to clue me in?" Shins asks.

Kendrick waves him off. "I told you not to let Rachel talk you into moving to Clarence. Now you're stuck out there with cozy racism and farmers' markets. Cap's girl moved to Buffalo."

"She's not my girl," I sigh.

Shins's eyes light up with the possibility of apple-picking double dates. "You're finally settling down," he grins. "You should bring her over for dinner. We'd love to have you."

"So Rachel can torture him with seasonless chicken?" Quincy's face twists at the memory. "Save your stomach, Cap."

"Y'all need to stop talking about my girl. She's trying," Shins snaps.

"To kill us," Quincy adds, causing everyone but Shins to snicker. "Should've left her in college, but *no*. You don't find it funny she picked a house in the middle of nowhere that looks like the one from *Get Out*?" He whistles.

"Shut up before I fling your little ass!" Shins shouts. Quincy is five seven to Shins's six three and remains unbothered. Shins, on the other hand, is ready to pop a blood vessel.

The team knows Shins's relationship with Rachel is a sore spot. He comes from money and has dated the daughter of his parents' best friends since high school. It's an arrangement he doesn't seem to mind. Couldn't be me.

"Chill, Quincy." I tap him and the smug grin he's wearing to fall back. Shins might come from the suburbs, but he will lay Quincy's ass out if agitated. "I'm not bringing my girl over to dinner because I don't have one."

That, and I don't want that bland-ass chicken. When we say we let our ancestors guide our cooking, that doesn't apply to everybody.

Kendrick eyes me with suspicion. "Miriam hasn't been here a week, and she already has your nose wide open."

"Bullshit," I toss. Now he's telling stories.

"Really? Explain why you stayed in your unit the entire night." Quincy smirks. "Lala came by looking for you. Says you never answered your door."

They wait for an explanation.

I shrug. "I was tired."

"Bullshit!" They yell.

"Why y'all so obsessed with this? I wasn't interested, okay?"

The excessive parties at Steel House was me years ago. I did all of that ten times over, and I only entertain them now as something to pass the time. I'm not a prude like Shins, who only comes out when his girl allows it. I want something else, something other than a splitting headache the next morning and a woman whose name I forgot. I call up Jalisa or Lala if I need to get off, but I didn't want the company on Monday.

Wonder why.

"Miriam moving to Buffalo has nothing to do with it. I skipped one party—one—and people want to act like I'm committing to a life with a white picket fence and babies," I say. I'll commit myself to an asylum before that happens.

I'll admit that having her here comes with a certain level of excitement. I look forward to learning more about her, just like I've been counting down the days until I see her on Friday.

We've barely texted since running into each other at the MLK event two days ago. I didn't want to bombard her. I'm giving her the space to sort out her life, which is packed in boxes, and answer the million-dollar career question that's been following her since college. Outside of a text to check in and confirm we're still good for Friday, all communication is silent.

It's hard not speaking to Miriam, but I'm not confessing a damn thing to my nosy teammates, who are still staring at me.

Since they want to be in my business...

"Remember when you told me to stay away from your sister?" I remind Shins.

"Yeah?"

"Daisy is safe with me, but this one fell in love when he saw her during her summer visit." I crack up at Quincy's glower before the shock that I outed his secret registers.

"Not funny!" Quincy sprints away from Shins, who catches him by the back of his jersey collar. Their eight-inch height difference has his feet dangling off the ground.

Shins does not play about his baby sister.

"Cap!" Quincy screeches in a high pitch for help. He wiggles out of his jersey but gets stuck in his compression shirt underneath. "Don't leave me hanging!"

"Too late," I laugh.

Kendrick is cracking up like he didn't try to make me a hot topic.

"Aye, Shins! Kendrick said he wanted to motorboat your mama's booty." I back away from the grenade I launched and smirk at Kendrick. His eyes are wide, and his jaw is on the turf.

Teammates and staff gather around the commotion. Shins is a raging bull caught between Quincy and Kendrick. The furious lock tosses Quincy into a trash bin before sprinting after Kendrick.

"Give me those fast feet every game!" Coach Titan nods at Kendrick's Olympic run down the pitch.

"Cap!" Kendrick wheezes. "You ain't—"

Shins tackles him at full speed.

"Shit..." he groans.

Chapter 8

Miriam

"**I**'d kick Mitchell Slate square in the dick if it wouldn't land me in jail."

On a good day, Marcela grits her teeth dealing with Buffalo's mayor. Meditation. A Bible app. Boxing. Whatever it takes to keep her out of the Erie County Holding Center.

Today, she's out for blood, contemplating ways to put her years of soccer to use. It's my first time witnessing her fire up close and not on the other end of the phone.

The mayor should fear for his life. And his penis.

Marcela's black blouse slides against my retro dining chair. Her legs are planted wide in black vegan leather pants, and her matching stilettos scrape over the speckled linoleum floor. She flexes her fingers next to a glass of water she hasn't touched since storming into my house from City Hall.

The flattened line in her plump lips matches the slash of her threaded brows.

"Is there anything I can do, minus bodily injury?" Her large brown eyes meet mine from across the tiny white table. The soft pairing with the seafoam green dining chairs is a contrast to the red seeping into my sister's mocha complexion.

Her "No" comes with a tired smile, accompanied by a long exhale. She rubs the back of her neck below a high bun of Marley twists. The mask eldest daughters wear to prove they can handle the weight of the world slips.

Marcela is the strong one, overprotective and intrusive, but my hero nonetheless. Her stubbornness and inability to ask for help make it hard for me to show up for her in the ways she shows up for me. I'm here for her, but I won't survive jail.

"I'll handle him," she says in a promise to herself.

"I take it your meeting with the mayor didn't go well?"

She snorts. "The prick pretended he wasn't in his office, like I didn't see him peek out of the door when he thought I was gone." Her lips spread into a grin. "You'll see me on the news."

"Please tell me you left Knuck and Buck at home." It's rare for Marcela to leave her house without her brass knuckles.

"Am I calling you for bail money? I simply vented my frustrations to news cameras that were covering a rally about Buffalo's budget deficit. Can you believe one was happening at the same time I had a scheduled meeting with scary-ass Slate? Talk about timing."

"Right," I chuckle. "Always with a backup plan."

"Don't leave home without one. Anyway," she laughs, her tone back to its usual playfulness reserved for the people she doesn't want to kick in the penis. "What's going on with you and the job search?"

"Don't start. It will take more than a week to sort out my life." My clothes are still in boxes. "I don't know who's worse, you or our father. Acting like I'm a baby," I sigh.

"You are the baby."

"I'm thirty-four with a whole doctorate!"

"Dr. Baby." The clementine I toss at her head misses its mark. She pulls the bowl from the middle of the table to her chest. "Age-wise, you're grown and smart as hell."

"But?" Because there is always a but, and it's fat and intrusive in my family.

"But," Marcela says gently, "your life experience could fit on a report card. Let our father help."

"You tell me all I do is spend time in a classroom, and now you want me to go back inside one?"

"How do you plan to use the doctorate that took five years of your life?"

"I—" Don't know.

I want to pop the smug smile off of Marcela's face, but I know better. I'm not a fighter, and she'll have me cowering behind a locked door like she did the mayor. She and my father mean well, but, goodness, would it be nice to have a little time to figure out who I want to be now that I've finished school.

Do you know how diverse the field of mechanical engineering is? I could create technologies to address world hunger, the climate crisis, transportation needs, and fix every McDonald's ice cream machine in the country.

I just parted ways with my lab wigs, and my family expects me to decide if I want to spend the rest of my days in academia, industry, or the public sector.

Hell if I know!

The minute you hit thirty, every piece of who you are and what your purpose is needs to click into place. God forbid you're in your mid-thirties and still trying to figure it out. Apparently, the world will end if you don't have it together.

Marcela pats my hand. "No need to talk to yourself, Miri. You're turning red." Dang it. "Your savings is a good cushion. Sooner or later, though, you need to find something that will keep the lights on. Our father is a lifeline if it comes to that. Just expect strings."

He's a loan shark with a heart. Minus the extortion.

Excellence is in our DNA, a reminder he sends in my annual birthday card. Years of his sacrifice working for the State Department came with long hours, divorce, and an understanding that the next generation of Beckfords will carve out their own pathways to success.

Engineering is honorable so long as I don't act like Lynn from *Girlfriends*, earning degree after degree with only student debt, a band, and "the Lynn Spin" to show for it. I can't carry a tune or twirl on a ding-a-ling to make anyone proud.

"Hey, it's Friday," Marcela says to lighten the mood and the pressure to solve the equation of my life. "You're out of wine, and I need something stronger than filtered water. A few sorors are meeting at The Pine Room. Get dressed. We'll leave in twenty."

I glance at my leggings tucked into knitted socks. The Sunnydale sweatshirt hanging off my shoulder doesn't constitute "going-out attire." Not that I planned to leave the house.

"I'm staying in."

Marcela's brows knit. "Are you not the one who told me you wanted to do stuff outside the house besides grocery shopping? This is stuff."

"I do, but tonight isn't good for me."

"Why not?"

The doorbell rings.

"Because I already have plans," I say.

The heavy lashes shadowing Marcela's cheeks fly up. "Plans? Who is making house calls?" She hops up from the table, the determination to sniff out my business set in her smirk.

"Nobody."

The doorbell rings again.

"That doesn't sound like nobody," she teases.

My sock catches on the kitchen threshold. "A friend!" I hop after her with a throbbing baby toe.

"You have no friends here—*ouch*!" She rubs the arm I punch.

"I'm working on that!" I whisper-yell, now feet from the front door. "There's a meetup next week for people over thirty who are looking for new friends."

"You're going to a group event with strangers *willingly*?"

"Don't laugh." It's embarrassing enough trying to make friends at this age.

To her credit, she lifts her hands and zips her lips. "Good for you. Want me to come for moral support?"

"I don't need a chaperone. I'm capable of interacting with people at a function alone." I might vomit a little in my mouth, but I'll manage.

She forces a smile to keep from calling my bluff and tilts her head toward the door. "So who's that?" A glint of humor sparks in her eyes when it clicks—I only have one friend here.

I don't ask God for much, but I'm silently praying in King James English that Marcela does not embarrass me.

"Antonio." There's no point in glancing up to catch the grin that's ruffling her mouth.

"We're friends."

Friends can do lots of things. Have dinner. Watch the news. We've been platonic since life knocked us upside the head on that New Year's Eve we've never discussed nor attempted again. Antonio doesn't think of me like that anyway.

The doorbell rings again, followed by a knock.

I'm an awful host. The man is probably frozen whole on my porch by now.

I shoo Marcela away. "Please don't act a mess."

She frowns. "What kind of big sister would I be if I didn't?"

"Nice and decent," I shoot over my shoulder. Whatever rebuttal I have for her snappy comeback dies on a squeak. It's more of a gasp that becomes a cough.

Sweet muscles and thigh meat!

"Hi." Antonio's voice is a silky rumble with no signs of hypothermia. It's gentle, a far cry from his athletic form, which is suffocating the life out of my doorway.

His weatherproof pants shouldn't tempt any fantasies about the hard muscles beneath the fabric. How they exert energy when provoked. The planes of his legs are carved from hours in the gym and on the field. His chest is no exception. Broad lines molded over thick pecs lead to the protective arms I've seen cradle a rugby ball and fling other men his size.

I'm eyeing him like a Cyber Monday sale. How do I expect to make more friends if I can't stop ogling the only one I have?

This isn't a date. Friends pay house visits all the time. Even friends with penises.

"You okay, Doe?"

"Huh? Yes." I push up my glasses and blink at the team logo that's stitched on the black hoodie stretched over his torso. The ox-like animal taunts me over "Buffalo Steel" written in white letters wrapped in black. "Hi."

"Is this a bad time?" His eyes shift to Marcela. "Hey." The word lacks its usual vigor.

Is he nervous?

"It's nice to see you again," she offers.

"You too, ma—"

"Don't 'ma'am' me. I'm only six years older than Miriam, and I'm no one's elder or auntie."

Antonio nods, his gaze sweeping over me. The casual perusal activates butterflies in the pit of my stomach. "N-Nice couch," he stutters. "You picked a good color."

"It's limestone," I confirm. "Not exactly beige or gray but has a warmer undertone. There's a bifold memory foam mattress. I heard they're good for pressure relief and spinal alignment."

I'm rambling.

"That's good." He nods again. "I need to run home for a quick shower, but I wanted to drop these off. I stopped by the store." He squints with an expression that's hard to decipher.

Did I say too much about my new sleeper sofa?

Oh, he's holding a reusable grocery bag. Right, his trip to the store.

You're staring.

Antonio clears his throat. "Fridays were your no-study nights with sushi, wine, and *Buffy*, if I remember." He glances at my sweatshirt.

"Yes—right! I figured we'd order in, but this is very thoughtful." I bite my lip. "Thank you."

"No problem."

The night air crackles with the faint scent of firewood in the distance. It mixes with the lingering threads of Antonio's cologne. The below-freezing temperature frosting the cars parked in the street is no match for the heat that's painting our breaths.

Marcela cuts through the silence with a bark of laughter. "Let me go." She reaches for her coat on the hook next to the door and aims a defiant smile at me. "Enjoy dinner with your *friend*."

Don't start, I mouth. Her stilettos put her a few inches taller than Antonio, blocking his view.

So finish, she mouths back, faking a shiver. "It's cold out. Be a good host and invite Antonio in. I'll text you about Sunday's brunch."

He shuffles out the way. "Need help to your car?" He motions to the six-inch contraptions attached to her feet.

"*And* he has manners? I got it. Thanks, though. Bye, you two. Don't forget to wrap it up!"

I groan at her deep grin, tempted to take her out with my snow boot, which is within reach.

"The food, I mean," she adds. "In case you want seconds later. Gotta keep it fresh."

"Get out before I yell that you're voting to raise taxes. Drive safe." I stick my tongue out, pull Antonio inside, and slam the door shut. Her chuckle vibrates from the other side.

"I have towels and washcloths here if you want to shower," I tell him.

Now wait a minute.

His eyes widen below his Buffalo Steel winter hat. The cute kind, with a tiny ball on top. "Nah. I don't want to put you out."

"Oh, stop." I smack the brick that is his chest. "You need to shower, and I have one. We can eat faster this way."

A brow rises. "Are you sure?"

"Do you not trust my soap?"

"Not if it's a bar. Those collect pubes. I'm joking!" He lifts his arms with a laugh and thumbs at the front door. "My gear is in my trunk. I always keep a change of clothes with me."

"Okay," I say.

"Okay." He hands me the grocery bag with our dinner and sets off in high-tops to his car.

"This is silly," I tell myself from the front window. There is no justifiable reason to peek out the blinds. Antonio doesn't need a lookout or a witness should he bust his tail on a patch of ice.

Simple, box-shaped homes with overhanging eaves and sash windows—like the one I'm pressed against—frame the quiet street, which is painted in quilts of snow.

"A shower isn't salacious," I confirm to my half-unpacked, half-boxed-up living room. "It's hygienic, and it conserves gas by saving him an extra trip."

I jump when he looks back at the house. Then I make a run for it to the kitchen, where I search for the common sense I must have lost in the junk drawer.

Friends can eat raw fish without it being weird.

Chapter 9

Antonio

"Get your shit together, Knight."

I angle my head under the steady spray. The polished chrome showerhead resembles a 1950s relic, but it funnels enough pressure to knead my tired muscles from today's practice. Water drums over my head, running in rivulets down the nape of my neck to my back.

Bundled eucalyptus mixes with steam. My muscles aren't screaming anymore, but nothing has worked to calm my dick. It's ready to knock a hole through the tiles.

I've been hard since I froze my ass off on Miriam's porch waiting for her to open the door. Aside from the good blood circulation, I'm not proud of it. Her black leggings, curved to the smooth lines of her hips and succulent thighs thick enough to crack watermelons, had all of me leaning forward.

Whether she's a siren in a tight red dress looking for a one-night stand or in a loose sweatshirt with her hair pulled back into a curly puff like tonight, her existence demands a response.

One glance and a whiff of that rose oil is all it takes. Her scent invades the tight corners of the tiled shower behind a simple cream shower curtain. I soaped myself twice in Miriam's shea butter body wash to keep from beating off in the smallest bathroom in Buffalo.

"Fuck." I drop my head and widen my stance to welcome hard strokes.

Plump lips and wide eyes appear behind my eyelids. Miriam is the complete package.

Sweet.

Intelligent.

Full-bodied.

And you're about to come in her bathroom.

"Shit!" The thought snaps me away from the woman who's starred in my dreams for the last eighteen years. She's under the same roof but still out of reach.

I've wanted her since I knew of her. She stayed on the fringes of our mutual circles for so long, I never pictured us being friends. I can't help the physical response she excites by just breathing in my direction, but I can get a grip. One that doesn't involve jerking off in her tiny-ass bathroom, fantasizing about something that will never happen.

"Pervert," I mutter, and rinse out the wash rag.

Coming here wasn't a big deal until it was. Masturbation in a porta-potty-sized shower wasn't on the agenda, but neither were the nerves I felt seeing her in person for the second time since we decided to be friends.

I clammed up ringing the doorbell and clenched my ass, if I'm being honest. Tonight isn't a date—I don't date—but I found myself checking my breath and second-guessing the dinner I grabbed after practice.

The whiplash of my heartbeat and that prickle I feel down my spine whenever I'm near her will fade as we spend more time together. I don't want to ruin what we have or the peace she brings to my life.

I turn off the water, exit the shower, and frown at the towel on the toilet. It's the size of an oven mitt. She'll get a show if I cough wrong.

My rugby bag, which has my clothes and a towel for people my height, is in the hall. This bathroom barely fits a toilet and tub, so I couldn't keep it on the floor. I was tired of tripping over it, shuffling between the sink to brush my teeth and getting the shower ready. How Miriam fits in here with all that ass is a life hack.

Don't think about her ass.

I peek outside the door to make sure the coast is clear. The hall is an empty space of white walls with molding and aged wood floors that creak beneath my tiptoe. I reach one of the zippers before I sprint toward a yelp.

"Doe!" I call out, my hand on the towel, inches from exposing my dick. The smart thing to do would've been to grab a pair of pants. But my feet took off faster than my common sense could catch up.

What I find when I enter what I assume is her room has me laughing to the point of tears.

She's hanging from a shelf inside a narrow closet. A step stool is on its side on the ground as her feet flutter in the air to find it.

"Doe," I snicker.

"I'm okay!" She can't look back or down. Her head is sandwiched between her arms as she forces a pull-up.

"Just let go."

"I don't want to land wrong and twist my ankle. The step stool is here somewhere."

She's only two or so feet off the ground, but she's so focused on the foldable platform she doesn't notice that the boxes stacked above her are now leaning.

"Doe!"

"Ahh!"

The shelf buckles under her weight, taking her and the cardboard boxes with it. I run to her and dive at the last minute. The boxes pound over my back as I curl Miriam into me.

"Are you okay?" I'm panting from the adrenaline high.

"Yeah." She swallows a heavy breath and fixes her glasses. "Thank you. Marcela must've stacked those. I was on my tippy-toes on the stool."

"Let's not put things where you can't reach. You sure you're not hurt?" I scan her face for any signs of discomfort.

"Except for your bodyweight pressing into my ribs? Just peachy," she grunts.

"My bad."

I push up to a squat and gasp at the cold air creeping up my thighs.

Miriam's eyes bulge.

My towel is gone.

"Oh my—"

"Shit! Close your eyes." In a scramble to not assault her with my dick, I pick up the closest object and use it to shield her eyes.

"Did you really just toss a box on my head?" she asks through a muffled cackle.

"If it's any consolation, you're still beautiful." I tap the cardboard that's swallowing her from the shoulders up and speed walk to the bedroom door with my nuts in my hand. "Don't look at my ass!"

She giggles. "Too late. Hey, Antonio?"

I lean through the doorway and catch the dawn of a smirk. Miriam's hair is a splatter of curls bungee jumping from her head.

"Yeah?" I ask.

"They have tanning salons to help with that."

The melody of her full belly laughter surrounds the chaos of boxes and the contents of her closet.

"Oh, you got jokes about my ass now? Caramel doesn't sugar cookie in the winter. Just for that, you can fix the shelf you suplexed yourself."

The corners of her mouth ribbon. "My team's solar-powered refrigerator system won a senior design competition. I can handle a shelf."

Refrigerators were never a turn-on for me, but the way she's talking has me hard again.

Down.

I clear my throat. "You want company? A safety monitor so you don't take out another shelf trying to scale it?"

"I had a step stool!"

"And still looked like you were trying to dunk." I dodge the slipper she chucks and laugh.

"I'd rather fight gravity than have cheeks as white as the moon."

My mouth slacks, and I do a double take at my so-called friend. "I'm eating everything I brought by myself when I get downstairs."

"Don't be sour!" Miriam yells through her laughter.

"As a Sour Patch Kid!" I grin and lengthen my stride to scoop up my rugby bag and change in the bathroom.

This, the jabs we toss back and forth, is one of my favorite things about her.

She's funny as hell, with a sense of humor most will never see because of how quiet she is around groups. I love it, even if I'm on the receiving end of her corny jokes.

"My ass is fabulous," I mumble to the mirror on the medicine cabinet.

I step into my boxer briefs. My toe catches on a strap on my open bag when I lift out a pair of sweats. It sends me backwards, straight into the shower curtain, which is clearly unable to support my weight. I tumble into the damp tub, feet and bootyhole in the air.

Miriam rushes into the bathroom. "Are you okay?" She frowns when she sees her shower curtain wrapped around me like a toga.

"Win any design projects fixing a shower rod?"

A metal ring rolls off and smacks me in the head.

"Ow."

Chapter 10

Miriam

"So you don't want to talk no more, ah? Why I have to call you every time?"

Patricia Rojas is consistent with, if not dedicated to, guilt trips and Saturday morning cleaning. My mother calls at ten thirty every week, and she always acts like it's been years since we last spoke.

The bright pitch of "Gotas de Lluvia" sways through mariachi instruments down the other end of the line. That song was a wake-up call before I'd spend hours cleaning the kitchen, bathrooms, and living room. My father had enough money to hire a full-time cleaning staff, but no stranger was seeing what our floors looked like.

Marcela and I *were* the cleaning staff.

"Hi, Mama. How you doing?"

"I'm here," she says, her words a hum above the Spanish lyrics about tears from heartbreak and no trace of love. A common soundtrack to dousing the house in Fabuloso and hanging the laundry on the clothesline outside.

"I was calling Xiomara," she says about her younger sister. *Here it comes.* "But the phone just ring, ring, and ring again. She says she's coming by, *pero ya tú sabes. Ella no se acuerda de nada.*"

"Mama, be nice."

"I am!" She feigns innocence. "Just keeping it real, as you kids say."

Tía Mara and my mother are like rubbing alcohol and bleach: a combination that makes chloroform and might compromise your organs.

Maybe you pass out, or maybe you die.

As a member of the youngest sibling committee who gets spoken about and to, I empathize with my tía. Marcela treats me the same way. Her heavy-handed tendencies are courtesy of the oldest child hardwiring that keeps her telling me what to do. Yet, we love each other without causing a chemical reaction or a state of emergency. Unlike my mother and her sister.

"You out of bed and on your way to work?" My mother's West Indian accent is a heavy syrup over "out" that sounds like "oat," and "work" that's closer to "werk."

Translation: *The grace period for earning a PhD ran out. How are you paying bills?*

Walking away from job offers keeps my family's side-eye chambered. I don't know if I want to recommit to a lifetime of labs or lecture halls. There's also management. Maybe I should've studied rocket science to figure it all out.

My mother has her own way of expressing loving concern. Like reminding me I'm inching closer to forty, am not investing in a retirement savings plan, and have no prospective life partners, because grandbabies.

She means well, but she has always said what she felt and felt what she said.

My parents never told Marcela and me the reason they divorced. My mother was a couple of years older than my sister is now when she filed. That was almost a decade after we moved to Maryland. I was two when we came to the States. My father always travels for work. That's how they met in Panama, during his time working for the US embassy. If I had to guess, his work schedule is what sent her back to Panama a single woman.

"I'm at a home improvement store," I say to change the subject. I pick up a paint sample. The mint green matches my sweater. It's my favorite color, one that reminds me of the sun reflecting off the water near my mother's property in Coronado.

"Eh?"

"*La ferretería*, Mama," I say about my impromptu trip. "*Tengo que arreglar un estante que se cayó y la barra de la cortina de ducha.*"

"My goodness, Miri. *¿En qué tipo de casa vives que se está cayendo a pedazos?*"

"There were a couple of accidents," I say.

"Accidents," she repeats. "*No has estado allá ni un mes y ya estás destrampando la casa.* Have mercy, Jesus. What happened to the shower rod?"

The answer is riding the shopping cart like it's a chariot.

What should've been an in-and-out solo trip became a joint expedition down every aisle. Now the cart is full of things I don't need. I found a new closet shelf that I got cut down to size and a shower rod to withstand the weight of a rugby player.

Everything else in the cart is Antonio's doing.

He talked me into grabbing "a few things": plants, kitchen counter appliances I'll never use, and accent pillows for the sofa I didn't let him sleep on last night. He's buying everything as a housewarming gift, committing me to more things to unpack and store in my home.

Once we soothed our injuries, we crowded around the tiny kitchen table Antonio engulfed with his body to talk and eat. Six hours passed with no signs of fatigue. He left around midnight, which surprised me as much as his eight a.m. "Good morning, whatcha doing today?" text did.

I wasn't expecting to hear from him so soon, but he told me he was free today to help. Then he showed up at my house at nine with two coffees and a smile. I whipped up eggs with toast, and here we are.

Not once did I get lost in my head trying not to act odd. I was safe being me. Comfortable.

Antonio pushes the cart in a circle. He accelerates down the aisle and kicks up a Timb, shifting the shopping cart at the last minute to avoid crashing into a display of light bulbs on sale. He bounces back at the force of his torso colliding with the metal handlebar with an "oof" and catches a potted plant on the cart's bottom shelf.

I muffle a laugh at him scratching his beanie, which matches his orange coat. Our eyes lock as an employee calls for assistance in the tile department over the PA system. A smile creeps into a grin above his trimmed boxed beard. It spreads the smooth, wide lips that came dangerously close to mine last night.

The proximity of our mouths and the Skinemax nudity of his body covering mine shut off my ability to process. Everything in me overheated.

Panting in Antonio's face like a Boston terrier or him sprinting into my room wearing a towel the size of a washcloth wasn't how I imagined his first visit to my house, but it happened. Just like the eyeful of bulge against the white cotton between his gladiator thighs did.

God, those thighs.

The weight of them almost sent me through the floor. I didn't get a full look at him mid-fall, but you better believe I snuck a peek at them...and at the butt I've seen stretch out his rugby shorts.

"Miri!"

I jump when my mother's voice cuts through the inappropriate replays of my bestie, who's staring like he's onto my secret.

Am I that obvious?

"You listening, child?"

The number you are trying to reach is not in service.

"Yes, ma'am," I say without a clue what we were talking about.

Antonio pushes the cart closer. His smirk pulls his lower lip between his teeth. I reroute my attention to something that won't fog up my glasses or get me cussed out from Central America.

All-purpose caulk.

Great.

"Don't use any power tools while you're spacing out like that, Miriam. Your Tío Chucky almost burned off his hair and scalp messing with a blowtorch. *Para qué lo necesitaba ese tonto, no lo sé.* What's got you distracted?"

I eye Antonio. He smiles and mouths, *You in trouble.*

"Nothing." I back away from him and the caulk.

My faculty for scientific analysis hiccups. I have a mental catalog of numerical methods to approximate answers to problems I can't solve through algebraic procedure.

The Finite Element Analysis is a go-to for how a complex mechanical structure will react to different conditions that impact its stress distribution. Yet no method helps me comprehend why I can laugh with or at Antonio one minute and want to test how much body heat we'll generate the next.

Urges come in waves when I least expect them. Like right now, in a home improvement store, while I'm on the phone with my mother. It happened briefly last night when he came over, and then upstairs when we were sandwiched together.

There has to be an academic journal with published research that explains the biological effects of a friendship with someone who is hide-in-the-bushes fine, with a kind heart and a good butt to match. I need that analysis and proposed solutions so I'm not staring at a tube of caulk, imagining how thick Antonio's container is.

What is wrong with me?

"Don't spend all your hours on drill bits and shower curtains," my mother snaps.

"*No lo haré.* We're wrapping up." I wince the moment *we* slips. This is why I don't like talking on the phone, or in general.

My mother latches on to the confession before I can take it back.

"Marcela is there?" The pitch in her voice shifts. "Pass the phone. I tried calling her and kept talking to her voicemail."

"I'm not with Marcela," I clarify.

She went to meet her sneaky link in Crystal Beach late last night, to deal with her stress. Does the Canada Border Services Agency know she's hopping countries to bounce on penis?

Is that what you need? International peen?

Do I?

The other end of the line goes quiet. "Then who are you with?"

Fluorescent light beams down on buttery caramel skin. The sleek lines of Antonio's cheekbones shift when his mouth tips up. Under a hood of lashes, brown eyes wander from the phone pressed to my ear, down my oversized sweater, and to my hand stationed on my hip.

He's waiting for a response, and he gestures for me to go on.

Jerk.

"A friend, Mama," I say with nonchalance.

That's what he is, even if he excites tingles in places that shouldn't tingle. Well, one place *should*, but not because of him.

A tingle-free friend zone.

"What friends do you have there?" I snort at the question. My mother is no better than Marcela.

"I have one! I plan to add a few more next week."

Something I can't interpret flashes across Antonio's face. I motion toward the self-checkout lanes and dip my brows at his head-shake. "Mama, I have to go. Love you."

"Love you too, baby."

I stuff my phone inside my winter coat. "Why aren't we leaving?"

"We're not done here." He folds his arms over his chest, forcing the material in his jacket to strain over his biceps. "Who are you meeting next week?"

"Nosy much?" I huff. "You and my mother will get along just fine."

He nods. "Can't wait to meet her. Same question."

"What else do we possibly need?" Our shopping cart looks like it ran away from an HGTV set. All that's missing is a high-performance toilet and shutters.

"*We* don't need anything. You're getting cans of that paint color you keep eyeing. I'm getting a juicer." He nudges me out of the way with the cart. "What's next week?"

My nose wrinkles. "Why a juicer? I don't juice."

"But I do." He glances at the aisle signs above us. "The guys keep breaking the ones I buy for Steel House. I like juice in the morning and after practice. This way."

We pass another aisle. I snag a couple of outlet covers to replace the ones in my bedroom.

The scene of last night's—

"So what's happening next week?" Antonio asks again.

Tingle-free friend zone.

I blink. "Huh?"

"The few friends you plan to add next week."

"Oh. That." I fidget with my jacket zipper and look down at the salt streaking my winter boots. "There's an event that takes you around the city on a bus and drops you off at different bars. It's for people who want to make friends. Organic opportunities to establish friend groups don't happen as often as they did when we were younger.

"Research suggests that our number of friends peaks in our early to mid-twenties, then goes down. I'm already fighting an uphill battle, and I want to better my chances in a controlled environment with like-minded people who are also looking for friends. I don't need a lot. I just want more than one, and someone who isn't my sister."

It's me again, rambling.

Antonio's face sours. He opens his mouth and closes it.

"It's okay to laugh," I say quietly. "I wouldn't expect you to understand."

"Why would I laugh?" His voice is smooth and low. "There's nothing wrong with trying to make deeper connections. I inherited most of what you'd consider friendships from rugby. But the only people in my life I call beyond wanting to have fun, the relationships that go deeper than surface-level shit, are Julian and you."

"Oh."

"The quantity isn't as important as the quality."

I smile. "So you don't think what I'm doing is weird?"

"Oh, I do." He scratches his beard and laughs. "Only because it sounds like speed dating. Do you get a steak dinner if you both swipe right at the end of the night? I'll go, and we can pretend not to know each other."

"Shut up!" I reach for the cart but come up short.

"Do you want a wingman?"

"A what?"

"A wingman," he says again. "Someone to be your emotional support or sing your praises. Point out people with ulterior motives."

A crease burrows between my brows. "Why would anyone have ulterior motives?"

His stare is the most serious I've seen him. "All those book smarts and not a lick of street—Doesn't matter. There's always some asshole waiting to take advantage. They'll pretend to be your friend and like what you like until the minute they slide the panties to the side. Once they get their nut"—he shoots his hand into the air like an airplane—"gone."

"This is why I stay in the house," I mumble.

"Stick with me, kid. I'll keep you safe." He winks and pushes the cart.

"Did you forget I'm older than you by five years?"

"I haven't. Doesn't mean I can't teach you a thing or two. I'll meet you at whatever bars you go to, and I'll sit off to the side if you want."

Having someone there I'm comfortable with will make the event less awkward.

Hopefully.

"I'd like that, thank you," I say.

"Good! Now back to my juicer. I'll grab one for your place too."

Antonio's eyes light up at appliances I have zero interest in or room for.

"What makes you think you'll be at my house enough to need a juicer?" I ask the back of his puffer coat. My line of sight remains on his belt and not the gym booty or the tree trunks for legs under the pair of jeans that are sculpted to his form.

"Friends let friends juice," he says to the shelves of counter gadgets. "And before you say something slick, I'm not sharing with any new friend you might make. Ooh! This one has a thousand-watt motor."

"Antonio," I sigh. "You've seen my kitchen."

"It's cute, and this will look nice in it." He grabs a box with a lopsided grin that deflates when he sees my glare. "What if I keep it in my trunk?"

I snort at his pout. "You want to keep a juicer in your trunk for when you visit? I don't know who's more off their rocker, me or you."

"Both of us, bestie. Is that a yes?"

I'll regret this. "Yes."

He fists the air, then assesses our already full cart. "We should've gotten a flatbed." He frowns at the jumble of random supplies and accessories we accumulated over the last hour. "Let's get your paint for our painting party."

"Our what?"

Chapter 11

Antonio

E.U.'s "Da Butt" slides through the Bluetooth speaker I brought from home. I kicked off the night with Silk's "Meeting in My Bedroom" but almost found myself on the other end of Miriam's front door. In my defense, we do have plans to fondle her walls, but she says, "that's nasty."

The bass of the DC go-go classic is no match for her cackling. I lost track of how many times she snorted today and had to check her pulse twice to confirm she was still breathing.

She does this silent laugh, like she's choking. She's wheezing now, tears streaking her makeup-free face, which is mushed up like she's reaching for one of Fantasia's high notes. Her eyes are closed, and her body convulses with a force that would make people call an ambulance if we were in public.

Watching Miriam be so carefree is an experience that requires earplugs at times, with her high-pitched squeals, but demands a front-row seat. She never laughed this much in the years we circled each other from a distance or when she was wrapping up her PhD. She put so much into her studies, it was hard to get her to come up for air.

This is the first time I'm seeing *all* of her, the layers buried beneath her sixteen years of chasing after degrees that consumed her identity. Those layers are slowly shedding away to reveal a woman who's ready to let loose with the right encouragement.

"You done yet?" I say to her body curled into a ball.

She snorts. "Your p-penis is missing." My phone falls out of her hands as her head tips back, inciting another soundless cackle. "Oh my—" She snorts again before a wave of giggles takes over.

"I. See." Snort. "Person." Her laugh hits a high pitch.

It's an annual tradition for rugby players from the league to hit up Vegas the weekend before the season starts. Everyone dresses up in costumes during one of our nights in Sin City.

Last year, the Steel were Troll dolls. The ugly ones from the '90s that look like foreskin with hair. It took a full-length bodysuit and a few tips on tucking from Queenie LaCreme, a Buffalo drag queen, to keep my dick down without cutting off my circulation.

It wasn't long before I tossed the belly jewel and bare bottoms for basketball shorts and slides. It would take a magician to make these inches disappear, but Miriam doesn't need to know that.

I shimmy across the drop cloths to her. "Come with us."

Her face scrunches, shifting her glasses to the bridge of her nose. "What? No."

"Why not?"

"Because."

"You already graduated, and whatever job you land wouldn't start until after we're back," I say. "One weekend, Doe. Consider it a party to kick off the season and celebrate your next chapter."

The last twenty-four hours are the most time we've spent together without interruption. It's hard not to want to be around her now that we're in the same city. I want to see her with her hair down, like it is tonight. After years of studying, she deserves it before she goes back to a life of classrooms—or whatever engineers spend their time theorizing about.

Miriam bites her lip and stares at the stack of cardboard in the corner. We unpacked every box and had groceries delivered so she can cook tomorrow. We would've finished painting her room if I hadn't distracted her with random rugby pictures on my phone or dance moves she's been dodging.

Two dimples pop. She adjusts her glasses. "I'll *consider* going under two conditions."

"Name 'em."

"We have separate rooms, and I get to skip any activities that require a year's worth of energy."

"Deal." I nod and stretch out my hand. When she shakes it, I pull her off the floor.

"Antonio, no! I didn't say yes!" She cackles in a weak attempt to shoo me away. "We won't finish at the rate we're going."

"I think we're done. One last dance."

"No!" Her snort causes a hiccup. "I'll pee if I laugh any harder."

"We got the drop cloths down. Aht—no, you don't." I chuckle at her attempt to go limp and take her painter's brush between my teeth so I can hold her up.

"Antonio!" Her palms press into my white tee. She tries to push me away, but there's no force behind it.

"*E-yea-e-yea-e. E-yea-e-yea-e-yea-e-yeah!*" My words muffle around lacquered wood. It's a challenge to serenade her like this, but I do it with a George Jefferson two-step and a hip bump.

Her shoulder lifts before she fully commits and moves her body. Her black biker shorts have been fucking with me all night. The nylon spandex rests above her knees but clings to her fleshy thighs like paint. There's no gap, only curves and wide hips that mock me for missing out on the chance to access the feast between her legs.

I spin her and adjust myself in my jeans. Her rose body oil lingers under my nostrils as I twist and turn her, savoring every giggle.

"Okay, okay." Her laughter bounces off her simple V-neck shirt and the large breasts beneath it. *Eyes up.* "The paint needs to dry, and you missed a spot, Happy Feet."

"The hell I did!" I snatch the paintbrush from my mouth. "My side is immaculate."

We transformed the room from a basic white to a light green shade. I've helped D with his construction business enough times to know how to paint and how much to apply.

I always lay it on thick, but my shit is even.

Miriam lets out a breath. "I don't know. That spot looks bare to me."

My nostrils flare, but I'm all bark and no bite. "Okay, Bob Ross. Here you go." I hand her the paintbrush so she can inspect the built-in shelving above the headboard.

She wanted to do this side of the room herself. It made no sense since she had to use the stool she fell off of yesterday to reach everything. I kept an eye on her just in case and was surprised she stayed upright the entire time.

Miriam is the clumsiest person I've met—*with* glasses on.

"I know I didn't miss a spot. I don't miss," I mutter over a half-used can of paint next to the discarded brush. "Watch her trip over the tarp trying to reach a spot at my height." I shake my head and stand. "Miri—"

I'm halfway up before she hits me with paint. It's a direct chest shot that ricochets across my arms.

A sinister grin stretches across her face. "Now we're done."

"You're gonna get it."

She yelps and attempts to run out the door, except I'm pulling on the drop cloth to bring her back to me. A laugh morphs into a squeal when she falls. I pounce, dragging her weapon of choice up her thighs to the strip of mocha skin peeking out from beneath her T-shirt.

"Not the hair!"

I push back her loose curls and swipe her neck. "Missed a spot." My voice softens when I paint her chin. "Got another."

She bites her lip to stifle a giggle and looks away, unaware of the effect she has on me. My throat knots at the unwelcome urge to drag my thumb across her pulse point, which is now decorated in her favorite shade. None of my body weight is pressing into her, but I feel her heart thudding against the thin material of her shirt.

The urge to close the short distance between us and tease her lips apart with my tongue is there, but I won't do it. But I won't. Having her in any way that compromises our friendship, which took years to build, risks losing her. It kills me to deny the feelings that won't go away, but I have to, because not having Miriam in my life is an agony I never want to experience again.

She stills. Shit, did I go too far?

We always play around, but I don't want her to feel uncomfortable.

"Hey, sorry," I say through a frown and push off of her. As I do, a smirk flashes before she grabs my paintbrush and smears my jaw.

"Got ya," she teases.

I graze my beard and gape at the paint coating my fingertips. My shock fades fast enough for me to grab her ankle and drag her back under me.

Her brown eyes widen, and her skin tints a shade of pink. "I take it back! Truce."

I grin. "Can't do that, Doe. We're just getting started."

Chapter 12

Miriam

"You missed a spot." Antonio motions to the space between my jaw and ear. He dodges one of the new throw pillows I toss at his head. "You started it."

That I did.

I never had a paint fight, much less one involving gallons. We managed to keep the walls safe, but the floor and furniture covers were casualties. I scrubbed my crack and creases three times to remove the paint from my body. My hair is a lost cause. There are mint green splatters across my coils.

Antonio fared better, with only paint on the beard he washed and all over the shirt and jeans he replaced with sweats and a tee he brought from his place. Our near-foot height difference was not to my advantage. A reminder he hasn't let me live down.

"Want me to lick it off for you?" A smile toys at his lips.

"You're such a flirt." I roll my eyes and dab a napkin from the tray on the end table into my water glass. "Did I get it?"

"Yeah," he says, a splatter-free poster child of peace, shoveling complex carbs and protein into his body by the mouthful.

We've been together over thirteen hours today—not that I'm counting. Aside from my mother's call and a text from Marcela reminding me about brunch tomorrow, I barely looked at my phone. I don't have people trying to get in touch with me like Antonio does, but he hasn't checked his phone either.

I put us straight to work after our trip to the home improvement store. We painted, sorted through most of my boxes to unpack the lifetime of books I've acquired, and built bookcases. Antonio's jaw remained on the floor when he learned engineering encyclopedias are a thing. I'm the proud owner of twelve, including one on vibrations, which he thought was code for something else.

Those vibrations are in a small box inside my bedroom closet. I'll unpack that one once a certain guest goes home.

"Want more before I kill it?" He lifts his container of citrus barbecue chicken with broccoli and brown rice from the other end of my sofa bed.

"No thanks, I'm stuffed." I pat my stomach, satisfied with the chicken and rice I inhaled. "Thanks for bringing dinner."

"I got you."

Today wiped me out. I was too tired to cook, not that Antonio would have let me if I'd tried. He grabbed two meals from the weekly prep packs he orders for the team. A walking testament to the wonders of good nutrition and big muscles.

The weighted blanket I found at the store swallows me in my pink and white pajama set and everything but his torso. Neither of us has moved since we sat down for dinner. The way my muscles are screaming at me for what little manual labor I did, I'm done for the evening.

Note to self: Find a method of physical fitness you'll actually tolerate.

As predicted, the dance-offs and paint-tossing banished me to the couch for the evening.

Still.

"I had fun today."

Antonio mirrors my smile and leans back into his pillow. "Me too."

The glare from the TV he set up dances across his caramel complexion and the hard slab of his chest. His gaze is a silent expression I struggle to translate, which breaks when his phone rings.

"Excuse me," he says, halfway off the sofa bed and on his way to my little kitchen that could with the phone to his ear. The ringtone is different than his usual factory-setting jingle. So is the care in his tone when he answers, "Hey."

Hey, who?

"Not my business," I say under my breath as I turn onto my side to scroll through movie and show options.

It's not my place to care about Antonio's sexual partners. Unless they support something harmful or have secret children.

I'm very much aware of his activities. There are years' worth of stories, and I've seen the texts roll in firsthand like emergency alerts. If you're sending rapid-fire messages like that, the ding-a-ling must be exceptional.

Antonio is a shower, and he has thumped me a time or two with his—

Stop thinking about his penis!

I flip to a baking competition, which, thankfully, has no phallic symbols that will keep my mind in the gutter.

"Peanut butter blossom cookies are a fine choice," I say to the screen.

They look like nipples.

So much for baking.

I switch channels with unnecessary aggression and lean over the arm of my sofa bed when I hear faint laughter coming from the kitchen. He's not visible from the doorway, but his hushed whispers echo in the distance.

What's so funny?

The living room's long shadows contour in streaks of light from the TV and the candles scattered around the room. Antonio asked who we were conjuring, like an appreciation for clean-burning soy and relaxing your nervous system through scent means séance. I lit five, not twenty.

The light above the stove keeps him from standing in total darkness while he talks to whoever.

A booty buddy?

A lover?

An enemy he likes to penetrate?

He's never reacted so quickly to a woman before. That's a lie. He's chased plenty with his tongue wagging behind him. But hurdling over the blanket to answer a call? She's special.

Why do you care?

I don't. I'm merely acknowledging an observation.

The shuffle of Antonio's socks over hardwood stirs me into action. My hand slips off the armrest, which is surprisingly high in this position. The struggle to lift the half of my body that's hanging over the arm is another reminder of my lack of physical strength. I tip forward to catch myself from face-planting.

"What are you doing?" There's a trace of laughter in Antonio's voice when he sees my butt tooting in the air.

"Stretching." I grunt as gravity and my underdeveloped muscles battle it out with my breasts as they try to punch me in the chin. I reach for my glasses, which are slipping off my nose, and buckle further over the edge. "It's, um, a nighttime routine."

"A nighttime routine," he repeats. "Why are your arms shaking?"

I pant. "They're not."

"Okay," he says, not believing a single word out of my mouth, which is about to kiss the ground.

I push off my hands, but that proves to be a mistake. They go limp and send the rest of my body over the sofa arm. I squeak, but my face never connects with the floor.

Protective arms hoist me up by the waist. Every ounce of color would drain from my face if I were upright, but my crack is right under Antonio's chin. I can't verify how close it is to his mouth, but I suspect he could nibble on the cheek meat hanging out of my shorts. The only thing visible are the three bookshelves lining the wall and mild embarrassment loading.

"You need a helmet," he jokes. He lays me on the plush mattress like I'm a feather and not the one-eighty he casually lifted like a handbag.

Who is his rugby team's strength and conditioning coach?

My forehead is battling a downpour of sweat after holding myself up for two minutes. Antonio is a different story. There are no heavy breaths or signs of strained muscles.

But there is a frown etched into his face. "I have to go."

Oh.

He stuffs his hands into his sweats and looks off. "I'll send you details about Vegas if you want to come. See you this week for the school bus event to make friends?"

I laugh and adjust my glasses. "It's not a school bus."

He shrugs. "It might be. You need a helmet regardless. Come lock up."

I'm unsure why my chest is tightening at him leaving. He got the boot last night when he attempted to test-drive my sofa. Him sleeping over makes no sense, but leaving so abruptly after a phone call doesn't sit right with me.

"Is everything okay?" Something happened from the time he was on the phone, trading quiet laughs, to now.

"Yeah," he sighs. "Need to take care of something, but I'll check in later." He pulls me into a hug and kisses the top of my head. "Try not to break anything stretching."

"Hush." I try to push him away, but he doesn't budge. So I sniff his armpit and inhale the fresh scent of his soap and what I assume is oak in his deodorant. "Can't. Breathe," I mumble around cotton.

He lets out a short laugh and goes through what's now his post-bear-hug routine in search of injuries. His eyes soften. "It's been good spending time with you. I've missed it."

I chuckle. "We never spent time together, unless you count me checking your homework before you went to bed."

Middle school Antonio was a handful. He'd fight to stay up and ask twenty-six questions about a problem we already solved just to annoy me.

His back straightens, lengthening the distance between the top of my head and his chin. "It counts for me. Lock up, Doe. Goodnight."

The timbre in his voice lingers long after he leaves. God bless the woman's organs he's about to rearrange.

"Knock it off, Miriam."

I blow out the candles, resettle under the weighted blanket, and fall asleep to a cake bake-off.

No sugary cookie nipples in sight.

Chapter 13

Miriam

A good way to stir up childhood trauma is to sit through a church service three hours long or an overpriced meal with somebody's lawn clippings as garnish.

And *Howard the Duck*. The Dark Overlord possessing Dr. Jennings disturbed me.

Marcela is responsible for the first two today. If our server hadn't dropped a basket of artisan bread on our table, I'd never speak to her again. Snatching off her lace front came to mind, but I'd be on the receiving end of her hands, feet, and elbows if I even hinted at the slightest desire for a physical confrontation.

We survived Sundays in church. Not for a couple of hours—the entire day. I love Jesus, and I have the Vacation Bible School certificates to prove it, but He doesn't need to see me from sunup to sundown every weekend as proof. Had it not been for the chicken plates they served in the basement, I would've called CPS several times on behalf of my anxiety.

There is no logical explanation for why my sister didn't tell me she wanted to visit a church that started at eight and let out at eleven thirty. I ran out of Twizzlers after hour two. By hour three, I contemplated fainting. The only thing that would've come of that is a prayer cloth over my lower half and church aunties reviving me back to consciousness by speaking in tongues. No one to rescue me from sitting between a man with breath in need of an exorcism and the woman swatting me with the side of her hat.

Strike two came after Marcela insisted we eat brunch at an upscale restaurant with no weather mats to stop me from electric sliding over the marble floor. I almost went back to church in a casket the second my ankle boot hit the ground. Between the slush outside and the frozen stares, staying at home and not spending a small fortune only to still be hungry was the better plan.

Which brings me to strike three: Marcela's line sister inviting herself to our brunch.

Lisa insisted we sit in the private dining room with a wall of expensive wines the second she trotted into the restaurant wearing heels that would have me calling the injury attorney with the catchy jingle.

I was never a fan of her or her attempts to weasel her way into my time with my sister, the same way I'm not a fan of her plus-oneing herself to our family events and the annual DC galas my father forced us to attend. All Lisa cares about is herself and being seen.

She always steers conversations to who she's with or the luxury trip someone else financed. I'm not mad or jealous. I also did not risk slipping and falling to sit through another story that strokes her ego.

"Aruba was beautiful," she coos, with an emphasis on "beautiful." Her accent is foreign to her Buffalo roots. "Low humidity. Warm sand. Luxury brands. Come next time."

"Did you forget I have a district to run?" Marcela lifts her Bellini to her lips. "I can't just disappear for a week."

"Four days," Lisa corrects.

Marcela waves her fresh manicure. "Same thing. I have commitments."

"Like traveling to another country for dick?" Lisa arches a brow. "How is that not the same?"

My sister leans her forearms on the polished wood table, careful to keep the sleeves of her tweed pencil dress away from the croque madame in front of her. We're the only two at this table that seats ten who aren't eating a small plate of sprouts to look cute for the few people who walk by the street-level window.

"First, the dick lives in Amherst," she says about her senator sneaky link. "We go to his house in Canada to keep people out of our business. Second, I'm an hour away. Third, and most important, I don't fuck for handbags or trips I can't afford myself."

I choke back a laugh.

Marcela and Lisa's relationship is interesting, and by "interesting," I mean unnecessary but tolerated. Lisa is building up her event-planning business. She hangs around my sister for access to her contacts, former corporate clients, and associates. Marcela's star is on the rise as a councilmember, garnering state and national headlines. Lisa wants a piece of that and leeches where she can.

If this is what friendships look like, I'm glad I keep to myself.

"Something funny?" Lisa's glare sears into my profile.

"Nope." I cut into the tiny crab cake on my plate. Not bad, but it could use some Old Bay.

"Do you even know how to compute being around people? A man?"

"Not too much." My sister's tone is her first and last warning to try me in her presence.

"Sorry." Lisa feigns innocence. My smirk lifts her high cheekbones into a phony smile with perfect white teeth. "How are you liking Buffalo?"

"Good," I say, "but we don't need to pretend you care. Go back to trying to impress Marcela." Her face falls, and my sister bites her lip and drops her head.

I never understood small talk or communicating with someone you don't care about. Both seem pointless.

Lisa's jaw clenches, and her eyes narrow. "I'll do no such thing. I'm friends with your sister, and I hope we can be closer now that you live here."

"Okay" is my response.

Lisa has known me since she came home with Marcela during winter break of their freshman year of college. Never once did she display any signs of caring about me. If anything, she'd take jabs about my clothes and my K'nex set. I was twelve at the time.

I frown at Lisa's playful shove and look at Marcela, who lifts her shoulder before finishing her glass.

"Come on, we're older now." Lisa laughs and tosses the twenty-eight-inch bundles cascading down her back. I twirl my coils, which are sitting high from my wash-and-go. The shrinkage is real, but it's moisturized.

I giggle to myself at the double entendre. Antonio is rubbing off on me.

Lisa's face lights up. "What's got you grinning? Is it something, or someone?"

"Nothing." I sip my mimosa.

"It could be her friend." Marcela shrugs with an apology and a smile I want to knock off with my baguette. "Sorry, sis."

"Oop! Did Baby Beckford find love in the Rust Belt? So soon too. You've been here, what, a week?"

"I'm not in love, nor am I dating," I say to Lisa and cut my eyes at my sister. I'll thank her later for not disclosing Wednesday's find-a-friend bus tour. She still needs to zip it.

"I have a friend who's up here from DC," I reveal, much to my annoyance. "We've spent some time together now that I live in Buffalo and have finished my PhD. He's—"

"He?" Lisa's eyes widen.

"Is fine," Marcela says. Her hands fly up at my glower. "What? You see him twice with those glasses on. The man *is* fine and has body for days. That's all you, little sis."

"It's not like that at all," I protest. "Two people can share platonic interests without it meaning a trip to Canada for secret sex, or Aruba to score a handbag."

"Hey!" they shout in unison.

"We've been friends for a few years, but we've never spent time together. That's all we're doing. Painting walls and building furniture." I leave out the near peen sighting and the glimpse of Antonio's muscled butt, which would make a person with 20/20 vision lose sight from crossing their eyes.

"I'm sure he did paint your walls all night," my sister snickers into her glass.

"That's all I hear from you two—penis, penis, penis! There's more to life than a hard dick!"

A throat clears. Our server stands frozen, and nearby diners shift back in their seats for a better look at the woman who's shouting about shafts at brunch.

I force my eyes shut and rub my temples. "We'll take the check, thank you." I don't bother looking at the server, who rushes off like the building is on fire. I'm embarrassed for both of us.

"Miri. I didn't mean to get you worked up." Marcela's voice is low and holds a degree of what I assume is concern.

"I'm not worked up," I mumble.

"Your face is red, and your glasses are two seconds from cracking. I won't poke fun about you and Antonio." At least she has the decency to push down the humor in her tone. "Sidenote: I think this is the first time I've heard you say 'dick.'"

I drop my hands from my face and give her a deadpan glare. It morphs into a snort at the pride beaming across her face.

"You bother me."

"Love you back," she says.

The truth is, I don't want to think about penises because I'm struggling not to think about Antonio in that way. What he would feel like. How he'd make *me* feel.

I see clearly—glasses on or off—how attractive he is, along with the benefits of adding rugby to your workout regimen. His voice alone licks the shell of my ear, and I don't need to test the theory of what will happen between my legs if we step beyond the boundaries of a platonic friendship. Said boundaries are in place so I don't ruin years of friendship for one night of pleasure. I can't. He's my only friend, and he's too important to me. Not that he would see me that way.

What if he did?

Please.

I never gave thought to an "us" because it has no chance in reality. He'll screw just about any woman, and his history proves he will leave this earth a bachelor, sowing every oat in his box. He doesn't do relationships, and he enjoys a new woman to replace the ones who temporarily have his attention. I've seen him and his charm in action. I know better.

Something we do have in common is our lack of experience as someone's significant other. I've never had a boyfriend in order to keep school a priority; he refuses to settle down in order to keep multiple options in rotation. The difference is that I do want love and commitment one day.

Dating was never top of mind for me because of my studies. With that lengthy chapter of my life closed, I have time I'm willing to dedicate to seeing who's out there.

And fulfilling any physical urges my box of goodies can't satisfy.

"Antonio." Lisa chews on the name with a crease between her brows. "Antonio Knight, who plays for the Steel?"

"That's him," I say.

Marcela frowns. "Since when do you watch rugby?"

Lisa swipes her mouth with her napkin. "We're acquainted." Her gaze swings to mine. "*Well* acquainted."

The implication doesn't go unnoticed.

"You're sleeping with him?" Marcela asks.

Her mouth lifts. "I wouldn't call what we do sleeping, but I was at his place last night."

My fork slips from my hand, and I rush to catch it. I adjust my glasses and say nothing.

What is there to say? One call, a few whispered laughs, and Antonio was out my door. Onto the next. We haven't spoken since he left my house last night...for her.

I push down the images of them together. Her in his arms, kissing every defined muscle that stretched and bent to unpack my boxes. Her mouth around the length indented in his sweats.

It makes sense, their pairing. Lisa—or Jalisa—is attractive. Tall. Long legs. Toned. Perky breasts. She favors Maia Campbell and gives twenty- and thirty-year-olds a run for their money with her skincare game alone. Fashion too.

Her thigh-high boots and belted sweater dress are a far cry from my leggings and blazer, which I found stuffed inside one of my boxes. Lisa is the physical embodiment of Antonio's type. A reminder that whatever cues I think I receive are part of my imagination. Not that I would pursue anything.

Friends, I remind myself. Buddies without bumping booties and complicated feelings.

You're still talking to yourself.

I'm done.

Lisa offers a wry smile. "Will that be an issue for you?"

"Nope," I say, much to the surprise of my sister, who hasn't stopped staring at me. "Like I said, we're friends. Pass the salt, please."

Chapter 14

Antonio

"**U**p! Up! *Up!*"

I bob my head to Anite's cheerful cadence as she bounces and reaches for the ceiling. She recites the word with a clap that has my eyes shifting from the fourteen-month-old to the staircase.

Ain't no way Ella and Julian let this baby listen to Cardi B. Is "Up" one of those Kidz Bop songs remixed for today's youth? There are only so many ways to make lyrics about tight asses and men who don't deserve pussy appropriate for the playground. Maybe Elmo can do it?

I'm halfway through humming the verse when her chubby legs drop into a squat. She propels herself to jump but tumbles forward.

Shit.

I scramble off the sofa and freeze. Whatever baby gymnastics class Ella enrolled her daughter in is paying off. Anite tucks her head and flops onto her back. Then she sits up like the Cabbage Patch version of Michael Myers. Her tiny chin wobbles, her big eyes on me, wondering why I let her bust her ass.

"Nice one!" My standing ovation is thirty seconds too late, but it does its job.

Anite's brows pinch then slowly relax. She's back on her feet, her Godzilla steps summoning gravity only to knock her down again.

Ella advised me not to freak out over minor falls. Her exact words were, "If you stress out my baby, that's your ass." It's taken a lot of practice to not dive after my goddaughter, but I'm learning. Plus, I don't doubt that El and Morgan, Julian's sister and Anite's godmother, won't fly to Buffalo to fuck me up in some alley.

I'd never let anything happen to Anite, but I don't want her freaking out because I am when she falls.

"You good, little one?"

Anite bares all of her baby teeth in a slow grin. "Hee." She's adorable, but she scares the shit out of me when she acts possessed.

"Easy, Annabelle," I say, holding my hands out for her.

"You calling my baby a demon?"

Julian takes two steps into the living room before his daughter reroutes. A head of black coils and a snowflake onesie shuffle around the coffee table into his waiting arms.

"Is Uncle Ant behaving?" Julian asks his giggling daughter as he kisses her cheeks.

"Ant." She shifts in his arms and points to me.

If it weren't for their matching hickory-brown eyes and chocolate hue, I'd question if my best friend was in the room when Anite was conceived. Seeing him hang on to his daughter's every word tugs at the very small part of me that's curious to know how it feels. Fatherhood looks good on him.

Julian is still the same person who likes anime and old jazz records. We've been friends since our dads put us in rugby when we were kids. He's four years older, but my size and speed had his coach poaching me for scrimmages after my practices. He'll say I followed him around, which is a bald-faced lie.

We grew up in the same neighborhood and have been rocking ever since. Julian tries to act like he wasn't one of DC's notorious bachelors. I let it slide because bro is crazy in love.

Life shifted for him the minute he met Ella and her two kids. His house, once a destination for game nights that ended in X-rated sleepovers, is now babyproofed, with gates and outlet covers overtop the fossils of a former bachelor pad.

El rushes up from the basement like she just worked a double at the childcare center she runs. Her hair is frizzy on one side and falling out of the bun that's struggling to stay up on the other.

"Who jumped you down there?" She had one of those messy updos during dinner less than an hour ago.

"Very funny, Antonio." Her eyes cut to me before she motions for her carbon copy. "I'll take her."

"*Èske ou gen dòmi*?" Are you sleepy, little one?" Julian asks in Haitian Creole. "*Li le pou kouche.*" He kisses Anite and passes her to me. "Say goodnight."

"You're growing too fast." It was only yesterday Julian smacked me upside the head for palming Anite like a rugby ball after Ella gave birth. I promised to visit at least once a month, no matter how busy the season gets.

Anite sprouted from a tiny thing with new-car smell to a joyful soul who plays with her shadow and performs pop-rap when her parents aren't watching.

Mini Ella stares with thick brows, big cheeks, and a pouty mouth. I tickle her sides and blow raspberries on her neck. "Sweet dreams, Annabelle. See you next month."

"And we're done." Ella bumps me with her hip and takes Anite.

"Hey, Ella Bella? Your shirt is inside out." I point to her sweater.

Her eyes glide down to ivory seams that shouldn't be visible. "Oh." She looks everywhere except at her husband. "Sundays are laundry day."

My ass!

"Laundry, huh?" I scrub my jaw and peer down at her. "That's one hell of a spin cycle, to flip your sweater inside out."

Never mind the fact that the washer and dryer are *upstairs*. Not in the basement—a soundproof basement Ella snuck in and out of when Julian stayed down there before they got married.

The guilty party, the Lance Gross look-alike of DC, hasn't stopped shooting fuck-me eyes at his wife since she stumbled up here. Can't say I blame him. Ella is a beautiful medley of natural hair, curves, and child-bearing hips that Julian keeps begging to spread. Bro inherited Jackson, his eleven-year-old son, Haile, his almost nine-year-old daughter, had Anite with Ella, and still stays on his wife's ass.

Between Jackson playing youth rugby for a team Julian coaches, Haile's Brazilian jiujitsu competitions, and chasing after a fourteen-month-old, it's a miracle these two have the energy to run off like teenagers.

"Did you two dip off for a quickie and leave me on babysitting duty? Minute Man here wasn't gone that long." I dodge Julian's fist, laughing at the times he told me he ran out of the basement to come through the kitchen. His white tee and gray sweatpants are the perfect 'fit to drop dick and dash.

Freaks.

"Don't shortchange my sister," I chide.

Ella's smile widens. "He's been up here for longer than a minute, running my bath after checking on the kids. I'll get Anite down and say goodbye before you leave."

"Need me to double-check the water temperature?" Julian gazes at his wife with a tone that borders on Barry White.

"Hello, you have company," I remind them.

"I'm sure it's hot," she says.

I wave. "Still here." If they start fucking, I'm out.

Ella rolls her eyes and takes Anite upstairs. Julian's stare trails after her, his lips pulled between his teeth like they didn't just get it in.

I waste no time going to the kitchen to refill my water bottle. Paintings and certificates of achievement decorate the refrigerator. Paper snowflakes hang from the ceiling and match the feathery ice crystals scattered across the cabinets.

"How's Mom Dukes doing?" Julian joins me at the kitchen counter.

"Better," I sigh. "They're keeping her three more days because of the appendectomy."

I was on the last plane out of Buffalo after my mother called me from the hospital. Her appendix ruptured while she was at home alone. I held it together in Miriam's kitchen, laughing at my mom's poor attempts to make light of the situation and keep me calm. I was in shock, far from calm and so far away, even if "far away" by my definition was an hour flight. I didn't want to freak out thinking about her being by herself, and I made it to the bathroom on the plane before I lost it.

That woman is the heartbeat of my family. She assured me they gave her good drugs and to stop fussing over her.

My pops is out of the country on a business trip, and he got a call before I did. He canceled the rest of his time away and got in a little after four this morning. He hasn't left her side, no matter how much she snips at him to wash his ass.

"I'm glad she's doing better," Julian says. "I'll go over on Tuesday to give your dad some time. My mother already dropped off meals and has *te jejanm* by the gallon ready to go."

"Appreciate it, bro." I run my fingers over my waves, which are in need of a shape-up. "I don't like the idea of her by herself. Pops is slowing down and getting ready to retire, but look what happened the one time he was away."

Had my mom not had the strength to call 911 and let them in, she wouldn't be here to shoo me away after I climbed into that thin-ass hospital bed with her.

Anything could've happened.

Sepsis.

Organ failure.

Death.

The thought of losing her forced me to stay awake while she slept. In true Chrishelle Knight fashion, I got a kiss on the cheek and a boot from her hospital room hours after my dad arrived. They didn't want me to worry, and they encouraged me to visit Julian and El, who've kept my mind occupied, before my flight back to Buffalo.

Said mind has been so all over the place that I forgot to text Miriam after leaving the way I did.

"Didn't your mama tell you to stop stressing yourself and her out?" Julian nods at my thumbs as they race across my phone.

"I'm not texting her."

I'm sorry I left the way I did. My mom is in the hospital with a ruptured appendix, and I flew out to be with her. She's doing better. I should've told you, but I wasn't in the right head space and didn't want to put that on you. Send me the details about Wednesday.

Julian chuckles into a Roblox cup that's likely filled with all gin and no juice. "You've got forty-five minutes before you head to the airport. Unless *you're* a minute man, keep it in your jeans until you get back to the tundra."

"Far from it. My stamina is at an elite level, unlike some." I smirk at his middle finger.

He only plays rugby occasionally with the DC team we started on as flankers. Bro is a few inches shorter than me and a touch leaner on the muscle side, but he still keeps himself in shape.

My phone buzzes.

Miriam

I'm sorry and am happy to hear she's okay. Do you need anything?

I smile at the text. It's just like Miriam to get straight to the point. When she's not rambling from nerves, she doesn't waste words and only says what she means.

> Thank you, Doe. I'm good. Got scared for a minute but I'm okay since she is.

Miriam

> It's okay to share your feelings. You don't have to keep them in around me. I would freak out if something happened to my father. He knows nothing about home remedies or taking care of himself.

The tension in my shoulders dissolves.

> I appreciate you. What did you end up watching?

Miriam

> I fell asleep on a baking show. Never made it to a movie.

> Redo soon? I'll bring popcorn and a pillow.

Miriam

> Nice try, Romeo. You're not sleeping here.

Romeo. That's a first.

I'm far from romantically inclined, but I would climb a balcony outside of Miriam's room just to mess with her.

> Do I get a nickname now? I'm flattered. Also, you're real cold, bestie.

Miriam

> **Cold as the sofa bed you won't be sleeping on.**

I let out a laugh and pocket my phone. Julian stares at me with a knowing grin.

"Miriam, I take it?"

I nod. "I was at her house last night when my mom called."

Jalisa blew up my phone yesterday and invited herself over last night. I nearly missed my flight getting her out of Steel House.

Under normal circumstances, I'd welcome her open legs with open arms. But my mom was my priority last night.

And before she called you?

"Why are you looking at me like that?" I frown at Julian, who smirks and rests his chin on his fist. "Get your head out of the gutter. We were on her sofa bed eating dinner, fully clothed and showered." That sounds wrong. "Separate showers."

"And why were you two eating dinner on a sofa bed after separate showers?"

"I don't know, counselor. Because we got tired after a day of shopping for her house and painting her room. Don't cross-examine me. Save your legal tricks for daddy's law firm."

He always does this whenever Miriam comes up.

"We're friends," I add.

"How many friends have you spent nonsexual time with for a day—"

"A day and a half. I came over on Friday." Shit. I roll my eyes at the low rumble rattling his chest. Here we go.

"My apologies. It all sounds...cozy."

A grin flashes across his face, but he conceals it with the rim of his kiddie cup. It's the same look I gave him three years ago, after he told me Ella and her kids were staying with him. She was going through a bad divorce, and his sister offered up his Georgetown townhouse as temporary housing. She left out the part that Julian still lived there and often came home between his stints in London.

He showed up one night.

She was in his bed.

And they lived happily ever after.

They fell in love, which is different from Miriam and me. I care for her—a lot—but there's no "us," and there never will be.

"Save your dad speech for your kids," I jab. "I like talking to her, and I'm happy she's in Buffalo with her sister and finally has her head out of a book. Nothing sexual is going on, unless you consider arranging encyclopedias on a bookshelf foreplay."

A small part of me is relieved that Miriam and I never went through with our one-night stand. At some point, I always grow tired of the person I'm sleeping with. It feels too much like monogamy, and that's not a diagnosis I want in my life right now. If we fucked, it would change everything. I doubt we'd be as close as we are. She'd go back to being a stranger, someone lost in a long line of forgotten women. Losing her isn't an option.

I never told Julian about what happened three years ago for the simple fact that I don't want to hear his dumb conspiracy theory about me becoming Russell Wilson like he did. My pops still pursues my mom like he did back in college. He hasn't slowed down after thirty years of marriage. They met at twenty, conceived me during Freaknik at twenty-three, and tied the knot the same year. I'm not anti-commitment, but I'm not in a rush to settle down.

It's why I never had a girlfriend and haven't switched up my routine to accommodate one. A relationship isn't top of mind because it's not a priority.

Being a professional rugby player is my commitment. We're busy during the preseason, we travel during the regular season, and we keep busy during the off-season. I'll reach peak age to play once I turn thirty this year. There's still a lot I want to accomplish without a partner or family tying me down. I have enough responsibilities as captain, and with Steel House.

"I watched you watch Miriam for years. My high school yearbooks always went missing and magically appeared in your room." Julian chuckles and shakes his head. "You're different with her. Less impulsive."

Miriam is still the finest woman to walk the earth. I don't know what it is about her that makes time stop, but I felt it when I first spotted her at the ripe age of eleven. Julian was a freshman in high school, and he took me to an anime club that met across from a science class.

That's where I saw her.

Thick-rimmed glasses.

Curly hair.

Oversized sweater.

A pile of books in her hands.

My pops mistook my newfound interest in shadowing Julian during his extracurricular activities as an excitement for higher learning. But it was always her.

She still tilts the room without trying. No matter how much charm I put on display or how hard I worked to earn her attention, she never saw me. Now that we're good friends, I won't sacrifice the years we've spent getting to where we are for a nut. She's too precious, and I'd hurt her if I tried to be someone I'm not. Someone who wants to commit and slow his life down for love.

"I'm good with what we are," I say. Going back to a life of watching her only in glimpses won't work for me.

Julian drops his cup in the sink. "If you don't want to explore what could be, keep doing you. Just be careful. All of that time together has a way of changing a man's tune."

"I know what I'm doing."

His grin widens. "I told myself the same thing. Now I have a wife, three kids, and am researching minivans." He pats my shoulder on the way out of the kitchen. "Don't let a hard head make for a soft ass."

"We're just friends!" I call out.

"Famous last words!" he volleys back.

Chapter 15

Miriam

Father knows best is a guaranteed way to freeze to death.

Buffalo is disrespectfully cold during winter. It's the kind of chill that makes leaving the house a life decision. Every day I say it won't get worse, and every day the weather shows me how low it can go.

Outside is a *Silent Hill* simulation of cloudy skies and a barely visible sun. It's enough to summon seasonal depression. There is no reason for me to be away from the comfort of my weighted blanket and wool socks, which brings me back to my first statement.

Father knows best is a whole lie.

I knew the job my father pleaded for me to check out wasn't a good fit the minute I stumbled to the front door of the stone-and-brick building. He's the personal headhunter I never asked for, who would use LinkedIn as a matchmaking service for my career and my malnourished love life if he could.

The slightest hint of anything technical means a call or email in non-yelling caps to "GIVE IT A LOOK." He means well but still hasn't grasped the concept of specializations. You wouldn't ask a podiatrist to do open-heart surgery, but I'm expected to know every facet of engineering. My bachelor's, master's, and PhD—all in mechanical engineering—are forgotten alongside my requests to stop meddling.

Maple King is a juggernaut in the engineering industry. My father was correct to assume this consultancy focuses on engineering projects. Civil engineering. Not mechanical, like my degrees.

It shouldn't bother me how easily my parents forget what I've spent a decade studying and testing. Pardon my saltiness at the tiny fact that academia was my life. I never pledged a sorority, played soccer, or danced like Marcela, unless you count dancing alone in my dorm.

I did one thing, and it's not memorable enough to remember.

M is for Miriam.

Mechanical engineering starts with M.

Miriam is a mechanical engineer.

Simple, if you ask me.

In fairness, it's my fault I stuffed these hips and this waist into the suit. It was one size too small before I left the house, and I still forced myself to perform the magic trick of breathing without collapsing a lung or popping a button. It's not vulgar, though the ruffles exploding from my chest scream, *Check out these titties if you can find them!*

The shoes? Another fail. My heels caught every crack and patch of ice on the sidewalk. The way I slipped and slid across the floor of this fancy lobby, I'm walking evidence that some people should enjoy a life of flats. I was too busy fighting for my life to let humiliation to sink in, and I couldn't quite care about my yelps bouncing off the panes of glass.

But this potential job could fund a home lab in my second bedroom, which is the only reason I came downtown. I can't afford CAD software for design and simulations yet, but I want a dedicated space for skill development and personal projects. I also want an annual subscription for a program I used the student version of in grad school. The license alone is thirty grand I don't have, unless I show off my toes on a fetish website.

Software and prototyping materials cost money. I need a high-paying job to make money. Hence the ruffles, sausage suit, and heels.

The receptionist, who's in stilettos and not playing tag with her shadow, helped escort me to a chair. To her credit, she wasn't too disturbed by someone dressed like Prince and the Revolution doing a James Brown impression with half the coordination.

"Someone will be with you shortly." The brunette offers a smile mixed with a frown before she struts back to her desk. On its front is "Maple King" in gold bold letters, a reminder that my future, if I work here, means controlled pantyhose and practiced runway walks.

A knot forms in my throat.

I can wear high heels for software, I tell myself. It might mean relying on the company workers' comp, but I'll become a *Top Model* contestant if it means full access to technology.

Don't think about a future of blistered feet.

I cringe at the beads of sweat gathering across my forehead, streaking the liquid foundation I misapplied because I don't wear makeup. Contouring and blending aren't a skillset. At best, I'll mimic a five-year-old's fingerpainting project instead of the Bob Ross masterpiece that women with more patience have mastered.

Heat, conduction, and gravity are much more intriguing to me than face glue. I prioritized safety over fashion in labs, but something tells me Maple King will require shopping trips to stores that don't sell eggs or tires.

Is it too late to leave?

The slippery trek through the Antarctic I battled to get here is a cautionary tale to stay put. Jarvis, my trusty hybrid sedan, is parked down the opposite end of the street, which means more figure skating for me. If I take off the patent leather choking my feet now, I'll at least have a fighting chance of making it to the elevator.

"Miriam."

I push down the compulsion to jump into one of the trees outside and face the gravelly baritone. The owner of said voice's lips ribbon from a trimmed beard under deep cheekbones. He's in a cream dress shirt that's missing a tie and tucked into olive slacks over a long, lean figure.

I adjust my glasses and recoil. If he's an engineer, I want a list of who else is on staff...for research purposes.

He's still waiting.

"Coming." My scoot off the leather chair comes with the bonus of quick grunts to prevent a *Basic Instinct* moment.

My steps are a calculation of weight distribution from the balls of my feet to my heels, but I reach him without injury.

"Hi," I say through a heavy breath, careful not to swallow the jasmine and spice cologne that's emanating from the man in front of me. My heels add four inches to my five-four height, but I'm still half a foot from meeting his eyeline.

His eyes crinkle under a fan of dark lashes. He extends a hand. "I'm Kieran, nice to meet you. Can I get you anything? Coffee. Water."

"Have any ventilators lying around?"

His brows kiss against his caramel hue. "Excuse me?"

"It was a joke. These heels are a self-inflicted accident waiting to happen. I probably need another PhD to walk in them."

Don't ramble.

I adjust the grip on my briefcase and follow Kieran down a long hall. My father swears every professional needs one. This overpriced display of Italian leather and brass hardware holds my résumé, my old dentist's pen, and an emergency stash of Twizzlers.

"Funny" is all he says, with the slightest trace of humor. "This way."

He motions for me to enter an office with a desk and an executive chair in front of a long strip of cabinets. There are floor plants near a side chair in the corner, reaching for strips of the gray daylight coming in through the window.

"May I?" Kieran nods to my peacoat.

"Yes, thank you." I shrug it off and frown at the pit marks soaking my blouse. This is why you don't wear dark colors in the daytime!

"Have a seat," he calls from the coat rack near the door. I use the opportunity to stuff tissues from a box on his desk under my arms and plop into the chair. Sweat is trickling down my back, but one problem at a time.

I don't know why I'm so nervous. Defending my dissertation involved more people and less sweating. Then again, no one on the panel looked like Ghost from *Power*.

The crispy fade is there. So are the big brown eyes that played in Tasha's face. The muscles aren't the same—not that they need to be. Just an observation.

"Mr. Fils apologizes for his absence." Kieran takes his seat behind his desk and pulls out what I assume is a folder on my academic career.

If it's a folder on my life, he's in for a disappointment.

"Your father spoke very highly of you and your accomplishments."

Unforgiving leather assaults my butt, pushing an uncomfortable thong farther into my crack. I wince and shift in my seat. "My father called?"

Kieran smiles. "Just to tell me that we'd be fools not to hire you. I must say, you are impressive." He peels his eyes away from the folder and scans the blouse that has so many ruffles I look like I sat at the signing of the Constitution. Assuming I wasn't Black, or a woman. He clears his throat. "Our primary focus at Maple King is civil engineering projects. However, your research and designs are intriguing. What was your dissertation topic?"

I sit straighter and adjust my glasses. "The hierarchical organization of multiscale material systems. It was a follow-up to my thesis on an optimum maintenance model based on a Markov chain."

Silence.

"Need me to explain?"

"Wow." His eyes widen before taking another casual stroll over my face. Is my makeup running again?

"Do you have an interest in research and design, or are you looking for a research-only position?"

"Are you kidding? I'd love to develop new products. Troubleshoot too, but if there's an opportunity for prototyping, I'll take it. Some engineers excel at application. Others thrive creating designs. I'm the rare unicorn who does both," I say with a giggle. "What software do you use here? I've been trying to get my hands on one I used in school for structural stress analyses. The student version had limitations, but I assume a place like this can afford it, no?"

My long exhale is met with silence. Too much?

"I mean"—I fix my glasses—"I appreciate data, evaluation, and conceiving design plans. A good portion of my time in the lab was spent analyzing failures to make recommendations on how to fix them. Concept and creation are fine. Design, I mean. Do you design?" I try again, glancing at the lone degree on an otherwise blank beige wall. A bachelor's of science in civil engineering from Buffalo College.

"Oh no, I don't," Kieran chuckles. "I am good at deals and negotiations." His gaze shifts. He mirrors my frown and shakes his head. "We'd be a team. You would oversee the data and analysis, testing equipment for implementation and evaluating its performance. You'd also have access to the lab for any useful designs. I handle the boring stuff—the goals, budget, permits, and navigating regulations. Client satisfaction. We're wrapping up a lead line replacement program and working on a design-build project to expand Toronto's subway system."

"Toronto, as in Canada?"

"The one and only. Travel is part of the job, but only to touch base with our clients and partners." He tilts his head. "Does any of this interest you?"

Does it?

I never asked myself what I wanted to do after my PhD. I love analyzing how materials operate under different stressors. The professor life doesn't interest me. I also don't want to exclusively confine myself to the four walls of a lab until my eternal slumber. I want to be around people—not enough to overwhelm me—and be part of projects that make a difference. Not just a bottom line.

I want my work to mean something.

"I might have an interest based on the information I have thus far," I say.

Kieran flashes a smile that I'm sure electrocutes and causes third-degree burns. He's handsome, with a nice set of teeth. But that zing is missing. Not that I'm trying to rub materials with anyone at a potential place of work.

An image of Antonio pulls me back to this past weekend at my house. The softness of his hands and his hard body during our paint fight. That forehead kiss before he left.

I draw in a deep breath and try to forget the smirk on Lisa's face at brunch. Who lies about sex with someone who's running off to be with his mother in the hospital? Technically, he flew, but her audacity must have frequent flyer miles. Unless they hooked up before he went home to DC. That's an image I don't want roaming around in my head.

We don't fantasize about friends who sleep with your sister's friend, least of all in a job interview.

"Miriam?"

"Yes?" I swing my gaze up from the name plate on Kieran's desk. I never understood the redundancy of having one inside an office if there's one on the door. *Focus.* "Sorry. You were saying?"

A ghost of a smile appears. "I was wondering if I could answer any questions you might have about the position over dinner."

Is he...no. Right?

I'm an overheated puffer fish sitting in his office, and he's thinking about dinner. With me. *Why* is he thinking about dinner with me?

"You mean just the two of us?" Why do we need dinner plates to fill in the blanks?

Maybe he thinks you're pretty.

"Sorry. I'm not good at this. Engineering, yes. I didn't mean to imply any unprofessional behavior on your part. Potential colleagues share meals all the time. Fraternization policy or not."

In case it wasn't clear, I never miss my daily dose of putting my size ten in my mouth.

I die from embarrassment three times. Once from the verbal diarrhea I spilled all over Kieran's unnecessary name plate. Another from my pits, which are reactivating sweat stains through the tissue clumping to my skin. The third is from the beads of sweat between my toes, of all places.

"It was nice meeting you." I stand and retract the hand I offer because of the sweaty tissue pits. "Best of luck with your projects."

"Is that a no on dinner?" Kieran asks my back.

The look I aim over my shoulder inquires what the hell is wrong with him. I'm a mess with questionable common sense. He should be calling security, not confirming a meal.

"Does tomorrow at six work? I'll make reservations at The Boathouse."

I'll need to cancel the friendship event. Not that I'm in any shape to meet new people if I can't get through an interview my father set up. "Sure, sounds good," I say. "Okay, bye."

I swear I hear a rumble of laughter on my way out of his office.

Chapter 16

Antonio

Who got locked up? crossed my mind when Coach told me he wanted me in his office. Nothing good comes from an unscheduled meeting before training.

Shit, did somebody die?

"Come in," Coach Washington calls from the broom closet we transformed into his office. The knock on the door was a courtesy. It opens from the outside.

D pulled the impossible out of his toolbelt. No way should a desk and chair fit in here, but they did, along with the extra seat he motions for me to take.

Deep frown lines raise above thick glasses aimed at a stack of papers. Coach Washington has what you'd call a baby face. It's fighting against middle age and wear and tear from years of play. The gray at his temples is slowly creeping into the blond hair he keeps long on top.

"Have a seat."

The tiny folding chair whines under my weight. I shift my knees so they don't dig into the front of his metal desk. Anyone with claustrophobia would pass out in here.

"Who's in trouble?" I ask.

Coach sighs and says, "We are," squeezing the bridge of his nose.

"How? Season passes are up twenty percent. Same with merch. Last year's playoff appearance and the PSN deal have given us more visibility. They show league games on the network now." I don't mean to scowl, but he better look at his notes again and carry the two.

The RLA, or Rugby League of America, is still young. There are ups and downs in the seventh season—shitty pay and short-term contracts that create more questions than job security—but the eleven teams that represent professional rugby in the US give their all on the pitch.

"We bust our asses," I bark.

"I know." He sighs. "Miami is gone."

"What?"

"So is New Orleans and LA. Utah is at risk, but their finance department is confident that play will continue for at least another season."

The blow of dropping to an eight-team league is a shot to the chest. There are good people on the receiving end of those decisions. Guys with families who work two and three jobs. Staff who pour into us and put us back together.

"Fuck." I run a hand through my waves.

Coach's frown deepens. "We have enough money in our budget to grab one player. The others..." He forces out a breath and leans into his chair. "It's fucked up. The RLA is shortening the season from sixteen games to twelve. We'll still have our bye weeks, and you'll play five teams twice. One home game and one away."

Simon Washington is one of the best coaches I've had since I picked up a rugby ball as a kid. He played overseas for years as a flanker before retiring and joining the Steel in a coaching capacity. He's a stand-up guy who believes in transparency and wants what's best for the team.

"What aren't you telling me?" Three teams collapsing and another on the brink of stepping away from competition isn't the reason he called me in before strength and conditioning.

He considers me, the stress evident in his light brown eyes.

Frank Mancini.

Buffalo Steel owner and one of the biggest pricks in the game.

Our team is an afterthought, another item in his large portfolio of investments. Mancini has his hand in everything, with real estate being his primary focus. He doesn't come to games, barely pays players, and gives minimal health coverage during the season.

The RLA needs a players' union to fight predators like him.

"Mancini might offload the Steel," Coach reveals.

I huff and rub my jaw. "What should I tell the guys?"

"Nothing for now. It's still speculation. Analysts have us as a favorite to win this year, which should help. Let's focus on the season as planned." He eyes me. "If I hear anything more permanent, we'll have the talk. This is more than a job to me. The team is family. I wanted to tell you what I know, but I don't want the guys getting in their heads with this shit."

If the Steel was to fold, I'd be okay. Between my investment portfolio and the security of the family business, I'm set. But that's a privilege not afforded to most players in this league.

There's no pension, and sponsorship opportunities are limited. The market for rugby in the United States is small. The league needs more time to develop, and we deserve an owner who's invested in us as much as we are in the game.

"We'll leave it on the pitch like we always do." I stand and dab Coach.

"I appreciate you, Antonio. You're a good captain. I'm sorry we have to deal with this shit, but I'll do what I can from my end. For now, keep up the good work. The more wins and publicity we get, the more we have a shot at getting another season."

"Will do."

I head to the locker room to get ready for the day, pushing the fate of the Steel to the back burner. It's what I do best, take on stress so the people around me don't have to worry about it.

If Mancini needs a show to remind him who the fuck we are, he'll get one.

They all will.

Chapter 17

Miriam

Never in my life have I wanted to go upside someone's head with a taco. But Marcela isn't worth wasting the marinated pork and fresh pineapple. I'm hungry, and I wouldn't make it three steps before she tossed me into Lake Erie.

I still thought about it.

There are days when I dislike my sister, and tonight is no exception. Who ruins Taco Tuesday by poking fun at their sibling? Mine, apparently.

Marcela's face is stuck between signs of a seizure and a hard fart. She's been like this for the last six minutes and eighteen seconds—I counted in case she needs medical attention. Her head is tipped to the popcorn ceiling, her cornrows, which are woven up into a braided bun, touching the back of the chair as she slides down it.

Pure foolery.

I wave off the server, who's been hovering around our table in case my sister needs carted off to a place with padded rooms.

"People are staring." I kick her pantleg under the table. The only part of her that's visible is her bun.

Her response is a muffled snort. After a few more snickers, she finally comes up for air.

"It's just—" She snorts again and uses a napkin to blot the thick lashes fanning tears down her cheeks. "Only you would get asked out during a job interview while wearing that blouse."

My forehead creases. "It's a professional dinner, and I found this blouse in your closet." If she plays "When Doves Cry" on her phone one more time, I'm gone.

"Be that as it may, this is your sign to put yourself out there. I get not entertaining distractions during school. Now that you have a handful of degrees, put that mechanics knowledge to use."

"Mechanics is a branch of physics that—never mind." I sigh at her smirk. "I should cancel."

"To what, stay in the house and count the fake lemons in your display bowl?" Marcela raises a brow and wraps her lips around the blue rim of her margarita glass.

"That's the last time I tell you my business." I snatch the nearest taco from the platter between us. Everything from barbacoa to tripe is present, next to a side of rice and beans and pico de gallo. The one thing my sister and I agree on is not playing cute when it's time to eat.

El Teke Taqueria is a small box. The floors are sticky and the heater sputters, but the food is amazing. The best meals come from holes in the wall.

"All I'm saying is it's okay for you to *get* the business." She winks, grabbing a tortilla chip. "Work dinners aren't uncommon. If you're comfortable, shit, go for it."

A work dinner.

At a boathouse, which happens to have a live jazz band that evening.

"I saw the photo on the company website. He's attractive. You know he has a good job. If there's no policy against dating your coworker, give him a test drive."

"Marcela," I hiss.

The restaurant is too crowded for anyone to hear us. I still wouldn't like talking about sex in public, and I definitely don't like *having* sex in public, though the risk of getting caught has made me curious on occasion.

"Look at that brain, hard at work." She grins. "Get out your head."

"That's easy for you to say."

My sister's nonchalance is nothing new. Neither of us grew up imagining our wedding day or waiting for a man to gallop up on a horse and rescue us from the single life. She surprised us by getting married to her high school sweetheart, but then she course corrected to stay away from any hint of forever.

Her divorce took two years to finalize. Raheem couldn't keep a job to pay a bill but found a way to drag out the proceedings like the leech he is. My sister learned a costly lesson, and now she refuses to entertain a man beyond casual sex.

Unlike her, I want a commitment with the right partner. My lack of experience with love is neither evidence of missing self-confidence nor immaturity. Many people roam the earth who lack a basic aptitude for decency and pass around STIs like Tic Tacs.

Coital chaos demons.

I might be awkward at times, and I might get in my own head, but I have boundaries. I won't waste my time seeking validation through an unnecessary relationship.

While I'm open to love, any man I choose will complement me, not complete me. I'm inexperienced, but I'm whole.

"It's okay if you don't think Macaulay is cute," my sister says.

"Kieran," I snort. "His name is Kieran."

She shrugs. "I said a Culkin. No one expects you to go on a dick binge. But"—her head cants, and she purses her lips like Robert De Niro—"I won't say anything."

"Good to know." I roll my eyes and tap the rim of my margarita glass. "I've thought about dating. I'm not fully sold on algorithms being equitable on apps, which leaves finding someone in person." Where it gets weird fast, and I usually end up wanting to run back to the house to organize my lemons. "Kieran is cute. I just don't feel the spark."

"Spark?" Marcela crunches into a birria taco.

"You know, that electric charge. A zing. Our father had it with our mother."

"And look what happened to that," she scoffs.

Okay, not the best example since they ended up divorced. But the love was there. Remnants still linger in the way they try to brush off asking about each other. My mother is loud and outspoken. My father is reserved and quiet. Put together, their differences are what made their relationship, until his career got in the way.

"My point is that I don't feel anything for Kieran, other than nervous that I fumbled my interview. I'm also not actively searching for anybody right now. If it happens, it happens."

More people are having babies in their forties. The taboo of being single later in life is losing its stronghold, taking the pressure off of procreating within the time frame that society dictates is "reasonable." I'm not rushing or stressing myself out with what anyone else assumes is best for me. I'll know when it's the right time, just like I'll know who my person is.

Maybe.

"Would a certain rugby player have anything to do with you swiping left on Culkin?"

I frown. "Did you hear me say I'm not actively searching for anyone?" What's the proof in this tequila?

Marcela purses her lips again. "I did. That doesn't answer my question. Nice try."

God, why did you make her so annoying?

"Antonio has nothing to do with this." I poke at a taco with my knife to keep from poking the person across from me, who's a second away from demonstrating what a "blood" relative is.

"So you haven't felt the zing with him?"

"Yes—no!" *Please give me strength with her.*

Every hair on my neck stood up when Antonio walked into that Adams Morgan bar. My heart always skipped a beat when I'd see him on the rugby field. It made zero sense, because I once babysat him! It was only a handful of times before he went to high school, but still.

My attraction is more of an anomaly, an unexplained scientific occurrence. I like him, and I won't sour our friendship over an orgasm I can give myself. Plus, he's a player. The only reason he showed interest in me three years ago was because I was a consenting vagina.

I push my glasses up my nose and sigh. "For the last time, he is a friend who, last I checked, is doing your friend."

"Miriam." Marcela chuckles.

I lift my hands. "I'm fine. We don't need to talk about it again. They're free to see each other. It doesn't involve me."

My sister raises a brow. "Sex for some people is just that—sex. No emotional attachments or feelings involved. I do it all the time."

"I know you do." I giggle into my glass.

"Don't brush this off."

"What do you want me to say, that I don't like the idea of him with Lisa?" I push my plate away and fold my arms over a million and one ruffles. "He comes from money, and I'll kick her wig off if she tries him like the elders she uses for paid vacations."

"Not kick a wig!" Marcela hollers, earning the attention of our server.

Chucha madre.

"*Estamos bien,*" I tell his narrowed brows. "*La cuenta, por fa.*" He bumps a table on his escape route. I don't blame him one bit. Now I'm laughing.

"Her wigs do look like mops," Marcela says.

"Don't talk about your friend like that."

"She's not my friend!" My sister whines, which activates my wheeze. "I don't invite her anywhere. She just shows up. Her humping got her cut off anyway."

"You don't have to do that for me."

"And did." She straightens to adjust her blazer. "I caught the smirk Lisa thought she was hiding. She can play games with her mama before she plays with my sister. The fuck?"

"I love you, Cela."

"Love you too, girl."

My phone buzzes.

Antonio

Hey! Did they roll out the red carpet for you? I meant to text earlier, but we started at six this morning.

Sounds rough. The interview was okay. Not sure I'm completely sold, the more I think about it. They're making a position for me.

Antonio

That's what's up! Don't settle for less. You deserve it all. I'm beat. Showering, eating, and going to bed. We still on for your friendly school bus event?

It's not a school bus! Change of plans. Kieran, the guy I might work with, asked me to dinner to discuss the position. You're off the hook being my wingman. Get some rest!

"Why are you looking at me like that?" I ask Marcela and her smile.

She picks up a chip. "You and Antonio are both in denial, but y'all will figure it out one day."

"We aren't. We're—"

"Friends," she mocks in a kid voice and winks. "Antonio looks at you like he'd hang the sun, the moon, and every star for you. Got him calling me 'ma'am,' being all polite and grabbing sushi because you said you ate it on Fridays back in grad school. If you don't get out your own way and get your fairy tale…"

"He's being nice," I say quietly.

"He's in love. Probably waiting for you to give a sign that you feel the same way."

Never once have I heard of Antonio wanting to give up his bachelor life. We don't talk about who he sees or what they do.

I won't say things haven't been a little weird since he texted me on Sunday to apologize. His poor mother. It would be wrong for me to ask about Lisa, especially now. So I minded my business and left it alone. Between his mother and practice before the season starts, he's got his hands full.

I will too once I get a job. Maybe then I'll stop thinking about things I shouldn't. Like how long him and Lisa have been…active. If it's serious. If he could be with just one person.

"We like each other, but not the way you think," I say. "It's not my place to care about who he's with."

"Lisa didn't sleep with him," Marcela confirms.

"I don't need—"

"He kicked her out. Said he had to go to the airport. She called today to apologize. I told her trifling ass I wasn't the one who needed an apology."

The breath that was trapped in my lungs escapes in a slow release. I fix my glasses and nod without glancing at my sister. The confirmation that nothing happened between them shouldn't be a relief. But it is, and that confuses me.

Chapter 18

Antonio

Miriam is going on a date with *Kieran* "to discuss the position."

Why couldn't he answer any questions in the office, in broad daylight and with a respectable distance between them? You don't need linen tablecloths and three types of forks if you handled your business the first time.

I've dined with women after work. The only negotiations that came from that were if there were any preexisting conditions to consider and how many toys they wanted to play with before the main event.

Men like Kieran, who fish for pussy at their job, are walking red flags. Creating a business with a life partner is one thing, but asking for a date before an interview is over?

Fuck that.

"Just tell her that she has entrées at home," I say to myself from Miriam's front porch. "It's cold, and she doesn't see well in the dark to be driving."

Want him to come here?

"To hell with all of that."

Aged wood on the other side of better days groans under my Timbs. The porch light is on for Miriam and her neighbors to witness me pacing the small area. They probably think I'm a robber who's contemplating a life sentence in an all-black sweatsuit. I came straight from practice, unable to answer why I felt the need to drive over instead of letting Miriam enjoy her fake work dinner in peace.

I can't *let* her do anything. I'm not trying to control her life. I'm just looking out as a friend who's thought with his dick more than I care to admit.

Oh hey, you're home. Small world.

Where did you expect her to be? In the sewer?

I was just in the neighborhood—

The practice field is twenty minutes in the other direction.

Did you get that call about extended warranties?

I scrub a hand over my face and stifle a groan. There is no reason to be over here before her date.

Why don't you tell her the truth?

That the idea of her going out with this guy, or any other, itches my ass to no end? It shouldn't, we're friends, but it does. I have no—

I dive over the banister at the laughter behind the front door. The plastic trash can and recycling bins soften my landing, but they bang against the house. A dog barks a few doors down. I freeze, which isn't hard to do in this weather, and shut my eyes.

The door opens.

I right the bins and tippy-toe run to the back of Miriam's house. The back door swings open, and before I have time to react, a dark figure leaps off the steps and tackles me to the ground. I land on a pile of snow with a thud.

"What the—" My words are muffled by a lotioned hand covering my mouth. I push it away. "Please tell me that's a gun digging into my hip."

"With bullets just for your stupid ass, sneaking around my sister's house. What are you doing?"

It's hard to answer Marcela when the weight of her breasts is smothering my windpipe.

When I tap her hip, she lifts off of me and all but drags me to my feet by my hoodie. Unlike her sister, Marcela and I are similar in height. She's got a Coke bottle figure with extra curves. Not that I'm looking at her like that. It's just hard to miss thighs like hers and what I assume are E cups jutting out like a shield she's not afraid to wield.

The only ass I care about is Miriam's. To keep it in the house and away from potentially dangerous future colleagues.

"Hey, hey!" I back up at her shoves. Each one lands in the center of my chest. "Ow, stop!" I rub what will surely be a bruise tomorrow. "I had a hard practice—hey!" I turn my shoulder to dodge another direct blow.

Marcela's hands anchor on her hips. "Are you in the habit of snooping around Miriam's house?" If I didn't know any better, I'd assume she came to fight. She's wearing sweats, a tee, and...are those combat boots?

"What?"

"Oh, you can't hear now?" The inflection in her voice rises. "You're about to be acquainted with some real Buffalo *steel* in a minute." She reaches for her waistband.

I drop to my knees and raise my hands. Call me what you want. I'm not leaving here with bullet holes or in a body bag.

"Please don't shoot! I saw she was home. I was in the neighborhood, and I had questions about extended warranties."

Idiot.

My answer appears to do the trick. Marcela's hands fly to her knees. I assume she's choking until she lets out a wheeze followed by a loud snort.

"You should see your face," she cackles.

"Yeah? You try getting tackled to the ground and nearly pistol-whipped." It's a blessing I didn't pee myself.

Her laughter is the same silent strain as Miriam's. "Boy, ain't nobody shooting you. My gun is in my purse upstairs. This is a stapler." She raises it and cracks up louder at my deadpan expression. "I heard your simple ass talking to yourself on the porch. Miriam was doing the same thing before she left."

"She's gone?" I frown.

Marcela nods. "Left a little after you knocked over her bins being a creep."

"I'm not a creep. I have a good reason for being here."

What *am* I doing here?

I've never shown up to a woman's house, and I sure as hell never dove into trash bins. Miriam is smarter than I'll ever be. She can take care of herself and make her own decisions. But I drove over without a second thought. It just felt right to be here.

Marcela shakes her head. "No answer?"

"I just..."

"Care more about my sister than you like to let on?"

Do I care for Miriam? A hundred percent. It's not a stretch to say I love her. Being *in* love with her is a different story. I never loved any woman I was with or saw myself wanting. Miriam is different. But me, in love?

"The Boathouse."

"Huh?"

Marcela chuckles. "She's meeting him at The Boathouse. While you're thinking about extended warranties, maybe you should swing by for something to eat?"

~ele~

"This steak is juicy. Try some."

"Nah, I'm good." Kendrick pushes Quincy's fork out of his face and laughs. "I ain't never seen a filet over a bed of French fries."

"Don't knock it 'til you try it, big bro. I have everything I need for our mission on this plate." He shovels a broccoli floret into his mouth. "That's what we're doing, Cap? Spying on your friend?"

"I'm not spying," I tell Quincy for the second time. "I heard she'd be here, and the food sounded good."

Kendrick cuts his eyes at me over a plate of Bolognese. "Yeah, okay. Go over there and let her know you're here." I stay silent. "Exactly."

After getting caught at Miriam's house, I ran home to shower. Marcela suggested The Boathouse for dinner, and I figured why not?

I invited Kendrick and Quincy in the event she saw me and asked what I was doing here. In my defense, she never told me the restaurant where she's having her "work discussion." I'm a safe distance away in case she needs me.

"Scoot over. I barely have elbow room." Quincy attempts to push me and Kendrick away with his forearms. He's sandwiched between us, and there's not a damn thing any of us can do at this small table. We look like we left a JCPenney catalog shoot in variations of jeans and long-sleeve tees.

"You got a problem with my thighs touching yours?" I rub my denim against his and laugh.

"It's all fun and games now, but wait until *their* knees touch." Quincy nods at Miriam's table. Her hands are in her lap. Dickhead's legs are spread in a tired tan suit like some damn mating ritual. "You gonna crash out?"

"No." I stab my swordfish into rice.

To Dickhead's credit, this is a nice setup. The Boathouse has nautical vibes and wall-to-wall views of Lake Erie. Off-white wood beams hang high against a navy room with dark wood floors and dim-ass lighting.

The perfect ambiance for a fucking date.

I glance at Miriam. It's hard to tell if she's enjoying herself, but judging by her *date's* inability to shut up, my guess is no. Her shoulders slump slightly, and her focus is on the plate of salad she pushes around.

The outfit she wore is very her. An off-the-shoulder sweater and black leggings isn't a popular choice for an upscale restaurant, but you won't hear me complaining about the material hugging her thighs, waist, and that ass that spills over her seat. She's comfortable as herself and doesn't feel the need to conform to a specific standard. To her, practicality matters above all else. It's one of the many things I admire about her.

She's a natural beauty who wears little to no makeup. Her mocha skin glows without it. So does the smile touching her plump lips, but that isn't visible tonight.

"This jazz band is a vibe, low-key," Kendrick says, snatching my thoughts from my friend to the quartet in the corner. "We might need to come back next week."

"After an ice bath," Quincy groans. "Coach Titan really hates us with those sprints after a scrimmage."

I laugh at the scrum-half who's rubbing the collar on his polo and make a mental note to buy another ice bath for the house. "Gotta get that stamina up, Baby Q. Endurance is key."

The coaches are putting us through it. We face Houston in their house in a few weeks, and we are coming with that heat. They knocked us out of the playoffs last season, and they'll be a force with the two trades they picked up. We need to come out of the gate strong, especially after the news Coach Washington dropped about Mancini.

My phone dances across the table.

"Look at that goofy grin," I vaguely hear Kendrick say, too focused on the message preview.

Hey, did you eat already?

"Is she texting him from her date?" Quincy asks.

"Stay out of grown folks' business," I counter.

I could eat. Dinner not going as planned?

Miriam

You could say that. I'm trying not to be rude and fall asleep.

I roll my lips.

Want me to help you fake an emergency?

Miriam

What?

Her brows fold. Kieran is too caught up in talking to notice that she not only checked out of the conversation, but is texting another man.

Play along.

"Let's go." I stand and motion for Kendrick and Quincy to come with me. My phone is already to my ear.

"Hello?" Miriam's voice is cautious.

"Pretend I'm your sister and I busted my ass on some ice." I nod to the server for the check and point to the host station.

"Oh no," she says, convincing absolutely no one. "Are you okay?"

"Not with that fake concern. I could be in the hospital with a dookie bruise that wraps around my butt."

She snorts but catches herself. "Sounds like you need medical attention. Should I come to you?"

I sign my credit card slip and wink at the older woman behind the host stand. "How about I come to you? I can get dropped off. Text me your location."

Kendrick snickers behind me. "Lying ass."

"Okay. See you in ten?"

"Works for me. See you soon, Doe." I hang up and meet three sets of eyes.

Kendrick's are wild with mischief.

Quincy's are amused.

The gray-haired woman I winked at has hearts in hers.

"Can you two drive yourself home?" I toss Kendrick my keys as Miriam sends a text with The Boathouse's address.

"Like we got a choice," he chuckles. "Come on, Baby Q. Let's hit up a drive-thru."

"Not too much junk so close to the season," I call after them.

"Yes, Papa Smurf," they groan in unison.

They dip out while I jog off to the end of the street to wait for Miriam.

Wingman to the rescue.

Chapter 19

Antonio

Nipsey Hussle's "Dedication" blares across the pitch under dim lights. Sweat and exertion cling to the now-empty turf. The team and coaches left an hour ago. Only D and I are still here, a row of orange cones separating us.

I bob my head to the lyrics and tighten the harness across my bare chest, adjusting the compression shorts underneath my basketball shorts. I peek over at Darius, who gives me a nod. On my go, we take off.

Loaded sled sprints down a ten-yard runway isn't what I'd call a fun Friday night. I'm tired as hell, but I'll put in extra time after practice if D asks. He matches my speed and drops into a set of twenty push-ups before jogging back.

Show-off.

"Who you trying to impress? Your fan club president is right here," I say, stretching my arms, exhausted from the day.

D unhooks the harness clinging to his drenched shirt and takes a towel to the sweat coating his chest and tatted arms. "Funny." He rolls his eyes. "For real, though. I appreciate you for staying after."

Darius, or D, and I both joined the team as free agents. We're both pushing thirty and incorporate more training and recovery to compete with the younger guys. We eat right and stay in shape year-round so we can have a fighting chance of extending our careers.

The preseason cycle is winding down, but not the intensity.

Tactical training.

Endurance.

Agility.

Speed.

Match intensity.

The stakes are higher. So are the expectations.

Bro is a killer as a hooker. He wins the ball for us during scrums and is responsible for lineout throws to restart play. You have to be good at playing with your balls to make split-second decisions. D is a specialist who could teach a masterclass.

He usually can't stick around after practice because of his daughter or the construction business he co-owns. How he juggles it all and still brings his A game is crazy. Like I said, he's good with handling balls. Jokes aside, I look up to him. Well, down, since he's five ten.

We walk our route to collect the cones. "How's Aeris?"

He laughs, grinning from ear to ear about his daughter. "Ten going on forty. One of her friends, who's a year older, just got her period." He shudders. "I'm not okay."

"I don't know how you do it."

"Ain't got no choice but to." He shrugs. "Baby girl deserves the world. Whatever I don't know, I'll learn. Ms. Thomas keeps me right."

D is a single dad. Aeris's mom left when she was five and only calls when she remembers their daughter's birthday. He's a year younger than me raising a whole child. I can't keep plants alive, and he's out here learning about training bras and Common Core math. Sometimes, he leaves Aeris with me or Kendrick while he works nights. She's finally playing *Final Fantasy VII*, the game that inspired her name.

I lock up the equipment we used and motion toward the locker rooms. "Will you be good this season, with coverage and stuff?"

He nods. "Yeah. She'll stay home by herself more as she gets older. Ms. Thomas has a key in case of emergencies, and she'll keep her during away games."

"Don't tell her daughter," I chuckle. "Ms. Thomas is a respected block club leader, but Brianna is campaigning to be Aeris's stepmama."

"Don't play. There's no space in my freezer for any more home-cooked meals. You'd think somebody died the way she's been hanging around the house. The last time she came over, she brought light bulbs."

We bust out laughing. That's a new one.

"Maybe it's time to try out women in their early fifties." I retrieve my bag from my locker and pull out a fresh shirt. The shower pressure here is shit. Driving home musty it is.

D throws a vest over his thermal. "I'm good on that. Speaking of trying out..."

"Don't start, Shemar," I warn. If he wants to be an ass, two can play. "Don't you have a *Soul Train* line to terrorize with your light skin behavior?"

"Man, fuck you," he laughs, pushing a beanie over his low fade buzz cut. "I heard your friend is pretty. Maybe I should see if she wouldn't mind playing house with me."

"Keep *playing* and see if we don't end up on *Criminal Minds*." I slam my locker shut harder than necessary and stuff my arms into my jacket. "Miriam is off-limits." D is a good dude, but I'll be damned on her behalf.

Our staredown is reminiscent of *Drumline*. All that's missing are drumsticks pointed at each other and our faces on a Thanksgiving meme about whose auntie makes better mac 'n cheese.

D rubs his jaw with a smirk. He's what you'd call a pretty boy, but he can run his hands if necessary. They'd find us knocked out on these benches tomorrow. I play about a lot, but not Miriam. I have no say in who she's with, but the idea of her entertaining anyone bothers me more than it should. Especially someone on my team.

"Chill." His laugh is playful as he raises his hands. "You know I don't move like that."

"So move *around*." I smile, brushing his shoulder on the way out. "Some of us got things to do besides help with homework."

"Oh, this is wifey," he says through a cackle.

I don't bother looking back. "She's a good friend."

"We all have that someone we call."

I shake my head. "Not her. We're not like that."

"So you *like* her like her." He hits the lights while I get the alarm.

"I like my best friend, yes." I lock the door behind me and autostart my car.

"Want Aeris to make you friendship bracelets?"

It's not a bad idea.

"Could she?" I ask for real.

"Yeah, this is your future wife. Wait 'til I tell the guys." He's hollering now.

"Who's ashamed of friendship bracelets?" I ignore his "future wife" comment.

People wear friendship bracelets, and Miriam likes throwbacks. If she's not watching *Buffy*, she's searching for random shows, like *The Secret World of Alex Mack*. The series aired the year I was born and had something to do with inherited superpowers. Or was it chemical goo? I asked if Alex Mack was like Spider-Man and got the side-eye.

"The team would probably want bracelets too," I add. Crafts are a surprising way to destress after a game. Fucking too, but that comes with more strings.

"Tell you what. Get the materials, and I'll swing by tomorrow with Aeris." D points at me. "You're paying my baby."

"Consider it an investment in her college fund."

Miriam is out of town with her sister for the weekend. Catching up on sleep, laundry, and making sure no one blows up Steel House with the microwave sounds like a plan.

Chapter 20

Miriam

"There are these things called restaurants that cook food. Traveling with fish in your purse is insane."

"It was in my suitcase, not my purse." A storage bag of the red snapper I cleaned, scaled, and marinated in another bag for safe-keeping.

I cut my eyes at the passenger princess sitting on the counter. The kitchen in our rental at the mountain resort is a galley with pea-green cabinets. Marcela is taking up what little counter space we have with her big mouth and her bigger ass.

"Do you want to help with dinner or run your mouth all night?" I scold with a spatula in hand.

The only time she lifted a finger was to uncork the wine bottle. Did she offer me a glass? Of course not. She gets to sit pretty in a full face of makeup, a wrinkle-free pantsuit, and heels.

I pour the fish stew over rice into a bowl with a side of plantains and make one for my sister. She's free to clown me about the hour drive to Ellicottville with red snapper in my bag, but guess who saved us from spending forty dollars each on a salad?

I question who raised my sister to desire overpriced food with a sprinkle of salt and pepper. We come from a long line of aunties who cook for every occasion.

Quinceañera? Cooking.

Wedding? Cooking.

Funeral? Cooking.

Family reunion? Cooking.

Baby birth? Cooking.

Someone's in town? Cooking.

I picked up the tradition spending summers in Panama after our mother moved back. She would flip if she heard Marcela scoff at homecooked meals. She certainly did when I video called her to snitch.

Así que tú tienes plata? Compra tu marido y dame nietos.

Patricia Rojas will never not ask about the grandchildren my sister refuses to have. At some point I'll be in the hot seat, but I've been dodging bullets thanks to school.

My job situation is still up in the air. I haven't given Kieran a response. On paper, the position and salary are great, but something doesn't feel right. I don't know what or why, but I don't want to make the wrong decision.

"*Tu sabes lo que estás haciendo en la cocina,*" Marcela says after a spoonful of fish and peppers. She shakes her freshly pressed hair with a nod.

"Thank you."

If I close my eyes, we're in our mother's kitchen with the windows open to welcome the saltwater breeze from the ocean. It's twenty degrees outside, a far cry from Panama's dry season.

"Are we going out? You promised," my sister reminds me at my groan.

"And you promised me a low-key weekend with sister bonding." I grab my bowl for a second helping.

"We're doing that."

"I'm in a diaper!" Ice clinks as it shifts around in its plastic bag inside said diaper. At least I had the sense to pack my fleece onesie with a flap on the butt.

I agreed to come to Ellicottville for the weekend under false pretenses. When I said, "Sure, why not?" to a cozy condo with views of the mountain, it did not include me going up one. I'm not saying Panamanians don't ski, but this one doesn't. I never agreed to any snow sports, but I got tricked under the guise of a scenic tour and hot chocolate. I got both—after I rolled down a slope like an uncoordinated tumbleweed.

That slope I was on? It's the one they use for beginner lessons. I was the only adult in a class of twelve- and fourteen-year-olds. One of them told me I should've stayed at home.

Duh!

I've never been more grateful for my booty, a snow suit, and a helmet. The first was padding to prevent injury. The other two masked my identity.

Where was Marcela? Snowboarding down one of the steepest runs.

Only one of us channeled Queen Latifah in *The Last Holiday* if she didn't stick the landing. That person was me. My instructor was kind enough to escort me to safety. The kids were alright, but I was not.

"The bar seats have cushions." Marcela waves her phone in confirmation while doing her best not to laugh at the ice jiggling between my booty. My cold reality, all because she wanted to ski.

"No."

"One hour. The drink menu is good."

Dang it.

"One cocktail," I protest.

"One *hour*." She holds up a finger. "All drinks on me. I'll throw in dessert."

"You were paying anyway." I shake out a wedgie.

Marcela lied again.

The bar chairs do not have cushions. There is nary a fabric in sight, unless you count the cloth napkins I'm piling under my jeans. The drinks are good, though. I blew through the first and am now on number two. Sam, the bartender, makes a balanced raspberry mule, which made the trek out of my pajamas and into the cold worth it. For now.

Easy Daisy is a small bar at the end of Ellicottville's main street. Blink and you'll miss it between gift shops and restaurants that charge the GDP of small countries for the same lettuce I can buy at the store. The crowd here is small. A few of us are at the bar, facing a wall of illuminated bricks and shelves of liquor. Others are gathered around bistro tables with chairs that also lack cushions.

I won't admit it out loud and face Marcela's "I told you so," but this is nice. Relaxing.

"Don't look, but there's a guy checking you out."

And now my guts are touching my butt.

"What? Ow!" I squeak at her grip on my thigh.

"Don't look!" Her eyes lift above my sweater. "He's cute, and he's coming over."

"No. This was not part of the going-out deal," I hiss. "Drinks. Dessert. That's it."

Her smirk brushes the rim of her martini glass. "There's one more D to consider. Unclench your hands and breathe. You got this."

"I didn't want any—"

"Mind if I join you?"

I clench my butthole at the cool edge in his voice. Panic triggers the reminder of today's floor routine down the mountain as pain sprouts up my swollen cheeks, which are in need of a bed and not a hard barstool. My inhale is sharp, and it goes down the wrong pipe.

Marcela bunches her lips as she gently pats my back. I drain the last sips of my mule and swivel toward the man standing behind me.

He's in a dark gray sweater and jeans. Medium height with a round face, small lips, and wisps of chocolate brown hair underneath a knitted winter hat with a pom on top. It's similar to the one I'm wearing that presses down my curls.

My sister knees me after the sixth second of silence.

"Hi. Miriam." I thrust my hand out but pull it back when I remember my jagged cuticles are about to do show-and-tell. *Note to self: Add nail maintenance to the monthly routine.*

He flashes a smile. "Hart. Nice to meet you. May I?"

I don't own the establishment or the chair. "Sure, okay."

He takes the seat next to me. "What brings you to Ellicottville?"

"What makes you think I don't live here?"

"Oh, sorry. Do you live here?"

"No," I shrug. "Just curious as to why you assumed I'm not a resident. Do I not look like a local?" The total population here is the same as my high school.

"You're prettier," he says.

Don't blush. "Thank you." My eyes dance from my glass to the bar and back. How do people do this?

"Would you like another?"

"Huh?"

He points to the empty glass I'm holding. "Would you like another drink?"

"Oh," I chuckle and bump my eyeglasses with my thumb. "No thanks. I already had two."

More silence.

I chance a question that won't make me seem more awkward than I am. "Do you live here?"

Hart shakes his head. "Corning. I came over to ski."

"Don't remind me about the slopes." I wince. "I had a spill today." That's an exaggeration. I never even stayed upright on my skis. "Me and skiing don't get along."

"Maybe I could teach you if you're still around tomorrow?"

"Trust me, I'm helpless." My laughter fades at his eyes pinned to mine. They're blue. Not cobalt or sapphire. Still pretty, with a hint of gray.

I peek at Marcela for a lifeline and get a wink.

"This is my sister, Marcela."

"Hi." She offers a quick wave.

"Hey." He all but ignores her.

Well then.

What's the goal here? We ski. I fall. He takes me to the hospital and asks for my number.

Do we exchange contact information now? I don't like how he barely acknowledged my sister. Am I interested in a first date? Where would it be? Tomorrow? In Corning?

How does Antonio do this with multiple people?

I'm already exhausted.

"Um." I twist my glass. "I'd rather not risk more embarrassment to my family than I already have."

His brows draw together before realization dawns. He snaps his fingers. "That was you today! I saw someone rolling down the kiddie run."

I lift a hand. "Guilty."

He offers an apologetic smile. "We all start somewhere. How about snow tubing, or hot chocolate if you want to stay indoors?"

I jump as my phone rings in my purse. At least, I think it's my phone. The ringtone is off.

Hart's face matches my frown. "Are you carrying a modem around?"

"Of course not," I say, digging through my bag. "I'm not connected to a WAN. Aha!" I pull my phone out and laugh at Antonio's name on the screen. "Excuse me one second." I answer. "Did you change my ringtone to a dial-up internet sound?"

"Only for my calls," Antonio says without a hint of guilt.

"When did you do that?"

"On Wednesday, after I rescued you from that fake date."

"It was not a date!" I laugh and turn to Hart. "A potential colleague asked me to dinner to discuss a position. Now that I say it out loud, it does sound a little weird."

"Told you," Antonio adds.

I scoff. "Hush. I can decline any non-work-related dinners. Lunches too."

Antonio sucks his teeth. "Like that will stop James St. Patrick. I bet you he wears bow ties."

"He does look like Ghost," I giggle.

"I don't lie. But that's not why I called. Do you still like that mint green color?"

That's random. "Why?"

"I'm making you a friendship bracelet."

"A what?" I snort. Marcela grimaces.

"You heard me," he says.

"Antonio is making me a friendship bracelet," I tell my sister.

"Hey, friend!" Antonio shouts through the phone, earning a smirk. I put him on speakerphone. "You want one too? We got an assembly line going."

Marcela lets out a short laugh. "You two are a mess. I'm good."

"Suit yourself," Antonio says. "So, do you still like mint green, Doe?"

"Yes, but why are you making friendship bracelets on an assembly line at nine thirty at night?"

"I'm watching Aeris while her pops does night construction. He plays on the team. Speaking of which, say hi to Miriam."

"Hi, Miriam!" voices say in unison.

The visual of professional rugby players crowded around beads and accessories is one I wish I could see in person. Antonio describes Steel House as a place of debauchery. Not a Michael's.

"Hey, Maid Miriam!" Bread's voice is loud and clear. "Stop hogging the hearts, Baby Q."

"Aye, split those," Antonio cuts in.

"Mint green is fine. Thank you for thinking of me." I smile.

His voice lowers. "Always do."

A collective "Aww!" follows, flaming my cheeks.

"Shut up!" Antonio pauses. "Don't repeat that, Aeris. I'll let you go, Doe. Enjoy your weekend with your sister."

"Will do, bye."

There's a chorus of "Bye, Miriam!" before the line goes dead.

Antonio is something else. Silly but also thoughtful.

He texts a picture of his handiwork. On his wrist are three bracelets. The first spells "Mechanical engineer" with a mix of yellow and orange. The second uses the mint green color and says my name with a heart, followed by "BFF." The last one has his nickname for me: "DOE," in call caps.

> Does your team laugh at you calling me a deer?

Antonio

> That's not what it means.

I frown.

Three dots dance across my screen. I draw in a sharp breath at his response.

Antonio

> DOE = Design of Experiments. Isn't it an engineering term to describe the systematic approach to problem-solving?

> How do you know that?

Antonio

> I try to keep up.

I reread the words on my screen until a throat clears. I forgot Hart was still here.

"I take it we're not making plans?" At my sad attempt at a smile, he shakes his head, sighs, and leaves.

I wasn't interested, especially after Antonio's call.

Who spends Saturday night babysitting a teammate's daughter, or making friendship bracelets with other players?

Apparently, he does.

Antonio has layers that are hard not to love the more he peels them back.

He's full of surprises.

Chapter 21

Miriam

My father is a menace who must be stopped. For the second week in a row, he sent me on a scavenger hunt he calls a job opportunity. This one was with a nearby university and required heels and grace. The first I hate. The second I lack.

The interview could've been an email, one that started with me responding, "Thanks, but no thanks." It was for a teaching position I know wouldn't fulfill me. I don't want to spend my days educating twenty-something-year-old college students, and the thought of wearing "professional clothes" for the rest of my life gives me hives.

It's not that I'm trying to be difficult. I want a job. The problem is, once you reach my age, whatever choice you make sticks. There's no trial period to see how a role might align with your goals, no understanding should you want to make a life change and release what doesn't fulfill you.

Creeping closer to forty means permanent. Settled.

I want that for my career, which is why I'm not hopping to take the first position thrown at me. I'm not operating out of arrogance. It's just that chasing after degrees never gave me the chance to breathe. To figure out my *why* beyond research and diplomas. I don't have an answer, but I know what makes my spirit sing, and the position my father thought was perfect isn't it.

Across from Marcela's district office, I ease into a parking spot not covered in two feet of snow. She's on the ground floor of a corner mixed-use building on one of the busier streets on the East Side. "Meet people where they're at" isn't just a slogan for her; it's part of the values she lives out loud for the people of the Jefferson District.

"Hey, Trevor." I stomp my heels on the weatherproof mat at the front door. A gust of cold air creeps in, slicing through my peacoat.

"I almost sent a rescue team to help you across the street." Hazel-green eyes lift over a computer monitor and zero in on the patent leather shoes choking my toes.

"You saw that?"

Curly hair bobs above his brows. "The whole hood saw you. Always wear boots outside. You know the city don't salt for shit. Allow me."

He stands from his desk, which doubles as reception, and offers me a cardigan-covered forearm I happily take.

Trevor joined my sister's team a year ago, quickly working his way up to become director of community affairs. The twenty-five-year-old is the go-to for constituents and Marcela's guard dog. His Anthony Ramos features and penchant for sweaters and dress pants are deceiving. He'll knock anyone who tries to run down on Marcela into next week and not think twice about it.

"Is my sister free?"

"She's still in her one o'clock," he says. "Can I get you anything?"

I collapse into a chair against the window. "Water, if it's not too much trouble, please." The breath I release is heavy. I'm sore and overstimulated.

"I mean no disrespect when I say this." He nods to my feet. "You might want to rethink heels. They've been crying in syllables, the way you were dragging them across the street like unwanted kids."

"Go get my water and leave me be." I shoo him away.

Trevor is an unofficial addition to our family. I don't go out of my way to speak to him, but we've talked enough to develop a rapport that's similar to brother and sister. He doesn't judge my quirks, and I keep his obvious crush on Marcela to myself.

My sister's door opens to laughter in mixed altos and shades of melanin. Trevor takes one look at her mouth stretched into a glossy smile and the long column of her neck and freezes in place.

I clear my throat before kicking his black loafers to reactivate his common sense. He hands me a water and goes back to his desk, blinking away the hearts in his puppy dog eyes.

"Miriam! So nice to see you." I stand to receive Ms. Amber's hug. It's warm and scented in crayons. "I was just telling your sister how much the kids still rave about your station."

"That's very sweet. It was nice to work in a group setting again," I admit to her eager gaze and chocolate brown cheeks. "I enjoyed their enthusiasm."

"You recently graduated?" A woman steps around my sister and extends a hand. "Aanya."

"Miriam. Nice to meet you."

Unlike me and Ms. Amber, who hover around five four, Aanya is my sister's height. She's fairer skinned, with thick, arched brows to match her long flowing hair. Her round eyes stare into my soul.

Crap, do I have food in my teeth?

"You studied mechanical engineering, yes?" The question comes through a faint accent.

I nod.

"And your specialty?"

My eyes shift to Marcela, who's wearing the same stony expression. "Mechanics and materials?"

I don't mean for my response to come out like a question. My nerves are trickling down my anus. "I researched and tested structures and materials under extreme conditions. Fracture mechanics and some design optimization. That whole thing."

Why is everyone looking at me?

I'm ready to test my luck with not falling on the sidewalk when Aanya's features soften.

"Amazing," she says with a smile. "I run an organization that's focused on creating an equitable food system on Buffalo's East Side, to combat the legacy of food apartheid. The three of us are part of a coalition comprised of groups and people with generational ties to the neighborhoods we love and want to see thrive."

"The city has extracted and withheld resources from East Side communities for decades," Marcela chimes in, frustration evident in her tone. "They segregated neighborhoods that now rely on box chains for basic needs. The lack of access to healthy foods, like produce and fresh meats, is one piece of a bigger issue that forces us to reimagine our food systems."

"What's happened isn't a 'food desert'—that implies a natural occurrence," Aanya adds. "This is an intentional effort, through zoning laws, lending practices, and other shit policies, to drive racial segregation."

"Aanya is one of a handful of trusted advisors from the East Side who are informing me on solutions to push in City Hall," my sister says. "Food is a priority in my office because of the ripple effect on families. We want to cultivate a food infrastructure that's rooted in and run by East Side residents."

Ms. Amber's grin stretches. "We created a position at the community center to educate kids about STEM and work with organizations like Aanya's on urban farming initiatives. It's part-time for now, while we secure more funding, but it comes with benefits. You'd have the creative freedom to mold the role how you see fit."

"We could use someone with your background. Think it over," Aanya says, her light blue suit catching in the light that reflects off the snow. "I'll work with Ms. Amber on a job description and salary. We have some funds in my organization to hire you as a consultant. It was great to finally meet you."

Ms. Amber squeezes me into another hug wrapped in White Diamonds perfume and a hint of school supplies. The tips of her curly pixie cut tickle my chin. "It would be wonderful to work with you. I know you have a lot of options. Please consider us."

The pair leaves into the tundra.

Marcela bumps my shoulder. "Look at you making connections. How was the job interview?"

"Not a good fit," I sigh. "Maybe I was supposed to swing by your office."

"Maybe you were."

I know absolutely nothing about food equity, but creating solutions to help families put food on their tables would be fulfilling.

"We get to work together!" Marcela squeezes me to her chest and proceeds to smother me with her cleavage while jumping up and down.

"Please keep your titties away from my mouth," I mumble and push her away. Mine are big, but hers are flotation devices. "I haven't agreed to anything, and I don't know how I feel about being responsible for kids."

Keeping the plants Antonio bought me alive is one thing. Kids are a different story. At least no heels or suits are required.

"We should celebrate."

"I haven't said yes!"

Marcela's smirk activates a smile. "You will."

Chapter 22

Antonio

Miriam is full of surprises. Like choosing violence for fun.

"Doe, I swear to—*Doe!*"

My fingers fly over the controller, but it's too late. Miriam's character not only decapitates me but manages to rip out my spine.

Shock with a hint of pride have me looking at her cackling figure sideways. She's curled on her side on my sofa in my damn sweats and jersey. Her shoeboxes for feet flail in the air as she hiccup-snorts, tears rolling across her cheeks.

I check the controller for signs that the game didn't freeze on me before shifting my attention back to the world's cutest serial killer. Miriam has no bodies buried in real life—at least, not that I know of—but she sent every character I played to a gory death.

We came back to my place after grabbing dinner at a nearby burger joint. When I asked her how she wanted to celebrate her new job opportunity, I was happy she chose something low-key.

It's her first time at Steel House, first time in my apartment of bare walls and honey-colored wood flooring. The space is smaller than my DC condo, but it fits a large sectional and an eighty-inch television in the living room, the current scene of the crime.

Training kicked my ass. Now, she is.

Miriam talked big about beating me in a game I've played since I was little. No one, not even Julian, can touch me in *Mortal Kombat*.

"You cheated."

Miriam holds up both hands, wearing a straight face that cracks under my glare. She's cold as hell.

"Let me see your phone."

"What?"

"Your phone." I motion for her to fork it over. When she does, I hold the screen in front of her face to unlock it and go to her contacts.

Her brow lifts. "What are you doing?"

"Getting to the bottom of this." I stick out my tongue and hit speakerphone. "Councilmember? I'd like to report a crime."

"Oh my gosh!" Miriam falls back on the couch and holds her chest in a fit of laughter.

"Antonio? I know good and damn well you aren't playing on my line at ten at night," Marcela spits.

I glance over at the clock on the oven. "It's nine forty-seven."

"Boy!"

I mush Miriam's head when she reaches for the phone and jog around the couch. "This is an important district matter." I dodge a smack to my chest.

"For the last time, I'm not your councilmember," Marcela grits out. "Where is my sister?"

"Right here, cheating."

"I didn't cheat!" Miriam cries.

"What kind of household raised her to be a liar and a cheater? I'm calling your mama next. Aye! Watch my nuts." I raise the phone over my head, out of Miriam's reach.

She uses the couch to climb up my shoulders. "I promise I didn't cheat!"

I swat her hand away. "How do you explain killing me for two hours straight, huh?"

The beatdown was a massacre if ever I saw one. I never stood a chance and had to keep pausing the game to make sure Dr. Engineer over here didn't rewire my system during my quick shower.

"Miri," Marcela sighs.

"*Dime*," she responds, strangling my traps with her thighs.

"*Mátalo y vayan a culear*."

Miriam gasps. "*Deja de joder. Solo somos amigos!*"

I don't catch anything but "friends" in the sibling exchange before I'm falling backwards to catch Miriam from breaking her neck. I grip her thighs, which are now smothering my face, and brace us for impact. She uses her bodyweight in a last-ditch effort to flip us onto the couch.

She snatches the phone and tells Marcela, "I'll call you tomorrow," before hanging up. "Are you okay?" Her chest is heaving, her thighs still around my face.

I tell myself that the sharp inhale of her center is for breathing, but that would make two liars in this house. I'm fighting the urge to replace my nose with my mouth.

My apartment door smacks into the wall. Quincy rolls inside with a Nerf gun, followed by Bread in full tactical gear. Don't ask me where he got it from.

Quincy lifts the visor on his helmet. "You good? We heard a thud."

Miriam squeaks when I bench-press her weight. I slide her off of me and adjust my sweats. "We're good." I picture my granny at her eighty-second birthday last year to deflate my erection.

"If you say so," Bread says. He motions to Quincy. "Let's roll out."

"Don't forget to pack—and close my door!" I shout.

"Yes, Papa Smurf," they say on their way out.

I look back at Miriam. My eyes are on her face and not her sharp breaths stretching my jersey across her chest. "You sure you're okay?"

"I'm fine." She pushes me away with a laugh. "Thanks for tonight."

I shrug. "I'll always turn up for you."

"I don't have the job yet."

"It's yours if you want it." I brush her knee and take a pull of my beer. "You could be the next Tony Stark to those kids."

Miriam's curls tip back with her laughter. "I do like him."

"Is that what got you into engineering?"

She sips the red wine I picked up for her after training. *Bill Nye the Science Guy* and *Mighty Morphin Power Rangers.*"

"*Power Rangers*?" Her teeth seep into her lip at a dimpled grin. "How does that make sense?"

"Someone had to build Alpha 5 and make morphers functional. I tried to mimic the wrist communication but couldn't get the wiring down. What?"

How do I put into words how incredible she is? Everything about her is magic. "You're one of a kind, Doe."

Her blush resurfaces. "Thank you."

"For real. Those kids would be lucky to have you. I was jumping off roofs when I was a kid."

Her breathy laugh mixes with a giggle. "Which explains why you needed a babysitter in middle school," she says.

"I'm glad it was you. I'm happy to know you."

"I'm happy to know you too."

I ignore the ache in my throat and reach for the controller. "Well, Inspector Gadget. Round two?"

Chapter 23

Miriam

I did it.

For the first time in my adult life, I made a decision on a whim. I didn't consult empirical data or well-researched plans months in advance. I gave myself permission to live in the moment and get out of the bubble of routine.

I'm flying to Vegas to spend the weekend with rugby players.

My departure was far from the *Living Single* finale, which was on TV last night. Khadijah was a woman of habit who never veered from her life running *Flavor*. I don't have a boyfriend who showed up at my door to inspire a last-minute trip out of the country. But I do have a friend who invited me to do more than deep-condition my hair and fold laundry this weekend. Academia was always my excuse for not doing the unexpected.

So I packed the proper toiletries, ran through the pre-travel checklist for my house, and hopped into an airport taxi. Khadijah might have been comfortable leaving her house with only a purse and the underwear she had on, but I need extra clothes in case my pants snag on a door handle.

Marcela video called me to make me prove I was on my way to Sin City with the Buffalo Steel. Our flight left at seven and will touch down before midnight. Six hours and thirty-eight minutes is the total flight time, and it only took takeoff for the thrill to wear off.

"Breathe, Doe. You'll crack the armrest if you squeeze it any tighter. Want me to sing to you again?" Antonio's tone is playful, but he eyes me closely for signs I'll jump out of the emergency exit.

"Negative." Witnessing him attempt Usher's falsetto in "Superstar" with a straight face and the pitch of a wild goat is a one-time experience.

Our friendship bracelets touch when he reaches for my hand to rub my protruding knuckles. It's a weighted blanket on my nerves and kindle for a foreign sensation stoking embers to reignite.

"I like your bracelets. Mine too," I say to the trio on Antonio's wrist. He's wearing the "Miriam BFF" one. Underneath is the "Buffalo Steel" bracelet the team made, and one that says "Be Happy" with different smiley faces.

"Good." He nods. "You still got a baseball grip. Nervous?"

"Nope."

He grins. "If you say so. Did you run through your pre-travel checklist?" His gaze sharpens, and his head tilts. He's not making fun of me.

I follow his profile from his maroon beanie down to his bearded jaw. The detour to his heavy lower lip zeroes in on the slow bob of his Adam's apple as he swallows.

Stop it.

"My checklist," I blurt, drawing his brows together. My hands smooth invisible creases in my leggings. Traveling across the country in jeans is not a testimony. "I went through my checklist."

"It's a good system. I use it for away games and vacations," he says, his focus swinging above my face. "I like this. Your hair twisted up."

Oh.

My fingertips trace my pink and orange headwrap. I twist my hair and tie a scarf before bed. Nothing groundbreaking or fashion-forward, but it has Antonio staring. He does this more now, compliments my appearance. I always assumed he was being friendly. Now, I'm not so sure.

"Thank you." I give him a curt nod and fight the urge to purr.

I don't know what's going on, but I'm hyperaware of him.

His scent.

The weight of his undivided attention.

The planes of muscle contouring his Henley.

The friction of his jeans as they rub against my leggings.

The change in altitude must be the culprit. That, or Antonio's knee digging into mine.

Since graduating, a floodgate has opened that's hard to close. Sexual thoughts sprout like hot flashes, to the point I had a telehealth appointment with my doctor to weed out perimenopause. My kitty vibrates at random times and could win a strongest-person competition dangling a car from between my legs.

Antonio excites my pulse every time I'm around him. Not *every* time, but enough. I guess it makes sense. He is the closest man in my life, and he's a walking vessel of hallelujah.

"Doe. Did you hear what I said?"

"Hmm?" My teeth sink into my lip. His eyes are on me when I chance a glance. Capturing his attention shouldn't intrigue me the way it does.

Stop.

We both blink away.

"I, uh, I said that I'm happy you came," he stutters and clears his throat. His eyes ping-pong from the front of the cabin to the flight attendant light.

"Me too. You didn't need to buy my ticket. First class is spacious but overpriced."

Not that I'm complaining about complimentary champagne and a food menu that goes beyond cookies, pretzels, and canned drinks. It's nice, but it wasn't necessary.

"I told you, it's part of your belated graduation gift and now a congrats about your future job. Did you reach out about the position?"

"I did." A smile sprouts at the grin spreading across his face. "I spent the last two days looking into the organization and its efforts to make healthier food more accessible on the East Side. I start next week."

Ms. Amber and Aanya possess a synergy that drew me in before their pitch. A power from multiple elements coming together to yield greater results than the sum of their individual capabilities.

That's shared purpose, and I want in.

I blow out a long breath. "I hope I know what I'm doing with the kids."

"You will," Antonio says with finality. "Now we celebrate." He leans against the seat and pats my hand. "And first class was necessary. I didn't want the guys overwhelming you. All the starters plus the seven reserves are coming. I'm already a handful. Multiply me by twenty-one, and you'd be looking for a parachute."

I push the boulder that is his bicep. "You're not that bad. Your team, either."

The guys are rowdy at times, with the random cheers and hollering, but it's been fun being around them. Kendrick is here. So is Bread, who hasn't stopped poking his head through the barrier that separates first class from the main cabin to ask for snacks.

One thing is super clear: The team listens to their captain. They respect him.

"You've settled down," I point out. Three years ago, Antonio would've flown to Vegas from the wing of the plane.

He scratches his chin. "I have, haven't I? I feel a responsibility to set a good example. That crazy shit doesn't excite me much, anyway. Been there, done that, you know?"

"I don't," I laugh, taking in the lone reading light that illuminates our cabin. I should've brought my book. "The wildest thing I've ever done is come on this trip. I still don't know where we're staying, which is grounds for a private meltdown under normal circumstances."

"I canceled my reservation and got a suite in a different hotel."

"Antonio. I didn't ask for that, and I don't need to be treated with kid gloves." I adjust my glasses so he can see how serious I am. I'm tired of people treating me like a child for lacking certain experiences. "I'm thirty-four, not two," I say, my tone clipped. "I won't break."

"I know." His voice is a soft stroke as he takes my hand. "I changed the reservation because a K-pop band is performing at the original hotel."

"Oh." I take in our joined hands. His swallows mine, but they fit.

"You never needed kid gloves, Doe. Your comfort will always be my priority. Got it?"

I nod. "Got it. Thank you again for this weekend. I appreciate it...and you."

His eyes drop to my lips, jolting my heart to pound against my chest. I'm lightheaded, a symptom of being thirty-five thousand feet in the air, not feelings I shouldn't have for my best friend.

Our stare is a series of seconds lost in time until a *psst* breaks us apart.

Antonio chuckles. "You're being summoned."

My snort morphs into a laugh when I see Bread. Only his head is visible through the black partition.

"Maid Miriam," he whispers. "What you got for me?"

"Here." I hand him a half-empty bottle of champagne.

He takes it with a smile and, if I'm not mistaken, tears in his eyes. "You're cool people." He bows before the partition closes.

"We got extra booze!" Bread announces to the players. "What do we say?"

"Thank you, Maid Miriam!" the main cabin shouts.

A flight attendant stomps by and gives me the stink eye. "Please refrain from sharing your items with the other cabin, or you'll lose your privileges."

The cheers do a record scratch when she asks for ID. They're all over twenty-one. I thought it was okay.

Oops.

"Troublemaker." Antonio smirks before dozing off.

Chapter 24

Antonio

My last set is a slow grunt of force through exhaustion. Fuck, I'm tired. But if I didn't squeeze in a workout now, it wasn't happening. I rerack the ninety-pound weight, grab my gear, and travel through the maze of halls to the elevator.

I've been up since five, not because I enjoy waking up at the ass crack of dawn. The hotel I moved me and Miriam to fumbled my reservation, which meant finding new accommodations for Bread, Kendrick, Quincy, and three other players right after we landed. Shins is flying out today, and he'll be in a room with his girl until he gets a permission slip to come out.

The spot we're in had a suite available and another one with bunk beds in a large room. The guys and I slept two to a bed during our first year thanks to the league's limited budget. They'll survive a few days sharing one bathroom, and they can fuck in a dark alley for all I care, provided they don't get arrested.

That left one problem to solve. The reason I've been up for hours, unable to sleep.

Sharing a suite with Miriam didn't sound like a big deal at the time. Having rooms across from each other would cut down on the time it would take me to get to her. Separate spaces also guaranteed we wouldn't cross any boundaries.

The problem is, we're not in the two-bedroom suite I reserved at the previous hotel. We're in a suite with a panoramic view of the city and one bed.

Technically, there's a sofa in the living room, which became my space after I evicted her. She's so damn stubborn. Once she sets her mind on something—ignoring my pleas to take the bed, in this case—she'll stop at nothing to get it.

I didn't expect to go toe-to-toe with her, or chest-to-chin, given our height difference. I'm not arguing with anybody at one a.m., and definitely not after a six-and-a-half-hour flight to the other side of the country.

I rolled her suitcase into the bedroom.

She rolled it right back to the sofa.

I stood at my full height.

She stood on a chair.

The only reason we got what little sleep we did is because I waited for her to fall asleep before carrying her to the bed. Where she belonged.

I tucked the sheets into the mattress extra tight to keep her from getting up in the middle of the night. Then I spent an hour jacking my dick to the city skyline. Apparently, I don't know how to fucking act in the same space as the woman who's had me in a vise grip since I was a preteen.

I've been in bed with plenty of women. Hundreds, if I had to guess, and in multiple-player situations. The most I worried about was forgetting where I was during the few nights I partied too hard, or someone trying to steal my wallet. My heart never left my chest the way it does when I'm around Doe. It's already hard to breathe around her at times, trying not to sound like an idiot or let my attraction to her beat my ass like it has for almost two decades.

I'd be lying if I said the bond we've developed doesn't scare the shit out of me. I never let myself get this close to a woman, never worried about any emotional attachments. Miriam is different, and that makes our temporary living arrangement—with one fucking bed, no less—a challenge.

She doesn't see me as anything more than a friend, and I didn't invite her out here to run game. I want her to have a good time and feel comfortable being herself. If that means cold showers and tugging on my dick like it's a Nintendo joystick in order to keep it together, so be it.

I meant what I told her last night. Her comfort is my priority. Her happiness too.

The door to the suite opens when I wave my wallet over the sensor. I step inside and inhale the air, which is now saturated in the fragrance of coffee, eggs, and ham.

The growl I release while taking off my shoes is from my stomach touching my back. Another growl comes when I turn the corner to find Miriam seated at the dining room table.

Two parts of my body are starving for different reasons.

Her hair is still twisted up into a tiny bun that pokes out of the silk scarf wrapped around her head. Her foot is propped on a chair, summoning my attention to the thick, oiled thigh on full display.

The bottom half of her pajama set inches up to the source of her nectar, which I wouldn't mind with a stack of pancakes.

"There you are," she says around a mouthful of eggs. "I looked up what professional rugby players eat for breakfast." She aims her fork at the spread on the table that I missed. I was too busy imagining what else I'd like to spread. "Is this okay?"

I flick a glance at the overnight oats next to plain yogurt and bowls of fresh fruit and granola. There's avocado toast topped with eggs and bacon, and scrambled eggs and spinach.

"Aww, honey. You shouldn't have," I say, dropping my stuff to join her.

"Shut up and come here." She moves her foot for me to take the chair. "How was your workout?"

I reach for the avocado toast. "Good."

"I can tell." Miriam gestures to my gray shirt soaked in sweat. Black basketball shorts cling to my legs. I need a shower.

"Anytime you want me to work you out…" I waggle my brows at her and flex my bicep at the sting of her slap. "Sleep okay?"

She huffs. "After I extricated myself from the straitjacket you created with the bedsheets? I slept good. No waking up remembering that my savings isn't limitless and the job I'm taking is part-time."

"You know I got you." I motion for her to hand me her empty coffee cup, which I refill.

"I got *myself*, Papa Smurf." A smile spreads over her lips, and I return it at her use of my team nickname. "You've already done enough. With my housewarming presents and all of this." She waves a hand in the air. "Ms. Amber said she's looking for additional funding. Hopefully it will go full-time soon, but I'll figure it out. For now, I want to enjoy my weekend. It's my first time in Sin City."

The suite at the twenty-one-and-over hotel we're in is nice. There's a full bar, floor-to-wall windows, and a dining space big enough for us to take down the feast she ordered. The navy and cream color combo is a welcome change from the suites across Las Vegas that are drowning in beige and marble. Some people might enjoy living like they shit gold foil, but I'll pass.

Miriam butters a piece of wheat toast. "At least let me cover our food and drinks. You can't be that stubborn," she says at my headshake.

I stab a piece of strawberry and cut my eyes at her. "Who waited for who to fall asleep before moving them to the bed?"

She scoffs. "You should've left me on the sofa. This is your suite."

"*Our* suite," I correct. "It will be a cold day in Hell before I put you on a sofa when there's a bed in the room." My father would slap me from DC and ask who raised me.

"Do you ever let people take care of you the way you take care of them?"

My fork hovers inches from my lips. When was the last time I let someone do something for me? Other than give me head, I've got nothing.

"I've always been this way," I admit, unable to meet Miriam's eyes. "Done things to be useful."

As an only child, it was easier to make friends if I was more outgoing, more giving. Kids flocked to my house to play the latest video games or attend one of the infamous house parties I hosted whenever my parents were out of town. After a while, the expectations stuck, and I fell into them because I like being liked.

Miriam's hand on top of mine pulls me back to reality. Hairs prickle when her thumb rubs circles into my skin.

"Want to know something?"

"You'll tell me anyway. What's up?"

She leans forward, granting me the brilliance of her deep brown eyes and intoxicating smile. "You don't need to prove your worth for someone to like you. You're a good man, Knight."

"That might be the nicest thing anyone has ever said." She thinks I'm joking, but I'm not. Outside of Julian treating me like a brother, and the rugby team who appreciates my Papa Smurf tendencies, no one has shown much interest in me beyond what I can do for them.

Miriam reminding me that my worth isn't attached to my acts of service means more than she knows.

"How about this," she says. "You let me express my gratitude the way I want, and I'll work on coming out of my shell."

"Don't change for anybody, Doe. I'll be part of whatever adventure you want, but you're perfect the way you are."

A blush creeps up her cheeks. "Okay. I still want to try new things." She stretches out her hand. "Do we have a deal?"

"Deal."

Our conversation wanes into silent chews and reloading our plates. Spending time with Miriam has quickly become my favorite pastime. Aside from enjoying everything about her, she's making it easier to open up—even when I don't want to burden people with my shit.

"The league is struggling this year," I say, my voice drifting above a whisper. "A few teams are folding, and Coach Washington told me there's talks that the owner wants to offload us."

"Antonio."

I rub the space above my brow and sigh. "Forget I said anything. I don't want to ruin breakfast."

"Hey. We tell each other when something is wrong, remember? You don't need to keep anything in. I'm here to listen if you need me."

I'll always need you.

"I'm the only one on the team who knows. Nothing is set in stone, so there's a good chance nothing will happen." My gaze sweeps across her face. "It feels good to get it out. You're the first person I've told."

Miriam's dimples frame a smile that brightens the room. "Well, consider me honored. I'll always be here for you if you let me. I am your emergency contact, after all." I crack up at her wink. "Is there anything you can do for now?"

"I don't think so. The Steel is getting good press. That will likely mean more interviews and a busier media schedule. All good stuff for the team." I pat her leg. "I don't want what I said to mess up our weekend. In Vegas, we turn up."

She raises her coffee mug. "Here for it. How do you quantify turning up?"

Chapter 25

Miriam

"**A**bsolutely not!"

"We had a deal!"

"That didn't include cutoffs!" I stretch my fingertips at my sides. There is no hem. Only frayed edges of jean shorts that are three inches from showing a coochie lip.

I don't know what Antonio was thinking buying this outfit. Half of it is still at the store.

"Doe," my sleazy stylist begs from the other side of the door I pushed him out of before squeezing myself into these scraps. "*Please*. I have your hard hat."

"A hard hat?" I snicker.

"You wanted to try something new, right? We do this every year. I promise we're dressed alike."

I doubt it.

Try something new was today's motto. Antonio kept his word by tagging along to the haunted museum, where we promptly made a U-turn for the front door. He stuck it out at the Pinball Hall of Fame before I agreed to an open-air leap eight hundred-plus feet in the air.

Yes, there was a cable attached.

Yes, I still peed a little.

We made good on our vow not to let the uncertainty of the Steel's future thwart our weekend. The man is living his best and fearless life, whether on the 108th floor of a building or in the living room getting ready for a night on the Vegas Strip. The only "strip" I'm interested in is peeling off this ridiculous outfit and showing the shower jets every angle of my body. This suite is a beautiful mix of modern amenities in a soothing color palette of blues, gold, and cream.

I have no business being outside dressed like I'm responsible for street repair.

Antonio taps on the door. "If you really want to stay in, I'll leave. I'm not taking any photos tonight. Promise."

My toes sink into plush navy carpeting on my way to the full-length mirror. The shorts are short, but they're not awful. The high waist keeps me tucked in, but my thighs threaten to swallow what little material stretches across my legs. At least the sleeveless white body suit covers my breasts, though I'm showing more cleavage tonight than I have in years.

"Yes to new experiences," I tell my reflection through a shaky breath. How many people can say they flew to Vegas on a whim with a professional rugby team?

Fine.

I toss on the orange work vest that came with the outfit and open the bedroom door. It takes a miracle to defy the laws of gravity and keep my tongue from rolling out of my mouth.

Antonio is in a pair of jean shorts that match mine. Large, carved thighs protrude from the tiny material, flexing cords of muscles that reach all the way down to those Teenage Mutant Ninja Turtles calves. His chest is bare underneath a construction vest, immaculately sculpted and teasing dark nipples. Do they match—

Don't think about his nipples!

I open my mouth, but the heat in his gaze melts the words. He hasn't said anything either, just stares with an unreadable expression.

This would be the point in a horror movie when a jump scare occurs. For the record, I don't like to jump or be scared.

"Should I change?" I ask, second-guessing if a night out is worth it.

He blinks. "No—no. You, uh, you look..." His eyes stall on my hips. "Damn—I mean. You look nice."

Nice is good.

"You don't think it shows too much?" I spin around to show the back. The vest covers the top half of my butt. One wrong dip or bend, and the good people of Las Vegas are seeing my peach.

"Antonio?"

He's in the kitchen with a glass of water to his lips. Is his hand shaking?

I frown. "Are you sick?"

The glass slams to the counter. He wipes his mouth with the back of his hand. "Nope. Just hot."

"It is a little warm in here," I say on the way to the thermostat. "I'll set it a few degrees lower so it'll be cool once we return."

"Great," he mumbles, brushing down his vest over a washboard stomach. Sweet goodness.

Eyes up.

"The helmet looks good." I point to the hard yellow plastic resting over his brow. "Functional."

"Ready?"

"Yes," I nearly pant, suddenly too hot myself. I grab my shoes near the door.

Don't ask why, but I packed open-toe stilettos. They're black with a four-inch heel and thick elastic bands around the soles. I hate when my baby toes dangle from thin straps like they're bungee jumping. Not that I wear heels often. I'm a fan of flats, but I figured why not?

I've never worn this pair, and we are in Vegas.

At my new height, I'm closer to Antonio's eyeline. So close I can see the beads of sweat forming under his hat in high definition.

I press the back of my hand to his cheek. "Are you getting a fever?"

He sniffs and shakes his head. "No. Come on."

I'm guided out of the hotel room by hand. The fanny packs he got us will keep our wallets, phones, and hotel key cards safe for the night—but not my feet. I trip on the lip of the elevator.

"Are you sure you're good in those?" Antonio directs the question to my shoes.

My nod rattles my hard hat. "Should be. Trying something new, remember?"

The elevator is a glass structure that faces out to the hotel casino. Gamblers come into focus as we descend from the tenth floor. The cold whisper of air conditioning is a reminder of the skin I'm showing.

"Are you sure everyone else is dressing up?" I swallow, determined not to run back upstairs. Well, walk. I don't doubt I'll trip over my own shadow.

Antonio squeezes my shoulder. "I promise, Doe." He turns me to face the glass. "Our night is just beginning."

Every Steel player is shirtless in construction vests, hoochie shorts, and Timbs. A few wave from the cluster of yellow hard hats as our elevator comes into view.

They yell in unison at Antonio, who presses one hand to the glass and body rolls. The muscles in his abs contract as he thrusts his hips toward the ceiling.

"What are you doing?" I cackle.

His head tips back to flash a grin. "Getting the party started."

I am no better than a man.

With the amount of legs, wings, and thighs on display, it's a miracle I haven't run into a wall or tried to order a to-go box. I did trip into the private bathroom, but that's unrelated.

Hundreds of bodies grind to the Ying Yang Twins' "Shake" under the glow of LED lights. Rugby teams from across the country have invaded the nightclub, wearing every costume imaginable. There are elves, scuba divers, cheerleaders, and vampires. Flooding the Spirit

Halloween fashion show are the hard hats that took over the dance floor three songs ago.

It's pointless to count the number of times my eyes gravitated to Antonio. Even in a crowd of contoured back muscles and a buffet of booties, I still find him. When he's not laughing, he's pulling out every '90s dance from the vault. The man knows how to move his hips, and how to annoy me every six minutes.

I'm not upset, but I did banish him from the VIP suite he insisted on renting. Yes, it's as extravagant as it sounds.

The skybox isn't too far up from the main floor, but I'm the only one using it. Antonio, too, before I told him to go hang out with his team. I was perfectly fine blending into the back wall for the rest of the night without special accommodations. My discomfort and mild panic couldn't get cozy before I got a pat on my hard hat and a "No."

Who needs bottles of wine and a snack board all to themselves? Scratch that. I appreciate a good rosé and some sea salt pretzels. I had a glass in his honor. Three, to be exact, and counting. I feel nice, cocooned from the chaos of the big crowd and able to enjoy myself with snacks and wine.

The music changes to Faith Evans's "Love Like This." Fists holding twenty-dollar bills reach for the ceiling as confetti explodes into the humid cloud of sweat and pheromones. From my perch on the balcony, I have a full view of the bumping and grinding below. I've dipped it low from up here with a drink in the air.

Bread jogs out of the private bathroom, waving his hard hat. "Don't go in there for thirty minutes. Forty to play it safe."

Ew.

I slap his hand as it reaches for a Twizzler on my plate. "No, sir. Did you wash your hands?"

His brows dent. "What kind of question is that, Maid Miriam? I did. Twice." He snatches a piece of licorice and grabs a water bottle. "Having fun up here?"

"I am," I say with a shimmy to the music. "No drunk people stumbling into me. More air to breathe. I like it, but I also appreciate the company—when you're not blowing up the bathroom or raiding the snacks. Are you staying?"

"Nah. I'm not getting in trouble. Everyone knows you're Cap's girl."

The alcohol must be messing with my cognitive function, because I swear he said I'm Antonio's girl.

"Did you get concussed in the bathroom?" I ask. "Antonio and I are not together in any way, shape, or form."

One edge of Bread's mouth curls. "Okay."

"I'm serious."

"You got it." He bops his head to the music and nods at his teammates.

My hands find a home on my hips. The pose is one my mother always struck before the *chancleta* came out.

"You think I'm lying, M'Baku?"

"Yooo," he snickers like he's never called somebody a bald-headed demon. "You both are. He doesn't realize his own feelings."

He definitely got smacked in the head.

I refill my wineglass and search for Antonio. He's at the bar, talking to a beautiful woman in a Jessica Rabbit getup, long-flowing red wig and all. Her whisper in his ear activates a slow smile.

"See." I point to the pending sexual encounter.

Bread smirks. "That's nothing."

"Looks like something to me."

He leans on the railing so I'm not talking to his neck. "Nah. She's interested, but he's not matching her energy. Bro's eyes haven't left her face. The old Antonio would've led her out the club and resurfaced tomorrow afternoon."

"Likely story," I mumble.

Sure, he's been attentive to my needs. He's good to his friends, and I'm no exception.

It's only a matter of time before he finds his way into someone's bed for the night. It better not be the sofa, because I need at least seven hours of sleep to function. I also don't want to hear him putting Jessica Rabbit or any other woman through the frame. I'm so worked up, I might hump a pillow if it bends right.

Bread snickers. "Go ahead and process that, Ms. PhD."

"I'm not—this is my shit!" Bread catches my glass when I toss my hands in the air at the DJ playing a throwback I kept on repeat in the lab.

"Fuck it up then!" He urges me on as I belt out the lyrics to "Get Money." Something behind my back catches his attention. "That's my cue."

Bread nods to Antonio and takes the steps two at a time to rejoin the Steel, who are standing in front of the balcony.

I don't dance in public.

Ever.

I stay far away from anything that resembles attention and don't give people a reason to look at me. Crowds make me nervous, and I would rather throw up before I let my Mary Dance see the light of day.

I never felt comfortable doing what's common to everyone else. Yet here I am, twisting my heels on the floor like I won't break an ankle.

Whistles and hollers come from the group of hard hats cheering me on. The Steel shouts, "Go, Mimi!" to replace "Get money" in the song's chorus. Bread and Quincy lead a two-step to match my own. The smile I aim at Antonio grows at the grin playing against his lips. He's posted up on the wall, watching me.

I found the courage to try something new tonight because of the space he gave me so I wouldn't feel overwhelmed. An entire VIP suite with wine and snacks is excessive, but it's thoughtful nonetheless.

Antonio is a good friend. My best friend.

I spin, allowing my hips to move on their own. One song becomes another and another.

By two a.m., I'm done.

I sweat my curls out, am seconds from crashing on this couch, and I've lost feeling in my feet, which are still shackled to these shoes. My buzz wore off, along with some of my deodorant. But it was a good night.

"Come on, Doe. Let's go back." Antonio rubs my knee.

"How do you still smell good?" I grumble.

"You smell good too." He leans in to take a whiff and coughs. "On second thought."

I pop an eye open and slap his vest. "Turd."

He laughs and pulls me to my feet. "It got you up, didn't it? You good in those?"

I shrug. "Might fall. But if it gets me down the steps and into my bed faster, I won't complain."

Antonio's hand runs over his beard. "Take them off."

"Excuse me?"

"Your heels. It's faster to walk back to the hotel. We'll switch shoes."

"You're joking," I huff, ready to use our construction vests as a blanket and sleep right here.

He's already out of his Timbs and waiting for me in basketball socks. "Need help with yours?"

Guess we're doing this.

He squats in front of me and smacks my hand away when I sit back to unzip my heels. His touch is soft as he guides the zipper down and removes each one. I groan at the hard press of his palm to my foot.

"Don't tell me you give good foot rubs." I moan at the pressure to my arch as he kneads away years' worth of knots.

His laugh is a low rumble. "I can be good with my hands."

I clench my thighs and ignore the voice that's daring me to ask him what else those hands can do. I'm so caught up in sleep and sex deprivation that I miss him slipping his boots onto my feet. My feet are swimming in his Timbs, but they're no match for his situation.

Thick tears gather through soundless laughter that activates a snort. By some miracle, Antonio managed to squeeze his feet into my stilettos. His toes stretch over the lip, and his socks are poking through the elastic.

A rugby player in hoochie shorts and heels is a look he pulls off with his toned calves and sculpted hamstrings.

He tosses my purse over his arm and extends a hand. "Come on."

"You might want to hold on to the railing," I giggle.

He scoffs. "I could run fifty yards in these." To prove it, he does some type of football fake-out—or rugby fake-out, I guess. I still struggle to follow the game.

Whoever said pride comes before the fall did not lie. Antonio takes one step down the staircase and slides the rest of the way down on his knees. Everything happens in slow motion to Celine Dion's "My Heart Will Go On," which is in my head courtesy of the alcohol in my system.

The good news is the private staircase is away from the dance floor. The bad news is the whole team is at the bottom of the steps he slid down. They're all laughing.

He rights himself, flicks hair he doesn't have over his shoulders, and sashays away with his chin high.

Tonight is a night I'll never forget.

"Doe!"

"Coming!"

Chapter 26

Miriam

When Antonio suggested swimming, I imagined an indoor pool with those lounge chairs and annoying straps that swallow your foot when you get up.

Maybe some Venetian marble.

Definitely the stench of chlorine.

Indoor being the key word.

At no point did outside come into the equation. Who in their right mind wants to bounce around half naked in February? Though sixty degrees does feel like Panama after fleeing Buffalo's mere twelve. Anything warmer than frostbite would, but I still wasn't convinced to parade around in a swimsuit like I was on *Baywatch*.

Yet here I am. Still waking up after our night out, with a one-piece and a robe under my puffer coat.

I'm a complete fool waddling up to the biggest swimming complex in America. I don't know if it really is the biggest, but there are eight heated pools, and they lured every rugby player on the Steel who received an invite to the pool party we're hosting. *We* aren't hosting a thing, but the digital invitation floating around says otherwise.

It took pouting and whining on Antonio's part for me to leave our suite. I caved, because new experiences and all of that.

The bass from Wreckx-n-Effect's "Rump Shaker" spills across open pools that face a drive-in-theater-size screen. Daybeds and poolside couches hold forgotten towels and flip-flops as players throw it back and gyrate like it's *MTV Spring Break*. Their ringleader joins a circle of Bobby Brown thrusts. He pumps his hips before hitting the worm to wild cheers.

Antonio is in his element. An Energizer Bunny with no off switch, bouncing from guest to guest with the same enthusiasm. He rented a suite big enough for his teammates. It has a lounge area encased in glass walls that open up to a private pool. The indoor cabana is a heated escape with a bar, bathroom, and extra seating.

To my credit, I haven't hidden in there once this afternoon. The views are immaculate, and I don't mean the surrounding Vegas backdrop of commercialism and the occasional palm tree.

Muscles are on display. A fine assortment of hard, sturdy legs and veiny arms. Swimming trunks never made me wet until rugby thighs became part of the equation.

I got caught staring at the chest Antonio's teasing underneath an unbuttoned tropical shirt. How could I not? It's smooth, with a solid wall of thick muscles to match the tree trunks he calls legs. On his swimming trunks are tiny cacti-shaped penises.

A lifeguard in a high-waisted swimsuit blows the whistle at Bread's attempt to cannonball into the pool. It's four feet deep and his second warning. Judging by his smirk, it won't be his last.

He adjusts his banana trunks as he makes his way over to her. She giggles when he whispers something in her ear, the whistle once dangling from her lips now between her teeth.

In case I didn't mention it, today's forecast is clear skies with biceps and quads.

"This next song goes out to the other cohost of the party," the DJ says over a record scratch.

No.

Between the Steel and the other hotel guests on the lower levels, there's enough people here to activate my emergency sprint. I was fine imitating a potted plant, going unnoticed aside from the occasional hug and hello from Antonio's teammates. Every eye wasn't on me then like they are now.

"Maid Miriam, I believe he called you," Quincy says with a grin. "Your coat."

Fine with me. I came prepared.

I shrug out of my winter shell to his laughter. My hands tighten around the belt on my robe. I slip my glasses on and slowly back away.

"Where you going?" Bread and his inflated muscles appear before me. "She's ducking you, Cap!"

"Quiet!" I hiss. "I thought we were friends."

Winston Fluke smiles. "We are, but I've known him longer."

"Traitor," I mumble.

"I'll be that," he says before yelling to Antonio, who's at the DJ booth.

A chant incites around the pools and sweeps over the entire stadium.

"Mir-i-am!"

"Mir-i-am!"

Antonio grabs the mic. "Come up out that robe and dance with me. Don't do me like that!"

"I'll do you, alright," I say before I catch myself.

Doing Antonio would be very bad, and probably sticky. I'm sure it would feel amazing, those hands roaming my body while his thighs smack against my skin.

Very good, but very bad.

At least twenty Kardashian replicas are here. It's the same blueprint: bundles of long hair, breast implants, and BBLs. I shouldn't be the center of attention, but I haven't left Antonio's sight since we arrived.

The corner of his mouth tilts as he pins me with a look that disturbs my breathing. "Ah, she wants a chase."

"Don't you dare!" I shout to his grin.

Fight or flight is an interesting phenomenon. One minute, you're contemplating where to hide a body in the desert. The next, you're on your feet running from a rugby player whose leg spans half your body.

The Steel make a path for me to run to the other side of the pool deck. The lifeguard blows her whistle, and I yelp when Antonio scales the steps like he runs track on the side.

His eyes are predatory. He anticipates every step I take until he flies over a row of seats and scoops me into his arms.

Bread, Quincy, and the rest of the Steel cheer like they just won the Rugby World Cup. My head tips back in a laugh that gets caught in my throat when Antonio lowers me to my feet.

The fire in his stare melts the chill creeping up my back. My anxiety from him calling me over fades at his gaze, which starts at my loose curls, wanders down my lips, and stalls at my cleavage pressing against the soft cotton of my robe.

"May I?" His voice is low, desperate for consent I give with a nod. He swallows hard and unknots my robe, gently pulling back the material to see what's beneath.

I'm shy, but I love my body. My five-four stature of wide hips and thighs that rub together is a departure from the sea of size-two women who are model height and wearing bikinis. You'd find a needle in a haystack faster than the string in my crack if I wore one of those bathing suits.

My one-piece has a tie in the front and a keyhole above my navel. The built-in bra keeps my double Ds from touching my knees. The spandex alone is worth the money I paid. Praise be for tummy control and no material bunching in my booty.

The first notes of UCB's "Sexy Lady" play in the background. My hips wind on their own to the DC classic that fed cookouts, clubs, and college campuses. I didn't get out much, but I still got down to this song.

I'm so caught up in the throwback track and the functionality of my swimsuit that it doesn't register—Antonio isn't dancing.

"What is it?" His eyes are still on my body. The mustard stain I tried to wrestle out of my bathing suit doesn't incite anger.

My eyes drift down to the place that has him twisting his mouth. Hamburger fiasco aside, my body is not up for debate or judgment. My stomach has a pudge, and my legs could start a fire rubbing together, and to that I say, so what? I feel good in this suit, and I won't let him or anyone else make me feel differently.

Now I'm pissed.

"You don't have to stare like that." I try to close my robe, but he's still holding the lapels. "Unhand me. I might not be your type, but you—"

Every word dies against his mouth.

Antonio's arm wraps around my waist. His fingers trace the small of my back and down the line of my swimsuit before he squeezes my butt.

My gasp meets his moan and the tongue passing over my lips. I've been kissed before, but not like this. Not since the New Year's Eve we don't speak of for fear of reanimating dormant feelings.

With shaky knees, a tear attempts to slide from between my thighs.

Jinkies.

Chapter 27

Antonio

I broke our friendship code. Balled it up, did a crossover dribble, and shot a three over whatever line Miriam and I told ourselves not to cross.

The line is more figurative than literal, but I'm pretty sure tasting her mouth isn't allowed.

There's no excuse. Everything went blank when disappointment weighed in her smile. How the hell does she think she's not my type when she's the fucking blueprint of my desires? My toes are scraping my flip-flops right now, trying to keep me from levitating off the ground.

Every dip and curve of Miriam's body excites me to the point of shame. She's right that the women I mess with don't look like her. Why would I want a copy when the original is right here?

The moment our lips touched, I saw a future with her. A house, and higher insurance deductibles. If today is my last day on Earth, I'll happily go to the upper room with a two-step and a smile.

I kissed her. I'm *still* kissing her, and I don't have the brain cells or the common sense to tell me how bad of an idea this is. I'm pretty sure you need blood to think, and every ounce in my body is headed south.

Words were a safer option, but I went with what felt right. Apparently, that involves my tongue massaging her trachea.

I swallow another moan, unsure if it's hers or mine. I inhale rose oil mixed with sunscreen when I kiss Miriam's neck. Her gasp pulls my lips back to hers while my hands toy with her hips under a layer of spandex.

I've never wanted to be a swimsuit so bad.

I'm high on her.

The lips wilting against mine.

The thighs teasing me in that one-piece.

At this point, detaching myself from her will take an act of God.

Or a bucket of ice.

"Shi—"

"Ahh!"

Ice cubes mixed with freezing water spill over my neck and down my shirt. I move Miriam out of the way to keep her dry as I squeal at the razors shooting down my back. There's ice in my ass.

"Yo!" A few pieces fall through my trunks.

"My bad, Cap! I was aiming for Bread!" Quincy yells, sprinting away with an ice bucket in hand. He knotted a towel around his neck to match his superhero trunks, and he'll need special powers to outrun Bread.

"You okay?" I cup Miriam's face. She blinks slowly but nods.

The party resettles to hits from the '90s and '00s. Drinks are in the air, bodies swaying through a cool breeze. No one is paying attention to us tonguing each other down. They either don't care or have seen me with enough women to know no one sticks.

Would you be willing to stick for her?

Everything is back to normal. Everything except us.

The water droplets scattered across her glasses catch in the sunlight. She wets her lips, drawing my mouth in to follow the path of her tongue.

The DJ's record scratch is another ice bucket.

"Whoa."

"I'm sorry!" I lift my hands and step back. "I got caught in the moment."

"Young's modulus—"

"It was an accident, Doe. I swear."

"—quotient between longitudinal stress and material strain."

I rub the back of my neck. "I'm fucking this up."

Miriam frowns. "I should go."

Shit, I'm scaring her off.

She disappears between bodies on the makeshift dance floor. I ball my hands into fists to stop myself from doing something else stupid, like chasing after her to kiss her again.

What the hell did I do?

I didn't mean to. At least, I don't think I did. She looked amazing, the opportunity was there, and I...this is bad.

It's been a minute since I kissed anyone. Come to think of it, I haven't kissed or slept with anyone since I ran into her at the MLK celebration. Maybe that's why I pounced, but that can't be true. I've been around half-naked women since we came to the pool and didn't brick like I did when I untied Miriam's robe.

The urge to satisfy my need for release with a random willing participant isn't there anymore. It's her.

"Someone's in love."

"Shut up." I have zero interest in Kendrick's poolside commentary.

His small braids are in a ponytail, his feet kicked up with a towel covering his blue swim trunks. He eyes me over the rim of his sunglasses and flips the newspaper in his hand. "Had your leg in the air and your toe pointed."

I collapse onto the lounger next to him and cover my face. "I'm fucked."

"The first step is admitting it, Papa Smurf."

Chapter 28

Miriam

"Come on," I pant in a mix of sweat and frustration.

Getting myself off has never been a problem. I'm well-acquainted with my body and the erogenous zones that will activate an orgasm. You wouldn't know it based on the hours I've spent trying to pleasure myself with the sex toys I bought. There's enough here to host a convention. Still no happy ending.

I didn't want to be outside dressed like Lil Kim in the middle of winter, but Antonio's kiss sent me out the hotel and onto Fremont Street like I was a track star in a past life.

My brain scrambled. I couldn't think straight, which is how I ended up searching for sex toys after venturing to the Strip.

Turns out my pre-travel checklist wasn't thorough. Every vibrator I own is at home, tucked away in the bottom drawer of my nightstand. TSA will likely flag my bag for the inventory I'm bringing home. How do I explain, in one of those tiny rooms with no windows, that I'm desperate to get off, but not from the only man who's touched me in *five* years?

I was determined to eradicate Antonio and his soft lips from my memory. I mustered up the courage to ask the woman behind the counter, who was assembling a literal bag of dicks, to point me to the good stuff. That statement got a quick revision when she directed me to the biggest silicone penis I've ever seen. The thing could plug a pothole and was going nowhere near my vagina.

I left with the anonymity of my hooded winter jacket and two discreet bags. A fairy wand, glass "juicer," tongue teaser, bullet, rabbit, textured finger stimulator, and clitoral suction device are spread over my rumpled comforter.

Seven toys.

Two hours and fourteen minutes of putting them to use.

Nothing.

I'm a problem-solver by nature. I defined the issue: me not getting laid. I identified the outcome: euphoria from orgasms. I brainstormed potential solutions: my hands and toys. I conducted experiments and evaluated the results:

A testament to good battery life but no resolution for my neglected private parts.

The only malfunction to report is me. My equipment works just fine. I'm the one who can't get into the right headspace.

Every time I close my eyes, I see Antonio.

His eyes boring into mine.

His teeth digging into his thick bottom lip.

The hands that gripped my waist.

No. The conclusions of *that* experiment will remain a mystery.

Would a one-night stand even work among friends?

What happens in Vegas—

"Leads to blurred lines, possible bruises, and offering our relationship to the altar of bad decisions."

Great, now I'm talking to myself.

I gather the toys to wash in the kitchen sink in a huff. Antonio hasn't returned since I came back from my pleasure expedition, which is ironic considering I didn't *come* at all.

He's probably on round three with a leggy influencer or a women's rugby player who knows how to scrum, or whatever it is they do. He's been thoughtful of me since we arrived, but I know him. A chronic bachelor in Sin City leads to one thing: all-you-can-eat pus—vagina, and sex on repeat.

I rip open the bedroom door and stomp down the hall in knee-length socks. I'm happy my friend is deep-sea fishing with his penis between someone's legs. His touch still haunts me, and I can't pleasure myself without seeing his face, but good for him. Doesn't bother me one bit!

Maybe if I tried—

Dear God, I'm being robbed!

The toys go flying, and my mumbles turn into a scream at the figure in the kitchen. It's completely dark, minus the lights from Vegas crawling over the living room. The sconces above the counter illuminate.

Antonio pulls out an earphone. "You okay?"

"You scared me," I say between breaths, gripping my chest. "I thought you broke in."

"To raid the fridge?" He chuckles. "Got washed up and wanted a snack."

"How?" The only bathroom in the suite is in the bedroom.

He lifts a shoulder and scratches his bare chest. "It's past eleven. The lights were off, so I figured you were sleeping. Didn't want to disturb you, so I washed up here."

Sure enough, there's a washcloth on top of a towel on the granite counter next to the sink I came to use.

My sex toys are still on the ground.

"Did you, um, hear anything?" I fold my arms over my chest. My ratty black nightgown is see-through from years of use.

Antonio follows the movement, and his gaze stalls at the swell of my breasts. A muscle in his jaw ticks. "I had these in." He pulls out the other earphone. "What were you doing?"

"Nothing," I blurt. "If you want to wash up with more than dish soap, feel free to use the bathroom. After your snack. With the food in the refrigerator behind you."

"What fell?"

"Why are you asking so many questions?"

"Why are you dodging them?"

"I'm not."

His eyes narrow. Light drips over his very defined deltoids as he leans over the counter. His lips quirk. "Want to know something fun about being your friend? Picking up on shifts in your behavior. You talk a mile a minute in detail when you're nervous, and your voice sounds like Regina Hall's when you're excited."

Where is he going with this, and why is he moving?

The toys aren't visible from where he is, but they will be if he comes around the counter.

"You don't lie often." He continues his impersonation of a nosy forensic investigator. I'm all for solving crimes, but he needs to mind his business. "On the rare occasion you do, you clench your throat and give vague responses. Like you are now."

"Not true."

He inches toward the end of the counter. "I see your sweat from here."

Our stare-off ends when I make the mistake of glancing down. He rounds the corner before I get the chance to kick away the sex toys.

I toss my hands up. "Fine. You caught me, though it's perfectly normal to enjoy self-pleasure. It's safe, and I don't have to worry about anyone annoying me or giving me the clap. I love touching myself, but I can't get off." For reasons I won't reveal.

"I tried for hours. I'm wound up so tight I could snap. I haven't had sex in years, and I would like to sleep without contemplating rubbing myself over a pillow to feel a tingle because the sex toys I had no business buying with a pending part-time job aren't helping. They're scattered all over the floor because I thought we were being robbed, and I tossed them. A thief making a snack before holding me at gunpoint sounds like the only action I'll see, anyway."

How's that for mile-a-minute details? At this point, I'll take a slice of cheese before bed. I need to pack my clothes and my unsatisfied vagina to fly back to Buffalo tomorrow.

I squat down and grab my waste of an investment. Fatigue and embarrassment are enough for me to bury my entire body somewhere in the desert.

Antonio drops to his haunches and holds my wrist. His quads are hard muscle under smooth caramel. His abs tense over the band of his boxer briefs, which holds a very noticeable bulge that's teasing me to stare.

Between his legs, chest, and that weapon he calls a penis, someone is enjoying the best sleep of their life tonight.

"Let me help," Antonio says, his silken voice a gentle whisper.

"Okay."

Chapter 29

Miriam

The walk back to my room is a silent rhythm of steps. Who needs an in-depth discussion about sex toys and their function? It's bad enough I can't get Antonio out of my head, only for him to find me with all of the clitoral stimulators I could carry.

He doesn't appear fazed. In fact, he hasn't said a word since offering to hand-deliver the objects of my displeasure back to the corner where they belong.

The stare that's trained on my back lifts the hairs on my nape under a bun of two-strand twists. I don't understand him. Why's he in our suite and not out doing whatever it is bachelors do in Vegas?

When we get to my room, I turn to face him. "Thank you for your assistance," I say to his chest and push up my glasses. "Breakfast tomorrow?"

"Sit on the bed."

"Pardon?"

"Sit. On. The. Bed."

I force myself not to laugh at the man in front of me, who has newly cleaned sex toys in his hands and a crease in his forehead. There's a joke here I'm not getting.

"I don't understand."

Antonio steps closer, forcing my eyes back up well-proportioned pectorals to a calm gaze that's masking something below the surface. It's the same stare he had right before he kissed me at the pool.

"It's late," I whisper over the uptick of my pulse. "I'm sure you want to go back out tonight."

"I came straight here after going out with some of the guys."

"Oh." I nod.

"Are you done playing with yourself?" He says the words like I spent hours stuck on a *Battletoads* level and not searching for the cheat code to my vagina.

My cheeks flame. "Please don't make fun of me." I prefer reason over emotions, but I still feel.

"I'd never do that, Doe," he says softly. "I want to help."

Is he...oh.

Antonio tosses the toys onto a chair in the corner and adjusts himself. The bulge from the living room is now a girthy outline across his left thigh.

How does he play in rugby shorts with that between his legs?

The question dissolves when his hand tips up my chin. "Do you want my help?"

"I—" Good damn, I can't think with him staring at me like that. My breath stutters at the gentle stroke to my cheek.

Logical reasoning tells me that no toy will solve the issue of Antonio's kiss extending beyond the platonic boundary we established years ago. My lack of orgasm suggests the need for an alternative, one I shouldn't consider. Based on testimonials alone, he has a history of satisfying women across geographic borders.

I'm attracted to him, but, more importantly, I trust him.

Ovulation plus his pheromones have me feral. I was one frustrated sigh away from howling at the moon, and that was before him and his chemical signals aroused my nervous system.

A night with Knight. "Just for tonight," I say.

He kisses my nose. "Go sit on the bed."

We're doing this.

Moonlight dips through the window, illuminating rumpled sheets and discarded pillows. The mattress gives beneath my weight. I release a shaky breath to steady my heart, which is somersaulting in my chest.

"You're beautiful."

I bite my lip. "Thank you."

My throat tightens at his footsteps. His knee seeks entry between my thighs, and I part them. I lean back to create space he suffocates with his hard body.

"Wait." My palm vibrates against his heart beating wildly through iron muscle. "No vaginal penetration." The hardware digging into my leg might leave dents. I'm also not playing with my health, assuming he was offering community penis on the Vegas Strip.

He lifts my palm to kiss the inside of my wrist. "Wasn't planning on it. Lie back."

How is he so calm?

At the low command, I sink back into the comforter, close my eyes, and release a calming breath that gallops when my nightgown lifts above my thighs. Heat presses into my dampened underwear, and I bite back a moan at the weight of Antonio's groin.

"Breathe."

"I'm finding it." My inhale is a slow, steady hiss at the friction between my legs, which have to stretch to accommodate his size. He's overwhelming.

Breathe in.

"Miriam."

Breathe out.

"Yeah?"

"Look at me, baby." I pop an eye open at the smooth, velvet edge of his voice. "Do you feel comfortable continuing?"

My nod takes a forehead kiss to dissolve. "It's been a while since—five years and eight months since someone was this close. I'm not...I haven't—"

The feel of his lips on mine snatches me off the raceway that is my mind.

I reach for the trimmed fibers of his beard and moan when he leans into my touch. Antonio is a skilled kisser. Dominant but also gentle, giving me the space to explore his lips.

I like it. A lot.

He pulls back to search my face. "Tell me if it's too much?"

"Okay."

His biceps flex as they cage me in. "Can I put my mouth on you?"

I huff.

"Just straight to it, huh? Yeah, okay."

The smile he gives me is deceptive. There's nothing friendly about the first swipe of his tongue over my neck. Or its trail from my collarbone down my cleavage.

"Oh." I pant as his breath fans over my right breast. The mix of heat from his mouth and cool air crystallizes the tip, and he swirls his tongue over it through my nightgown. Then he tugs on the wet cotton and grazes my nipple with his teeth.

"These are perfect." He tugs my straps together to expose my nipples and skims them with his thumbs.

I nearly come from the sensation and his deep groan. He's staring, marveling at their size. "Fucking perfect," he whispers before pushing them together to suck. The laps of his tongue and the scrapes of his teeth put my toys to shame.

"Antonio."

"Stay still for me."

I writhe beneath him, rocking my hips into his. Pressure builds before it shatters. I moan loudly and fight a cramp in my toes.

He releases my breasts to grip my chin. "Good?" His tongue dips into my mouth at my nod, and then he's off the bed. His eyes never leave mine as he removes his boxer briefs. The breath in my lungs snags on his length. It's firm and thick with a slight curve.

"On second thought, maybe I'll stick with the toys." He snickers, but I'm dead serious.

What does he expect? I've only had sex twice in my life, and I'm nowhere near prepared to deal with *that*.

Game over.

"You'll get used to me." He bites his lip and runs his hand from the base to the tip. The motion contracts the muscles in his torso as he steps between my thighs and balances his weight on his forearms.

Inches apart, he kisses me with a softness that rivals the penis that's hardening against my leg. But my nerves subside, and I get lost in the ecstasy of his tongue.

"I've wanted to do this for three years," he murmurs against my lips. His erection rolls over the seat of my panties.

A slow hum builds in my core as he lifts to a push-up and thrusts harder. The cotton between us is a flimsy barrier he pulls to the side to drag his thumb over my seam. I gasp at the pressure on my clitoris.

"You're fucking soaked, Doe," Antonio grunts. "Can I taste you?"

"I—what?" My heart rate is running for its life. "No one has ever done that to me."

He looks up. "Will you let me be your first?"

My last sexual partner only cared about getting himself off. Never once did he stare at me with affection the way Antonio does.

"Okay."

The lingering huskiness in my tone fades when his hands travel to the apex of my thighs. "You know, we could skip this." I squirm. "Ice cream and brownies! You like sweets, and isn't today your cheat day?"

"I got my brownie in front of me."

A finger breaches my barrier.

"Oh, but I heard their sweets are world-renowned. Imported chocolate."

"Have it here." He kisses my sensitive flesh, dangerously close to my opening.

I muffle a gasp. "Caramel."

Another kiss. "Have it."

My hips buck at his breath over my skin. Down there. Where no one's been.

"What about—"

He replaces his fingers with his mouth, and I lose it. The sounds coming from me are a mix between a broken respirator and a skipping record. I grip his head to ride the tidal wave that is his tongue as it crashes into me. Why on earth did I spend years filling my head with engineering and science instead of *getting* head?

It's fantastic.

It's—oh!

Antonio pins my thighs apart and eats me like a mango from my mother's tree. The slurps and strokes of his tongue are a deadly combination.

Did he skip dinner?

My cries rise into an aria when he stretches his mouth to cover me and sucks. His tongue is back on my clit, strumming another orgasm to the surface. His hand flies over my mouth as I shout like Patti LaBelle selling one of her sweet potato pies.

Antonio reaches my lips. "Taste your pussy." He feeds me his tongue. I do my best to oblige, but my soul is stuck on the ceiling.

How do people have sex for hours?

I cut my eyes at his chuckle. "Don't tap out now. We're just getting started," he has the nerve to say.

My brows snap together, and he rolls that magical length over my soaked vagina.

"Look at us," he mumbles.

I lift onto my elbows, my hair a mess, my breath running in circles. My jaw slacks at his penis gliding over my damp entrance. The sensation shoots a flare through my veins.

"Don't stop," I moan, rolling my nipples between my fingertips. Let my soul stay on the ceiling. She's fine there.

"Fuck, Doe," Antonio growls.

He presses himself against me with more force, careful not to penetrate the boundary I set. He wraps my panties around his shaft and strokes himself while thrusting harder.

My juices drip down the sheets I'm squeezing to death. The squelches from his body on mine are a soundtrack to our moans. My breasts bounce, and my breath becomes a spurt of pants as another orgasm awakens.

Antonio slows his pace to quicken his hands working over his shaft. His eyes are on me when he comes undone. The muscles in his abs tighten as cum saturates my underwear and skin.

It takes a minute for the high to wear off. "Was that okay?" Sweat covers his brow.

For reasons unbeknownst to me, I laugh. It's delirious, because who am I?

"No notes." I fall back on the bed and savor the remaining tremors heating places no man has touched until tonight. I always dreamed about getting eaten out. Now I understand the concept of crashing out over someone. Antonio isn't my man, but he would have me catching arson and battery charges like Mario coins if he thought about dropping off this dick to someone else.

It deserves its own *Magic School Bus* episode, exploring the wonders of humping and the joys of orgasm.

I'm happy, sleepy, and doped up on oxytocin.

"Bless your penis," I say through a yawn.

He cackles and pulls me to my feet. "Let me clean you up."

"I got it."

Gravity and shaky legs prove me to be a liar. My hands fly to his chest, and I grip it to keep from falling over. I need a shower and some Icy Hot.

"Don't laugh!" I snicker. I look like Kym Whitley after Shemar Moore put his mouth on her.

"Can you make it to the bathroom by yourself?"

I trip over my foot but catch myself. "Yes."

"No." I'm scooped up bridal style.

"Put me down! I can walk."

"Into a wall." He adjusts his grip.

The bathroom comes to life with the flick of a switch. Gold and white wallpaper reflects in the mirrors across from the frameless glass shower. Antonio sits me on a stool and fiddles with the settings.

"I'll join you after I get our bed ready," he says, halfway in the glass enclosure to check the temperature. His penis slaps his thigh.

Focus.

"Our?" I adjust my glasses. It's a miracle they haven't fogged.

"I'm pretty sure we sweat through your sheets."

"You want to shower and sleep together?"

He steps out and folds his arms. "Did I not just have my mouth on your pussy and my dick on your stomach?"

We crack up.

"Don't be so vulgar." I snort on accident.

He shrugs. "Why be shy now? I'll order the brownie you were moaning about."

"I wasn't moaning."

"Fooled me." His eyes snap shut, and his voice rises. "'Antonio. They're world-renowned!'"

"Get out!" I push his body, which is doubled over in laughter, and fight back a smile. "This night with Knight is over."

He stills. "What?"

"Don't act like you don't know. I've heard stories."

"What stories? My eyes are up here, Doe."

Then tell your penis to stop waving at me.

"What stories?" he repeats. The playfulness in his tone is at a simmer now.

My smile falls at his stare. "It's no secret how you are."

"How am I? I want to hear you say it."

"Friendly with your—" I gesture to his length, which is about to take a bow. "Lala. Lisa."

"Lisa?"

"Jalisa."

He frowns. "How do you know Jalisa?"

"She went to college with my sister. They're somewhat close, though that's questionable," I say, uncomfortable with having a conversation about the degrees of separation between me and his hookups. "I'm not judging. Do you—or them." I look away. "I know what this is."

He steps forward and lifts my chin. "What was tonight for you?"

"Satisfying. Confusing. A line we shouldn't cross again."

It takes several seconds for Antonio to blink. "You want things to stay the same?"

A crease burrows between my brows at the scowl marring his face. "I'm not naive. I know what this is: you getting me off. I'm sure it's not the first or last time you'll help one of your friends."

"Friends." He laughs to himself. "Yeah, sure. Go get cleaned up. I'll call down for new sheets and hop in after you."

"Okay," I say to his back. "Antonio?" He glances over his shoulder halfway through the door. "You don't need to worry about me catching feelings. Nothing will change between us."

I get a nod before I'm left in a cloud of steam.

Chapter 30

Antonio

"Need a hug?"

"I'm fine." I wave Shins off.

"You sure about that?" He raises his hands at my glare. "Just asking."

Someone needs to ask himself why he wears Carl Winslow sweaters in public.

"I told you I'm fine."

"You've been staring at the wall in the kitchen for twenty minutes."

I fold my arms over my chest. "Thinking about changing the backsplash."

The lie does not take my mind off Miriam. In fact, it does the opposite. I bet she could renovate my entire apartment in half a day. I've seen her calculate figures in her head and criticize what she deemed to be overcomplicated instructions.

She probably has a toolbelt too. One of those good suede ones with compartments for protractors and compasses and shit.

I swat Shins's hand away from my face. "Are you following concussion protocol?"

"I don't have a concussion," I mutter, shifting to look at the movie and not the unwanted houseguest in my personal space.

My sectional seats six, eight if they're not ruggers. There's more than enough space to stretch out without him breathing down my neck.

Shins hasn't been home since practice ended. He comes to Steel House to kick it from time to time, but he's been here for three hours. Spent all of them on my last nerve.

"You took a hard blow during the scrimmage."

"I've been hit harder," I point out.

Jones, the other starting flanker, tossed me on my ass. Hard. I wasn't paying attention, and he capitalized. Simple as that.

How Miriam and I left things in Vegas messed with my head during practice.

Two knocks rattle the front door before Bread pops his head in. "Got any honey I can borrow?"

My face twists. "Why are you glistening?"

He grins. "Baby oil."

I need to move.

"Bailey, so help me God, if you stain the floors again." I groan, a hand over my face to block out flashbacks of the berries he stomped into the hardwood. Every year, it's the same thing: me reminding him not to act up, and him finding new ways to cross the line. I don't want to know who or what he's doing in his room.

Bread steps into my apartment shirtless in silk boxers and rainboots. "I remember from last time. Why you sulking in your bathrobe? Need a hug?"

It's a sad day when a man can't sit in peace.

"I'm not sulking. I'm processing."

I haven't seen or heard from Miriam since she hugged me at the airport and hopped into Marcela's car.

I kissed her.

Tasted her.

Came on her.

I gave in to the will to press my body against hers and drink from her mouth. Miriam doesn't see herself when she's turned on. How easily she brings me to my knees with a single look. How could she think she'd be a notch on my belt after all of this time? She should know me well enough to understand how important she is to me.

What happened between us—what's *happening* between us—isn't because of my friendly dick. She's changing me.

Having her that way was a dream come true. I saw stars and galaxies—shit, the meaning of life—after I released almost two decades' worth of tension. Imagine my surprise when I thought we'd spend the rest of the night together, only for her to split the brownie we ordered and send me on my way. Her snores floated into the living room, where I was up half the night wondering why it was so easy for her to dismiss me. I gave her my best strokes.

She's never judged me for the women I've entertained. I never brought them up. No one lasted long enough to be relevant in my life. I'm not interested in catching feelings, but here I am, tight-lipped and in my robe—pissed at life.

I miss her, but I'll respect her space. She made it loud and clear that she regrets what happened in Vegas.

"He's doing it again."

I jump back when I find Shins and Bread inches from my face. One looks like he belongs on a '90s sitcom. The other needs a shower and an exfoliating brush.

Bread's big head leans closer. "He's been like this all night?"

Shins nods. "He put on a rom-com too."

"Bullshit!" I look between the thorn in my ass and the team's next PR crisis. "Shins found it on TV."

I forget his character's name, but the doctor from *Grey's Anatomy* is an idiot. Dude should've professed his love to his best friend before she left for Scotland and fell in love with the other doctor from the same show.

Couldn't be me.

Sure about that?

"Would you give me space?" I kick my teammates away. "I don't want grease on my couch."

Bread steps back to study the log-throwing scene on my eighty-inch. He grins. "You miss Maid Miriam."

I tighten my robe and look away. "She's safe and breathing. What's there to miss?"

"The friend he likes and won't admit it?"

"The one and only," Bread says to Shins, on his way to my kitchen for God knows what. He pulls open the refrigerator and dips his head inside. "I saw the way you were looking at her all weekend. Shit, we all did."

"Don't forget the kiss at the pool," Shins adds with a proud smile. "You like her, more than any woman we've seen you with."

"If I had to approximate, you don't know how to deal with having her so close. No more late-night conversations on the phone or texting." Bread sets a carton of eggs, chocolate syrup, and whipped cream on the counter.

"Since when do you say 'approximate'?" I skip over him raiding my fridge.

He lifts a shoulder. It's sparkling from all that damn baby oil. "Heard Miriam say it once. The shit stuck. She's cool, Cap. Likely won't stay single for long."

"And what's that supposed to mean?" I'm out my seat, hands on my hips. Ain't no way a man drenched in oil will school me in my house.

Shins chuckles. "It means don't be an idiot and let a good thing pass you by."

"Moping like Lance after his wife died," Bread huffs. His fingers hover over a cereal box. "Too far?"

Shins and I nod.

There wasn't a dry eye in the theater during the funeral scene in *The Best Man Holiday*. My mother and aunt were sniffling with big tears like Monica Calhoun died for real. I won't lie and say it didn't make me squirm. The shit was sad.

"Miriam wouldn't want me anyway." I kick at the rug with my slipper.

Knowing Lisa, she gave Miriam and Marcela a full outline of what we did together, including footnotes. Her beauty couldn't mask the jealousy that broke through her smile when she heard I was out with someone else. Popping up at my crib unannounced already had me off of her.

I never fuck anyone in Miriam's circle. No wonder she thinks I'm handing out dick like breath mints.

Shins and Bread get the redacted version of my history with Miriam and what happened during our trip. By the time I'm done, they're both on the ground, hollering.

"Bro, you met your match," Bread cackles, soaking his baby oil into my hardwood floor. "She pulled a you by kicking you out and leaving you on read."

I scoff and step over their gyrating bodies to grab water. "You make it sound like I'm heartless."

It's true that I don't like for women to spend the night. I prefer to pay for their car service and text to make sure they get home safely. Miriam handled my ass the same way. She doesn't do small talk or lead with emotions. I expected a long conversation about what we did and what it means for our relationship. If we want it to mean something. She said she was fine, ate her brownie, and went to sleep.

It was back to normal the next morning, like we didn't rub our body parts together. Three days later, and I'm in a robe and sweats, pissed off at rom-coms.

How does she not feel the way I feel?

"Welp." Bread swings two reusable grocery bags over his shoulder. "Hopefully she's still on the market after Friday, so you can figure it all out."

My frown deepens. "What's Friday?"

"Valentine's Day, the holiday you always dodge by running off." He yawns. "Miriam's sister hosts an annual district auction. It's a fundraiser to bid on items, including Buffalo's most eligible bachelors and bachelorettes. I did it last year and spent the weekend caked up with an attorney who helped me get out of parking tickets. I signed you up this year."

"You did what?" I shout.

"Shit." He chuckles and grabs an apple from the bowl. "I knew there was something I forgot to tell you. Show whoever the winner is a good time, dick out or not."

If we didn't need Bread in the season opener against Houston, I'd put him in a deep grave. Not only did I forget about Valentine's Day, but I now have to take a stranger out for charity.

We fly out first thing tomorrow, which means I won't be around to intercept whoever goes for Miriam.

"Stop stressing Antonio out," Shins chides. "Who says she'll participate?"

"*Shiit*. I'd make her participate if I were her sister," Bread says. "She's fine, smart as hell, and thick. Maybe Maid Miriam will find someone to scoop her up like homie in the kilt." He points to the television. "Women like her don't stay single forever. Going to get my dick sucked. See you bright and early."

Bread bops out like he didn't just fuck up my mental while stealing from my refrigerator. Miriam has been off-limits for so long, I wouldn't know how to approach her.

Would she say yes to giving us a try?

Am I ready for an us?

Shins pats my shoulder. "Need a hug now?"

Chapter 31

Miriam

Entertaining sixth and seventh graders is no walk in the park. I was dabbling in electrical circuit kits at their age. When I'd visit, my mother would accuse me of trying to blow up the house because science and technology held my interest over makeup and boys. I knew what I was doing back then. Right now, I've got no clue.

I'm officially the STEM program coordinator at the Jefferson Moselle Community Center, and I've only thought about crying in the closet once. My father didn't miss the opportunity to remind me how "unbefitting" the title is for a woman with a PhD, but I'm enjoying the work.

The kids are quick to crack on me for wearing leggings two days in a row or rambling about formulas. They're happy otherwise. Every child who steps into our gathering space of worn rugs and painted cinder-block walls has an appetite for creativity and hands-on application. I'm not a teacher—at least, I wasn't before this week—but I'm happy these kids want to learn. Engineering and the ability to problem-solve shapes societies. I'm guiding the next generation of world builders who will bring their imagination to life through practical solutions.

Today's project is Valentine's Day-inspired. I'm not a fan of the holiday, but the kids wanted to make gifts. So, we're coding. They're using a binary code alphabet reference to write "secret notes like they did in the 1900s." A direct quote.

I advised against the practice in school. The last thing I need on my conscious is an eleven-year-old telling another child to suck a fart out of their butt, as Harmony so eloquently spelled out in zeroes and ones before I took her paper.

Flatulence aside, the coding bracelets we're creating are keeping them hard at work. We're spelling out "Love" and "Peace," using pink beads for the zeros, red for the ones, and white for the spaces between the letters.

"I finished, Ms. Miriam." Marc shoves his bracelets in my face with a gap-toothed grin. "I made three."

I smile. "That's nice."

"One for each girlfriend."

The smile is gone.

"You have *girlfriends*, with an *s*?" Marc is nine and cried until he was allowed to participate in my after-school program. He's decked out in a Roblox shirt and sweats, and his love life puts my nonexistent roster to shame.

"Yup." He lifts a finger to describe each one. "Monica goes to my mama's church. Kiana I see at the Y. Angel is in my homeroom. My brother says I'm too young to be locked down by one female."

I bet your brother says, "Grand rising," and talks about ancient Egypt too.

"That's...something," I say.

He points to the craft on my desk. "Did you make that for some-one special?"

My fingers graze the friendship bracelet Antonio made me on my wrist. "You could say that."

Antonio is special to me. A good friend, I remind myself, and nothing else.

It wasn't my intention to create distance, but I was at a loss on how to solve the challenge of us. There is no *us*. What happened last Saturday was…well, there are no words—at least none that I'll repeat here. I thought I could separate my need for physical gratification from my feelings for him, which aren't going away. I pretended what we did had no effect on me, but the truth is that it does. Compart-mentalizing might help with complex projects, but it doesn't work with matters of the heart.

I can't fix the hunger to be touched again, but I can prevent the recurrence to ensure my heart, head, and vagina don't get the wrong idea. "Antonio" and "relationship" have never appeared in the same sentence. I'm not ready for one this second, but I will be at some point. Falling for my best friend would lead to hurt, not to mention an imploding friendship. There's too much to lose if we cross the line, and last weekend proved it.

I haven't seen him since we flew back to Buffalo. Yes, I could've reached out, but I know the drill. The start of rugby season is always busy for him as the Steel make last-minute adjustments ahead of their first game. He texted to wish me luck on my new job before he flew out yesterday.

It's weird. Missing someone you have no romantic connections to but have somehow threaded your life with theirs.

Marc runs back to a table with construction paper and markers. Resources are a mere wish list buried underneath maintenance and general operating costs, but we make it work.

I slip out my phone from a desk drawer to send Antonio a picture of the bracelet I made him.

> Hi. I made this for you. It's a binary coding bracelet that says "Peace." The kids are making them for Valentine's Day.

It's not a peace offering. Maybe an icebreaker?

> Happy Valentine's Day BTW. You might be out with the team. Did you know that the International Space Station has a Houston area code?

> Houston also has the largest freeway in the country, with twenty-six lanes at its widest point. You're probably better off walking to the stadium, depending on where your hotel is. There's also a six-mile underground pedestrian tunnel system.

You're rambling.

> Anyway. I hope you have a good time.

I type "I miss you," but I erase it to wish him well on his first game. Saying I miss him after what we did is a bridge too far with hurricane consequences. "Break a leg" didn't sound right either, in case he actually does.

"Stop thinking about him," I mumble to myself.

"Get your big toe out of my butt!" I swat Marcela's foot, which is burrowing into my crack, and block her smack with a to-go cover.

Our sisterly fight scenes are a time. At any moment, a flick or gesture could ignite a choreographed kung fu film mixed with MMA.

Marcela assumed that because she's older she'd get the drop on me—literally, in this case, with the elbow she launches from two feet above my head. I roll off the couch moments before the moisturized joint slams into the cushion.

"Bitchhh! My wig!"

She's stronger, but I'm faster.

I twirl the glueless hairpiece from a safe distance away, between my couch and the kitchen doorway. It's a cute cut with bangs and wavy layers that reach beyond her shoulders.

Well, *reached*.

"Don't mess up the curls. I'm wearing that on a date this weekend," she snaps with a hand on the stocking cap that covers her cornrows.

"Don't put your toe in my butt."

"I wasn't trying to. My feet are cold."

She stares but sighs when I raise a brow. Every younger sibling has their limit. I'll set this wig on fire and not think twice about it.

"Miriam," she says through gritted teeth, "I apologize. May I have my hair back please, and a pair of socks?"

"You can." I hand her the ombre brown wig and retrieve some socks from the basket of folded clothes next to the steps.

Popcorn, raspberry mules, and rom-coms are the highlight of our Valentine's Day. I planned my evening in on the couch for a party of one that became two after Marcela texted she was on her way. Based on the scowl and the bag of liquor in her hand when she arrived, her date with Ian in finance didn't end well.

Her phone has been blowing up all night with texts from the senator she sees on the side. I asked why they're not together for the holiday and got a snort.

Marcela settles under a blanket and grabs a bowl of kettle corn. "Can we watch *Waiting to Exhale* after this?"

I frown. "How is that a rom-com?"

Her shoulder lifts. "It was funny to me," she mumbles under her breath as another message lights her screen.

"Why don't you go see him?"

She sucks her teeth and pulls the blanket over her little black dress. "He's at dinner...with his wife."

"Marcela!"

"Technically *estranged* wife. They've been separated for over a year and live in different houses."

I fold my arms over my "I like cheese" PJ set.

"They're both miserable. They're only married because of their families." Marcela tries to explain her situation like it will justify entertaining an undivorced penis.

"They haven't made an appearance together in two years. They'll file for divorce once their youngest graduates this year."

"And you're okay with being a mistress?"

"He's not my man, trust. I'm not interested in a commitment, with him or anyone else." She tosses popcorn into her mouth. "The only reason we meet up twice a month is because his dick has girth and he eats my pussy for thirty minutes straight."

I really needed that visual—said no sister ever.

Her eyes soften under the bangs of her wig, which is now sitting two inches crooked. "Don't worry about me, Miri. I'm not breaking homes. Hearts is a different story. He wants a relationship beyond sex. Not interested."

We settle into the sofa and *My Big Fat Greek Wedding*. Gus, the father, was so cute with his Windex home remedy. I empathize with Toula and her thick glasses. Contacts feel like condoms over my eyes, so I can't give up frames for good, but there are pieces of myself I see in her.

Awkward.

Unmarried in our thirties.

Still figuring it out.

"I'm thinking about dating. For real this time," I announce to the bowl of popcorn in my lap. Marcela's stare burns through the silk scarf that covers my nightly twists. "Do not make this weird."

She raises both hands. "I'm not."

"It's just...I think I'm ready. Not to settle down and get married tomorrow. Maybe I'll find a guy who believes in monogamy and wants to see where things go. Someone who isn't technically married." I giggle at her swat to my shoulder. "Someone who isn't—I'm ready."

Antonio never read the texts I sent. I got curious and went on social media to check out what the Steel are up to. The answer is a night out with Jell-O shots and women with long hair and short dresses. He didn't post any photos, but Bread did. Video of Antonio shirtless in a gold chain and jeans, looking down at a woman who was grabbing her ankles, was the reminder I needed to snap out of whatever feelings I think I have.

Marcela's four-month marriage to her on-again-off-again high school sweetheart taught me not to dive headfirst into a relationship, especially one that sweats your hair out and ends with ulcers and a night in jail after busting out every window in his car.

The weight of Antonio's penis alone would have me popping out his trunk with a tire iron. He's charming, sweet, and *fine*. Forget the width of those thighs that drove into me, or the beard that scratched against my lower lips. I'll catch feelings and federal charges behind him.

Any thoughts that veer outside of platonic are wrong. He's clearly enjoying the single life of a professional athlete, as he should.

I don't expect Vegas to mean anything more to him than helping a friend in a bind. Like changing a flat. My vagina was the tire, in this case. His penis was a *very* effective jack, hard as iron without causing puncture wounds.

"Will you stop staring at me please?" I fix my glasses and push away Marcela's foot as it creeps back to my butt. "It's not a big deal."

"Does that mean I can count on you to come out tomorrow?" She drums her fingers together with a face-splitting grin.

My sister hates the idea of love and celebrates Anti-Valentine's Week religiously each year. Tomorrow is the kickoff, with her annual charity event.

"It means I'll come, but I'm not subjecting myself to a date with the highest bidder," I warn. "You and your district can kiss my ass."

"Miriam Yamileth Beckford. Did you just cuss at me?"

"Stick around. I'm just getting started."

Chapter 32

Miriam

A fish fry with throwbacks is always a good time.

Marcela's fundraiser for the Jefferson District isn't the convention-center soirée I'd imagined, with overpriced parking and bland food. It's the place to be on a Friday night in your Sunday best.

Worn pine softened from decades of neighborhood gatherings and gospel brunches creaks under two-steps to Tony! Toni! Toné!'s "Let's Get Down." Elders hold court at spades tables around the hem of the dance floor. The crackle of fish searing in the kitchen floats through the double doors, separating greens, cornbread, and catfish recipes passed down generations.

Tonight reminds me of nights in Panama City during the rainy season, when we'd open the windows and doors to listen to the percussion of water droplets and "Patria."

Rubén Blades isn't in rotation, but the heart of the community is here, which reminds me of home.

I beat my chest and swallow a cough when the sting of bourbon incinerates my insides. Samford, the gray-haired bartender with bifocals, put more than a "splash" in the lemonade cocktail he swore would change my life. More like send me into the afterlife with a hangover.

I'm barely hanging on, with only prayer and a plate of fish keeping me steady on the barstool.

This is my first drink, by the way.

I did my part tonight. I came. I saw. I bid on a spa treatment with mud and seaweed wraps.

My social battery is travel-sized at best, which meant two laps around the cozy hangout to snatch more catfish from the buffet before I parked myself in the nearest corner.

Me being here in a knee-length black dress I keep in the back of my closet is a miracle. So are the heels strapped to my feet, which I haven't tripped in yet. Marcela, by all accounts, is a local celebrity. With that comes an interest in me by association.

The hugs.

The handshakes.

The business cards.

Why must people insist on invading your personal space to tell you about themselves? Most are people my age who are more focused on candid selfies and feigning importance. No meaningful conversation whatsoever—not that I need it. I'm good with being ignored, but that wasn't an option tonight.

Does it look like I care how quickly you became a project manager in two years? Or that you were photographed with the mayor last week?

The third person who introduced himself with his LinkedIn profile got the hint and left me alone with my catfish. I'm one "Can you introduce me?" away from sneaking out the back. Marcela already caught me and redirected my butt in wobbly heels right back to the bar, where I've been munching on the best golden-crusted marine life in the city.

For all of the interviews and line dancing she's done, my sister's hair—a sharp bob I didn't snatch off—remains in place. So does her glossy smile that matches the amethyst jumpsuit sparkling against her skin. Her makeup is flawless, and her breasts are sitting high and pretty, tempting men, women, and a few acne-faced teens. She contained her cleavage, but there's a lot of circumference peeking out of the top. It's hard not to notice.

Poor Trevor was sweating like the Jordan Peele meme. He managed to keep his tongue in his mouth but hit his breaking point watching Marcela electric slide. There was a shot, a swipe right on an app, and he was off for the rest of the night.

"Not bidding?" I freeze at the familiar voice.

My brows knit as I slowly turn to face the last person I expected to be here.

"Kieran. Hi."

"Didn't mean to interrupt your dinner."

"It's my third plate," I admit with zero shame.

His chuckle rattles his Adam's apple. "You're really fucking up that catfish."

"Slipped a twenty to one of the grandmas in the back for a couple of to-go plates. I'm not cooking this weekend, and Ms. Ethel promised me extra cornbread."

My finger breaches my lips to savor the final notes of the love letter to the Jefferson District the cooks wrote with seasoned batter and oil. Kieran's eyes lock on the movement. His nostrils flare, and his jaw tightens.

"Are you okay? There's still plenty in the back. I swear I didn't eat it all."

His laughter is faint. He runs a thumb across his lower lip. "My appetite isn't for fish. Did you bid on anyone? Me, maybe?"

"Oh God, no," I snort. "I mean—that's not what I meant."

Do you see how awful talking is? One minute, I'm eating in peace. The next, I'm disrespecting a man who was almost my boss.

With a flushed face and regret that I didn't stay in the house, I try again. "What I meant to say is, I'm not bidding on anyone. I've never been on a date, and I don't want my first to be one I paid for."

Unless Kierra dragged me somewhere, I kept to myself. Dating required time I refused to spend and an interest in young adults who were still very much big kids with facial hair.

The two times I had sex never included a happy meal, much less food outside of what I had in my dorm room. I was horny. Josh Alby's penis was available. We consented. He finished in under three minutes each time. The end.

Nothing memorable. Not like—

Access denied.

What happened in Vegas will stay in Vegas.

Kieran's gaze roves over my nearly makeup-free face, down the silhouette of my scoop neck dress that screams more *Who died?* and less *Slide me your digits.* His eyes stall at the outline of my breasts and dip to my thighs stretching polyester above my knees.

I tuck a loose curl behind my ear and jolt when he leans forward. One of his hands is on the black granite. The other is on the back of my barstool, and he uses it to turn me to him. The scent of his cologne, a woodsy aroma mixed with citrus, toys with my nose.

Was he always this forward?

Shadows dance across the sharp lines of his cheekbones and down to his trimmed beard. His lean figure fills out the all-black suit pulled over his shoulders.

"You really do look like Ghost from *Power*," I giggle into my water glass. Omari Hardwick is alright with me.

"I get that a lot," he says in a low tone. His stare smacks the breath from my lungs as he closes the distance between us. "I'd like the honor of taking you on your first date. I'll make a bid."

I frown. "On yourself?"

"I consider it an investment."

"In?"

He studies me. "Possibilities. I've been searching for a way to approach you without pulling your number from your résumé."

"Because that would be weird." I went to Maple King about a job, not for a man.

Kieran's fade catches in the light when he nods. "I took a chance you'd be here tonight."

"And if I didn't come?"

He shrugs. "I'd find another way. We're problem solvers by nature, Miriam. I was disappointed to hear we won't be colleagues. But perhaps we can still collaborate in a professional sense outside of the office."

"I already have a job," I say.

"I heard." He lets out a chuckle at my brows threading. "Buffalo is the second-largest city in the state, but it's small in many ways. News about you travels fast. Do you think teaching STEM after school will satisfy you? Our offer still stands."

"Teaching kids is only part of it. When I'm done, they will have built equipment to help sustain urban farming efforts across the city. These kids are future engineers who look like us, and they will go farther than we ever have. It's more than just after-school teaching. This is a generational investment."

The pieces of my life clicked together when I stepped into the Jefferson Moselle Community Center on Monday. I was a child who naturally gravitated toward science and technology. My parents recognized the spark and invested in me, the same way I'm investing in these children four days a week.

They're eager to learn, and they deserve more than the scraps the city gives them in funding every year.

"You sound happy."

For the first time tonight, I smile and actually mean it. "I am."

He considers me. "I would like to support you. Our lab is open if you ever need it."

"I might take you up on that."

"Now, about that date."

Kieran isn't unattractive. By conventional standards, he's handsome, with good teeth and a top-paying job at a prestigious engineering firm. I don't feel a zing with him, but maybe that's okay. It's dinner, not a hand in marriage.

I reach for my cocktail but think twice. "A dinner would be nice."

He chokes back a laugh. "All I get is one?"

"Do you think you're entitled to more?" I shake my head and sip my drink before covering the unsexiest cough.

The bartender refills my water with an apologetic smile.

"Thank you, Samford," I say.

"What are you looking for?" Kieran asks.

"A signature drink, apparently." I push away the cocktail.

Thick lips split into a grin. "You're funny. Beautiful too." He nudges my knee. "Don't get shy. What are you looking for?"

"Nothing," I say, matter-of-fact, and straighten my glasses. "I wanted degrees, not a life partner by a certain age. Love will find me when I'm ready."

He nods. "Any traits you like?"

"Someone who makes me laugh and accepts my quirks without trying to change me." I smile to myself. "Someone kind, considerate, and honest. Loyal. Someone I'm enough for, who won't dim my sparkle to shine on their own."

Despite my best effort, Antonio skates back into my mind.

The hours we spent together in the hospital.

The care we held for each other throughout a long-distance friendship.

Our home improvement trip that ended in a paint war.

Video games.

Vegas.

He makes me feel comfortable to try new things. To explore more. To be me.

Antonio checks many boxes, but he isn't wired for love in a romantic way. Going cold turkey from each other is the safest solution. Minimal contact to ease back into random texts and late-night calls will fight off any physical attraction.

"I fly out for a client meeting in the morning, but I want to see you when I get back."

I smirk. "I'll have to check my calendar, but I should be free. Good luck with the bidding."

The corner of his mouth lifts. "Don't need it. I put down two grand in your name."

The water I gulp goes down the wrong pipe. Who in their right mind drops thousands for a chance at a date?

"Too much," I push through a cough.

"It's a start. Your sister is doing good work. As for us, I look forward to exploring more ways to collaborate."

Kieran walks over to the bidding table in the corner. He grins at something Marcela says when she passes by and winks at me before leaving.

Two thousand dollars—in this economy!

Marcela rests her forearm on the bar and motions for water. "Look at my little grown sis, pulling dates from the bar. And he bid thousands on himself? That man in sprung."

"Hardly."

"Thousand*s*." She emphasizes the *s*.

"It's for a good cause, and the fish is good," I counter.

"*Thousands.*" Her voice rises an octave, drawing my frown. "Fine," she sighs. "I'll leave it alone."

"Thank you. I don't want to make a big deal about Kieran's—" I roll my eyes and laugh at her palm propping up her chin. "Change the subject, please."

"I'll let you off this time. Your bestie brought in a nice amount. Five thousand, to be exact."

"What?" My stomach plummets.

"Antonio was a last-minute entry. We've had a player from the Steel for the past two years. Lisa went back and forth before she got outbid and stormed out. Serves her crooked-ass wig right."

"Who was the lucky winner?"

Marcela puckers her lips toward a woman with a crowd gathered around her. She's easily over six feet tall, in black-strap stilettos that show off even, painted toes—professionally done and not a rushed hack job while hopping to the door in open-toed shoes that are too tight.

She's slimmer than me, with perky breasts on display in a V-neck evening gown with silver sequins. Crystals, maybe, judging by the diamonds dripping from her ears.

"That's Kenya," my sister supplies. "Former cheerleader for Buffalo who does some type of TV work. I don't remember what she said. She's in town as an ambassador for the children's hospital."

Charitable and looks like Rihanna.

"She mentioned she and Antonio are friends. Sounded like they were close a few years ago, before she moved away." Marcela tilts her head. "Didn't he tell you about tonight?"

"No," I mutter. He's been quiet all day, with a one-word response here and an "I'm good" there.

It shouldn't surprise me that his "friend" is here, dropping thousands for a date and possibly recording an R&B album later. She's gorgeous.

Out-of-your-league, I-laser-off-every-ounce-of-body-hair beautiful. Of course they would be familiar.

A night with Knight.

"I'm going to go."

Marcela frowns. "Do you want to talk about it?"

"Nope. Just tired." I offer a quick smile and steal a final glance at Kenya. Even her teeth are pretty. "The farm tours are this weekend, so I better pack. Congrats on a successful fundraiser."

I need a distraction, far away from the feelings I can't shake.

Chapter 33

Antonio

"**R**ight there! Don't stop!"

"Shit!"

"Oh!"

"Yes! Yes!"

"Give me that pussy juice!"

"*Ahh!*"

"Give me that pussy JUICE!"

The art hanging feet above shakes at the force of the headboard colliding with the wall. It clangs three times before a high-pitched squeal threatens to rupture my eardrums.

Fucking should be an Olympic sport, but not the night before a game.

"He better not pull a damn thing," I mumble from under my forearm.

I warned Bread countless times to save it for after we play. If he wants to drizzle chocolate syrup all over his body and bedazzle his dick hole in sequins, I'll support him. *After* the game.

"Who are you calling?" I ask Kendrick.

"The front desk." He sucks his teeth and rubs the sleep out of his eyes with the hotel phone pressed against his ear. "I'm no snitch, but

I've had enough of him and the hyena. Ain't no way that's the same woman from earlier, hollering like she got shot."

I toss a pillow over my face to keep from cracking up. He's dead serious.

"Aye. The team paid for the room. No noise violations," I say through a shaky laugh.

"Yes." He cuts his eyes at me and answers the person on the other end of the line. "If you could send someone up to tell his Black a—to keep it down. Thank you." He hangs up, tightens the string on his flannel pajama pants, and mumbles to himself on the way to the bathroom.

Kendrick and I agreed to share a room during away games. Shins must be on a couch in the hotel lobby, the way Bread is murdering that woman. I can't complain, given my own track record with disturbing the peace. But I'd usually stay in a separate hotel room, or her house if the vibe was there.

Except this year.

My sex drive is never satisfied, but the urge to get a nut off with someone whose name I won't remember in the morning just isn't there.

Many of Houston's finest women were out last night. A few caught my eye, but none held my attention enough to take it farther than a nod or a dance. I haven't been out in a minute, and I came back to the room with Kendrick. Between the early flight, team meetings, practice, and dinner at the bar, I passed out the minute my face hit the pillow after a quick shower.

I didn't read Miriam's texts until I woke up. My phone was on airplane mode, and I missed wishing her a happy Valentine's Day. Not that I celebrate. This time every year, I'm hundreds of miles away from anyone I've been inside of who expects flowers, candy, and an invitation to give love a try.

I bought Miriam a few gifts from the Space Center, which I visited today before our final practice. A 3D-model kit, astronaut kitchen mitts, and freeze-dried ice cream aren't much, but they're things I figured she'd like. A "thinking of you" gift in a miss-your-friend kind of way, because I do miss her. Not talking to her is eating at me. It didn't bother me in the past, when she lived in a different state, but it does now.

Valentine's Day falling on the exact date I happened to be near the Space Center is just a coincidence. Dessert and some trinkets aren't a declaration of love. I don't make those, and I won't start on this holiday, of all days.

Kendrick pads across the room in his house slippers. He has a newspaper tucked underneath his armpit, his signal for me to not go into the bathroom he blew up. Our hotel room isn't the biggest. The mattress barely accommodates my height, but the sheets are soft.

"Maybe he fell asleep," he says about the welcome silence.

"Let's hope so. We need to be at the field by nine." I roll over to the shared nightstand and grab my phone.

DMs I ignore and a text from my mom.

Nothing from Miriam.

"Does that tight lip mean she hasn't hit you back?" A hint of humor laces Kendrick's tone. "Maybe she's out."

Miriam did text that she was spending time with Marcela before she went silent. I'm just checking to see if she made it back home safely. It's midnight in Buffalo, an hour ahead. There's black ice on the road and pool-size potholes she'll hit if she's not careful. What kind of friend would I be if I didn't verify proof of life?

I scroll through the photos of tonight's fundraiser Marcela posted on her social media. The only reason I follow her is because her sister refuses to get online. The event was packed with people laughing and dancing. My brows narrow at an image of Miriam at the bar. She's in a black dress that curls up her thighs, sitting next to the guy from the workplace she turned down.

Dickhead.

Heat flares inside my chest. My jaw clicks, and I resist the compulsion to fly home. They're not touching, but his big-ass knees are disrespecting her personal space, if you ask me. He's staring at her. Hard. Her smile lifts her dimples, and I don't like that shit.

I have no right to be this tight over a photo, but seeing all of her teeth on display for him fucks with me.

Maybe Dickhead was a guest, but he's one more eye-fuck away from visiting somebody's hospital.

Something about him is off.

Or you have an issue with anyone pressing up on her.

I scoff and type a quick message.

Did you make it home?

Alone.

"Can't ask that," I mutter to myself.

Respectful and within the boundaries of our friendship. If she asks, I'll tell her I was online and saw the fundraiser photos. Harmless. She doesn't need to know I've checked my phone all night in case she wanted to talk.

"You good?" Kendrick asks my profile.

"Smooth."

What is she doing here?

Kenya Thomas is in the second-to-last photo. I haven't seen her since she retired from professional cheerleading and left Buffalo. That was, what, two years ago?

We met during the Steel's first press conference. Players from Buffalo came out to support, and she was there. You can't miss her in any room she enters. We kicked it and quickly learned how much we have in common. Both of us come from families that own financial businesses. She was busy with her career and finishing up grad school. I had no interest in anything beyond linking up. The only flaw Kenya had was cheering for Buffalo. I don't care how long I play for the Steel, it's Baltimore football all day.

An explosion of knocks hits the door.

"What now?" I rip off the sheets and adjust my boxer briefs. "Did you order room service?"

Kendrick sucks his teeth. "This late, the night before a game?"

Another knock.

I damn near snatch the handle off and squint at Shins. He's in an undershirt and sweats, gripping a pillow to his chest.

"Can I sleep in here?"

"What's wrong with your bed?"

A loud moan cuts through the wall that separates our rooms. The headboard sends another tremor through the art, which Shins points at and says, "That."

"Didn't you call downstairs?" I frown at Kendrick, who's on his knees praying.

He rubs his temple. "I did."

"Ahh!"

"Did they not send someone up?" I ask Shins.

"Yes! Right there!"

"Oh, they did." He pushes his way inside. "Kendrick, can I share with you?"

"Ride my shit, then!" Bread shouts from the other side of the wall.

"Why can't you sleep with Cap?" Kendrick huffs.

Shins and I shrug. "You're smaller," I say, like it's not obvious.

Kendrick's glare bounces between us before he sighs. "You owe me—both of you. Keep your ass on the edge."

Shins moves to the open side of the bed and tosses a pillow between them. "Thanks, man. The noise-canceling headphones don't work. Do you think we could find a bigger room this season for the three of us to share?"

"To hell with his." I hop into a pair of basketball shorts and slides. I didn't sign up for a threesome, and I'll be damned if I sit my ass on a toilet seat I'm sharing with two other people.

It takes four hard knocks for Bread to answer. I smack his big ass in the forehead and tell Front Desk Brenda to go back to the job that pays her. I know good and damn well her job description does not include riding dick.

There is no reason for the room to smell like pennies and coriander.

Kendrick and Shins are holding each other while summoning the dead with their snores once I get back.

"Come *on*," I mumble.

I consider suffocating them with my pillow, but I choose a safer option, one that won't end in fifteen to life. Reaching for my phone, I glare at the screen.

No new messages.

Things are about to change around here.

Snore.

Starting with my room.

Chapter 34

Miriam

I had my suspicions about Kieran, but I didn't want to judge prematurely. We all have a skeleton or two in the closet, but he's stashing corpses in the wall.

"Stop looking at me like I'm on a most-wanted list," he laughs.

"If the ice boot fits."

Walking outside in freezing weather *willingly* is suspect. My aptitude for social activities is still in preschool, but that's an invitation for frostbite, if you ask me.

Kieran's gravelly voice lifts into a chuckle. "It's called winter hiking. You should try it."

"Not even if Hell offered hand warmers. I tolerate my insurance premiums where they're at, thank you."

Serial killer hobbies aside, tonight has been enjoyable. Kieran made good on the date I pushed off until this week. I had my reservations, but I stepped out of the comfort of my tube socks and sweater for fine dining and conversations about questionable behavior.

We're in an upscale restaurant in Elmwood Village, a few blocks from my house. The food is incredible, and the space is surprisingly quaint. Half a dozen square tables are scattered across a dining room surrounded by exposed brick walls. Our table is in the corner, tucked away from other diners under a black ceiling and dimmed lights.

The cranberry sheath dress I'm wearing was option number four for my first official date. Bile only rose up my throat once, so that's a good sign.

"So, what do you do to decompress?" Kieran washes the question down with scotch and rests his forearms on the white tablecloth.

Antonio's smile enters my mind. The deep lines of his mouth and those crinkled eyes bring memories of being me without reservation.

"Play video games," I say, my thoughts back at Steel House with laughter and *Mortal Kombat.* Antonio was so mad I beat him in every game we played, and he tickled me to prove I wasn't hiding a book of cheat codes under my shirt.

Where did he think I went before I came over, Radio Shack?

Kieran grins. "We might need to have a go."

I force my dimples into a smirk.

I'm breaking dating etiquette thinking about another man. But everything reminds me of Antonio. The fancy-name appetizers he'd swear the chef picked up from a grocery store and added asparagus to in order to charge twenty dollars a plate. The complicated pasta dishes he swears he can cook, even though I know he struggles to boil water.

Random texts kicked off a friendship neither of us expected. Now, I'm lucky if I get a response the same day.

Eleven days came and went since we last saw each other. I assumed some distance would reset us back to where we were, before lust and complicated emotions got in the way.

I was wrong.

The here and there messages are harder than I anticipated. I don't want us to hurt each other, but I don't want this.

"What's on your mind?"

"Hmm?" I readjust my glasses.

Kieran studies me. "You look deep in thought."

"Oh. It's nothing." I smooth down my twist-out.

Kieran, by all accounts, easily charts any most-beautiful list. He's the proud owner of a full set of lips, high cheekbones, a crispy fade, and groomed facial hair. All of the ingredients are here except the spark. Maybe that comes with time?

The tips of my fingers burn to reach for my phone. I haven't touched it since we sat down, to resist watching Antonio's PSN interview. He left on Tuesday to record it after returning from Houston late Sunday night. I was in Central New York last weekend, visiting farms that are part of a food equity collective with urban growers. By the time I came home, he was gone.

"Miriam, are you okay?"

"Yup," I lie. It's a struggle to sip my wine with a straight face. Pounds of sugar in my glass aren't a requirement, but good gracious, this is dry. "What did you ask me?"

"Did you always want to be an engineer?"

"Back to shop talk, huh?"

His shoulder lifts. "Indulge me."

"Yes and no. Most of my toys as a kid were robotics and science kits."

"Legos?"

I smile. "Those too. What about you?"

Kieran's mouth tangles in a frown. "I didn't have a choice."

My face sours. "What does that mean?"

He laughs at my grimace. "It could be worse. My family's legacy is at Maple King. My father. My mother. My grandparents."

It sounds like a cult where you sacrifice newborns every generation for wealth and status, but I keep quiet. Maybe I should send my parents a thank-you for not forcing me into a career. Not that they could have if they'd tried.

"What would you do if you could choose?"

It's a simple question, but it catches him off guard. He stares with narrowed eyes and a creased forehead like I asked him to explain theoretical physics.

"I don't have an answer."

"That's sad." I pop a shishito pepper into my mouth. "I'm sorry if that was insensitive."

He laughs. "You fascinate me."

"I don't know why."

"You're honest and don't seem rattled by what people think."

"Don't forget clumsy and smart."

"And stunning." He eyes me. "Are you doing what you want to do?"

Saved by the server.

I say a quick prayer before digging into my Cajun salmon. It's not the ideal dish for a first-date kiss, but I have no plans to kiss anything but my toothbrush before I go to bed.

"I enjoy applying what I learned in practical ways," I say. "I want to own patents. Wow, I never admitted that out loud until now."

An idea formed during a recent visit to an urban farming site in Buffalo. Climate resilience is a concern. Summers are hotter. Blizzards are more commonplace. Machinery struggles to withstand extreme weather with its current materials.

"I'd need the proper environment to conceptualize and prototype my idea, and programming," I say out loud to myself. "I can do it."

Kieran studies me. "A patent is ambitious."

"But not impossible," I add.

"Correct." He smiles. "The offer to use our lab still stands."

"That would be amazing."

Kieran and I talk about my time on the farms this week and the Afro-Indigenous practices used to cultivate the land in an effort to repair the earth and the communities harmed by generations of predatory practices. There's so much to unpack.

"That's something." He scratches his chin. "Commendable, but it won't fix the problem."

"What do you mean?"

"I mean Black farmers are barely a blip in the industry. Working against a billion-dollar industry isn't a good use of time or resources. You won't produce the changes you want to see without corporations' support."

Time for a side-eye. "I'm no expert, but even I'm aware of the effects of unchecked power on agriculture and the environment. The pesticides we ingest. The poor conditions for workers and animals. Don't you want better?"

He scoffs. "Of course I do, but we live in reality, sweetie."

My lip coils at the pet name. It's a pat on the head, a sign to not step out of line.

"I thrive in possibility," I counter. "Create solutions to improve reality." I already have ideas about how to enhance infrastructure through design to make farming more sustainable.

Teaching kids engineering at the community center is only the first step. We'll put what they learn into urban farming efforts around the city.

A small piece of a larger ecosystem.

I use the opportunity to peek at my phone and stifle a laugh when Kieran excuses himself to take a call.

Video of the Steel in the locker room after last week's win replays during the PSN segment. Half the team is shirtless, wearing grins wider than their chests. The camera pans through a tunnel of biceps and chiseled torsos until it reaches the star of the show. I snort as Antonio gyrates to "Atomic Dog." He flexes for the cameras with his tongue on display.

He's in his element and doesn't miss a beat winking for the camera. That lip bite and those muscles rippling across his hard body will send half of America into a hot flash—assuming his thighs in the team's rugby shorts don't cause instant cardiac arrest.

All of him is a work of art, but it's Antonio's aura that will make him a household name. Everything about him is magnetic.

I minimize the screen and text him.

> Look at you on prime time! I'm so proud.

We're not in the best place right now, but I'll always root for him.

The clip fades to an empty locker room. Antonio sits on a stool in his team travel gear with a mic clipped to his collar. Light catches on his waves and his smooth caramel face splitting into a wide smile.

I enlarge the video as he pulls Kenya into a hug. She's camera ready, with straight black hair flowing over a sleeveless blouse. I have no right to be upset—that's the wrong word. What am I? Disturbed by the weight in my chest at their exchange of laughter and the *be my man* in her eyes. But Antonio isn't my man, so what do I care if two old friends demonstrate affection in front of millions of viewers?

They're familiar with each other, the same way we are.

Friendly.

Bet his mouth is real friendly.

"Antonio Knight, impressive start to the season." Kenya crosses her legs, angling herself toward Antonio.

"The Steel aims to please."

The pain in my jaw from clenching my teeth becomes a full-blown scowl. They look good together, like one of those couples who post unblemished photos and cutesy videos involving a surprise trip to Greece and a Bichon Frisé.

Jealousy isn't a shade I wear often, but my growing appetite to choose violence over tiramisu says otherwise.

I reopen my messages to the thread with Marcela.

> Is it too late to go to Toronto with you this weekend?

Marcela

> Of course not. You good?

The melody of Kenya's laughter stomps on my last nerve.

> Yup! Looking forward to it!

It's not a lie, though staying up past my bedtime for forced socializing is not my idea of bonding. If it gets my mind off Antonio, I'll take one for the team—the team being these feelings that won't unhand me.

Kieran slides into his seat. "Sorry about that." His gaze sweeps over me. "How about I show you the lab now? That is, if you're up for a detour before I take you home."

An opportunity to get lost in software that costs more than my car *and* not think about my friend servicing a booty buddy?

"I'm coming for the programs," I say.

Kieran laughs. "I'm under no other impression. You made it clear tonight is a singular date."

Was I too mean?

"Relax, Miriam. I'm happy to have whatever time you allow."

"Alright. Let's get dessert to go."

Chapter 35

Antonio

I rush into an opposing player with the speed of a freight train. The impact lifts him into the air before I drive us both into the grass, landing with a hard thud. The player under me groans, and I smile as the ball rolls out of his arms.

Cho grabs it and sprints off to our try zone in a race against time and the three Seattle players who are on his tail. He breaches the try line and taps the ball in the middle, earning us five points.

"Tee!" Kendrick shouts, catching one thrown from the sideline.

He lines up the seam of the ball with the posts and takes six steps back to the left. The opposing team charges, but Kendrick sends the ball over the crossbar between the posts. Weight transfer and the ability to control his speed is why he's the best kicker in the league.

Flags raise to confirm the two-point conversion kick. The loud peal of the ref's whistle slices through the air. Halftime.

"Nice one." I slap hands with Kendrick.

"That was all you and this one." He tips his chin at Cho, who's jogging back to us.

Jiwon Cho, or "Cho," is the resident pretty boy on the team. We're still getting his head checked for delusions. He's a fort when it comes to ball carry and one of the slipperiest motherfuckers you'll meet charging through a gap.

"You on that juice, Cap?" Cho grins, scratching the jersey gripping his chest.

I flip him off. "Your headband is too tight."

Cho grew out his loose waves to his ears last season and added "cinnamon" highlights for sex appeal. He has his own fan club, the "Cho-Hards," who travel to different games for a glimpse of his muscles and the stupid-ass wink he does for attention.

"He's working through some shit," Kendrick offers. I graze the top of his braided ponytail with a slap.

"With Maid Miriam?" Cho's eyes light up. He's far too excited to talk about my business.

"The only thing being worked is my last fucking nerve." I cut my eyes at them. Kendrick motions that his lips are zipped, and Cho backs away.

Anyone can get it today, nosy teammates included.

I've been on ten since the first whistle, and I haven't let up. My stats in this game alone might break league records the way I've been bulldozing through the Seattle team. A few ran away to steer clear of my path of destruction. At one point, Bread shouted, "Get 'em, CT!" when I was carrying defenders on my back. I high-stepped my way to a try like it was an elimination battle on *The Challenge*.

On the outside, I'm having the best game of my career. On the inside, I'm barely holding it together.

Miriam texted two nights ago, after my first PSN interview aired. I was on cloud fucking nine after a practice that could have made me a leading man in an Icy Hot commercial. I pictured those dimples denting her cheeks. Then I pictured my mama sobbing in front of a courthouse in the blue suit she only wears for special occasions before my televised hearing for killing a man.

In no universe did I expect a "What are you doing?" text would lead to her responding, "On a date with Dickhead." She didn't write "Dickhead," but what's understood requires no explanation.

I sucked on her pussy like it was a special dietary need, only for her to run to Kieran? They're not coworkers, or friends that I know of. Why are they enjoying shared meals? Her happiness is all that matters. I want what's best for her. If that means supporting her with a suit-by-the-pack-wearing asshole who probably took her to an expensive place with complimentary bread imported from France and fine linens, I'll support her. I won't like the shit, but I'll do it.

Miriam altered my life the second she drove her stubborn ass up here in that moving truck. I'm not acting how I used to, and it hasn't bothered me. Much to my surprise.

I've never been with only one woman in my life and wouldn't know the first thing about relationships. But I can't shake what I feel for her. A friendship isn't enough, and I sure as fuck don't like her entertaining dickheads who will break her heart.

Shit, maybe she's right. I don't commit, and I'm not about to fail trying with her. I'm already losing her, and messing up what we have isn't an option.

So we're standing by while Dickhead swoops in?

"Fuck all that."

Usher's falsetto whines float over from the sidelines. Cho holds his phone in the air with his other arm around Kendrick. The two idiots sway to "U Got It Bad." Bread hits a dolphin dive, humping the ground without a lick of sense.

"What the hell is this, a match or *Dancing with the Stars*? Get your asses in the huddle!"

Steel jerseys scramble at Coach Titan's glower. Our assistant coach never found an *American Ninja Warrior* challenge he won't use as punishment. His Rick Fox curls and puppy dog eyes are for show. He will knock your head off of your shoulders and do it wearing a sweater vest.

He's still popping blood vessels shouting at Bread and Cho. Serves them right.

"Bring your ass too, Lover Boy!" he snaps at me.

"What did I do?"

We win by fourteen.

Cameras were on the pitch right after the ref blew the final whistle. My energy was somewhere on the ground next to the bodies I laid out, but I did my best to hold a smile with the flashing lights spotting my vision. The Steel stay in weekly highlight reels across sports networks. It keeps us relevant and keeps the reporters chomping at the bit for interviews.

I'm tired, hungry, and could really use a blunt.

"Great game, son." Coach Washington pats my shoulder and motions for me to follow him out of the empty locker room. Anyone who wasn't part of the Steel got the boot, and I swear a little "Hallelujah" slipped out of me.

The stadium corridor is a quiet pathway of overhead lights that lead to the parking lot. The team is on the bus. Some already hit the streets to celebrate.

"PSN wants live coverage of our matches," Coach says. "Your interview was a hit. With today's win, we'll have the airtime to increase our fan base."

I nod. "That's what's up. Any news from upstairs?"

"It's been quiet." He strokes his brow. "Keep up what you're doing. Back-to-back wins is a great start to the season."

"I can handle that."

"I know you can. See you on the plane tomorrow."

Coach shuffles off in the team's track suit to catch up with one of the analysts.

The team bus shakes from the bass of "Turn Down for What" and hollering like we won the championship. I pull out my phone to respond to the texts from my parents and Julian congratulating me on the win. A few DMs from women I've linked up with in Seattle trickle in, which I delete.

There's only one person I want to call.

It's ten thirty back in Buffalo, too late to call Miriam. She's probably asleep on her couch while a baking show plays in the background. I want to hear her voice, that giggle when she gets excited.

I want her frustration when she asks if I remembered to take my vitamins and I say no.

I want…her.

My fingers glide across the screen as I type out a quick message.

Hey! We won our game. Press was hectic, but it's fun. How's your night?

"Yo, Cap! You coming?" Kendrick leans out the door to the bus.

Between travel and trying to keep the Steel alive, maybe it's foolish to think about what I want. There's so little time for anything else.

A grin spreads at my buzzing phone. She's up.

Kenya

Are you still in the stadium? I'd love to get an interview before you leave.

She's here?

Dumb question. Kenya's new role at PSN covers the RLA. If she flew up from Cali, she's with the Seattle team.

Tuesday's interview was a whirlwind of cameras and a crew hovering mics and lights above my face. We didn't get a chance to catch up after, but maybe we can tonight.

"I'll get up with you later," I call over to Kendrick. I don't miss his frown, and Bread damn near pushes him down the steps to lean over the front seat.

"Don't make me snitch to Maid Miriam!"

"Chill," I chuckle. "Another interview came up." I'm single. I can be outside, deep in pussy if I want to. I'm not on that kind of time, though.

Bread nods. "Be safe, and look both ways before crossing the street."

"Why aren't you going out?" Kendrick mushes Bread's face as he squeezes up the stairs.

His smirk says it all. "Got a shorty coming to my room."

There's a collective groan on the bus.

"Not again!" Shins cries.

"I got you. See you, Cap." Kendrick waves.

I can shower in the locker room. I wasn't planning on going out, but I can take one more interview.

Chapter 36

Antonio

"Thank you for waiting." Kenya slides a nail across my back and sits on the open barstool next to me.

"And miss dinner at the Seasons?" I point to my glass. "You're paying, right?"

She swats me with her pocketbook, which is the weight of a brick, and tosses her hair. "You wish! Do you ever dine with a woman at an actual table?"

I stroke my beard. "Does McDonald's count?"

"Stop!" Kenya's laughter floats down the bar. It's not packed, but a few heads turn. "Still noncommittal. One of these days, I'm getting you to change your ways." The split in her dress spreads over one leg as she crosses them.

Eyes up.

"Many have tried."

Commitment isn't an issue. I committed my ass to staying in the hotel lobby when Kenya invited me to her room after our interview. There's no guarantee we'd mess around, but I wasn't leaving anything to chance.

No tables is a preference. I'm not allergic to them—I have one at home—but with a dinner table comes assumptions. Food and drinks tend to be a promissory note for more. Bars are less messy, minus the communal peanuts with medieval diseases. Complimentary bread on a high-end tablecloth can get taken out of context fast.

Miriam got complimentary bread the other day.

Does she like him that much, to push around another salad on her plate?

I grab my phone off the bar and check my messages. Nothing.

> Did you fall asleep on the sofa bed again? Don't forget to blow out the candles. That's a fire hazard.

I should call to double-check she's safe.

Straight to voicemail.

"What are you having?" Kenya motions to the tumbler in front of me.

"Between the sheets," I rattle off, my mind on whether or not to have the fire department do one of those wellness checks.

"Tempting."

"Hmm." What if she's in her bedroom, knocked out in a bonnet and no bra? The fire department doesn't kick down doors in non-emergencies, does it?

"Everything okay?"

"What? Yeah." I reach for my glass and smirk at Kenya's head-shake. Guess it's hers now. "How's the new gig?" The bartender nods when I gesture for another drink.

"Good. I'm getting more airtime, and I negotiated better accommodations in my contract." She waves a hand around the smoke-gray room dressed in candles and shelves of aged scotch. The

Seattle Great Wheel towers Elliott Bay from the large window across the dining room.

Candles.

Miriam.

"I know they have good toilet paper."

"What?" Kenya snickers.

"Nothing," I say absentmindedly. What was the name of her neighbor with the dog? Maybe her number is public.

The bartender sets a new cocktail in front of me. "Are you two ready to order?"

Kenya's eyes drift to the menu. "I'll have the squash soup and tuna tartare. What do you want, Antonio? Tonight is on you."

"Yo!" I laugh. "I'll take the shrimp and grits, please." I eye Kenya. "Since I'm paying."

She raises my old glass. "To the new season."

"To you running my pockets." I lift mine.

"I paid five grand for you tonight. At Marcela's fundraiser."

Alcohol shoots through my nose. "What?" I cough.

Kenya's shoulder lifts. "It was for a good cause. I wanted to send a message."

"Which is?"

"You invest in what you want."

There's no trace of laughter in her voice, no mistaking what she means. Kenya is a knockout who's surprisingly down to earth. We always had a good time when we linked up. No drama or expectations. I'm flattered. Maybe under different circumstances, I'd consider the possibility of more than sex. But I'm wrapped up in a woman I haven't seen in weeks.

Kenya's fantasy material, but she's not Miriam.

"I'm considering moving back to Buffalo," she says.

"Why now?"

The charms in her bracelet clink when she twists her glass on the counter. "I'm interested in covering the Steel permanently. Some of my best memories are in Buffalo. It makes sense."

"Here you go." The bartender sets down our plates, cutting through the silence.

"No one died," Kenya laughs. "We have a good time together. Maybe we can see where it goes now that we'll see each other more."

I sigh. "Don't move for anyone but yourself."

"Are you still single?"

In one ear and out the other. "Technically, yes. I'm not trying to be mean, but I would've pursued something with you years ago if I felt it. Don't let me be a factor in your decision."

Kenya blinks at her plate. She's got an iron grip on her fork, like she might use it to draw blood. "Let me worry about me," she says through a whisper.

"I'll pay back what you spent at Marcela's fundraiser."

Marcela!

I knock over my fork and knife to get to my phone.

"Are you okay?"

"Yup. Shit." My phone scolds me for entering the wrong password twice. "Just checking something—aha!"

If Miriam isn't answering her phone, maybe she's with her sister. That would rule out the potential of a house fire.

My fingers run a mile a minute to pull up Marcela's social media. What pops up on her personal page has me swearing under my breath.

The video is dark, but strobe lights capture Miriam in the club clear as day, She's in a black dress that hugs her ass and heels that require a special license to operate. She fidgets with her hands and gets a slap on the ass from her sister when she tries to sit down.

Two other women surround her, making a half circle. Cheers ensue, and the smooth hips I've kissed flare to life with Mariah Carey's "It's Like That." I grin at Miriam's dimples tipped to the ceiling, along with her hands threading through the air.

Her joy is contagious, a high that requires a daily hit and protection at all costs.

"Get it, sis!" Marcela screams from the other side of the camera. "You might bag another engineer."

I beg your fucking pardon.

"Are you okay?" Kenya's brows knit. "You have a vein the size of a hose poking out your forehead."

My throat tightens, and my lungs constrict. "I'm fine," I growl.

There's no way Miriam found love in the two weeks we haven't seen each other. She's not dating. That's need-to-know information for your best friend, along with hand signals when you're over a party or what music to play at your funeral.

She wouldn't. Not with Dickhead or anyone else.

Hopefully she's still on the market.

I'll be damned. Bread was right.

"Ready to go?" I pull out my wallet.

"You barely ate." Kenya frowns at my plate.

"Right."

My phone is burning through my pocket, trying to keep Miriam out of sight. But she's still on my mind.

"Am I your one phone call?"

"No."

The line goes dead.

"No he didn't," I whisper-shout. Kendrick is knocked out in his bed. Shins is in mine, hugging his pillow.

I brought my sad ass back here after dinner, which ended in a hug and Kenya's disappointment. I'm not the kind of man to fuck while thinking about someone else. It's not fair to the woman I'm with, and it doesn't change the fact that I don't have the one I want.

I call again.

"You better be dying," Julian yawns.

"So much for our friendship. I doubt Matt Damon talks to Ben Affleck this way," I protest.

"He would if he called past midnight."

"Julie, who is that?"

"Antonio being an idiot," he tells Ella.

"*Hey!*" My tone hardens.

"Why are you whispering?"

"Because I'm trying to be respectful," I say. "Kendrick and Shins are asleep."

"Yet you called my phone to wake me up."

"I'm in a bad place and need advice."

"Put it on speaker," Ella says.

There's a muffled conversation. Julian lets out an exaggerated sigh.

"What? It better not be some bullshit, like someone's handcuffed to your bed again."

Ella gasps. "That happened?"

"Afraid so," I admit. "She put herself in a headstand and refused to leave."

"Oop!" Ella giggles.

"Get to the point, Antonio."

"Geez, so testy." I take a deep breath. "When did you know it was the right time to pursue Ella?"

"Aww," Ella coos. "Is this about Miriam?"

"Yeah." I grip the back of my neck.

"I believe he asked me the question, while you're climbing over me to get to the phone," Julian grumbles.

"Then answer," she challenges.

"It caught me off guard how quickly I cared about her. Her well-being, and the kids," Julian confesses. "I didn't think I was in a place where I was ready to settle down. Even in London, she had my heart. It got harder to stay away and deny what I felt. There was peace in pursuing her. Our timing wasn't perfect, but it felt right."

"Aww," Ella and I say in unison.

Bro kept his cards close to his chest, but the way he moved said it all. He cut off being outside to be with her.

Ring a bell?

"What's got you acting like I'm that lady with the couch?" *Smack.* "Ow! He called me, sweetheart. Obviously something happened," he says. "No more self-defense classes with Erica. I know you're giving Levi hell."

"She went on a date. A second date, with Dickhead," I mutter. I fill them in on Doe and her almost-boss. She's never hinted about liking him. Did I miss the clues?

"Something ain't right with him," I say. "Dude looks like Ghost from *Power*."

"He can't be trusted. What?" Ella sucks her teeth. "What role has he played where he's not causing trauma? *Being Mary Jane*."

"*For Colored Girls*." I shudder.

"I'm not staying on the phone going over that man's résumé," Julian snaps. "The point, Antonio."

"The point is, I don't know what to do! I like her. Hell, I love her."

"Aww," Ella says.

"I just…" I sigh. "This is all new to me. I've tried to ignore what I feel, but I can't stop thinking about her. I told myself we're better off as friends, but that doesn't feel right. We've been…intimate. Not *that*, but yeah."

"Bro." There's a smile in Julian's tone. *Smack.* "I can't be happy for my friend now? He's loved this woman since middle school and is finally admitting it."

"Have you told her how you feel?"

"No, El." I blow out a breath. "The last two times we were around each other, we didn't exactly talk. I don't know how to get her to see me differently."

"Show her," Julian says.

"I do! She's the only woman I talk to on the phone willingly. I took her shopping for house supplies. I painted. I rented a VIP suite in a Vegas club so she could come out and not get overstimulated. I made friendship bracelets."

"Now that's cute," Ella swoons.

"I don't know what else to do, and I don't want to lose her."

There it is, what I've been so afraid to admit out loud. I'm so far out of my element with Miriam, it scares the shit out of me.

"Tell her how you feel, but show her that the non-platonic side of you can be loyal and love her how she needs to be loved. Reassure her that taking your friendship to that level doesn't come with your track record in the streets. El wasn't around to see how I used to get down."

"Thank God!" she huffs.

Julian snickers. "Miriam needs to know it's safe to love you outside of the boundaries of your friendship. Your actions need to follow your words. That means no sides."

"Bro, I haven't been with another woman since she moved up here. The carpal tunnel in my—"

"Too much!" Julian and Ella say.

I drag a hand over my face. "You know what I mean. I'm serious."

Julian's tone lightens. "Sounds like it. You've been pining for her for almost two decades now. If you want her, go for it. Just give her the space to process. You're on her time now, and you have to respect whatever decision she makes. Ella tried to go on a date once. I shut that shit down." *Smack.* "Ow!"

"You did no such thing," Ella snickers. "The date was awful, but Julie ordered me tacos all the way from London to make up for it."

"I'd do it again, sweetheart."

Not again.

"I'll let you two go. Thanks for talking this through with me."

"We're always here for you." Ella squeals, "Julie, stop!"

"I'll hit you later." Julian's voice trails off, but not before he says to Ella, "Don't roll over. I'm up now."

The line goes dead.

I sit in the armchair across from my bed and scroll through pictures of me and Miriam. There aren't many because of the years of long distance, but we're making up for lost time.

My thumb hovers over the one from three years ago, of us in the emergency room. I pulled her in for a selfie. My smile is a grimace thanks to the tampon up my broken nose. Miriam looks off, like she's frustrated with the smile that's tempting her lips to curl. Even with her *Set It Off* braids and her wig stuck on my watch, she was the most beautiful woman in the room.

If you want her, go for it.

"See you soon, Doe."

Chapter 37

Miriam

I am not cut out for turning up.

This weekend was a reminder of why I keep my butt in the house. I spent two nights in Toronto with my sister, and it only took one to realize that regret would be in the room with us until we checked out.

Marcela wasted no time getting the weekend started. Our three-hour drive to Toronto ended in a late boozy lunch and checking into our hotel.

By five, we were out for dinner. Two hours later, we pregamed at her line sister's house like we were in undergrad and not nearing perimenopause. By ten, I was in a lounge with Marcela and her friends with a dead phone, sore feet, and a forgotten charger. Could I have picked one up earlier in the day? Yes. Did I keep my battery life in its coffin in order to not revive thoughts of Antonio? Also yes.

He goes silent before a game, doesn't check messages or talk to anyone except his coaches or teammates. I figured it wouldn't be a big deal to revert back to life in the Stone Age since he's usually busy anyway.

I miss him. His laughter, and how easy life is when he's around. It's impossible not to think about him physically now that our toes went over the line, but I'm trying. I try to forget his hard body exerting energy on the field in those tiny shorts. Or the parts of said body that almost put me through a mattress. Especially if they're satisfying other women.

With a new season comes new hookups and "old friends" who are apparently back in town. But do they know the real him?

Does Kenya get pieces of his joy, the Ace Ventura dance he does when he finds a snack buried in the pantry? How he lights up during off-season, when he gets to just exist in sweats, a tee, and no obligations? Or when hotels have two-ply toilet paper and prioritize liquid soap over recycled bars that resemble prison weapons after use?

Antonio is more than his looks and his wallet. He's one of the best people I know, with a heart bigger than every muscle on his body. A heart that draws me to him in ways I never predicted. We're magnets, total opposites in every way, and it's getting harder to fight the pull.

Distraction was my cognitive strategy to bury the feelings that followed me home from Vegas. Keeping myself busy was starting to work. Until Sunday, when he blew up Marcela's phone looking for me. I won't lie and say it didn't feel good for him to call her three times on his way to the airport. He got a tongue lashing in English and Spanish for bothering her before eight a.m., but he didn't care.

Ten minutes later, the concierge delivered a new charger to our room. I scrolled through the messages he left, but only one sent my heart through the wall.

We need to talk.

"Toro Mata" trumpets through my tiny kitchen. Celia Cruz always makes everything better, but she's doing nothing to calm my nerves right now.

What's so important that he'd get me a charger in a different country? He's not injured. The hospital would've called me since I'm still his emergency contact.

I expel a sharp breath and lift the ladle to my mouth to sip the *sancocho* that's been simmering on the stove for the last hour. When life becomes a complicated mess, I cook.

Rice with pigeon peas.

Patacones.

Potato salad.

It will take a week to eat through everything myself. Five pounds added to my hips, and I'll still be right here thinking about the potential soft launch of his first relationship. The chemistry between them was obvious based on what little I saw from the interview.

Kenya seems nice. She looks like she flosses regularly, does charity work, and gets to see him more during the rugby season. I should be happy at the possibility of my friend finding love. That's a big step, and I wish him a lifetime of happiness with whoever he chooses. Any woman would be lucky. Antonio is sweet. And hung.

I sigh and shake my head. Here I go, thinking about another woman's man. I know better.

We'll both find life partners at some point, and I don't want to lose him. If we want any chance of maintaining our friendship, we can't be so close. The texts, the late-night calls before Vegas. His skilled mouth on me.

That last one. *Whew.*

Focus.

The point is, I'm not supposed to fall for him.

With the burner off, I shuffle to an overhead cabinet for a bowl and scream at the figure on my back porch. It's more of an *eep!*, one Celia's version of the Afro-Peruvian classic smothers. So much for signaling my pending doom to the neighbors.

I twist down the dial on the portable music player Antonio bought. Another housewarming gift that fits perfectly with my retro-style kitchen. It will be the final memory I have before the person outside of my home goes on a murdering spree and steals my food.

Hiding isn't an option. The blinds are up on the back door. Whoever is out there has a full view of me frozen in place like a deer before it messes up your deductible. The window isn't big enough to climb through. Breaking in through the door is a different story.

I'm not ending up on *The First 48*.

I reach for a weapon and startle at a tap.

"Doe, it's me," Antonio says against glass now painted with his breath.

"Why didn't you go to the front?"

"I did. I rang the doorbell, and I called."

I wipe the sweat from my brow and roll my eyes at the tongs in my hand. What was I going to do with these, flip him over in a skillet?

I expected him to be on my front porch when I got home around noon. He wasn't, and he's been silent since yesterday's vague text, which I have yet to decipher. My exasperated sigh becomes a gasp when I open the door.

Light from the kitchen streaks the edges of Antonio's face. Our gazes catch like it's the first time we're seeing each other, but it's only been two weeks—fifteen days, if we want to be specific.

My bare feet retreat on their own once he steps inside and locks the door. His eyes slide down the blue paisley midi dress I wear around the house and land on my cotton candy pedicure. My kitchen is functional, but it's tiny. Now that he's sucked all the air out of the room, it feels the size of a dollhouse.

"Food." I blink away the lust clouding my judgment and my urge to crack a window. "I made food. For dinner." I fumble with the spatula and stir *sancocho* that doesn't need stirring. Fluffing rice and checking an oven I never turned on buy me time to slow my heart rate.

My breath gets more audible with every step he takes to reach me. His chest rises and falls when it makes contact with my back, the hard ridges of muscle under a cream Henley pressed firmly against me.

Do not inhale his pheromones. He must be jet-lagged. Maybe a little high.

I do a Jean-Claude Van Damme split reaching for a formula or equation, something to focus on that's not Antonio's hands trailing up my arms, which are now peppered in goosebumps.

"I missed you," he says, prickling the tiny hairs on my neck.

"Yes, same." I double-check that all of the burners are off. He must really be jet-lagged. "It's part of the season, right? You away in different cities." An image of him impaling Kenya flares my nostrils. *Be his friend.* "Meeting new people and playing different teams. Old friends. Do you want rice? It has pigeon peas. Not sure if you've had them before, but they have a nutty flavor." *Don't think about nuts.* "Great source of protein and iron."

"Miriam." His thumbs rest over the straps of my dress.

What is he doing?

"Th-the *patacones* are a little crispy but they still taste good."

"Miriam."

"This confuses me," I whisper, damn near out of breath. Between my stomping heartbeat and the sensation building between my thighs, I'm at my limit. "Whatever this is has to stop." I won't let him mess up his first relationship.

"Yeah?" His voice is low, rough.

"Yes." I swallow a moan at the heat from his fingers down my back.

Be strong.

"I don't want to ruin our friendship," I say.

"I won't let us," he counters, twirling a curl from my twist-out between his fingers.

Be strong.

I grab the skillet. "What about Kenya? A-aren't you together?"

"Not even close. She's not the one I think about."

Bitch, be strong!

My breath hitches at his hand on mine. Every ounce of resolve drains from my body.

"If we cross this line—"

"We already did."

I turn just enough to look him in the eyes. The air is knocked out of me when Antonio's mouth crashes onto mine. His hands hold my face as he tilts my head to suck on my lips. I stumble at the force of his body pushing against mine before I'm lifted into the air.

Where the hell is my strength?

Girl, it's gone.

His lips on my skin isn't what shocks me. What shocks me is that I'm kissing him back.

A moan slips, and he chases it with his tongue. My arms wrap around his neck as our kiss deepens. Searching. Unleashing.

He walks us to my kitchen table and clears it with a swipe of his hand. The salt and pepper shakers and the lemon bowl I spent an hour rearranging crash to the floor.

"Sorry," he mumbles against my mouth.

"It's o—" I groan at the erection pressed between my parted legs. My hips buck, an invitation for him to rock the weight of his length into my center.

"Let me take care of you," Antonio says, showering kisses down my neck.

I lean back on my palms, anchored to the table. At no point does common sense activate to tell me that this is a bad idea. My common sense is grabbing her ankles in the air.

My breasts are in his face, and he caresses them, massaging the plump curves between his hands. I widen my legs so his tongue can continue its voyage down my body. Our eyes meet, and I bite my bottom lip when he pinches my nipple between his fingertips.

Cotton skates over my sensitive buds, and I free them with the push of my straps.

He's practically drooling when he dives in. The suction of his mouth and the pull of his teeth are enough to send me through the wall. I hiss at the pads of his fingers over my clit, and it becomes a cry when he pushes inside of me. He moans at my lack of panties and pumps in and out.

It should be embarrassing how wet I am. The echo of my desire is louder than Celia Cruz. My hips buck at the pressure building between my legs.

"Fuck my hand." Antonio pecks my lips and fists my throat. "Yeah, that's it. Harder, Doe."

My body must have received a memo that said we like being choked on a kitchen table. My back arches off the table when his other hand presses down on my abdomen. He inserts a third finger and increases his speed.

I jerk from the explosion of pressure, short-circuiting in English and Spanish curse words when I come.

Antonio squats, tossing my legs over his shoulders. I get a kiss to the thigh before he latches on to my engorged hood.

He sucks hard, pulling my clit deeper into his mouth. I push him away once it's too much, but he pulls me back in. His tongue spreads, and the room spins as his pace quickens.

"Slide it over my beard," he commands, separating my thighs to lick me in long strokes. His deep moan is all I need to ride him and his beard.

I know for a fact this man licked his plate clean when he was a child.

He meets me thrust for thrust until I come hard.

Antonio kisses up my thighs until his mouth returns to my lips. The scent of his cologne mixes with the taste of my arousal.

"Hi," he says, his face satisfied.

"Hi." I'm panting like I ran to the mailbox and back. "Are you hungry?"

He smiles. "I could eat again."

Chapter 38

Miriam

"Cela, I let him put his mouth on me again."

"Are you pooping? I hear the vent fan."

I frown. "No. I'm sitting on the toilet—"

"Girl, we are not that close." Marcela sucks her teeth.

"Wait! I'm not using the bathroom. I'm in here to call you."

"Who did what with a mouth?"

This is why I need actual friends. Ones I don't let put their fingers and tongue inside me. The high from the kitchen vanished after I peeled myself off the table.

"Antonio is on the couch."

"*Okayy*. He's been over there before," she says.

"We...Well, he—"

"You finally did it?!" I tear the phone from my ear and stare up at the ceiling. I don't know if my sister cheering for my vagina is a sign of support or cause for concern.

My glasses shift with a pinch to the bridge of my nose. Any minute, she'll stop hollering.

"We didn't have sex!" That gets her quiet. "I mean, he gave me oral and fingered me—"

"TMI, Miri," she warns.

"Sorry. I like to talk in facts, and I don't know how to act around him since it's the second time."

She gets a summary of Vegas and what transpired after. I leave out specific details, like the weapon between Antonio's legs and how much I soaked the sheets. By the time I get to me being the unexpected appetizer on my kitchen table, I'm out of breath from my brain trying to catch up with how fast I'm talking.

"Say something, please." Marcela's name is still sprawled across my screen in white letters. "What do you do when you cross the line with someone you care about?"

"What do you *want* to do?"

"I—That's why I called you! I don't have experience with this, and I don't know how to go about determining the best solution."

Bossing me around my entire life with nothing to say now?

Why is she laughing?

"My sweet sister. Love is not an equation to solve."

It'd be easier if it was.

"This isn't helping! You're supposed to tell me that messing around is the fastest way to send our friendship straight to Hell. That these urges are because of our proximity. That he doesn't love me like that."

"We're talking about the same Antonio, right?" Her tone is full of sarcasm. "The fool who called me because he couldn't reach you, who had a charger sent to the room? That boy loves you, and I'd bet he's loved you for some time."

"I like him, but I don't want to get hurt. We've never been this way, and I'm afraid we're going to ruin what we have." I roll the toilet paper back and forth over the holder.

"If he only cared about sex, he wouldn't still be at your house." Marcela's voice softens. "For someone like Antonio to dedicate time to you means you're special—as he should! You fools have fallen asleep on the phone. You've kept a level of intimacy for years now. You said you're open to dating. Whoop, there it is."

The toilet tank's cold porcelain digs into my back. "Our pairing would be illogical."

"And yet, he's your person."

There's a knock on the door. "You good in there, Doe? I can get you something for your stomach if you need," Antonio says.

I bite back a smile. "I'm fine. I'll meet you in the kitchen to eat."

Marcela's chuckle tempts my eyes to roll to the back of my head. "Don't overthink it, Dr. Baby. I wish I had someone who cared about my guts after using his tongue to play with my stomach lining. Love can be scary when red flags aren't smacking you in the face. Trust your instincts. You'll do what's right."

"For the record, I had no intention of eating your pussy when I came over."

I snort into my soup. Here I was trying to find a way to break the ice after Antonio had my legs reaching for the ceiling on this very table.

"I wanted to put eyes on you and talk. I'm sorry if I made you uncomfortable."

Oh, you did the opposite, friend.

I adjust my glasses. "It's...We're okay."

He stares, deadpan. "You look like you're ready to cook oxtails and run to the store for scratch-offs."

After my call with Marcela, I went to change. I didn't want any distractions for the conversation we needed to have. A muumuu was appropriate.

My "don't touch me" outfit did nothing. Antonio is eyeing my ornate display of ruffles like I can get it with a promise to pay all of my bills.

He's still in the Henley pulling across his chest and loose denim teasing those thighs. Hot and unbothered.

"More rice? Potato salad?"

The deep rasp of his chuckle forces my attention back to my plate. There aren't enough sides on this table to mark me safe from his stare.

Antonio wipes the mouth he used to lick me clean. "Relax, Doe. I know what to do if I want seconds."

He means the food.

I clear my throat and spear a bite of potato salad. "How was Seattle?"

"Seattle was good."

"Oh nice. It must be beautiful. The parks and greenbelts." I fiddle with one of the plants on the table, courtesy of the man across from me. The breath lodged in my lungs burns with every second that passes.

"Can—"

"I don't want to lose what we have because our comfort keeps fueling these outbursts," I say before my nerves take over.

My gaze slides over the spoon hovering inches from Antonio's lips. "I was going to ask you to pass the potato salad."

Oh.

"You think what's happened between us is because of comfort?" His brow raises.

"What other explanation is there? We were fine for years."

"Because of distractions." He regards me with a look I haven't seen before. "You were finishing school. I was entering the league. Don't you see how special you are to me?"

The weeks apart have been unbearable, but they're a far better option than the alternative should things crash and burn. Not having Antonio in my life wouldn't just hurt; it would change the DNA of my future.

He's the one I went to when I was stressed with school, the one who'd listen to my engineering rants. He's the person who reminds me there's more to life than structures and equations.

Marcela is right: He's my person.

I expel a long breath. "What if you get tired of whatever it is we're doing?"

Antonio unfolds himself from his chair. He pulls me to my feet and wraps me in his cologne-scented hug.

"We can't go back. You know it, and so do I," he soothes, kissing the top of my head. "If you knew how long I've wanted you. You're the first person I think of when I wake up and my last thought before I go to sleep. Our friendship is our foundation, not the ceiling. There is no pressure because it's us, Doe."

His grip tightens against my waist, molding my body to his. No scientific principle will help me make the right decision. My heart has to take the lead.

"Can we take it slow?"

"I'm on your time," he whispers into my curls. "We go at your pace. No pressure, remember?"

"Just us," I repeat to release the weight of the what-ifs caving in my chest.

"Miriam, if I have you, I want all of you. Give Dickhead his walking papers before I send a cane to his house."

A cane?

Antonio's eyes slide down to mine with an expression that has me cackling.

"You're serious?" I muffle a laugh.

"I don't play about you."

"We went out because he bid on himself so he could take me to dinner. He let me use the Maple King lab after—"

"At night?"

"No sunlight was in the sky," I confirm, rolling my lips at his scowl. "I'm not the one with the reputation of slinging dick across states. Remind me who should be worried?"

"I haven't been with another woman since I ran into you at the MLK celebration." He has the nerve to look offended.

"And Ms. Pon de Replay?" I hike a brow. "You two love putting on for the cameras."

Whatever fear shifts to a premeditated felony at the thought of Antonio swiping his player card like a Costco membership.

"You're wild for 'Pon de Replay.' She's not an issue." He snickers and shakes his head. If the Rihanna song fits. "Setting boundaries with Kenya will be easy because I already have. Outside of interviews and the dinner for your sister's fundraiser, there's no reason for us to see each other. I wouldn't pursue you if I still wanted to fuck other people."

"You better set boundaries if you want access to me. *¿Qué crees?*" I scoff, my lips balled like a fist. "If you think you get to hop around in booty shorts—"

"Booty shorts?" Antonio's head tips back with a laugh.

"—and hump on whoever while you're home or away, forget it."

The Buffalo Steel would need to replace their star flanker. Permanently. Thoughts of sex tapes and secret families in Iowa cloud my vision just to piss me off.

"Doe!" He cackles like his mother wouldn't iron her favorite suit if he tried it. "I respect you and what we have too much. No one will come between us, I promise you that. I can't take back what's in the past, but I can protect our future." He pecks my lips. "I'm already committed to you. Trust me please. We'll go at your pace, okay?"

"Okay," I say.

My skin prickles at his mouth over mine. The kiss is slow, and he follows it up with one to the bridge of my nose.

His stare lingers. "I have to go."

"You just got back," I pout.

"I know." He sighs. "Kendrick and I have some press lined up in New York City before we join the rest of the team in Chicago."

Well, damn. I'm losing my man faster than I got him.

"Come lock up." Antonio steps into his shoes near the back door without lacing them up, then pats his pockets for his keys. When our eyes finally meet, there's a sadness he masks with a half smile.

"Our schedule is crazy this week, but I'll call you every chance I get." He tips up my chin. "I'll never get tired of you. Not in any scenario."

Antonio drops a kiss onto my lips before stepping into the winter night.

Are we really doing this?

Chapter 39

Antonio

"Here are the approved questions we went over on the plane. They're straightforward—what position you play, how rugby is different from football, and if you bench-press cars to maintain your physique. Phylicia likes to put her guests in the hot seat. Expect at least one question about your personal life, but don't feel like you need to answer if she prods too much."

"Hey, Reese?" Her dark brown eyes lift from the tablet that's now pressed to her chest. "I got it," I say.

"Of course you do." At her energetic headshake, a thick strand of hair falls out of the nest pinned to the top of her head. "You've been great! Your interviews stay on message and keep viewers excited. *The Borough Squad* airs live and streams to social media. There's a fifteen-second delay to catch profanity, but keep it clean, please."

"Reese?"

"You got it," she says.

If she didn't naturally operate like a squirrel who snorted a line, I'd tell her to sleep off the gallon of coffee she ingests before noon. She is as efficient as she is thorough in managing the Steel's media. Full of energy and sometimes forgetting to breathe.

Today has been a nonstop tour of New York City traffic across three of the five boroughs. It's been quiet at the top with management, and it better stay that way with all of the press we're getting. You'd think I have a movie, an album, and a memoir dropping. Many professional athletes dream of getting to this point. I'm grateful, but I want to dream in my own bed, in the house I pay for that has good toilet paper.

"Kenneth, are you satisfied with your prep? I'm happy to hold a quick session before you go in."

Outside of Kendrick's mama and grandma, Reese is the only person who calls him by his government name.

"Kenneth, are you okay?" Reese asks, her brows tight, her body angling to spring into action.

"Y-yeah." Kendrick clears his throat and tugs at the collar of his button-down. "I'm straight, thank you."

"Okay! I have a few calls to make, but I'll stop by before your interview. See you soon!" Reese strolls off with a smile in her *Baby-Sitters Club* outfit. I only caught a few episodes when I was younger, but I know a Mary Anne 'fit when I see one. The long socks tucked into patent leather loafers, corduroy skirt, and a blouse under a sweater scream, *Here come the '90s.*

"You should ask her out," I say to Kendrick. He's still staring down the hall.

"We're here on business, Cap." He digs his shoe into the graphite carpet lining the way to the studio.

"Business." I volley back his bullshit.

Bro is dressed to knock on doors on Saturday. Never once has Kendrick willingly signed up for media training, or to speak in front of an audience. He's a man of few words and no close-ups. But guess who volunteered to spend the day with me in New York City, bouncing between studios to help promote the Steel?

"I'll fall back with this interview since you got it." I grin at his scowl. "That's what I thought. Let's go."

I bet he laid out the white button-down and black slacks last night. After he booked a last-minute appointment for fresh twists and a line-up.

All for business.

Reese waves from inside a glass room. Kendrick swallows and averts his eyes while mumbling to himself.

Yeah, he's got it bad.

I squeeze his shoulder. "Take it from me, don't wait eighteen years to ask her out. She might be married by then with six kids and two dogs."

Kendrick is quiet before he sighs. "It's not like that between us. What you worried about me for anyway, Papa Smurf? You ever gonna make a move on Miriam?"

"Already did."

It hasn't registered that Miriam and I are together. There's no title yet, but I want this if she does. Travel and these media commitments are a boil on my ass. It's been impossible to stay in Buffalo for more than a day—two, if I'm lucky. Being away was never an issue when she was in Baltimore. I kept busy to pass the time and never had a reason to be home. She *is* my home. I'm not wasting any more time. I'm doing what I should've done years ago.

Hold on and never let go.

"Papa Smurf is in love." Kendrick's twists shake with his laugh. "It's nice to see it finally happen. You two are a good look, for real."

"To think we could double-date." I fold my arms over my sweater and stop outside the room of our radio interview. "Why do you insist on hurting my feelings, Kenny?"

"Chill," he groans. "She's cool, but she—"

"Good, you're still here!" Reese zips around the corner, panting. Her cheeks are pink against her maple complexion, which is covered in a thin layer of sweat. "We had a last-minute cancelation today, but that's okay! I pulled some strings and confirmed another interview after this, with chicken wings. Possibly a dunk tank. We'll end closer to nine, and I'll have you two on a plane to Chicago before midnight. There's one more change in the schedule."

My brows furrow. "What?"

Reese bites her lip and glances at Kendrick. He lifts his hands. "Whatever you're about to say doesn't involve me."

"It's not bad news, but it will require a few adjustments," she says, assuring no one. "We'd like for you to take on a few events on the west coast, after next week's game against Utah."

"Define 'a few,'" I say.

"A late show, two podcasts, and another PSN in-studio. I can get you back to Buffalo on Wednesday."

"That's halfway into our bye week." It's also three days too many away from Miriam. "I want the first flight out on Tuesday after that game."

"I'll see what I can do. And I'll work on a schedule for home games. It won't be as hectic moving forward."

"Appreciate you, Reese," I say.

"No problem! Let me see if *The Borough Squad* is ready for us."

The way today is going, I'll be lucky to get ten minutes to call Miriam once she's off work. Something will need to give.

All of this means nothing if it costs me her.

Chapter 40

Miriam

Time-out with a Lego set isn't so bad, especially when you're done adulting.

I'm not on punishment, but I've met my quota for talking and being around people over five feet tall. Hence my own exile to the quiet corner of my classroom that I use for sensory play. Decompressing is real, and building creates a flow state to channel stress.

Today was a lot—an aspirin and an animal tranquilizer to put me out of my misery kind of day. I also got a parking ticket three minutes after my meter expired!

The morning was a block of meetings I managed to survive from the corner of a cramped conference room with a large table, no windows, and a fan plugged in to circulate air between the bodies generating heat. Aanya called together food advocates, urban growers, block club leaders, and community members who could spare the time away from their jobs before we went to City Hall.

For years, there have been cries for Buffalo to use the thousands of vacant lots in its possession for public benefit. Most of that land is here on the East Side, unused and crawling with weeds.

What I learned from today's meeting in Aanya's office, which violated fire code, is that community nonprofits try to buy the lots but are hit with unaffordable market rates.

If there's one thing I hate more than a problem that doesn't want to be solved, it's having a solution that people in power refuse to implement.

And beads of sweat rolling down your back. I hate that too.

Marcela was a one-woman army during today's City Council meeting. She was the physical manifestation of patience, dressed in a blue suit and door-knocker earrings she surely wanted to pelt at her colleagues' heads. That didn't stop her from calling her fellow councilmembers and the mayor to the carpet for allowing vacant land to remain neglected.

The process to obtain lots is arduous, shutting out residents and community groups. Why is it so hard to do the right thing? People put you in office to uphold their best interests, not to waste their time and tax dollars making their lives harder.

Sitting bare-ass on thumbtacks would have been more comfortable than being inside council chambers. Stories of elders and others taking buses to reach food sources because the nearest supermarkets are miles away—in wealthier and less diverse areas—was downright shameful. Buffalo might be the City of Good Neighbors, but it's one of the most segregated cities in the country.

Marcela has been fighting for changes to local zoning laws to support more affordable housing and farming efforts, as well as land disposition policies that prioritize East Side residents in vacant lot purchases. She also wants to reserve at least thirty percent of available vacant land for sustainable efforts.

Farming.

Parks.

Community gardens.

Housing.

Public art.

The math maths, and the dollars make sense.

I left the council meeting out of Twizzlers and with a migraine. Testimonies fell on deaf ears. City Council tabled the conversation, shutting down my sister and community residents.

The chaos, masked as political process, was enough for me to take a vow of silence for the rest of the day. The kids also had a rough day, so we kicked off our shoes and pulled out Legos, kinetic sand, and slime.

"Jayden went home. You're out of kids."

I glance at Ms. Amber in the doorway. "That was fast."

"Time flies when you're having fun," she laughs, nodding to the tables of houses, skyscrapers, playgrounds, and farms. "You should keep these."

I smile. "Plan to. I asked them to reimagine a Buffalo they want to live in and build it. We have art to go with it. Cleaner waterways. More accessible harbor space. The city could learn a thing or two."

Kids have the smallest voices but the biggest imaginations, un-restricted by limited thinking, corruption, and how things "should be." They remind me of myself when I was younger. I fell in love with engineering because of the possibilities. They're endless if we only dare to dream.

"Speaking of reimagining." Ms. Amber steps under the fluorescent lights wearing jeans and a worn sweater. "I want to talk to you about your position."

The pit of my stomach drops, and I silently curse myself for wearing a blouse and dress pants. If I'm getting fired, I want to be comfortable.

"Okay." I push my glasses up the bridge of my nose.

She sits down at a small table decorated in Lego creations and brushes back a curl from her silver pixie cut. Charades and mind reading aren't talents I possess, so I sit there staring.

"We received a donation that's large enough to begin work on our renovation projects and expand our programming."

"Amazing! Congratulations."

"The donor requested we make your position full-time to support the incredible STEM work you're doing."

All I can do is blink. My position isn't publicly advertised as part-time. It's just my name and title on the website. Who would know I don't work full-time and invest in me?

Marcela doesn't have the funds. Her corporate job paid good money, but not like *that*.

My mother...no comment. And any funds from my father would come with a long lecture about using my talent.

Kieran doesn't know enough about my business to intervene. He also doesn't strike me as someone who would give without cameras present.

Which leaves one person.

My heart somersaults in my chest. "Antonio," I whisper.

"Mr. Knight, yes." Ms. Amber's tone is cautious, her brows creasing the fine lines in her chocolate skin. "But he asked to remain anonymous."

How did he not think I wouldn't piece it together? He's always doing things he assumes will go unnoticed, like the stash of Twizzlers that popped up in my mailbox. Even in his absence, he makes his presence known.

"I won't tell. He's my—my—"

The warmth of Ms. Amber's smile echoes in her voice. "He mentioned a friend when the Steel were here in January. Someone in engineering, whom he spoke fondly of. That was you?"

"Yes."

Her grin spreads. "He seems like a fine young man. Handsome too."

"The best," I say, my voice thick and unsteady.

Antonio never ceases to amaze. His attention to detail and care for my needs render me speechless. The simplest gestures—the non-Valentine's Day gifts from the Houston Space Center, ordering me a phone charger from a different country—are reminders he's thinking of me. He's very thoughtful, but this is love. Not just for me, but for the community center and the kids who fulfill me every week.

"I have to go," I say, already on my feet.

It's a fight to not break down in front of my boss with big, messy tears and Florida Evans theatrics. My emotions and I don't do PDA, but this man has me ready to be a spokesperson on its behalf.

I hug Ms. Amber, her price to enter and leave the premises, grab my bag and coat off the rack, and rush out the door. My boot buckles clink over worn linoleum. I want to sprint to my car, which is under the spell of never-ending winter, and drive to Steel House. But Antonio isn't there. He left for Utah with the team yesterday to acclimate to the higher elevation before Saturday's game.

One day together wasn't enough. By the time I made it to him after work, he'd fallen asleep with a granola bar dangling from his mouth. Sleep knocked him out for the rest of the night. I stayed in his arms on the couch, studying the shadows of his profile, which was softened from hard-earned rest.

Antonio and the rest of the Steel are getting national attention. The recent media blitz and their undefeated record are bringing more fans into the world of rugby. I don't like him being away for so long, but the videos of him online keep me company. They're slo-mo shots of the team's forearms and wide thighs. I'm not ashamed to say that I saved a few of Antonio's ass in rugby shorts, and a well-timed video of the deep cut of his abs clinging to his drenched jersey.

To them, I say, thank you for your service.

My pulse leaps when my phone rings until I realize it's the factory-setting jingle and not the dial-up modem that's sent me diving over the sofa on an occasion or two. Okay, six.

"Hey." My attempt to chamber the flat greeting fails.

"Don't sound so excited." Kieran's chuckle travels down the line.

"Sorry. Long day and a lot on my mind." *Like a man who isn't you.* I cradle the phone between my ear and shoulder to zip my coat. "Did you need something?"

"I wanted to see about dinner, if you're up for it."

"Tonight?" I scrub my brow and think of my date with the DVR and a pint of ice cream.

"I haven't seen you since our first date. We can go back to my office, and you can use the lab again."

Damn him and that beautiful space.

A man in a trench coat could lure me into a sketchy van if he promised a computer with finite element analysis software.

I spent hours in the Maple King lab, skipping down a long rabbit hole and into a wonderland of ideas for my job. Everything I needed was at my fingertips. My mind was on technology I hadn't accessed since I graduated. Not romance.

Kieran stayed in his office most of the night. He never tried to kiss me, and I showed no signs of interest. There were a few sidelong glances from my eyes to my lips, but nothing to suggest a future proposal.

Marcela always told me people set too-high expectations on first dates, and that leads to delusion or a misdemeanor. The allure of access to material properties applications and visualizing stress conditions is what drew me back to the state-of-the-art facility. I sent no calls or texts since then for Kieran to be inquiring about a same-day dinner almost two weeks later.

"I don't think that's a good idea." The chill in the air latches on to my breath on my way out the door. No spring in sight. Only Mother Nature's freezer.

Kieran stays silent as I open my car door and start the engine. A puff of frost billows from the vent. "Okay," he says in a clipped tone. "How about tomorrow?"

"I don't think us spending time together is a good idea." There goes my emotional high from earlier. I hate talking about feelings when it's not necessary. "I think you're nice, Kieran."

"But you don't see this going anywhere."

Well. He said it.

"Dinner was enjoyable—"

"Please don't tell me you went because of charity. I thought we were past that."

Had Kieran not bid on himself, we never would've gone out a second time. I wasn't obligated to go in the first place, but I don't believe in wasting money. If he thought he could buy his way into a relationship, it was a miscalculation on his part. I'll miss the lab, but I'm not about to end up in something I don't want, or in the trunk of his car because he can't deal with rejection. Those Netflix documentaries are terrifying.

Kieran's low chuckle has me checking my back seat. His tongue kisses his teeth. "I'm disappointed, Miriam. I don't like to waste my time."

Is this where people usually say, "It's not you, it's me," and "We can still be friends"? Small talk is so pointless.

"Good luck with your projects," I add, so I don't come off a complete jerk.

Click.

Okay, then.

I wave at my neighbor, who's rescuing the sidewalk from pounds of snow when I pull up to my house. Another storm blew through, dumping inches and trauma over the region.

Heat and the scent of vanilla greet me when I step through the front door. Inside is my daily reminder of Antonio.

The sofa we ate on.

The bookshelves he built.

The shower curtain he annihilated.

My bedroom he helped paint.

That damn kitchen table.

I drop my coat on the rack and fish out my phone. Antonio picks up on the second ring.

"Hi, Doe." His voice is a steady calm over the clang of dishes and chatter on the other end of the line.

"You're out." Of course he is. It's four thirty in the afternoon in Utah, two hours behind. "I'll talk to you later."

"It's okay," he says in a rush. "I can talk. One sec."

The noise dissolves.

"Hi."

I smile. "Hi."

A beat passes before we speak.

"I miss you," we say at the same time.

The strength in my breath crumbles at the distance between us and his three words. We've said them to each other before, within the security of our friendship, when they didn't mean more. When I didn't want more.

"How was your trip?" My throat tightens at the sting of tears.

"Cramped," he says. "I had the middle seat between Bread and Shins for the flight from Chicago."

I snicker at the visual. "Sorry to hear."

"You don't sound like it."

We let laughter take over.

"I miss hearing your laugh in person, Doe."

More silence.

"I wanted to call you to thank you for your donation to the center. I'm speechless."

"I told Ms. Amber I wanted to stay anonymous," he groans.

"You are. She never advertised my job as part-time, so it was easy to guess who the donor was. Why did you do it? I mean, you didn't need to."

The rapid beat of my heart reveals the obvious. I know the answer, but I've been too scared to admit what's been here all along.

"I love you, Miriam."

I exhale through shallow gasps. Tears tangle with my words. "I love you too." My voice trembles.

"Don't cry, baby. I'll always support you. Your dreams, your desires. All of it. I'm your biggest fan, and I'll show it for the rest of my life. How was your day?"

"Better now that we're talking." I wipe my face. "The council meeting was awful. They tabled the discussion to make vacant lots more accessible to the community. It's not surprising, but the mediocrity offends me."

"I'm sorry, baby."

I bite my lip. "I like when you call me that."

"Noted." There's a smile in his voice.

"Aye. Cap. Coach is looking for you," someone says in the background.

Antonio sighs. "I need a minute."

"They're keeping you busy." I sag into the soft fibers of my sofa.

"I'm ready to take a year's worth of naps," he says between a yawn.

"You look good on screen."

"You checking me out, Doe?"

A smile creeps across my face. "I'm your biggest fan who supports your dreams. Have you heard anything from the owner?"

"Nah, it's been quiet. I'm taking that as a good sign for now." Forever the optimist. "Mancini is a businessman first. Three consecutive wins and all this press brings in more team sponsors. He's an ass, but he's not stupid."

"Have you ever thought about owning a team?" I ask. "Maybe the problem requires a different solution."

"One day, when I'm no longer playing." He huffs, and I imagine him rubbing his jaw. "The annual operating costs are in the millions, not to mention the millions needed to buy in. I want to do something good, Doe."

"You are. You could've bought a bachelor pad for yourself when you moved up here, but instead you thought about your teammates," I say. "You've covered travel costs and accommodations. You babysit to help out a single dad. Your contribution at the community center not only helps me, but will get programming and much needed repairs off of the ground. You don't have to worry about doing something good because you are good, Papa Smurf."

"Thank you for the reminder," Antonio whispers, his voice gravelly. "Can I take you out when I get back next week? There's something I want to do with you."

"Antonio," I warn with a giggle.

He laughs. "It doesn't involve my dick, I promise. Just you, me, and fun."

I can handle that.

"Okay."

"Can I call you later if it's not too late?"

"I'll be here with my baking show."

"Talk later, bestie."

Chapter 41

Miriam

When Antonio said he wanted to take me out, rugby practice wasn't on my list. It wasn't anywhere near the vicinity of what I imagined our first date would be. He said his penis wouldn't be involved, but he failed to mention the rest of his body being on full display—or the testosterone soaking into the atmosphere.

My hands clench, and my nails dig into my palms at the heavy hit. A player falls to the ground, cradling the ball. He extends his arms to two approaching teammates who have red mesh jerseys over their compression shirts. Both are tall, loaded with muscles, and surely dedicated to counting macros and bench-pressing twice my weight in the gym.

Antonio sprints from the other side of the artificial turf and rams into both men like they're crash test dummies. His shoulders are low, and every back and leg muscle is teasing my thighs to start a fire by rubbing them together.

Arson is a stretch, but splitting holes in my control-top tights is imminent.

"Jinkies," I mutter, out of breath from witnessing the force of his body disrupt motion.

Antonio peels out the ball with his cleats, and another player grabs it and speeds off to the try zone. The man is a tank, forcing turnovers and knocking people down like bowling pins. How he maintains the stamina to pop up after tackles and run into players again defies logic. No amount of money or love of the game would possess my body to plow into a grown human at full force—*with* a smile.

A whistle blows. Antonio skips to the sideline through a procession of back pats. His eyes land on me in the corner, where I put myself to stay out of the way. I don't need the attention, and I certainly don't need anyone questioning if I'm having hot flashes because of the tiny shorts littering the AstroTurf.

My God.

He winks before walking off with a man holding a clipboard. To his credit, he's kept our date casual, with minimal chances to reexamine the strength of my kitchen table.

Our first date.

It still takes a minute to process that we're doing this, investigating an "us" outside of our friendship. I was nervous getting ready, but reality told my assumptions to have several seats once his car rolled up my driveway. Some nerves were still fluttering in my stomach, but most had subsided due to the safety already embedded between us.

I know him.

I've known him.

We met on my front porch, at Antonio's request, where I got a firm handshake and a pack of Twizzlers in lieu of flowers. I fell out laughing once I realized he was serious and taking no chances. But all cackling ceased when his hug wrapped me in his tobacco and cedar cologne. My toes curled, and my body vibrated from his nearness after so much time apart. I got a kiss on the nose and have been in this foldable chair next to the equipment locker ever since.

Only God's strongest soldiers are immune to thick thighs and good intentions. I'm not ashamed to admit the dizzy spells I get from his grunts and the way his teeth sink into his lip when he pistons into another player.

The Steel have a reduced practice schedule to reflect their bye week. Where we'll go after this remains a mystery. A few of his teammates are hinting at, and I quote, "an evening of charity and questions." The black turtleneck and gray skirt I dug up were the best I could do with little to no information about tonight. If it involves an auction of any kind, I'll personally tackle Antonio myself or end up in somebody's hospital bed trying.

My phone beeps.

Antonio

Hopping in the shower. Will be ready in ten. You look really pretty BTW.

Thank you. Do I get a hint about where we're going?

Antonio

Nope.

I snort at his response and shake my head with a promise to kill him later. The fact that I'm still calm and not hyperventilating over the fear of the unknown is a testament to my level of comfort with him. I trust him to keep me safe. But there better not be any snow or nudity involved. I do have limits.

I startle at a long sigh that belongs to a woman in a cream slip dress and chocolate thigh-high boots.

"They should be out by now," she mutters from under a canopy of layered brunette hair and pursed lips.

I'm unsure if the comment is for me or the empty indoor field, but then she aims a glare at me like it's my responsibility to supply an answer.

I state the obvious. "They went to the locker room."

"Who are you?" Her polished tone doesn't match the growing scowl that deepens as she examines my outfit.

I thought black ankle boots and tights were a sensible pairing. Clothing is functional for me. I don't want to look like I jump in dumpsters for fun, but I'm not letting fashion runways dictate how I accessorize my life. Not that sample sizes would ever cover these hips.

I won't judge someone's decision-making process, but I do question wearing thin silk in thirteen-degree weather.

"I'm Miriam. I'm with Antonio." I crane my head to reach her eyes.

She laughs. "One of those."

"Excuse me?"

"Antonio," she emphasizes, like I didn't hear the disrespect the first time. "He has *lots* of women who show up to his practices. I'll tell him you said goodbye."

Is Lea Michele dismissing me?

I adjust my skirt when I stand. It's a few inches shorter than what I'm used to wearing. With my ankle boots, I'm still half a foot shorter than the woman who huffed and puffed two minutes after she arrived.

"What's your name?" I adjust my glasses.

"Rachel," she says flatly.

"Well, Rachel. I've known Antonio for years. Our relationship is still new, but our friendship isn't. I don't need to leave, because he's my ride. Should I repeat?"

Comprehension looks different on different people. For Rachel, it's walking off in a trail of entitlement and high-end perfume.

Guess she understood.

Antonio's laughter rounds the corner before he does. My heart jolts at the anticipation of him and thuds when he steps out with a toothpaste-model smile crinkling his eyes. A teammate is next to him. He's handsome, around the same height, and has an aristocratic widow's peak like the Black duke in *Bridgerton*.

My eyes drift back to Antonio. Where the duke looks like he raided Carlton's closet, Antonio is Taye Diggs in *Brown Sugar* coded, wearing a cream cable-knit sweater, a matching beanie, Timbs, and jeans.

I roll my lips. "Nice outfit."

"This old thing?" His twirl flares his full-length peacoat. "Winter cream is a look."

Now I'm laughing in his face. "I'm pretty sure you saw that in a movie." My favorite, second to *Aliens* and *Alien vs. Predator*, an honorable mention. We watched *Brown Sugar* at his place the night he got tired of losing to me in *Mortal Kombat.*

"Hi, I'm Shayne." His teammate extends a hand that I shake.

"Miriam. They call you Shoulders?"

Antonio snickers.

"Shins," Shayne clarifies over a chuckle.

Bread.

Shins.

Kendrick.

What's next, Irish Spring?

Antonio bends to wrap an arm around me. "Ready for tonight?" We're taking things slow, though I have a feeling he'd speed to the moon if I let him. I want us to pace ourselves before we defy gravity.

"That depends on what we're doing." I raise a brow.

A grin spreads. " questions."

Ay, Dios.

"Welcome to The Newlywed Game!"

Applause erupts.

"I'm your host, Melvin Jones," the announcer with the Steve Harvey veneers says. The size of his teeth doesn't match his small frame. Neither does his brown suit. He looks like he's going to represent himself in court or sell you a vacuum cleaner.

When Antonio said tonight would be an evening of charity and questions, I was not expecting a game show in a South Buffalo bar. No wonder he insisted on driving.

"Stop eyeing the exits," my *date* says next to my ear. He reaches around me for his water bottle on the counter.

"I'm starting to rethink this whole trust thing," I grumble. "What made you assume I wanted to do this?"

"You said you wanted to go out more."

I gawk. "To the movies or something. Not"—I wave my hands around—"a game for married people."

He drags my barstool to the side as a man with no sense of courtesy or spatial awareness squeezes himself between us. My back is now against Antonio's chest. His arms cage me in to shield me from the people clamoring to get the bartender's attention.

"My family's investment firm co-sponsors this event every year," he tells me, his voice soft and low. One inhale of his cologne sends my senses into a frenzy. "It raises money for families around the city who are experiencing financial hardship, and it's a good boost in visibility for the Steel. We played Family Feud last year and Jeopardy the year before that."

"Your philanthropy is commendable, but we aren't married," I say over my shoulder. I shiver at his mouth inches from mine.

The kiss he plants is soft. "I know," he whispers. "Shins is playing with his fiancée, Rachel—"

"The one who's hard of hearing?"

"What?" Antonio laughs.

"Nothing."

"Bread and Kendrick are on a team. Then you and me. The winners get a trophy and a steak-and-lobster dinner at Amato's."

"Why didn't you lead with that?" Antonio will be on the receiving end of my wrath for this at some point, but Amato's is *famous* famous. The waitlist is a year out, and I heard every dish is based on the recipes of the owner's grandmother.

"Why am I not surprised?" He shakes his head with a grin.

"The same way I'm not after dealing with your antics all these years." I down the rest of my mule in one go.

He leads us from the bar to the half dozen steps next to a raised space where our fate awaits. His grip is firm on my hand, rubbing circles into my thumb as we walk by a large group. We pass a brick fireplace across from beams with hanging string lights twinkling over aged hardwood. Our seats are between the other two teams.

Kendrick stuffs notecards into his black pants. Were we supposed to study?

Rachel is talking to the side of Shins's face. Her hands and mouth are moving a mile a minute while he stares at the other end of the room. Completely bothered and unamused.

"Alright, teams. The couple that answers the most questions correctly will be our winner," Melvin declares. "Any questions?"

"I'm not fucking him." Bread points to Kendrick. "You're handsome, bro, but we're not like that."

"That's not a question," Melvin notes. He signals for his assistants to pass us whiteboards with dry-erase markers.

We're doing this for charity and steak and lobster.

Antonio leans over to me and says, "Don't overthink it."

Melvin strolls past us with a Vaseline smile like that man from *The Hunger Games*. "Before we start, tell us what you do and how you met."

Rachel pats Shins's thigh. "Since we're the only couple up here, we'll start." She stands and snatches Melvin's mic. "We're engaged." There's a squeal and a flash of a large rock. "We've been together since high school, but we've liked each other for much longer. Our families play tennis together. They're members of the same country club."

"*Country club*?" Someone in the audience scoffs. "Girl, this ain't *Laguna Beach*." A wave of laughter flows from one end of the crowded room to the other.

Rachel looks to Shins with a pout. He sighs and takes the mic after telling her to sit down. "We've been together for ten years. She's a real estate broker. I play for the Buffalo Steel."

The audience whistles for the rugby team.

Shins passes the mic.

"I'm Bread, and this is Kendrick."

"I'll take a bite of your loaf, big boy!" a woman catcalls.

"Who said that?" Bread shields his eyes from the spotlight on stage. "Don't play with me. You sound fine as shit. You can get these gluten-free strokes!"

"Bring the little one too!" another shouts. "I like short kings."

Kendrick drops his head.

Antonio steals the mic from Bread. "Sit your ass down," he grits before smiling to the spectators of this circus. "A round of applause for Kendrick and Bread. They both play for the Steel, as do I."

"Captain, my Captain," the three rugby players sing.

"Alright, enough," Antonio chuckles. His face softens. "This is Miriam. She has a PhD in mechanical engineering."

"Come on, Queen!"

"Let her know!" he shouts.

"Please don't encourage him," I groan.

"She's amazing, and she recently accepted a job at the Jefferson Moselle Community Center. We have a separate donation box for them near the bar. Please show your support."

I unshield my face from embarrassment. "What?"

He covers the mic. "Whatever we raise tonight, I'll match it."

"I—"

"Beautiful couple," Melvin says. "How long have you two been together?"

Antonio clears his throat. "It's new, but she's been my best friend for three years." His smile is wide. "I had a crush on Miriam for the longest. I first saw her in her high school while visiting a friend. She was on her way to an engineering club meeting."

"You never told me that," I whisper.

"It took a while for her to notice me. Years, actually." He bites his lip and stares down at me through a fan of lashes. "One unfortunate incident on New Year's Eve became the best night of my life."

"Aww," the crowd says.

Rachel's scoff barely registers. I had no idea that Antonio first saw me in high school. Most of my days involved my nose in a book, but still. I always thought he remembered me from the times I babysat him.

strumming his fingers on the steering wheel to whatever R&B mix he found on the radio.

Except I'm not.

My eyes haven't moved from the Polaroid a volunteer handed me before we left. It's a picture of us smiling with our trophies. Only I'm looking at the camera, and he's looking at me.

A fluttery sensation spreads from my fingers to my toes at the evidence that's been in front of me—clear as day, waiting for me to take notice.

Antonio has been in love with me for some time.

Every act, every display of affection, has come easily. There are slips and accidents, but it's pure. Just for us.

I feel like an idiot. Here I am, declaring I'm ready to date and that love will come when the time is right. Love never needed to find me; it's been here all along.

His SUV rolls to a stop in my driveway. The steady hum of my pulse and the scent of cedar with tobacco thicken the air.

"I'll walk you to the door."

I'm on him before his hand reaches his seat belt. My fingers dig into the short hairs of his beard, and my lips crash to his.

"Mir—"

This man has every right to be afraid. I would be too if someone mauled me in my car like they were possessed. Once I stopped thinking about all of the reasons we're not right for each other, desire took over. And she wants a word.

Antonio's eyes flare before he pulls me over the center console to straddle him. My winter coat traps my skirt from riding up my thighs. He widens his legs, focusing on stretching mine over his frame. A heat stroke might be in my future with all these extra layers, but for now, I throw caution to the wind and hump him in my driveway for all to see.

Our war of lips and tongue wanes when Antonio strokes his thumbs over my jaw. Each kiss is gentle, slow, and measured.

He presses his forehead to mine. "I don't want to rush this, Doe. I want you to be comfortable."

"I love you," I whisper, my body vibrating from the heat in his gaze and these damn layers. "Come inside with me."

"Are you sure?"

"Only if you want to."

Chapter 42

Antonio

Sex wasn't on my agenda tonight. Neither was Miriam jumping me in her driveway. The Miriam I know is calculated, risk-averse, and looks to data before making decisions. The Miriam here with me now threw caution and self-control out the window. It might still be at the bar or somewhere on the interstate.

Something shifted tonight, and I'm here to take care of her in whatever way she needs me to.

I can't keep my hands off her.

One, it's *her*. If Miriam so much as blinks my way, I'll get hard. Two, the level of difficulty walking up the stairs with her in my arms and my jeans around my ankles requires me to handle her with extreme care. In hindsight, it was a dumb decision, but I dare anyone to think straight when the woman of your dreams pushes you into a door and sucks your soul from your lips. There were a few technical difficulties with our height difference, so I picked her up, and here we are.

The whimper at my nip to her neck swells my dick. Her legs are too short to wrap around me, but what she lacks in height, she makes up for in grip.

We reach the top of the stairs without injury. I walk us into her bedroom two steps at a time, careful not to trip over anything that will prematurely send her through the headboard. Our coats and shoes are downstairs, which leaves a few more layers to peel off.

I put her on the comforter and kick off my jeans. Her breath hitches when my fingers curl into her thighs to roll off her tights.

"These are on there," I grunt, struggling not to rip the fabric in half.

She giggles. "They're a little snug."

"No shit. Let that pussy breathe."

Heat fans across her cheeks as she lifts the thickness of her ass to unfurl the nylon down her equally juicy thighs. The scent of her nectar between her legs invades my nostrils.

"Are you of sound mind?" My eyes are on the thong choking her lips.

"What?" she snorts.

I tear my gaze away to focus on the top half of her, minus the titties I want in my mouth. It's hard to form complete sentences with my blood traveling south, but I need her consent.

"Doe." I rub a hand over my waves, trying to remember how to speak. "You wanted to take things slow. Now we're here. Trust me when I say I'm in full support." My eyes roam over her valley of curves.

Fuck me.

Focus.

"I don't want you to regret anything. I'm okay with waiting." Even if I develop terminal blue balls.

Moonlight spills through the cracks of her curtains and onto her silhouette. I've been with many women, but none have turned my heart inside out the way Miriam does. She's one of one.

"My mind finally caught up to my heart," she says softly. "I'm not afraid anymore."

"You have no idea the gift you are."

Her eyes shine, and I look away to keep from crying myself. She really has no clue how long I've wanted her. How much I love her.

My steps falter on my way to the bed.

"I don't have condoms," I say. *Shit.* "I haven't carried any on me since...since you've been here."

It wasn't a conscious decision to not restock my wallet. Unprotected sex is a nonstarter, regardless of the person or the situation. I never paid attention because I wasn't having sex.

"I'll run to the store." On two wheels with no brakes. I'm knocking the lining out of Miriam's pussy.

"When's the last time you got tested?" she asks.

"A month ago." I grab my pants. "Players get a full exam before the season starts."

She bites her lip. "I haven't been sexually active for half a decade. If your tests are negative, I'm on birth control."

It takes a second for what she said to register.

"Are you sure, Doe?" I blink to refocus. My heart is pounding in my chest, and all of the blood in my body has rerouted south.

Her stare doesn't waver when she nods. "I'm trusting you with my heart and my body."

My phone flies out of my hands as I make my way to the bed. I catch it and give it to her. She scrolls through the lab results.

"I'd never jeopardize your health or intentionally break your heart," I tell her. "I can't guarantee I won't do or say something to piss you off, but you're safe with me. I'm also okay with waiting."

"I don't want to wait," she whispers.

I cup her face and press my mouth to hers. My thumbs run over her jaw as my tongue traces her lips. She opens to dip her tongue into my mouth, the sensation of her smooth lips exploding through my chest.

Kissing Miriam is a spiritual practice, one my body craves in every way. The fact that I'm with her right now is still a shock to my system. I've never wanted anyone more than I do her.

My senses spin with the scent of rose oil as I press her into the bed. Heat prickles my skin at her nails denting my shoulders. She sheds her skirt and turtleneck to reveal the soft lines drawn through every one of my fantasies.

Full hips.

Wide thighs.

Her black bra and thong don't do her body justice. Miriam was made for worship, so I fall to my knees at the altar of her thighs.

I kiss my way up her creamy legs, which she parts. My tongue traces a beauty mark, exciting her breath in long, surrendering moans. She trembles when my nose presses to her satin thong. She's soaked.

"Fuck, Doe. Do you have any idea what you do to me?" I inhale sharp, flatten my tongue for a long swipe up the silken material, and groan.

"I'm addicted to your taste," I hum over her skin. I pull the thong to the side to marvel at her pussy. Juices pool at her opening in an invitation for me to latch on to her pearl. I pull her clit between my lips, massaging the bundle of nerves in targeted strokes.

"Antonio," Miriam pants, her fingers digging into my scalp. My girl loves getting her pussy ate, and I'm happy to oblige. I thrust my tongue inside and push her thighs further apart.

"Play with your titties," I command. "Let me see those nipples."

She moans and lowers her bra straps, freeing her breasts and those deep brown areolas. Her lip rolls between her teeth as her fingers twist her tight nipples. I suck harder and ease two fingers inside of her to strum her G-spot. Her breasts bounce, and her legs jerk until her toes curl. She showers my mouth with her juices that drip down my beard. I blow on her opening and pull her clit back into my mouth.

That's one.

"Oh my—" She gasps for air. "I want to personally thank your mother for having you. Does she like fruit baskets?"

I lift my head and snicker. "Ask her yourself when you meet her."

"She's getting a fruit—*uhh*!" Miriam whines as her pussy sucks my fingers. I take a nipple into my mouth and bite. "Oh, she's getting a hand-picked basket. I'll pick the mangos myself in Panamaaaa!"

That's two.

The pressure against her G-spot rips the air from her lungs. I pull out my soaked fingers, wrap them around my dick, and revel as her eyes widen and her lips part with each stroke.

Her hands find their way back to her breasts. She's dripping, pussy engorged and leaking onto the bed.

I kiss her face and rub the head of my dick against her entrance. A shiver shoots down my back. "You have no idea how long I've waited to love you," I whisper, my eyes fixed on hers.

Miriam reaches up to caress my cheek. I peck the inside of her wrist through slow breaths in an effort to calm down my heart, which is thundering behind my rib cage.

"Are you nervous?" I ask.

Her smile is shy. "A little."

"Me too."

Our kiss is gentle, a vow we make without words.

"Go slow, please," she murmurs.

"I will."

I drop a kiss to her forehead, unsure how long I'll last.

"You're shaking, Antonio."

"I can't believe this is happening," I admit through a ragged breath. My eyes close, and I shake my head. "You're my first crush."

"I am?"

"My first love too, Doe."

I kiss her again and slowly push into her. My back tenses at the grip, strangling my dick with every inch I take. She pulls her lips from mine in a gasp.

"You okay, baby?" Beads of sweat form across my brow. It's taking every ounce of strength I have not to move too fast or nut too quickly. Fuck, she's tight.

"It feels like you're splitting me in two," she moans.

I freeze. "Want me to stop?"

Her eyes snap to mine. "Don't you fucking dare."

I snicker and thrust deeper. Miriam's eyes are closed, but mine are on hers, looking for any signs of discomfort. Tension eases into euphoria. The frown between her brows softens, and her lips part.

"Look at me, baby." I kiss her collarbone and roll my hips. "I love you."

She smiles, tears forming. "I love you too."

I keep my pace slow, swiveling into her spot, which I knock on repeat. My lips close over a nipple as I drive deeper. Miriam lifts to meet my mouth, her breath skating over my face in a chant. I raise her thighs and thrust until my dick is kissing her back wall.

Watching Miriam come undone is ecstasy. My hips jerk, and I hold her in place in a slow release.

She's a dream come true. One I won't give up without a fight.

Chapter 43

Antonio

Tonight is a redo of our first date, an opportunity to prove to myself and Miriam that we can be in the same room without my tongue or dick buried inside her. I promised to take things slow, only to reenact interpretive dance moves while folding her into different positions. Miriam did initiate what became a three-day marathon of waxing her cheeks, but I don't want her assuming she's like the women in my past.

I want more than sex with her. I want it all.

She asked me to surprise her tonight, which left me stumped and out of options. There was dinner, but restaurants with Resurrection Sunday linens are a hard no for both of us. A quiet night on her couch with a baking show or at my place with video games would lead to fucking. The botanical garden came to mind. So did catching a movie, with minimal fondling.

I settled on a date Ella recommended after I called her for advice. Yeah, I phoned a friend. My history of wining and dining outside of a quick fuck isn't stellar, and I want Miriam to have the best. Drinking and hurling axes never crossed my mind, but Miriam's snorts trapped in giggles proves it was the perfect choice.

If Ella's aim is anything like hers, Julian better rub her feet for the rest of eternity.

We've been at Hoppy Axe 'N Dents for a little over an hour. It isn't too far from Steel House and has cages with wood chips on the floor and targets bearing the marks of axes thrown with abandon. The number of people skipping away with grins on their faces after going to work with single-handed weapons should raise some type of concern. Miriam's *Xena: Warrior Princess* squeal terrified me.

Then there's the full kitchen, and the bar, which had me in front of the manager to confirm that my lady wouldn't be in harm's way. Her becoming a hatchet-wielding assassin is one thing, but her getting a scratch or a splinter is another. We're here for fun, but I'm not playing those kinds of games about her or her safety.

We joined another couple, which turned into a battle of the genders. Not my idea, by the way. Miriam is across from Jimmy, a bear of a man donning fully-tatted sleeves on both arms, a crew cut, and a dad bod. He's twice her height and size, served three tours overseas, and is good with weapons—knives and hatchets included.

His score is impressive, but it's nowhere close to the woman who barely reaches his chest in an oversized sweater, leggings, and high-tops.

Miriam eyes her target with calculated precision, her weapon of choice for the evening turning over in her soft hand. The slightest smirk appears before she raises the hatchet above her curly updo. Unlike Jimmy, she uses both hands. Her arms are close to her face when she sends it sailing through the air.

Bull's-eye.

I'm off the metal barstool on the outside of the chain link fence. My phone is out recording her, which is quickly forgotten when I pump my fist in the air.

"That's what's up!" I shout, like Miriam didn't hand me and Jimmy our asses.

Ask me if I care. The grin denting her dimples is worth losing every game.

She does her best to hide the blush that's inching up her cheeks as the instructor and nearby groups applaud her. Our eyes meet, and the smile she gives just for me shifts something in my chest. It's subtle, like her long exhale and the fire behind her eyes.

"How long have you two been together?"

My gaze swings from Miriam down to Sarah. She's around the same age as Jimmy, her partner, and is his complete opposite. She's in a button-down shirt tucked into loose-fitting jeans and Keds.

"About a week," I say to her smirk under honey-colored bangs. "But we've been friends for three years."

"You're a beautiful couple. Remind me of myself and Jimmy in our early years."

"She's special."

Her eyes sweep over Miriam's friendship bracelets before swinging back to me. My hoodie is pushed up to my forearms, so mine are visible too.

There are enough women in my life that I can decipher the look Sarah is giving me. My mama and granny share the same stare when they're waiting for me to catch on to something. It took a minute for me to admit my feelings, but there's no lesson to learn here.

"Miriam is someone you spend every chance you get loving."

"I speak from experience when I say the best love affairs come from friendships. It's the perfect foundation for a love you never imagined," Sarah says.

My smile grows. "That's the plan."

Miriam speed walks past Sarah, who meets Jimmy at the entrance to the cage. Her eyes are on me, her presence altering the rhythm of my heart, the way it always does. The draw to her is the same pull that stopped me in the hallway the first time I laid eyes on her.

"Can I get your autograph?" I swing her into a hug and kiss her grin. "Having a good time?"

She threads her arms through mine to grab my waist. "I think I missed my calling."

"No shit," I huff. "I'm hiding every knife in my house and yours when we get back. The can openers too."

"Hush!" Her head tips back with a laugh that exposes the smooth column of her neck, and I pepper it with kisses. My mouth moves from her chin to peck her lips twice.

PDA has become a love language we speak whenever the mood strikes. Miriam still recites formulas under her breath when she gets anxious, but she's more comfortable living outside of her shell.

She rests her chin on my chest. "Thank you for tonight."

I kiss her dimple. "You never have to thank me. I love spending time with you." I kiss the other one. "I love you."

"Mmm. And you're home for the next month?"

"Four whole weeks." The Steel's home opener against DC is next week. We have three more games after that, followed by a bye week.

We'll have an away game before we end the regular season at home with our final two matches.

Interview requests aren't slowing down, but I'll be closer so I can play in her guts and sleep next to her shadow.

I sit on a stool and pull her into my lap. "Ready for another round, or do you want to do something else?"

"I'm ready for another game."

"Alright. There's an arcade not too far from here. We could also try an escape room, but you're saving us." Miriam's hand strokes my thigh through my jeans. "Chuck E. Cheese maybe? There were a few coupons in the mail—Miriam. This is a dick-free date night."

Out in public with a dick print that's about to rip a hole through my pants is as maniacal as she is.

I grunt when she rocks her hips into my erection and presses her mouth to my ear. "I never agreed to that."

"I'm trying to be good," I grit. "I don't want you to think I only care about sex."

"I know you love me," she says with a gentleness in her voice that rivals her grip on my leg. "There's nothing to prove except your stamina."

"Bite your tongue. Are you finishing that?" I point at her red wine and pull her to her feet when she shakes her head. "Stamina. Bring your ass."

We'll see who's laughing when we get back to her place.

"Bye!" Miriam waves to Sarah and Jimmy. I'm halfway to the door with her wrist in my grip.

"Pack a bag and bring your vitamins. You're staying with me this weekend." In my bed, possibly tied to it if she keeps it up.

Her smirk teases her dimples. "It's already waiting by the door."

"I created a monster," I mumble.

"No. You unleashed one."

Chapter 44

Miriam

There is no such thing as "good luck pussy," but I'm bouncing on Antonio like my coochie will get him to the playoffs.

"You're going to be late," I heave, out of breath from using leg muscles I never use.

Less than two weeks was all we needed to christen every surface and corner in both of our houses. I'm pretty sure we did it in a day and a half. Engineers are curious by nature. It's a foundational trait I've put to good use. I understand the process of sex, but the beauty is in the complexities I've been soaking up, along with my sheets.

Continuous learning has been my foreplay, and I'm going for straight A's.

"I'll leave right after," Antonio says through clenched teeth. "Just like that, Doe. *Shit.*" His hands grip my hips to guide me up and down his length, which is slicked with my juices. His head lifts to lap a nipple before he pulls it into his mouth. I press my hands into his chest and grind down.

Cowgirl has quickly become a top-three position, second to missionary and my thighs spread for backshots. I lean back to cup his balls.

"Fuck, I love you, girl!" Playing with his testicles is a tip I read about, and it's paying off.

I love watching Antonio and his reaction to my body. The way his lips widen and his penetrating stares. How he's tuned into my needs, studying me for my pleasure.

"You feel so *good*," I moan, my back arched and hips steadied over his steel as I make it disappear.

Today's leg power is sponsored by yours truly. Antonio is happy to be along for the ride so he doesn't cramp before today's first home game. I swear he mentioned no physical activity the day of or before, but we broke that rule. It's a miracle we haven't broken his headboard.

Speaking of the headboard.

I grab the top of the wooden frame and lift to my feet. Just enough to swivel my hips over his mushroom tip before swallowing him whole.

"Fuck!" Antonio's grip tightens. He bites my nipple.

"Ahh!"

Sex with him has been a discovery of self. I've discovered that I, Miriam Beckford, the second of her house, love intercourse. I made up for five years in the almost two weeks our relationship turned physical. The sensation of his dick, how it stretches my walls and hits spots no toy can activate, brings out a side of me I never knew existed. I love being completely naked, feeding my arousal to him like an elixir, and riding him until his toes curl.

We were already in tune with each other, but this takes us to the clouds. Our hearts beat in sync every time our bodies become one.

My hands fly to Antonio's shoulders as the pressure of another orgasm explodes.

"*Uhh!*"

"Gah—Doe!" He comes in three rapid thrusts. Every muscle in his stomach coils at his release.

I giggle through gasps of air. "Why are you sweating? I did all the work."

"That last part was all me."

"Mister Three Seconds." I squeal at the pinch to my nipples.

"It takes Jedi concentration to not shoot into this sweet pussy, Doe." His lips press to my collarbone. "I've never felt this before, baby."

We kiss until it's time for him to go to the field with the team. I hop in the shower—well, walk, with fatigued thighs from mounting a rugby player—and get ready for the home opener.

Folding chairs line the manicured pitch under a bright blue sky. The weather is deceptively cool, but not cold enough for a full winter coat for Buffalo natives and transplants alike.

I text Marcela my location and adjust my knitted hat to keep my curls from blowing away with the wind. There may still be a chill in the air, but you wouldn't know it looking at the Steel in their short-sleeved shirts and shorter shorts.

"They better win on the strength of home-field advantage."
Marcela tightens her jacket and reaches down to hug me. "Hey, girl.
This me?" She points to the empty chair next to mine.

I nod. "Careful."

"*Eep!*"

"It rocks."

Her arms and legs flail, but she catches herself and eases into the
concept of a gliding folding chair. "Where did you get this?"

"Antonio bought them."

His eyes land on me from across the field. He winks and runs off
with Shins. A small smile plays on my lips at the all-black uniform
molded to every inch of muscle. His thighs are out, his back is
corded, and his biceps are on full display.

"Somebody is glowing," Marcela teases. "Would this have anything to do with your disappearance?"

"I did not disappear." I push up my glasses and swallow my
tongue as the Steel warm up. "I was occupied."

Tied up.

Facedown.

In the air.

Against the wall.

Over a sofa arm.

Bent on the steps.

Miriam was busy.

My sister smirks. Her cropped haircut accentuates her cheekbones. Her vibe today is an ode to the '90s. Loose-fitting jeans over

high-tops and a black windbreaker. Minus her jacket, we're match-ing.

"What's the matter, Antonio got your pussy?"

"Don't say 'pussy' out loud!" I whisper-yell.

She grins. "Since when do you say that word, Dr. Baby?"

I bite my lip. "Since he's been making mine purr."

"I knew it."

"Keep it down," I plead, pulling at my coat collar, now overheat-ed. "I'd rather not talk about my recent expeditions."

"Alright." She nods. "I'll leave it and your newfound glow alone. Just one question." She pinches her thumb and pointer finger to-gether.

Here she goes.

"Go ahead," I sigh.

"How are you still walking after all of that?"

Marcela motions to the Steel. They're on the ground in stretch-es that simulate a mating ritual with the grass. My eyes lock on Antonio. His mouthguard hangs from the side of his mouth as he rolls through a downward-facing dog. His forearms flex, and he straightens his leg into a side stretch. The mobility in his hips, the shift in his weight to activate his quads, which have pistoned into me on more than one occasion, is a testament to his flexibility. And my, is the man flexible.

"I'm small in height, but I'm a big girl," I say, my gaze trained on the mass of his legs as they widen into a child's pose. I never thought of myself as an ass person, but I shift in my seat at his back-and-forth movements.

"My sister is in love, and getting that back cracked!" Marcela cheers.

"I do love him," I say proudly.

"You and everyone else." Lisa drops her chair next to Marcela. Her stare lingers on Antonio, who's bending into a squat and touching his toes. "He is flexible." The snide remark leaves no room for interpretation about her history with my man.

Marcela whips her head in her direction. "I know I didn't call you to come over here and start shit. Matter of fact, I didn't call you at all."

Lisa purses her lips. "I come to every home game. I don't mind sharing with you, Miriam. Antonio has plenty of fans. There goes another one now."

Kenya marches onto the field with full glam and confidence. Heads from both teams turn to the woman in high-waisted pants that model her long legs and a blouse underneath her corduroy vest. Her outfit isn't screaming for attention, unlike Lisa's crop top and apple bottoms from Rainbow. Kenya is all business, and she grins harder when she reaches Antonio.

His eyes drift over her head to me before he nods at something she says.

"Like I said, he has lots of fans. You'll learn to share. We all did."

"Hey, Lisa?" I face her.

"Yes?"

"I know for a fact he hasn't called or seen you in months. The last time you tried to show up to his house unannounced, you were sent right back out. Antonio and I are together now—officially and in every way. If you want to test the theory that your tired antics will take him from me, by all means, give it a try. But I promise that your feelings won't be the only thing that gets hurt."

She grabs her chair and leaves.

"You dropped your dignity!" Marcela shouts at her former friend. She smiles at a family who says hello like she's not out here causing chaos. "Do not let that bitch see you sweat. None of them," she whispers to me. "I'm proud of you for standing up for yourself. There's always someone who will try to play in your face if you let them. Matter of fact"—she scans down the sideline for Lisa—"I owe her years' worth of ass whoopings. The nerve of her in that barely glued lace front..." Her voice softens. "You okay?"

"Yes," I snicker. "I know Antonio has a past. I just didn't expect it to come at me that way. I'm not used to being with anyone, much less someone who had a friendly dick."

It's not that I lack confidence. I know my worth, and I don't need it validated like parking. That doesn't mean I'm welcoming members of the I Fucked Antonio Fan Club into my space with stickers. I don't want or need any reminders of how other women writhed and sucked him. The thought of tackling Kenya and Lisa has crossed my mind, and I've only had the dick for two weeks!

Antonio only talks to Kenya because of work. Does it make me happy? No, but I trust him. He doesn't give her access to his personal cell and coordinates any interviews through the team's media manager.

"As long as he's not giving them a reason to think there's hope, sit high on your throne, Queen. You're the only one who could, and did, take him off the market."

"Thank you, sis." I smile.

The game kicks off at three, with screams and cheers from Steel fans in black and gray. I'm on my feet anytime Antonio has the ball or makes a tackle, proudly displaying his number six jersey. He scores twice before the last whistle blows, and the Steel earns their fifth consecutive win.

News cameras follow reporters who shuffle onto the field, vying for statements from the team that's projected to win this year's championship. Proud is an understatement. This team works so hard, and they deserve all of the coverage they're receiving.

"I don't know what the hell I watched. I was nervous and a little turned on from all those hits." Marcela grabs her chest to catch her breath. "They play at home next week?"

I laugh. "Yes. Post those pictures you took on social."

"I will. Looks like they have a shot at going to the championship. I'll speak with some people about possible funding."

"Any plans to talk to a certain senator?"

She rolls her eyes. "No. He's still on punishment from Valentine's Day. It might be the end of the road with that one."

Marcela never discusses her romantic partners, but that sneaky link lasted longer than anyone else. Two years is a long time to not catch feelings.

Her lashes fall as she clasps her hands. "Love is," she chuckles, "not for everybody."

"Are you okay?"

"I always am. Who is *that*?"

I follow her gaze and smile. Julian Brooke never fails to make an entrance or cause neck pain within a fifty-yard vicinity. All eyes follow the former playboy turned family man. His low fade matches a trimmed goatee, and his chocolate skin is tucked into a suit and long coat.

We've never said more than a few words in passing. Kierra had a crush on him for the longest, one that turned into a one-night stand and her binging every British show after he went back to London for work. He's '90s-leading-man fine, but there's no way I would ever stay under a blanket boo-hooing over someone who sent one-word texts after we shared bodily fluids.

It's part of the reason I never wanted to be the casualty of a hookup, especially with a known bachelor.

"Hi." I stand up to give him a hug.

"It's good to see you, Miriam." Julian greets me with a knowing smile. "I'm happy for you two." He squeezes me.

"Thank you." I blush.

His eyes lift to my sister. "Hi. I'm Julian, Antonio's friend."

"Marcela, this one's sister," she says, doing her best not to get lost in his rich baritone.

"And city councilmember." Don't ask me why I mention it. The man is married with three kids. I hate small talk. "How's Ella and the family?"

A smile crinkles his brown eyes when I mention the woman who did the impossible and made him fall in love. It's written all over his face, and the wedding band adorning his ring finger.

"Real good," he beams. "Jackson is about to video call me to catch the post-game press conference. You coming down for the rematch next month? We'd love to have you over."

"Oh. We haven't made any plans."

He grins. "I'm sure it will come up. Antonio always comes through whenever he's in DC. I'm gonna head in and call my son, but I wanted to say hi." He offers a parting hug. "I'm glad you gave him a chance," he whispers before turning to Marcela. "Councilmember, a pleasure."

"That's Antonio's friend?" Marcela's eyes are still on Julian as he cuts left to the field house.

"Since they were little. He's happily married with kids." If she didn't know that he was married, she'd kidnap him and keep him for herself.

"Damn. The best ones are always taken."

"You should know."

Her head flies in my direction. "Bitch!" I get a playful shove. "Are we following? And not because I'm trying to stuff him in my bra."

"How about dinner?" I start packing up the chairs.

"Did you forget your man is a professional rugby player who's in there interviewing with national networks?"

"I didn't. I was trying to forget the press, the networks, and all those rowdy fans stuffed into a small room." I'm getting better with crowds, but millions of viewers tuning in is asking a lot. "I'll wait in the car."

Marcela frowns. "Didn't you drive separately?"

"Exactly."

She cackles and grabs my arm. "Bring your scary ass."

Chapter 45

Antonio

"Congratulations on another win. What's the feeling heading through the season undefeated?"

I glance down the row of microphones to Cho, Kendrick, and Coach Washington. Three sets of eyes land on me.

Guess I'm taking this one.

"We've worked hard," I say to the cameras, folding my arms on the table. "The preparation is in the results and what we've been able to achieve. Coach is on our a—"—*family friendly*—"butts with the fundamentals, and we try to apply them every opportunity we get. The Steel are solid, but we're not sleeping on anyone. DC fought hard today. We'll see them on their pitch in a few weeks."

Concise.

Diplomatic.

No curse words.

Post-game press conferences are exhausting. The last thing any of us wants to do after eighty minutes of hard collision is answer the same questions over and over.

How do you feel after your win? *Good.*

What was going on with those errors? *If we knew, we wouldn't have made them.*

Are you happy with your performance? *Code word: I'm about to tell you how you fucked up.*

Media training keeps the smile on my face and the FCC away. I'm happy the sport is getting the attention it deserves, but I'd be happier if I could eat or take a shit without worrying about cameras and who still needs an interview. I haven't done either, and I have one more question in me before I pass out on this table.

I haven't spoken to Miriam since before the game. We tunneled up with the other team before we jogged off to the locker room for a few quick words from the coaching staff. Then came the interviews.

My phone is still in my locker. Knowing Miriam, she dodged traffic and overstimulation by hightailing it out of here.

Journalists and podcasters fire off questions the others take turns answering. The field house we're in isn't small, but the eight-foot table we're at, plus rugby staff, security, and on-air talent and their crew make it a tight fit.

Movement near the door pulls my attention. A smile lifts my cheek at the winter hat bopping to the corner.

She came.

Miriam is barely visible between the tripods and the press gunning for a viral clip. Her height does her no favors, but I don't need to see her. I feel her.

"There's speculation that Mancini might relocate the team to Toronto to solidify his business interests. Care to comment?"

What?

The question comes from somewhere in the audience. I force my brows to stay in place and my mouth not to twist. *Remember your media training*. My eyes dart to Coach, who leans forward.

"We're not aware of any rumors. We're focused on a healthy team, finishing the season strong, and making Buffalo proud," he says, scanning the room. "This team already makes me proud, and I'll continue to show up for them the way they show up for each other. If there aren't any more questions about today's game, let's get these guys home."

Coach Washington motions for us to leave.

"Did you hear anything about a move?" Kendrick asks through a practiced smile I return.

"Nope, but that might explain why the prick hasn't come to a single game."

In the grand scheme of things, moving to Toronto wouldn't be the worst news. At least we'd still have a team. I could figure out how to stay in Buffalo and make it to practice. Toronto traffic is a bitch, but it's better than being traded to another team on the other side of the country.

I lock eyes with Julian and nod at Kendrick. "See you back at the house."

"Thanks for coming, bro." I hug my best friend. "Is that Jackson on the phone? What's up, big man?"

"Hey, Uncle Ant," Jackson says. His low fade matches his step-dad's. "Good game."

"Thanks. One day, we'll be watching yours."

That gets a smile. "Maybe my dad can buy a team. We're good for it."

"Aye, you don't know what's in my pockets," Julian laughs.

Jackson's face turns serious. "Will you make it home in time for my game tomorrow?"

Julian's voice softens. "I'm on my way to the airport now. I'll be home before you go to bed, son. I'll see you soon, okay? Love you." He ends the call and rolls his eyes. "Don't start."

"You're a good man, Charlie Brown."

"Dumbass. Keep me updated with your team. My son might need one when it's time."

"Make it happen." Having my best friend own the team would be better than Mancini. "Thanks for coming over from New York City. Safe travels. Love to the family."

The room clears, leaving Buffalo Steel banners, empty chairs, and her.

"Hey, superstar." Miriam's quiet laughter floats across the distance I cut in three strides. "Congratulations."

"Thank you, baby." I kiss her once, twice, and pull her to my chest. The halo of her rose oil floats up to my nostrils. "I'm happy you came," I tell her with my chin on her head.

"Me too."

"Marcela bullied you into staying?"

"Pretty much—but!" Her dimples squeeze her cheeks. "I am proud of you, Antonio," she says, her voice soft and gaze steady. "I'd pass out in front of those cameras, but you're in your element. It's remarkable to experience up close."

"That means more than you know, Doe."

Her lips part, drawing my mouth to hers.

"You're still here!" Reese rushes in with caffeinated energy levels and a deep frown. "I took care of Aaron. That jerk is always fishing for a story, and he'll fabricate one to make his stupid podcast relevant. I blocked him on Match Meet. It's not surprising he acted a whole fool with that question about Toronto.

"Who knows where he got that conspiracy theory. It's rare to hear from Mancini, but what else is new? We're fine! I'll release a press statement if it comes to it. You have a meeting on your calendar with a furniture company who's interested in hiring you for a commercial. Legal is taking a look. Do you think you can squeeze in a quick school appearance before Monday's—Oh, hi!"

Reese peels her eyes away from the tablet in front of her face. Walking while scheduling is her superpower. She sure as hell doesn't watch where she's going.

"I didn't realize you had company." Her cheeks pink to match her blouse. It's tucked into light pink pants with polka dots and silk fabric patches. No doubt a Gordon Gartrelle original.

"All good, Reese. This is Miriam," I say. "Doe, this is Reese, the team's media manager."

"It's nice—"

"You're Miriam! I've heard so much about you—all good things. I'm a hugger. Is that okay?"

"Your tablet is digging into my chest," Miriam says from Reese's bear hug, which is smushing her glasses and face.

Reese's eyes widen. She steps back and smooths the edges of her high, loose ponytail. "Sorry. It's nice not breathing in testosterone for a change. I don't have many friends because of my job. I probably shouldn't admit that."

Miriam's lips quirk. "I don't either—outside of Antonio, who doesn't count anymore."

I frown. "Hey!"

She muffles a laugh. "You know what I mean. I almost went on a bus tour to meet new people after I moved here."

"The beer-and-greet? You didn't miss a thing." Reese rolls her eyes. "Only six people showed. They talked about football the whole night. Do I look like I watch? I missed an *Alien* marathon," she scoffs.

Miriam's grin widens. "I love the franchise. I want to rewatch all of the movies in chronological order. You're welcome to join me, if that's not weird."

"Sure! That is, if I'm not intruding." Reese peeks at me.

"Why don't you come to Steel House? My TV is bigger, and I'll stay out of the way." Kendrick will lose his shit once he finds out Reese is under the same roof.

"Perfect! Antonio can give me your number, if that's okay. I'll text you next week!" Reese bear-hugs Miriam again before bouncing away.

"I like her."

The smile in Miriam's voice sparks my own. "She's cool, but don't get any ideas about replacing me. Come on."

"From now on, we're staying at your house." Miriam's loose bun of curls rolls over my chest.

She moans at the steak fajita I press to her mouth. My dick stirs when her lips graze my fingertips.

I adjust myself and peck her shoulder. "You can stay here for as long as you like."

"Don't tempt me with a good time. This is amazing."

The jacuzzi in the backyard of Steel House has mileage. It's a place for recovery after practice, home games, and whatever else I don't care to know about. It gets cleaned weekly, which made tonight a no-brainer with Miriam.

The guys are out wreaking havoc in somebody's club, and I'm at home with my lady. I have her, the fajita platters we ordered, jets massaging my battered muscles, and the cold night sky.

"Are you nervous about the team's possible move?"

I lean back on the neck rest and open when Miriam feeds me a bite of chicken. Water droplets cling to her warm mocha hue. The jets' lights bathe her soft curves in silhouette. We're both naked, hidden from the world by the canopy of white fabric around the wooden jacuzzi deck.

"No," I say truthfully, my arms stretched along the back of the tub. "Mancini always acts like he wants to get rid of us. Same shit, different day. We'll be good, I'll make sure of it."

She sets the plate with the remnants of our dinner on the deck. Her heavy breasts lift from the water, granting me a peek at her dark nipples. The tips brush against my skin when she straddles me. I kiss the flesh above her heart and gaze into eyes I've loved for what feels like an eternity.

I always loved Miriam, even when I didn't fully understand it or believe I was capable. I adore her mind, take pleasure in her body, and will never get enough of her spirit. Her presence shattered the hard shell I built to keep myself from feeling or imagining more.

She's my person, in every lifetime. I'll never deserve her, but I'll wake up every day trying.

She slides her arms around my neck and kisses my cheek. "I believe it will happen. You have a way of making dreams come true."

"You are my dream come true."

The kiss Miriam initiates is slow. She tilts my chin to glide her tongue over my lip. I moan at the slow roll of her hips over my erection, widen my legs, and suck a nipple into my mouth. Miriam bites her lip when I slowly circle my tongue over the sensitive buds on her areola. Her eyes are closed, head tilted toward the galaxy we fly to whenever we're together. She lifts her body and shivers as she sucks me into her pussy inch by inch. Her jaw slacks, and she stares at me with the same reverence I hold for her.

Tonight, I don't want to think about rugby, my schedule, or what will happen to the team. Everything I need is right in front of me.

Chapter 46

Miriam

"My plant is thriving! You see this, Miss Miriam?" Harmony proudly lifts her half container of fresh basil.

"It's beautiful! You did a wonderful job," I say to the sixth-grader.

"Can I take it home? My mama is always killing plants. Maybe she can come here to learn. I'm too young to throw away so many dead bodies."

Kids are a trip. They'll toss you under the bus and pretend they weren't the one in the driver's seat, using your feelings like speed bumps.

We've been learning about hydroponics, a technique to grow plants without soil. Last week's hydroponic farm visit on the East Side prompted our garden experiment. Not only are my kids learning about the life cycle of a plant, they're learning how food grows and the importance of how it's sourced.

We'll incorporate more urban farming activities over the next few weeks in anticipation of the Buffalo Grows Coalition's efforts to solicit City Council for twenty vacant lots. The plan is to expand a local urban farm with space for a community-owned grocery store stocked with local produce and meat from farms within the food equity network across the state. The land is just a short distance away from Buffalo's historically Black neighborhood with a community land trust that provides permanently affordable housing.

Community nonprofits within the coalition hoped the City would provide the lots, but they saved enough to purchase them outright. It's all coming together. All I need is Oprah money to get this research lab off the ground.

The room, tucked away in the community center, is a collage of worn carpet and old furniture stacked like Tetris pieces, but I see it. A long table against the wall for computer stations. Small islands in the middle of the room to prototype. A retractable projector screen near the window, and one of those touch-screen whiteboards.

With the right financial support, the Jefferson Moselle Community Center will establish a STEM hub for children and community members to engage in hands-on learning. A place for them to build the Buffalo they want to live in.

The day wraps with the kids measuring whose plant grew the most. It's hard to keep a straight face when the rulers come out, but we get through it without name-calling or dirt flinging.

My phone rings. I wouldn't say it's odd for Marcela to call on hump day, but it's not like her. Today is her planning day in City Hall. She'll go off the grid when she gets home, closing the blinds and keeping the lights off so she's not bothered.

"Hey." I press the button for speakerphone and collect crayons and the other supplies that never made it back to their bins.

Silence.

"Marcela?" I lift the phone. "Did you butt-dial me again?"

"I just left City Hall."

"Did you remember to leave your brass knuckles at home?" I giggle. Putting a dent in the mayor's forehead is a good way to guarantee time behind prison walls.

"A friend from the Strategic Planning Department gave me a heads-up about a project the mayor is backing. It's from Hunter Development Corporation."

The company the Buffalo Steel owner runs. It's not a cause for alarm, at least not on the surface. From what Marcela tells me, Hunter Development has its hand in everything.

"*Okay*," I exaggerate, unsure why this warrants a call. My feet are screaming to get out of the Chucks I've been running around in all day.

"City Council will receive a proposal to develop fifty vacant lots. Frank Mancini wants to build luxury homes around Moselle Park to 'bring up the value,'" she scoffs. "The plans include a mixed-use building with rental space for a restaurant and an urban farm on the premises."

The hairs on the back of my neck rise.

"An urban farm?" I ask, for clarity. "That's specific."

"Maple King is working on the project. They say they have a patent idea."

A knot forms in the pit of my stomach.

"What idea?"

Papers flutter on the other end of the line. "To make buildings more durable during extreme weather events," she says. "Maple King has no urban farms in its portfolio, which makes this project oddly timed."

"It's my idea."

I collapse into a chair. My mind races for an explanation, but the betrayal makes the room spin. My eyes snap shut as a sour taste coats the painful lump in my throat.

"The night of our dinner, Kieran invited me back to Maple King," I say through the pressure constricting my lungs. "He told me I could use the lab. I—I toyed with a concept I didn't have the software to test out." I huff. "I haven't conducted any research yet to fully inform the requirements."

How did he save it? I erased my work before I left. I'm certain I did.

"Nothing is fully tested or close to completion," I tell Marcela, to explain why the betrayal is not only theft but illogical. "Is that why he went out of his way to ask me out? To profit off my ideas? This can't be happening."

Why would Kieran do this? Because I didn't want to date him or hike in the snow?

When he asked what I was working on, I gave a summary in broad strokes. I was being nice because of his hospitality. I didn't think he would steal my concept.

"He won't get away with this," Marcela asserts in her big-sister voice that leaves no room for bullshit. "I won't let him."

"You can't stop him." Tears fall. "He has the reach and the legal power to steamroll me."

Maple King has the capital to flesh out my idea. It will be a race to file a patent application for exclusive rights to use the concept while preventing competitors from exploiting it.

The irony, right?

My sister blows out a long breath. "I'm checking with someone who works in the legal department. The chief attorney's job is to defend the city in lawsuits, should it come to that. If there's some way we can prove it's your concept, I'll fight like hell to can it. But we need to be quick, Miri."

"How long do I have?" Acid burns my throat.

The line is quiet. "A month, maybe more if I can stall. The proposal is on the schedule for next week's City Council meeting. It will get kicked to the Community Development Committee, where it will get the votes to pass back to the council for a full vote. You should call our father."

"No." I sniffle. "I listened to him lecture me about taking this job. I can't stomach an 'I told you so.'"

"Miri, he loves you, and he wouldn't let this slide. I'll follow your lead, but you have an army behind you. I keep bail money in the bank for this reason."

An underdeveloped idea stolen by a man with an unnecessary plaque on his desk who can't deal with rejection.

I don't know what to do. What can I do?

Chapter 47

Antonio

"Excuse me. Do you have an appointment?" The receptionist is on her feet. Her slender hips switch in tall heels to beat me to the door next to her desk.

"Do you have an appointment?" she asks again, skidding to a stop in front of me. Her penciled brows slanted into toothpicks are a reminder of my media training. I'm a walking brand at all times, which is the only reason this door isn't modeling my silhouette. Flinging Kieran from a window is a different story. He'd fall four floors before he met the sidewalk.

Anyone who messes with Miriam can die twice.

I knew something was wrong with Dickhead. It was bad enough that he took my baby out for a tasteless salad and paid for a date to get close to her. I never thought he'd physically hurt her, but this? Stealing her idea to patent it for himself is sinister. The reason why he did it doesn't matter. He preyed on her, and that won't go unchecked.

"If you don't have an appointment, you need to leave."

Her again.

I could ignore Bobblehead Brooke and push past her. She's the size of my elbow, but that wouldn't end well for her or for me.

She'd weaponize her tears on a two-part prime-time special, while I'd be staring at a double-digit sentence for shoulder-checking her too hard.

Option number two it is. Charm.

"I'm sorry. I wanted to surprise a friend. Is Kieran here?" I practice my mugshot grin and point to the door.

Her softening scowl becomes wide-eyed. "You play for the Steel."

"Guilty."

"I saw you on PSN the other night. You're...fit." That nasally voice wanted to kick me out thirty seconds ago. Her gaze slides over my navy parka and down my sweats to my winterized sneakers. In hindsight, I should've worn steel-toed boots to stomp her boss's ass, but I had to improvise.

"Can I run in real quick?" I didn't come here to get eye-fucked. "Gotta get back to practice."

"Yes, of course!" Her lashes flutter. "He's free for the next hour."

"Which office?"

"Fifth door on your left. I'll be right here if you need me."

I won't. "Appreciate it."

Polished floors grumble under my feet as I make my way down the annoyingly long hallway. Miriam's tears play on an endless loop. She was still in her car when I pulled up to her house yesterday after practice. Her gloves gripped the steering wheel, her breath visible in icy puffs. Her eyes, full of light and my forever, didn't blink. She just stared until panic rose with the flush rising up her throat.

Doe is an angel among the living, too kind for this world. I don't deserve her, and she sure as hell doesn't deserve anyone playing in her face and stealing her brilliance. After I kissed away every tear, I promised I wouldn't do anything to jeopardize my freedom, but this motherfucker is seeing me.

Voices float under Kieran's door. I let myself in.

"What are you doing in my office?" His eyes double in size, like he's unsure if he wants to square up or stay behind the safety of his desk. Like I won't clear it feetfirst.

Kieran doesn't know who I am, but he's smart enough to realize I'm not here to talk about bridges. He eases back into his chair, doing everything he can to look important in a bland suit that matches his bland office.

I've seen his type on the pitch. Players who talk shit but flinch before a tackle. His breathing changed, and so did his heart rate, given the erratic pulse popping out of his neck.

Silence chokes the office until someone clears his throat. In the corner, next to the door, is the second man on my shit list.

Frank Mancini.

"Antonio, right?" His head tilts, shifting the light from his Chuck Norris toupee to a mole sprouting on the bridge of his bulbous nose. I don't know if the former action star wears a hairpiece, but Mancini would benefit from a trip to the beauty supply store on Bailey. A lace wig and some edge control might work wonders.

I tower over him by almost a foot. He's short, with leathery skin hanging from his meaty features and bony shoulders that barely fill out his gunmetal suit. For one of Buffalo's elite, he looks like he needs to check his drawers every time he farts.

"I'm here for Kerry."

"Kieran," Dickhead corrects.

"Kerry, like I said." I smile. "I don't see any accolades around your office. Is that why you get off on stealing ideas and selling them as your own?"

He swallows hard and looks away. "I think you're mistaken."

"Now that would make my lady a liar, and she's far from it. Miriam is brilliant, but you already knew that."

Kieran's eyes snap to mine, his face a shade of rage.

Yeah, she's mine.

I grin and cut the distance to put my palms on his desk. "You trying to get out your seat?"

"I suggest you go back to where I pay you, which is the field," Mancini cuts in. "My business doesn't concern you."

I whip around, careful not to give Kieran my back. His trifling ass might try to take me out with some scissors. "Oh, but it does when it involves someone I love. Fix it. Now."

"Or?" Mancini challenges.

"Or I have no problem going public." That is, once Miriam gives the okay.

Cold gray eyes flash black. Mancini's scowl loosens into a tight smile. "Good luck playing rugby after I release you. Nobody messes with my money."

"And no one fucks with my baby," I spit. "You own the team, not me."

His tongue drags over his veneers. "I do own you, boy."

I got your fucking boy.

"We'll see about that."

"Mind giving me a heads-up the next time you decide to wage war on the owner of this team?" Coach Washington rips off his glasses to massage his temples. "I've been on the phone all morning with people I've never spoken to before about you disrespecting Mancini to his face. Not to mention payroll will be late again."

My brow shoots to the ceiling. "And you think that's a coincidence? How the hell is that permissible in the league?"

Coach eyes me. "It's not. I reached out to a few people at the RLA to get to the bottom of it." He lets out a long breath. "We're already on thin ice with so many teams dropping. We don't need this right now."

I figured word would reach my coaches after I pulled up on Dickhead. Mancini is a coward. An aged version of Big Boy Caprice from *Dick Tracy*, who wants to punish me by punishing the team. I never meant for the Steel to get caught up in this, but I refuse to be silent.

"I'm not playing on Saturday."

"What?!" The walls in the office shudder under Coach's shout.

"I'm not playing on Saturday, the next game, or the one after that," I say to his deepening frown. "Mancini's real estate company is working with a firm that's stealing Miriam's idea. They're gonna patent it."

"Shit."

"Exactly," I nod. "I was fully prepared to stand alone, because it's not the Steel's fight. To be honest, I think we should sit out the rest of the season until the RLA investigates why payroll issues continue to occur. There's no players' union to protect us, but compensation violations are a big deal, no? It's not a coincidence to me that money starts getting funny around the time the Hunter Development Corporation announces a new project. All I'm saying is, it might be worth looking into at some point."

Coach drags a hand across his face. His eyes catch on the photos of the team that line his broom closet of an office. "A protest would yield consequences." His stare slides back to me. "Possible lawsuits, in the millions. Let me try to handle things on my end before it comes to that. Riggs can take your position on Saturday. Just give me some time, son."

I stand from the seat that's putting my ass to sleep. "Do what you have to do, and I'll do what I need to do."

If that means my time in the league is up, so be it. Doe will always come first.

Chapter 48

Miriam

Antonio has lost his mind. Not a fraction. Not half. His entire mind.

I toss my car into park. The door slams, and I march up the concrete steps to the indoor practice facility, careful not to slip on any remaining patches of ice.

Shadows cloak the field at rest. The faint glow of light down the hall illuminates my path to the man who's about to throw away his entire career for me.

I never asked Antonio to visit Kieran. That man is a coward who lies and steals. I wouldn't put it past him to say Antonio dangled him out of a window, and I don't want him attached to any controversy. I know he wants to protect me. I want to protect me too, and I want to do more than cry.

Like punch Kieran in the face.

Kick him in the dick.

Set his degree on fire.

Something!

I'm tired of feeling so helpless and used. Every time the reality of a multimillion-dollar company patenting my idea sinks in, I want to scream. Actually, I did, and it scared my neighbor's dog. He won't pee or walk within ten feet of my house.

I still question why I didn't see the signs—why I didn't do a better job of erasing my digital footprint before I left the lab I regret ever stepping foot in. I love Antonio, and I appreciate his fearlessness in his desire to do what's right. But missing Saturday's home game for the second week in a row will guarantee his end in the league once the Steel's owner paints him as aggressive and hostile. The press is already in a frenzy because of his absence, filling in the gaps with their own speculation.

There will be more ideas to protect, but there's only one RLA, and there's only so many years left before Antonio hangs it up for good.

Kendrick Lamar's "DNA" explodes from the iron paradise of free weights, cable machines, and squat racks. Antonio is in the corner at the pull-up bar, shirtless and covered in sweat.

The muscles in his back contract as his biceps uncurl on his slow descent to the ground. His feet never touch, his waist anchored in a weight belt that's connected to a metal chain and heavy plates. Every inch of my guts would be on the floor if I attempted to pull my chin to the bar, much less with weights dangling between my legs. But he has no trouble slicing through the air. Up, down, the man is a machine with an endurance I enjoy on the regular. With an ass like that, maybe he can perform miracles.

"I smell you, Doe." He startles me out of a flashback involving him, his stamina, and my feet touching the shower wall. His shower, not mine.

He dismounts from the bar and detaches the weight belt over his basketball shorts. I'm supposed to be mad, but it's hard to concentrate when his chest is out and his dick is making its presence known against his thigh.

"Come here," he summons from a stretch to touch his toes. His eyes lift, and off I go between workout benches and toward the scent of his cologne doused in the grit of his exertion.

"Was anyone out front when you got here?"

I crane my neck and accept a kiss on the lips. "No."

He frowns and reaches for the remote to lower the music. "I don't want you walking from the parking lot by yourself."

"You make it really hard to yell at you when you get all protective."

His brow crinkles. "Is that so?"

Don't look at his chest. "Yes. I'm not happy with you."

"Really?" He steps forward.

I step back. "Yes."

"Because I won't let anyone mess with you? Disrespect you? Hurt you?" He steps closer. "You think I could look at myself in the mirror and play for a team whose owner is complicit in the theft of your work?"

When he says it like that...

"There has to be another way," I protest. "Your absence is stirring up rumors you're becoming a problem."

"I'll be that."

I shudder when his arms slip up my back to pull me closer. "The team needs their captain."

"And I need to do what's right. You asked me not to go off publicly. I'm doing that. But don't expect me to sit by and do nothing. I'm coming behind you every time." His nose nudges my head back for a kiss that lifts me out my shoes. A growl slips out to smother my rebuttal.

The world falls away whenever we're together. Every fear, every care, gets pushed aside. Common sense too, because never have I ever humped a man in a gym.

"I didn't come here for this," I say through a deep breath and step out of reach. The tingling in my lips is grounds alone for a visit to my doctor to check my circulation.

Antonio lifts both hands to an overhead bar. The broad expanse of his pecs contracts, daring me to lick off the sweat. "My apologies, Doe. Do you want to yell at me some more?"

Idiot.

"No." I smile.

"Wanna spot me?"

"*What?*"

He motions to a weight bench. "I need to lift before I leave. Come spot me."

I choke back a laugh. "I can't save you in an emergency. I can barely lift three grocery bags with one arm."

"Indulge me," he says with a wink.

"I know what you're doing," I mutter, removing the flimsy coat I threw on before leaving the house.

"Finishing my workout? Quite observant, you are." Antonio slides under an empty barbell. He positions his grip, his legs spread wide to tease the heavy print that's summoning my heaux to come out and play. "You spotting or what?"

"Fine," I sigh. "Where's the weights?"

"Sit," he says low, his eyes on me.

There's no question the barbell can handle me. I've seen him bench-press well over three hundred pounds. The bar isn't the problem. Putting my kitty inches from his face is.

"Doe. I'm not asking twice."

I can't believe I'm doing this. "Fine. How do you want me?"

A foolish question that earns a grin.

Antonio eyes my flannel shirt and black leggings. "Take off your pants so you don't slide off."

"For safety?" I deadpan.

He nods with his lip between his teeth.

"If someone walks in here and sees me with my ass out, I'm choking you with the bar."

"So violent!" He licks his lips and sniffs the air when he sees my black panties. "Yeah. I smell you. Climb up. Spread your legs, and hold on to the rack."

"This is a bad idea," I grumble, but I follow directions.

The cold metal prickles my bare skin. I shift my weight and grip the rack for balance. My thighs spread like peanut butter, inviting heat from the air to press into the seat of the thin fabric soaked in my desire.

"You know I got you, right?" Antonio asks, his voice husky. "I always will."

"I know," I whisper down to his stare. "Thank you for the distraction."

All thirty-two of his teeth show. "Thank you for the snack." I moan at the first swipe of his tongue over my seam when he lowers the bar.

"Spread for me," he mumbles from between my legs. "Yeah, she's ready for me. Hold on, baby."

Antonio pushes up and lowers me to his chest without effort. The flex of his muscles and the sensation of the slow glide of his tongue over my underwear hardens my nipples. He's laser focused, his gaze locked and mouth latched.

We get to twelve reps before he racks the bar, and his lips are on me again. This time, he pulls my panties to the side to pull my clit into his mouth.

"Make a mess for me, Dr. Beckford."

Shit, say less.

The angle of his head and the power of his jaw crack my toes. My breath skips, and my thighs tremble. I curl into the fast strokes of his tongue and whimper.

"I don't like you wound up like you gotta carry this shit by yourself. Let it out."

A moan rattles his throat. I grip the barbell and cry out to the ceiling when he sucks harder. The release is sharp, demanding every ounce of air in my lungs. He holds me in place as I rock into him and slows his pace to lazy licks. My shoulders slump, and for the first time since Marcela called, I feel calm. Balanced.

Sex won't change my circumstances—or Antonio's hardheaded efforts—but his love and affection soothe the wounds. It also doesn't hurt that his tongue has magic. I can fly home as high as I am.

He helps me off the barbell and sweeps me into his arms. I wrap my legs around his waist as he guides us to a flat bench.

There are no words. Only a slow kiss that starts at my mouth and slides down the valley of my breasts with every button he undoes. He pushes my shirt open to palm my breasts, then frees them from the front clasp on my bra. My clit pulses at the drag of his fingers that dip between my legs. His tongue runs laps around my nipples as he cups me with his hand. The force strangles my breath and restarts my engine. Thick fingers spread inside me, and I ride the wave of another orgasm using his palm as a surfboard.

"I need you," I pant, reaching for Antonio's mouth to bring to mine.

"You always have me." He steps back and hooks his thumbs in his basketball shorts. His dick bobs free at a tug, hard and glistening with pre-cum. I wrap my hands around his length and guide him into my mouth. My tongue outlines his tip, salty from his sweat, as I breathe through my nose to take him deeper.

"Shit, Doe." The muscles in his quads flex through the slow pump of his hips. He cups my face and pushes in deeper.

Taking him to the back of my throat is still a work in progress. What I can fit in my mouth, I slurp and jerk with a hand, hollowing my cheeks while caressing his balls. My face burn from the stretch, my mouth wetter with the saliva running down my lips he swipes with a finger. He jerks at the flick of my tongue on the underside of his head.

"You look good with me in your mouth. Fuck," he hisses. His nostrils flare, and his eyes snap shut. He staggers back to catch his breath. "Shit. Should I send your mama a fruit basket?"

"Shut up!" I snort at him holding his dick in awe.

My laughter dies once he straddles the bench. He bends my knee and eases into me. Every inch is a slow burn until he's fully seated. My lips part at his tongue as he holds my other leg firm against his chest and pumps into me.

Antonio would bruise my cervix if it caused no pain and came with a speedy recovery. He's a mechanical bull who can hold a mean squat. His thighs are tight, his aim steady on the target.

I reach for the edge of the bench above my head to ride out each thrust. Two games' worth of unused energy pummel my walls.

"I love you, Miriam. I won't apologize for fighting for you," he says, his eyes low, focused on me. He thrusts faster, his balls smacking into my pussy. "She's singing to me," he grunts, rolling his hips to thrust deeper. "Eyes on me. Give me all of you." *Grunt.* "Your worries." *Grunt.* "Your fears." *Grunt.* "There's nothing I won't do for you, Doe."

Time loses its importance. My body shakes and my toes cramp. His release comes through his declaration to love and protect me.

I follow Antonio back to Steel House, where I wake up in his arms. Safe, well-rested, and thoroughly satisfied.

Chapter 49

Miriam

"I knew you'd call. Come in." Kieran holds open the front door to the Maple King office building.

"Thank you for meeting with me." I keep my tone even and swallow the urge to vomit. Flight is squaring up with my fight, but I'm here on a mission.

The walk to his office is quiet through traces of recessed lights spotlighting a pathway I thought I'd never take again. No one else is here. Not that I'd expect there to be at eight thirty at night.

My grip on my purse tightens at the feeling of his eyes on my ass. The weather is unseasonably mild for early April in Buffalo. I traded in my winter coat for long-sleeved tee and a vest to enjoy the weeklong warm front. Now I regret not wearing some type of Missy Elliott garbage suit to conceal my curves.

I wait next to his office with the stupid plaque and follow him inside.

"Close the door." He takes a seat at the front of his desk and crosses his legs.

A cold knot forms in my stomach. *You can do this.* I shut the door.

"You look good." His eyes swing to my curls, which are nearly touching my shoulders. I swallow hard when they reach my breasts. "Did you come to apologize?"

This n—

"I want to understand why you're patenting an idea that's not yours," I say, confidence finding its way into my voice. "Do you have any idea how hard it is for Black women in any field, especially engineering? That concept is mine, and it will do a lot of good for the community."

"We'll put it to good use on the East Side."

I gape at his audacity. "So, what? You ask me to dinner after my job interview, pay thousands to go out with me again, and let me use Maple King's labs just to steal from me? Was that the whole plan all along? To use me?"

"I wanted to fuck you." He chuckles to himself. "I still do. You had the opportunity to build with me here, for us to create a legacy. You chose not to." His nostrils flare. "Everything comes with a cost, Miriam. Lucky for you, I'm willing to start over."

The timbre in his voice sends shivers through me. His arms fold over his button-down shirt. It's fitting that he's in all black tonight, to match how evil he is.

I lift my chin. "Does that mean you won't pawn off my idea as your own and patent it?"

A dark smile spreads across his lips. "That ship has already sailed, sweetie," he says, amused that I'd think it would be on the table. "You worked on your concept in the Maple King lab."

"At your invitation, and after hours! I didn't give you permission to steal from me."

He pushes off the desk. "I never needed your permission. Don't be naïve, Miriam. You designed a concept using our property. What did you think would happen?"

"So you're confessing to taking my concept?" I spit.

He grins. "I don't need to. You were in our lab."

"I'll go public."

"Go ahead. You aren't the first and won't be the last."

Did I just hear him right?

I jerk away from his touch. "Don't take it personal, Miriam. It's just business."

"What would your parents say? Or the Hunter Development Corporation, having its name attached to theft?"

Kieran's laughter is dark. "Who do you think encouraged me to use what you designed after you dismissed me the way you did? As for Hunter Development"—I recoil at his breath fanning across my face—"it's part of our business practices, among other things. Come home with me. I'll make it better."

"You disgust me," I snarl.

"You came to me. You'll be back." He laughs as I sprint out the door.

I jog back to my car in record time, with no signs of collapsing from the cardio.

"Jesus!" I jump at the dark figure in my rearview mirror. "I thought you left."

"How can I keep you safe if I leave, Maid Miriam?" Bread scoffs before ripping open a packet of gummy bears.

I frown. "Where did you get snacks?"

"Ran across the street to the convenience store while you went up. Want one?" He extends the bag.

"No thanks."

He shrugs. "Did you get what you needed, or do I need to go up there and beat his ass?"

"None of that," I say through a long sigh.

Antonio would catch a manslaughter charge if he knew what I was up to and would beat Bread in the process. He sat out another game. The press is officially turning on him. Some are speculating he's hiding an injury. Others say he is dividing the team and not taking his leadership role seriously.

His head coach is forbidding interviews. With no one to set the record straight, made-up stories are piling up at his expense.

A gossip reporter spotted Antonio and Bread arguing in the parking lot after practice. Yards away, it was easy to assume a star player was beefing with his teammate. The reality is that Antonio had to talk Bread off the ledge before he took matters into his own hands.

The guys want to help, but Antonio won't let them. He can afford to face any consequences from his protest. Things are tense, but the team respects their captain. They ignore press questions and focus on winning games.

"Thank you for coming with me tonight," I say to Bread's hulking frame that's swallowing the back seat of my car. He's dressed in all black but too big to hide from anyone.

"Like you had a choice," he chuckles. "You know I got you and Cap's backs."

Bread overheard me on the phone with Reese a few nights ago at Steel House. I took the call in the main kitchen downstairs, hoping to avoid Antonio. Bread was grabbing a snack and told me he'd be my security just in case.

Reese picks up on the first ring.

"Are you safe?"

"Yeah." I draw in a sharp breath and tap the speakerphone. "I got what we needed."

Poor Reese is putting out fires left and right, trying to explain why one of the Steel's star players isn't on the pitch. I won't stand by while the press eats him alive. When I asked Antonio in Vegas if he ever lets people take care of him the way he takes care of others, I made a promise to protect him the way he's protected me.

Fuck Kieran and Mancini.

"Phase two," I tell Reese.

"Phase two."

"Hell yeah!" Bread shouts.

The incessant ringing of my doorbell wakes me from a deep slumber. Who is at my door trying to catch a toaster to the forehead?

"It's six thirty," I grumble from my pillow when I glance at the clock on my nightstand. The cocoon of flannel sheets and a thick comforter come with an implied Do Not Disturb sign.

It's not Antonio. He slept at his house last night to be ready for a five-a.m. session with D. Working out that early is demonic, and I won't argue the point.

Fridays are the one day of the workweek when I get to take it easy. I wake up at eight, read in bed, and get to the community center by ten thirty. It's perfect—except for today and the person fingering my doorbell with no couth.

I check my phone for messages, toss on a terry cloth robe, and stomp down my steps. If we're skipping the pleasantries of a courtesy call, whoever is on the other side of my door will get a front-row seat to my bonnet and eye boogies.

Did a neighbor get locked out of their house? Did a child miss the bus?

"Dad?" I gape at my father, who's standing in a suit and coat on the "An Awesome Engineer Lives Here" mat. One guess who found it online and shipped it to my house. "What are you doing in Buffalo?"

"The better question is why didn't you reach out sooner? I didn't call because I assumed your phone stopped working." He eyes me flatly, kisses my cheek, and walks inside.

I shut the door. "I'm handling it."

"How? By recording a conversation you hope will change hearts and minds?" He folds his arms across his black coat, his seawater and lavender cologne clinging to the tie I bought him two Christmases ago. "Why didn't you come to me?"

Why do I need to when Marcela blabs my business?

He motions for me to sit on the sofa. I cross my legs and sigh. "Because it's my problem. I don't need another lecture about how I chose the wrong job, or why my title is beneath me. I'm doing good work that will make a difference. I don't want your disappointment, but I don't need your approval."

My father runs a hand over his low taper fade. His Rolex peeks out from the cuff of the suit that's tailored to his six-three frame. He anchors his elbows to his knees and strokes his chin as he softly regards me with the dark brown eyes we share.

"You've always done what you wanted, since you were a kid," he says with a sad smile that lifts his chocolate dimples. He lets out a short laugh. "You never needed my approval, Lady Bug. If anything, I was searching for yours, to prove my usefulness. I'm sorry I've been so hard on you. I only wanted the best."

Not tears in a bonnet before seven a.m.!

He slides forward to hug me, and I melt into the protection of the first man I ever loved.

"You're never too old for me to defend you," he whispers with a kiss to my temple. "You have a family who loves you, even if we're overbearing at times."

I laugh and wipe away a tear.

"Don't put yourself in danger, Miri. Anything could've happened last night with you going over there by yourself."

"I know. I needed Kieran to admit what he did on tape."

My father sits back. "Why?"

"Because New York is a one-party consent state. Recording a conversation is legal as long as one of the parties consents to the recording. I planned to use it to get Maple King to reconsider stealing my patent idea."

"Lady Bug, your recording alone isn't enough. Maple King will explain away whatever press you garner." My father pats my leg and stands. "The best way to deal with them is to hit them where it hurts the most: fuck with their money."

My brows dip.

"Did you forget where your father works?" He smiles at my pinched stare. "Maple King relies on government contracts. One call to a friend in Toronto this morning terminated their latest one."

"Dad."

"I didn't build up years of relationships and a network of influence to sit back while some prick takes advantage of my baby girl. You've always stood tall on your own, Miri, but anyone who messes with this family will be handled accordingly. I'd like to take you to lunch to catch up. You can tell me about your new position and the work you're doing."

I smile. "I'd like that."

"And that rugby player you're dating."

Marcela!

"Your mother is expecting your call."

Chuleta.

Chapter 50

Antonio

"I made a lapse in judgment that caused harm, and I regret my actions. I take full responsibility. I deeply regret my decision. My actions were my own and do not reflect the values of Maple King. I am sincerely sorry."

Kieran's chin quivers. He hangs his head, crumpling under the spotlight.

"I don't deserve forgiveness, but I hope to earn it."

He sobs.

Punk ass.

"I'm so sorry," he says through a hiccup.

"How many times have you watched that video?"

"Not enough. Dickhead could fit three marbles inside each nostril with all the hollering he's doing." I kiss Miriam's smile and put away my phone.

Her pops threw down the gauntlet at Maple King two weeks ago. Executives wasted no time tossing Kieran in front of the cameras for a public apology. It's all bullshit. The only reason he's sobbing like he's on an Oprah special is because they hung his ass out to dry.

His reputation is dead—his and his raggedy-ass parents, who encouraged their son to steal from a woman who rejected him.

I still want to put his head through a wall, but I'm happy the apology was public. Kieran kept Miriam's name out of his mouth at her father's request. She doesn't want to be tied to any scandals. As far as I'm concerned, Kieran can spend his days hiding under whatever rock he crawled to after leaving Buffalo.

I damn near shit out my guts when she told me about meeting up with him to get his admission on tape. The president of Maple King released a statement after firing Kieran, and agreed to erase Miriam's concept to save face and their government contracts. That didn't stop Reese from contacting her investigative journalist friend. Wouldn't you know it, she uncovered a trend of predatory business practices.

Those government contracts? Gone.

Doe will refine her urban farming concept for submission to the patent office. She caught an attitude after I purchased the software and licenses she'll need for her research. I'll be damned if I let anyone take advantage of her again. Julian, my parents, and I pitched in with seed money to get her STEM hub off the ground at the community center. Even her pops donated, which helped to heal some of the tension between them.

I didn't have the pleasure of meeting her dad while he was up here, but I look forward to meeting him when the Steel play DC in a couple of weeks.

"You'll be okay over here?" I kiss Miriam's forehead for the third time, rubbing circles into her shoulders, which are covered in a blouse that has more ruffles than Prince had in his closet. I don't mean to stare, but damn.

I'm no authority on the dress code for press conferences, but my baby might have be okay with looking like the Quaker Oats man.

"Do you think this is too much?" She motions to the curtain of fabric on her chest.

Don't say it.

"Truth?" I wince, then attempt a recovery. "Someone might think you ripped the drapes off your windows, but you're gorgeous, baby. Look at it this way, you already have a costume for Hallow—"

"So help me God, if you say Prince..."

"I was actually thinking *Penguins of Madagascar*." *Not helping!* "I'll go now."

"You do that," she growls.

"It's not bad!"

My steps are cautious, but I give her a quick peck on the cheek before I take off for the stage.

"Ready?" Marcela asks.

"Let's do this." I shake hands with Coach Washington, who comes up the stairs in khakis, a polo, and boat shoes.

"Taking the yacht out after this?" I tease.

"Not all of us enjoy suits." He eyes my black slacks and Italian shoes, which are shined for my close-up. My dress shirt is unbuttoned at the top so my gold cross can shine.

Everything is falling into place. There's just one more piece.

Attorney General Kennedy Richards steps to the podium with a fresh press, buttoning a light gray suit. She scans the room with a silent authority emphasized by the shift of her hips.

Her tone is a smooth alto with zero tolerance for bullshit. "Good morning. Your attendance is appreciated. My office has initiated an investigation into allegations of misconduct and fraud within the Buffalo Revival Department, including real estate developers who have benefited from exclusive contracts through campaign contributions to the current administration.

"As your attorney general, it is my duty to protect our state from fraudulent, deceptive, and illegal practices. We will withhold details to investigate without prejudice while we determine whether charges and other disciplinary measures are necessary at its conclusion."

She steps aside for Marcela and the City Council president. Big sis is fit for war in her plum suit. I've never seen the council president before. Judging by the sweat beading at the top of his balding head, he doesn't want to be here.

"In light of the recent investigation, City Council passed a resolution to place a moratorium on the sale of vacant lots across the East Side of Buffalo," Council President Gallagher recites like he practiced in the mirror. "We've heard the concerns of residents"—he looks to Marcela—"and Councilmember Beckford to make development more equitable. We will conduct a series of public hearings over the course of the next two months to develop a strategic plan that considers all city residents."

"For years, community members have questioned who truly benefits from Buffalo's revival," Marcela says to the cameras and attendees. "We've questioned why the same corporations get to build houses across the city, houses that are neither affordable nor accessible to everyday Buffalonians."

"That's right!" an elder shouts.

"City Hall continues to operate through business-as-usual practices while passing off the buck. I applaud the attorney general for investigating the Buffalo Revival Department, an office chaired by our current mayor, with campaign contributors who have deep pockets and vested interest in seeing their projects thrive. Today, we say the buck stops here. It's high time City Hall works for the people, not the corporations that line their pockets. I look forward to working with my colleagues on City Council. We need more public servants to do what's right, even if it takes them a while to get there."

Mitchell Library erupts in applause. Marcela claims she has no interest in being mayor—"too many people are in my business already," she tells Miriam—but she sounds like the leader we need.

"We'll now hear from Bryan McCaw, Commissioner of the Rugby League of America." Marcela makes room for Coach Washington and I to take our places behind him at the podium.

"Thank you, councilmember," McCaw says, a touch of his Scottish accent peeking out. "In light of an internal investigation into the practices of Buffalo Steel owner Frank Mancini and the violation of league rules, the RLA is exercising its right as the governing body to issue an interim owner, effective immediately. Temporary management will run through the remainder of the year. Mancini, who also owns Hunter Development Corporation, which is being investigated, has agreed to sell the franchise after failing to cooperate with our probe. We hope to announce a new owner by the new year, and we look forward to seeing the Steel compete in the playoffs."

Who owns who now?

What I would've paid to see the smirk wiped off Mancini's face. It's too bad I couldn't see it in person. Guess who fled to Florida?

Whispers of his alleged involvement with the mayor in corruption and uncovering irregularities in his accounts fueled the RLA to take immediate action. I didn't think we'd see the day. The media has been running with the story since the RLA's decision earlier this week, and they're shining a light on the lack of a players' union, minimal healthcare coverage and benefits, and low wages.

Will all of that change tomorrow? I doubt it, but it's a start.

The press conference concludes. I make a beeline for Miriam and get intercepted by a five-foot-six ball of sunshine in box braids.

"We have you set up in the resource room. PSN has twenty minutes—no questions off-limits, per your request. But I'll be there in case there's something you don't want to answer. Just be yourself—"

"Reese?"

She nods. "Sorry. You got it."

"I was going to say thank you for what you did for Miriam. I appreciate you looking out for her."

"Oh, it was nothing." She dismisses my gratitude with a hand but offers a smile. "The Steel have become family, and Miriam is a friend. It wasn't right what happened, and Dickhead deserved what he got."

"Am I rubbing off on you, Reese?" I chuckle.

"A good girl never tells." She winks and skips over to Miriam, all but tackling her in a hug.

A tornado of white and yellow ruffles spins in squeals. Reese rubbed off on Miriam. Doe wore that Victorian-era top on her own, but she laughs harder and smiles wider whenever Reese is around.

I drop a kiss onto Miriam's cheek. "I gotta do an interview. See you over there?"

"I'll come with Reese in a sec."

It takes a few handshakes and photos to reach the resource room.

"Ready for your close-up?" Kenya tucks her hair behind her ear and stands from one of the two chairs in the middle of the small room. Two cameramen maneuver around short bookcases, setting up lights and microphones.

"Yup." I step back when she reaches for my arm. A frown draws her brows together.

We get mic'd up and take our places in front of three cameras. After a sound check, Kenya motions to start.

"Thank you for joining us, Antonio. It's been quite a month since we last saw you on the pitch," she says, her eyes steady, with no hints of softballs. Her legs cross in a knee-length blue dress. "How is the team handling the recent development with the ownership?"

"We're rolling with the punches, but we're happy things are finally coming to light," I say honestly. "I can't speak for other teams, but when we play at a certain level, we hope the higher-ups match that energy with equal investment. That hasn't been the case. Hopefully, what happened to us will set a precedent moving forward."

"You've been noticeably absent on the field. There's been lots of speculation about the reason you haven't started the last three games. Some reports allege disputes with the coaching staff. Others, the team. Care to set the record straight?"

I run a hand down my beard. "It's crazy how quickly the media turns on you based on assumptions. I consider myself to be a team player and a good captain. I respect my coaches, and I love being part of the Steel. I'm not a perfect man, but I am my parents' child at the end of the day."

Kenya leans forward. "What does that mean?"

"It means I've never been with the bullshit," I say. "Frank Mancini's development corporation had ties to a company that took something important from someone I care about. We exchanged words, and I sat out from there. What was done in the dark is coming to light. Quite frankly, I hope he gets everything he deserves.

"Mancini is vile, and he never cared about the team, in my opinion." I look directly into the camera. "He once told me, 'I own you, boy.' Karma isn't the only one who proved to be a bitch."

Reese will have my ass for this, but she'll survive.

"Well, then!" Kenya snaps her fingers. "You heard it here first. Now that we cleared that up, let's talk about what's next. The Steel are the front-runners to win the playoffs, with eight consecutive wins under your belt. Any plans you care to share if you come out victorious?"

I smile at Miriam when she walks in. "Yeah. I'm going to the Space Center with this one. Come here, Doe."

Kenya frowns when her eyes land on Miriam. "Who is this?"

"My future wife," I say, pulling Miriam to sit in my lap. She's a deer caught in headlights, likely because of all those damn ruffles on her blouse. "You interested in a trip to Houston?" I wrap my arms around her and kiss her lips.

"I'd like that, but I think our steak dinner at Amato's is in order first." The grin she aims up at me stirs inside my chest.

"Okay. How long has this been going on?" Kenya asks, doing her best to recover.

My eyes stay on my best friend, my forever. "You could say I've loved her all of my life, even when I didn't think I deserved her, or that she would give me a chance. We've been friends for years, and I couldn't be more grateful to have a partner who's kind, brilliant, and my favorite person. There is one question I never asked you, Doe."

Her eyes turn into saucers.

"Not that—not yet." I pull a sheet of paper from my pocket with a laugh. "You getting this on camera, Kenya?"

At her nod, I unfold the crinkled white page and hold it up. It reads, "Will you go out with me?" with a "yes," "no," and "maybe" box.

Miriam snorts at the *Brown Sugar* reference. Her laughter shakes her ruffles and tints her cheeks pink. "I cannot believe you."

"You gonna answer me in front of America?"

"Yes." She smiles. "Always yes."

Epilogue

Miriam

Eight months later

"What can I get you?"

"An Aperol spritz please." I offer the bartender, who's in classic black and white, a smile.

"Interested in a pomegranate Prosecco punch? It's our specialty cocktail for the night."

I remove my coat. "Sounds great, thanks."

"Your dress is a mirror ball!" The bartender nods at the shimmering material that stops above my knees. Its built-in shapewear keeps me snug and my breasts from spilling out. "Forgive me for staring, but wow. I'm Leah, by the way."

"Miriam. It's nice to meet you, and thanks."

She pulls a bottle of Prosecco from the refrigerator below the bar, which is illuminated by a wall of shelves. "I take it you have plans tonight? Can't let a dress like that go to waste."

"Coming back from a dinner," I say.

"An early New Year's Eve celebration?"

I smile. "Something like that."

The Buffalo Steel is officially under new ownership. The league agreed to let Four Kings Sports and Entertainment purchase the team. Julian is now co-owner, along with three partners—Preston Donnelley, Miles Walker, and Terrence Reyes. They're all friends, and they now make Buffalo the first Black-owned professional rugby team in the RLA. Preston, Miles, and Terrence flew in with their wives ahead of a couples' trip in order to finalize last-minute paperwork and celebrate. The signed agreement permits Julian to split his ownership with Antonio once he retires. He still plans to play for the foreseeable future, but he'll own a piece of the team he's poured into since its inception.

Leah sets my cocktail on a napkin and slides it over. "Thank you," I say after a sip. "This is delicious."

She winks and wipes down the onyx counter. A spiderweb tattoo on her hand peeks out from her cuff. It matches the one behind her ear.

"Heading home after this?" she asks.

"I hope so. I'm meeting someone here. I don't know his plans for the rest of the night, but I wanted a redo."

"A redo?"

"I was at this very bar a few years ago on New Year's Eve," I say, my finger tracing the rim of my glass at the memory. "I made a promise to myself but didn't get a chance to fulfill it."

Traveling down to DC before the end of the year required a detour to the place that changed my life. Antonio and I came back to this bar the weekend the Steel played DC before the playoffs. But tonight feels different.

The night I stumbled in here on shaky heels and in my sister's dress, I was nervous to take risks outside of the comfort of habit and empirical evidence. Forsaking the tradition of pajamas and snacks at my father's house not only led to romantic love, but it brought me to a version of myself I never imagined possible.

I gave up a life of hard wigs that night. I'm still the same Miriam with Twizzlers in my purse, but I now enjoy a softer era with more adventures and laughter. Settled and confident enough to assert my needs.

And tonight, I'm definitely sitting on someone's penis.

My pulse quickens when the front door opens. Tobacco and cedar drift over to invade my nostrils amid the hum of soft jazz. Smooth steps roll over concrete to excite my attention, the same way they did four years ago. Only this time, the shiver rippling through me is not of fear but welcome anticipation.

"Mind if I join you?" Antonio's voice kisses between my legs.

I wet my lips. "Sure."

He folds himself onto the stool next to me, swallowing my personal space. The swell of his thighs invades my legs, which he brings between his with a pull of my seat. He towers over me, the width of his chest and shoulders testing the flexibility of the button-down stretched over his frame.

We already tested my flexibility in his condo before the celebration dinner. No bloody noses or ER visits involved.

"Can I buy you a drink?" I offer.

He shakes his head. "We're not staying long." His gaze slides over my lips to my breasts and exposed thighs, which he squeezes. I draw in a sharp breath at his stare. It tingles the pit of my stomach and flares in silent expectation.

"You look edible," he says. His husky tone skates over my lips when he leans closer. "Can I take you back to my place?"

I giggle and push him away. "That's not how this is supposed to go."

He frowns. "We already knew each other back then."

"Knew *of* each other. What would you have done if I'd never revealed my intentions that night? Indulge me, please."

He lifts my hand to kiss the inside of my wrist. "I would have told you what I should've told you four years ago: that I've always liked you, and I want the chance to love you for the rest of my life. Then I would have grabbed your coat, paid your tab, and asked if you were ready."

"Just like that?" I ask quietly.

"You ready?"

I down my drink in two gulps. Antonio pays Leah and helps me with my coat. I get a forehead kiss before he interlaces our hands to leave the bar. A chill wind blows through the bare branches waving gently along the street. Colorful row houses light up with nightlife in a neighborhood that barely sleeps.

Antonio dropped me off at the bar before he parked the car at his condo up the block. He told me he has a surprise for us later, but he got caught in a work call before he could give any more details. I'm tired already just thinking about staying up late in this dress.

"There go those wheels turning," he teases.

"Can you at least give me a hint about what we're doing?"

"That's for me to know and you to find out. If you must know, we're swinging by the house first. I have something in the oven."

What?

"Are you sure it won't be in flames when we get there?"

He scoffs and puts a hand over his heart. "I take offense. Can't a man bake his woman dessert without involving the fire department? I made *concolón*, thank you. I can flambé."

"You burned the bottom of a pot of rice, and my mother helped you save it. We had to air out her house for two days." I crack up remembering Antonio's first visit to Panama over the summer.

We spent two weeks with my mother, whose exact words were, "If you don't marry this boy, I will." She fell in love quick with her "son-in-law" and is coming up in March for his first home game of the season. She's yet to visit me or Marcela in Buffalo but actively texts with Antonio throughout the week. He's earning bonus points for learning Spanish.

"I know what I'm doing," he says. "I left the plantains in the skillet on three before I came to get you."

"You *what*?! You can't leave hot oil unattended." I snatch the keys from his hand and sprint up the stairwell.

Don't ask me why I thought this was smart. There's an entire elevator to prevent me from wheezing or puncturing a lung. I don't exactly have Iron Man stamina.

The triathlon, not the Avenger.

"Doe!" Antonio calls from the lobby.

Who gave him the bright idea to flambé anything?

"We're never watching a baking show together again!" I shout back.

With sweat kissing my skin and the edges of my hair reverting back to its natural curl pattern, I reach the top floor. I made it six flights of stairs in platform heels and a wool coat that's about to incinerate my insides.

I'm a glistening mirror ball.

My breaths come in gasps as I thrust the key into the lock.

"You're fast as hell," Antonio says from behind me. Of course, he's breathing properly.

"You." *Wheeze.* "Don't." *Wheeze.* "Touch." *Wheeze.* "Appliances." I push open the door and stumble inside to find pink and white rose petals.

D'Angelo's "Untitled (How Does It Feel)" spills over the sound system into the kitchen and living room, which is somehow not engulfed in flames.

"What?" I pant.

I blink at the white floating candles in cylinder vases that line a path from the front door through the living area. Hundreds of white balloons float over the space, which is covered in rose petals. Tied to each gold ribbon is a polaroid of Antonio and me.

Our first selfie in the ER four years ago.

A photo of me laughing on the phone with my mother in the home improvement store after he broke my shower curtain.

Vegas with the Steel.

The summer vacation we took.

Apple-picking and hayrides with Bread, Kendrick, Reese, Shins, and his fiancée—who's still hard of hearing.

Marcela and I with community after the City Council voted for the Buffalo Grows Coalition to receive 20 vacant lots.

"Keep going," Antonio says over D'Angelo's serenade to provide everything I desire.

I walk through a canopy of our memories. Printed-out text messages, our words of encouragement during our biggest life transitions when we lived apart. There are photos of me at his games—when the Steel dominated during playoffs, and when they won their first championship.

"H-how did you do all of this?" I gulp hard, tears slipping down my cheeks.

Antonio wipes them away. "Ella did the balloons and photos at her house. Your sister handled the rest while we were at dinner."

"Marcela is here?"

"She's out with her friends, but yeah. She leaves Friday."

My sister said she was taking time for herself after her reelection. A few city councilmembers lost their seats, but she ran uncontested. With eyes on the mayor and whispers of more uncovered corruption, she's been working around the clock, and she deserves the break. We spent Christmas together, but I never expected this.

"Keep going, Doe." Antonio takes off my coat and kisses my neck.

Fresh tears gather, and my voice catches at the images Antonio took during his visits to the community center. Me with my kids in the STEM hub, and me in my home office dedicated to designing and prototyping my patent concept. I'm in the final stages before I begin the application process.

Every memory of us together is here.

I arrive at the corner window that overlooks DC. A white neon "Will You Marry Me?" LED sign hangs in the middle of a heart-shaped backdrop covered in white roses. At the base are candles in vases, bouquets of flowers in soft pinks and creams, and a faux fur blanket covered in rose petals, with my high school yearbook on top. It's open to the page with my photo from sophomore year. A heart is over the image. Next to it is the word "love" scribbled in the margin.

Julian's yearbook.

"Doe."

Antonio is on one knee with a black box in his hand. His coat is off. So is the beanie covering his waves. His smooth caramel skin anchored by a boxed beard glows under soft lights.

Jinkies.

"From the moment I saw you in the hallway, my world was never the same. I've loved you from afar, hoping to taste the edge of your laugh and catch the eclipse of your smile. I never believed I would have a soulmate until I met you. Every day we've spent together and all those years apart drew me to you. You've been my best friend, my person, and my greatest joy.

"Every milestone, every memory we've shared together is a reminder of our love. You are my home, Miriam, in every universe across every lifetime."

"Antonio," I sob. Damn me for wearing these condom-like contacts.

His smile wobbles. "I love you so much." He brushes away a tear and opens the velvet box to reveal a classic solitaire stone on a simple band. It's perfect. "Will you do me the honor of being my emergency contact for the rest of my life?"

We erupt in laughter.

I drop to my knees and kiss away his tears. "Yes, I will," I whisper over his lips.

His mouth trembles over mine as he cups my face for a kiss.

"I love you," he repeats with each brush of his lips.

"I love you too," I say back.

He lifts me into his arms, peppering my face with kisses on the way to his bedroom.

"Antonio?"

"Yeah?"

"Maybe lose the watch, just in case."

A smile toys at his lips. "Good idea."

THE END

Acknowledgments

Can I be honest? Writing Antonio's book came and went too quickly for me! He was one of my favorite characters in *Ella Gets the D*, and now his story is done (womp!). While we'll see him and Miriam throughout the other books in the Buffalo Steel Rugby Romance Series, I enjoyed writing their story and the friendship that blossomed after that trip to the emergency room.

While I'm being honest, I'm usually not a fan of friends-to-lovers stories—because what do you mean you've loved me for half of my life and never said anything?? Just sitting on your truth like a hard fart bubbling up in your stomach. (For what???) And yet, as I picked up my pen, this is where we landed, lmao.

It was a little intimidating to come back to the pair I quickly teased in *Ella*, as years have passed since I wrote that standalone. But there they were, waiting for me to wrap up the Chance at Love Series. Coco (@thechaoticlibrarian_) asked for an Antonio novella back then. I hope his story was worth the wait with this one! Who knows, maybe I'll write a short little something down the road with Miriam and Antonio and Julian and Ella. I don't want to say goodbye just yet!

One of the things that felt special with this one was the "first date" feeling of their friendship once Miriam moved to Buffalo. There's something to be said about investing time over distance and contending with feelings in person. The best romantic relationships are built on a foundation of friendship. I'm grateful to have it in my marriage to my real-life cinnamon roll, who inspired this book in so many ways.

My husband (first-gen Black Panamanian) has been asking for Panamanian rep in my books for some time. I wanted to center it in this book, as he's also played rugby (flanker) for over two decades and is an engineer. Quite a bit of this story overlaps with real life. From him and his team enjoying a night on the town in construction vests and hoochie shorts (I have it on video!), to the amount of dedication that goes into playing—and witnessing his teammates' shenanigans in bars (my God, today!). Rugby life wasn't just an investment; it was part of our story for many years. There were good times on the sidelines of the pitch, lots of photos (I was an unofficial team photographer at one point), use of super glue to fix cuts, championships, hard losses, and endless stories. Some of our best memories together came after games, and it will be fun revisiting them for this book series.

Rugby thighs, tackles, and stretches are very popular these days (trust me, I get it). Yet, as I write this, the Major League Rugby in the US will be down four teams ahead of the upcoming season. It's been a struggle to get professional rugby off the ground in this country. Players aren't paid enough and barely have insurance to keep them healthy throughout the year. I wanted to touch on some realities that often get overlooked in favor of the physical satisfaction of the sport, as professional rugby life in the United States isn't very glamorous. If there's a team near you (professional or not), consider attending a game. It's an amazing sport!

As with all of my acknowledgments, this is running long. Thank you for coming on yet another journey. We'll detour in Sicily next for a standalone mafia rom-com (the first release in 2026) before we circle back to Buffalo for Marcela's story (second release in 2026). The plot is *loud* in my head, and I already have a title that will turn heads more than *Ella Gets the D* ever could.

Thank you to all of the people in my life (too many to name) who keep me going and give me the space to dive into my imagination. It's been challenging given the realities we've been navigating, which makes shifting into the realm of shenanigans all the more healing.

See you on the pitch!

Stay tuned for more in the **Buffalo Steel Rugby Romance Series!**
Marcela is kicking off book two.

Want to read about Ella and Julian's love story? Check out **_Ella Gets the D_**, available on Kindle Unlimited and paperback!

© Frenchy Press LLC

Tanvier Peart is a future bestselling romance author with a healthy obsession for snacks and happily ever afters. She is a good girl with kinks who spends her days working on policy and enjoys the wild life of being a wife and soccer mom. By night, she writes and reads romance books with steamy scenes. When she's not lost in the land of smut, Tanvier enjoys long walks down snack aisles and the chorus of grunts at the gym.

Want to stay up to date on all of Tanvier's bookish news? Sign up for

her newsletter:

https://tanvierwrites.substack.com/

Connect with Tanvier online:

@tanvierwrites

(Instagram, TikTok, Threads, Facebook)